I0782157

HERO

SECOND OF THE NINE BLOODLINES

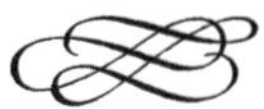

K.R. BADY

TANGLEWOOD PRESS

BOOKS BY K.R. BADY

THE NINE BLOODLINES SERIES:

Companion

Hero

Hero, Second of the Nine Bloodlines
By K.R. Bady
Published by Tanglewood Press, an Imprint of Woods Publishing
All rights reserved
Hero, Second of the Nine Bloodlines Copyright © 2023 by K.R. Bady

CHAPTER 1

$\mathcal{B}$lythe's gaze darted from her console to the sleek silver tower against the side of the gateway leading to the colony's transport station. Her dark skin itched under the faux leather of her bodysuit, where excess fabric seemed to clump into every crease of her form, and her leg bounced with impatience.

Now was not the time for intrusive thoughts, but the physical discomfort forced her to reflect on the ill-fitting gear. It was past time she invested in something more suited to her frame instead of snatching up the cast-offs of other star surfers. It was fine two years ago, when she first wandered onboard from lack of options, but now . . .

It was starting to get embarrassing.

Blythe rolled her shoulders back and refocused on the controls in her hands. Perhaps a bit snappily, she asked, "Why haven't we been hailed yet?"

"Don't worry," Tilla said as a heavy hand landed on the back of Blythe's neck. "Coast here until they call for our credentials. Remember, we're expected, and the sigils marking us as merchants are perfectly visible."

Blythe nodded, but her neck felt stiff.

There was no good reason to expect otherwise, but Blythe couldn't shake the feeling this routine procedure was about to blow up in her face. They were low on fuel, and it had been weeks since they left Earth. If the Lunar authorities chose to deny them entry the one time Blythe was in the pilot's seat at the point of correspondence, she would never live it down, as most of the crew was still wary whenever Tilla urged her into the chair, and her conversation skills tended to be less polished than her flying.

Tilla gave her a gentle shake. There was a deep huff of laughter in their voice as they said, "Relax. They might laugh at you if you get tongue tied, but that's the worst that'll happen."

Nearby, the crewmember manning navigation chortled and added, "And if they don't laugh at you, we will."

"True," said Tilla.

"I hate you all," Blythe grumbled.

As the command deck broke into pockets of snide laughter, Blythe cast a pinched look at the captain. Well over six feet tall, with heaps of muscles and a long mane of golden hair tied into a knot at the base of their skull, Tilla was an imposing figure. They were golden-brown and faintly furred, though only the skin of their face and ample cleavage were visible in the bodysuit.

The garment fit the captain like a second glove. Tilla made it look like the functional spacefaring outfit it was.

Blythe tried not to think of how such a suit looked on herself. There was nothing impressive about her anymore. Even the jaguar spots marring her skin didn't stand out among the crew.

The console's speaker crackled to life with an incoming transmission with perfect timing and redirected her morbid thoughts. The crisp and polished voice of a Lunar-raised man demanded, "Halt and identify yourself."

Around the command deck, the crew muttered snide comments.

The only remark Blythe could make out was Tilla's terse, "Someone's grumpy today."

Blythe cleared her throat loud enough to signal the crew for silence, then she reached for the transponder button. With utmost professionalism, Blythe provided the standard information.

"Intergalactic trading vessel, The SSC Zephyr. En route from Earth. Merchant Code," Blythe hesitated as she fought back a blushing grin, "Foxtrot-Romeo-one-five-Kilo-Yankee-eight-one-seven-Charlie-Hotel."

She cut the transmission with the last syllable, and not a moment too soon. The command deck erupted with laughter.

"Ha!" someone cheered, "Frisky bitch!"

"Classy!" snarked another crewmate.

Among the resounding claps and amused hollers, Blythe could finally take a full breath.

She popped up from the pilot's seat and gave a deep bow to either side of the room. There were only a handful of crew on the deck, but they roared like a rowdy crowd of drunks before a grand spectacle. Tilla's laugh was the loudest, the most familiar. Blythe caught the captain's golden eyes and was momentarily thrown back in time to a different audience.

A different life.

The surrounding crewmembers broke into a cheeky chant —"Frisky bitch! Frisky bitch!"—and Blythe felt her shoulders sag as the collective attention scattered. The only person not joining in on the inside joke was Tilla.

"Back in the chair, Blythe."

Tension flooded back into her every muscle like it belonged there.

"You'll never be a pilot if you don't learn how to land," Tilla said. While their tone was kind, it left no room for argument.

Blythe cringed. "You say that like piloting was my hobby of choice."

As usual, the captain ignored her pronounced reluctance. Despite herself, Blythe dropped into the seat like a rock, inflexible and cold beneath Tilla's guiding grip.

The rest of the flight crew was still goofing around, but their chortles dropped off as they noticed Blythe was back behind the controls. Maybe she imagined the notes of nervousness as their humor faded. Maybe not.

No one on board understood Tilla's recent campaign to pressure Blythe into learning to fly. Even Blythe wasn't sure, and she was privy to the minor lectures Tilla had been throwing at her, something about "goal setting" and "personal responsibility."

Tilla's hand stayed solid on her nape as they loomed over her shoulder. "Nice and easy. Just don't scratch my ship."

Twenty minutes later, Blythe scratched the ship.

It was ugly.

The Zephyr was a hunk of gray metals, consisting of two meager levels encased in a dinged and burned hull that had traversed Earth's decaying atmosphere more times than Blythe could count. Compared to other merchant vehicles, it was small and unimpressive. It was no more or less than its function demanded, designed for business, not aesthetics.

Even so, the fresh scratch across the starboard-side nose of the ship was a pronounced eyesore. It was superficial enough that it wouldn't interfere with the work roster, but the sight of it made Blythe's guts shrivel up and plummet to the ground. When Tilla had all but tossed her out of the pilot's seat to take over landing protocols, Blythe was torn between crying and heaving a sigh of relief.

Now, she just felt sick to her stomach.

"This was my fault," Tilla said, staring at the damage alongside her.

Blythe flinched. "No. This was all me—"

"You weren't ready," Tilla interrupted with a sorry shake of their head. "I shouldn't have pressured you."

Blythe bit her tongue. Reminding Tilla of her general disinterest in piloting from the start would do neither of them any good.

Without looking away from the ship, Tilla said, "You should go."

Blythe flinched, and a few locs whipped her cheek as if her hair were picking up Tilla's slack in chastising her. Batting the locs from her face, Blythe peered up at Tilla and tried to ignore how dry her mouth had gone.

"You're kicking me off The Zephyr?"

"No." Tilla blinked at the scarred hull of their ship and sighed. "We have a week before we fly out again, though. You should go home."

"Oh. Okay." Blythe tried to swallow the rising bile in the back of her throat as she turned to leave.

"Do me a favor?"

Blythe jerked around. It earned her another loc-lashing, but she didn't care. "Sure."

Tilla cast a somber smile her way. "Take a good, hard look at what you want out of this arrangement before you come back."

BLYTHE DRAGGED HER FEET THROUGH THE MILLING CROWDS OF spacecraft personnel and travelers in a lonely little pocket of her own defeat. She wasn't the only person departing the station from The Zephyr, but everyone else was ensnared in conversation or rushing by with pressing matters to attend. On occasion, someone would shoot her a wave or an errant farewell, but all Blythe had to do was lift her chin with a half-hearted smile, and the interaction would be over.

She never missed a step, sped up, or slowed down until she was outside.

The mass of commuters dispersed around her, and Blythe paused to raise her face to the sky. The transparent dome that protected the inhabitable areas of Earth's moon glittered with stardust far above the tallest buildings. The station was close enough to the perimeter that she could see the blue-gray rock beyond the barrier; as she watched, the light hit the dome just right, and it seemed almost pearlescent against Luna's dull surface.

It was nothing short of magical, serene and whole in ways Earth hadn't been in millennia. Blythe stared through the dome to the lifeless landscape and tried to remember the awe she'd felt the first time she stepped foot on this colony.

Lunar-5 was a fantasy come to life. Her childhood was sustained by daydreams of this place, of its breathable air and visible sky. It used to turn her breathless and weepy, overcome with Luna's beauty and promising implications.

Such a time was long gone. Two whole—but terribly short— years gone.

What did she have to show for it? Most of the small collection of treasures she brought with her from Earth were still collecting dust in a storage facility. Whatever items she sold in the past two years kept a tidy little studio apartment vacant and waiting for her whenever she made it back to the port, but she could barely remember what the space looked like.

She should probably go reacquaint herself with the space, as Tilla suggested. She could hole up in the apartment for the week and take her time reworking her locs; the hairstyle was good for long stints of interplanetary travel, but they were long overdue for some maintenance. It would be just her, her mess of hair, and her thoughts.

With a sigh, Blythe pointed her feet toward home. The apartment wasn't far from the station, and commuter shuttles tended to get too crowded for Blythe's liking. She could walk.

It wasn't like anyone was waiting up for her.

She made it less than a block before the sleek silver band on her wrist chirped with an incoming message.

"Yes?" Blythe huffed as she lifted her wrist to activate the comms.

She expected to see Tilla's face beaming from the device with an unfortunate summons back to The Zephyr. Instead, the bracelet hummed and spat out a projection of a different, but no less familiar face. The recognition stunned her silent for a few seconds.

"Hey, girl," Phink said with a toothy grin.

Blythe's heart gave a vicious pang of homesickness.

He was just as she remembered him. His beard was cropped short, almost indistinguishable from the fur covering all but the peach skin around his eyes and mouth. The dark hair sprouting from his head stood on end in its usual haphazard way, while the calmer brown fur on his face lay flat. His fearless embrace of splicing side effects was as admirable as it was stunning; he looked more bear than human at this point.

Blythe's heart twisted in a complex reaction at the sight of him. Phink had always been this way: a giant teddy bear with a perpetual frown to match the chip on his shoulder. If his animal features ever caused him grief, it was long before she met him.

Phink held no shame or discomfort about his splicing. Not like she did.

Stars above, but she missed him.

"Hi," Blythe croaked, choking back tears.

"Hey," he repeated, "I know we agreed not to contact each other, except in an emergency—"

Blythe gulped, going lightheaded. "Are you okay?"

He winced. "That came out wrong. Yes, I'm fine. Everything's fine. Just . . . different. I'm on Lunar-5. That's your home port, right?"

"You're on Luna?" Blythe reeled, pulling away from the comms as her emotions tried to adjust. "I thought you wanted to stay on Earth?"

He sighed. Blythe imagined his fur seemed to droop. "Things have changed. Can we meet?"

TANYA'S PLACE WAS A HUMANITY FETISH BAR THAT HAD SEEN better days. That much was clear to Blythe before she stepped foot in the building. It wasn't that the place was ugly or in disrepair; it was just dull and unembellished, with an overhanging sign that was decades out of fashion. Meanwhile, the establishments to either side were polished and gleaming, in fair competition with the sky-high barrier that secured a livable atmosphere on the moon.

It was a sad comparison.

The inside wasn't much better. The lighting was decent by Earthling standards, but there was only one stage at the far end and no obvious direction toward private lounges. Back on Earth, the stages were the focal point of every differentiated room in such a place of business, but at Tanya's, the bar reigned supreme; it spanned the full length of the central room, and the counter was a sparkling slate of geode-encrusted glass. Black high-top tables and stools cluttered the floor, with a row of upholstered booths along the wall opposite the bar.

For a bar, it would have been a crowning jewel in the few inhabitable port cities that remained on Earth. It never would have passed for a HEPP House. Unfortunately, it *was* a HEPP House, and on the moon, no less.

Blythe fought not to wince in second-hand embarrassment. She wasn't the only one.

Phink was seated at the bar, leaning back against it with his arms crossed over his bulbous belly as he scowled around the space. There was no one else around. He glanced at her as she approached, and for a moment, she thought he looked close to tears. That couldn't be right.

She gestured around the place. "What's this?"

Phink turned his glower to the ceiling with a stubborn jut of his furry chin. "This is my latest assignment from HEPP."

That gave Blythe pause.

Phink was the manager of the Human Existence and Preservation Project's entertainment House in the American Port. He made them good money, showcasing the rawest humanoid talent he could find on Earth. Thanks to him, HEPP's token presence in America was bolstered into a successful business, one that provided significant funding for the organization's off-world programs.

"They sent you away from Centrism?" Blythe gaped at him. "Why?"

Phink shrugged without tearing his gaze from above. "Petty politics. The European Houses have been pissy with me ever since I hooked Sly up with the Companionship of the century."

Blythe winced in sympathy.

Companionship wasn't common to begin with, and it never featured a human participant from the dirty little port she once called home. The fact that Sly, of all people, ended up in a contract with an elite Nocturnus was nothing short of a fluke of nature, and it had been an insult to the European Houses that usually monopolized such arrangements.

If the mention of Sly's name also made her want to cry, Blythe wasn't inclined to admit it.

Phink dragged a stern stare over her, and it rocked Blythe back on her heels with a sense of déjà vu. How many times had he looked at her like that, with such unsurprised disappointment? How many times had he sighed, aiming that expression from Sly to her and back?

The three of them weren't family. Not really. Even so, Sly was the closest she had to a brother. And Phink? He was . . . an honorary uncle? A pseudo-father figure? Technically, he was their former boss, but he'd always been so much more.

"So," he said, punctuating his tone with a slap to the counter as he faced her, "I'm here, either to quietly retire or pull another miracle out of my ass. I might as well try fixing the place up."

Blythe choked on a stunned laugh. "Seriously? Phink, I know it's been a while since you were here, but the moon doesn't have much of a market for HEPP Houses. The majority of the people who live here are Nocturni, and among the humans . . ." She trailed off with a careless gesture.

She didn't need to explain this to him. Phink was born on Luna. He knew.

"Yeah." He sighed, scratching through the fuzz on his neck. "The splicing culture isn't the same out here. People aren't as desperate for a reminder of their humanity."

Blythe gave a sympathetic nod as she patted his shoulder.

"I'm still going to try." He swatted her hand away as he grumbled. "What do you say, Blythe? Want to jump back into show business with me?"

Blythe reared back, blinking at him. "What?"

She turned to stare at the meager stage. It was smooth and whole, but it was also unpolished and sporting stains. She turned back to Phink with her eyebrows raised high.

"Seriously?"

He matched her tone as he snarked, "Obviously."

With an awkward chuckle, Blythe stepped away from the bar. "Listen, Phinkly—"

"Don't start—"

"It's been years, Phinkerton—"

He slapped a furry hand over her mouth. "Quit it. I put up with that name shit from Sly because he'll sic his vamp on me if I don't, but you don't have that kind of protection, girl."

Rolling her eyes, Blythe pushed his hand away. "And before you virtually sold him off to said vampire's Harem? What was your excuse then?"

Judging by his grouchy expression, Phink was not impressed with her comeback.

Blythe beamed at him. "Aw! You miss us."

"No shit." He scoffed as he hopped off the barstool. He heaved his dress pants up his hips till his belly interfered, then made his way behind the counter.

"I need a solid act," he huffed as he retrieved two whiskey glasses from a cabinet. "When I got your comms info from Sly, he told me you were still wasting time on that trading ship."

Blythe's spine stiffened. She shook it off with a shimmy of her shoulders and braced her elbows back on the bar.

Across from her, Phink brandished a bottle and caught her eye with deliberate gravity. "Was that boy lying to me?"

Blythe's face grew warm as she averted her gaze.

In her periphery, she caught Phink nodding to himself as he poured the alcohol. "I was sad to see him go," Phink said, but his conversational tone was laced with familial concern. "I mourned when he left. It was like losing a brother."

Blythe raised a brow at him without comment.

He snorted. "Fine. It was like losing a son. Or something. Whatever."

Blythe accepted the drink when he slid it across to her, but she couldn't bring herself to raise it. She cradled it between her palms, hyperaware of the wet chill of the glass against her dark skin. She studied it as Phink kept talking.

"But you know what? Once I accepted my personal loss for what it was, I was happy for him. Proud too. The brat I took pity on by hiring him all those years ago was all grown up and making moves, cutting loose the baggage weighing him down and building a life for himself."

Blythe nodded along. The sweating glass consumed her vision, but not her hearing.

"Now look at him!"

It was easy to imagine. Sly was a quarter of a galaxy away on a tiny outer planet called Ethos, happily playing lover and personal blood donor to one of the most renowned Nocturni in existence, Kahled Vauqeulin. Kahled wasn't just another vamp, he was a living descendant of one of the first vampires ever created; he was part of The Nine Bloodlines, and the chances of his Companion finding a better life elsewhere were nonexistent. At times, Blythe thought she hated Kahled. She didn't know him, but he was the reason Sly was gone, why Sly was his Companion.

A long-term commitment with the potential to impact future generations was usually called Companionship. Such contracts were signed between an individual vampire and a specific human blood donor. They were also consensual. As such, Sly was too busy making the vamp's life a fairy tale to be bothered with hers.

Phink pulled her from her thoughts by clanking the rim of his drink to hers. He tossed back the inch or so of liquid and set the emptied glass down with a solid thud, then he leaned toward her. His necktie pooled on the bar between them.

"That's our Sly," he said, "living large and as far away as he can get from the dying little rock we call Mother Earth. Sure, he's shackled to the Nocturni for the rest of his life, but he's happy. He's safe."

"He moved on," Blythe agreed, nodding as she forced herself to take a sip.

"Yeah, he did. For a hot minute, I thought you did too."

The alcohol soured on her tongue. She lowered the glass.

She wouldn't lie to him and claim she was happy with The

Zephyr. The work was long and tedious. There still wasn't a single bodysuit in her closet that fit her right. Even the glory of space travel had lost its shine after so many treks through the stars. Tilla was a good person who cultivated a good crew, and most of them were veteran star surfers with a long-standing fondness for The Zephyr and each other, but even after two years, none of them quite knew what to make of her.

But The Zephyr's people treated her the same as anyone else on board. Blythe's otherness could remain an unspoken element among them for a lifetime if she let it.

Phink's hands covered each of her wrists. He squeezed, firm, warm, and knowing. "You loved dancing. Do you love being on that ship even half as much?"

She slipped from his grasp to gulp the remaining whiskey.

"Tilla's teaching me to fly," she said. "I'm still figuring out the finesses of landing, but I'm getting pretty good at the actual flying part. It's all right. Lucrative."

"But do you love it?"

"No." Blythe's shoulders slumped as she returned his direct stare. "But it's safe. Can't that be enough for now?"

His frown made her feel like a disappointment. "Not forever, Blythe."

THAT NIGHT, BLYTHE'S DREAMS WERE FRAUGHT WITH MEMORIES.

She was eight years old, and Sly dared her to take off her protective gear in the midday sun. She watched in amazement as raw sunlight glinted off her nails, only to start screaming as blisters blossomed across her skin.

She was twelve when she began elective splicing. It was the first time she introduced feline DNA into her physiology, because what kid wouldn't want the increased speed and strength of an ancient predator? Overnight, the backflip she'd been struggling to execute for weeks became effortless. Before that point, all her genetic splicing was limited by medical necessity on a planet that had grown hostile to humans. It made her ill, but oh, it was worth it—until suddenly, she wasn't twelve, but thirteen, and her parents lucked into a pair of shuttle tickets to Luna and Sly's dad refused to let a "polluted" foundling take sanctuary in his home.

Then, she was eighteen, and HEPP had finished their task of ensuring her survival to adulthood. Phink was there waiting with the job of her dreams on a silver platter. She jumped on the opportunity. She jumped again when it was suggested her lack of visible splicing side effects could be a hit with a certain clientele, ignorant to the risks it might invite.

She was twenty-four years old when she watched her home go up in flames. Beneath all the protective layers hiding her from a murderous atmosphere, Blythe's bruised cheek throbbed, and her eyes watered with the understanding that nothing would ever be the same again.

CHAPTER 2

*B*lythe woke up the following morning in her own bed without a shipmate snoring in the bunk above her. For all her body felt rested, her head and heart felt heavy.

The apartment was a cozy closet with lush carpet, a spotless paint job, quality air, and a communal kitchen decked out with cutting-edge coffeemakers and cookware. Blythe took full advantage of her private toilet, and she was still seated on it as she used her comms to add her name to the waitlist for the building's baths. By the time it was her turn, she was fully awake with a satisfied stomach, but the mundanity only served as an added weight hanging from her temples.

Soaking in a hot bath didn't help, so Blythe dressed and slicked her edges with an irritated snap to her movements. She had to pluck the leotard out of her ass more than once, and it was an unwelcome reminder that her days of wearing skimpy dance outfits like a second skin were well and far behind her. The sight of her ill-managed locs in the mirror only added insult to injury—once upon a time, the idea of wearing locs on a stage, even for a half-hearted audition, would have been laughable; she certainly hoped Phink didn't expect her to show up with the smooth waves she once favored.

Stars above, but it was like squeezing into a costume she long since outgrew. The dancewear fit her form no better than the flight suits she used on The Zephyr. It only showed off more of the damn jaguar spots.

The chip on Blythe's shoulder chased her halfway across the city and through the front door of Tanya's Place. As she glanced about the bar, Blythe was glad she hadn't primped more for the occasion. Tanya's Place was better lit, but no more encouraging than the last time she visited.

"Blythe!" Phink greeted her at the entrance in his customary business attire. He looked like a polished gem surrounded by crude rock. "I knew you'd come! See? I told you she'd come!"

Blythe peered around Phink's girth to see who he was talking to. She was unsurprised by the pair of suits lingering by the bar. Phink already knew she could dance; the audition was bound to be for strangers.

The two suits, a man and a woman, stared them down as Phink led her over. While the dark-haired man remained seated on a barstool, the woman stood tall beside him with the rigidity of a sentry.

She was tall and curvy, with her substantial weight squeezed into a resplendent business suit of molten grays. Her honey-blonde hair was coiled into an artful bun, and her eyes were striking. It was no trick of her dark makeup, but a splicing side effect; the pupils dilated and slitted with every shift of the light, the irises wide and bulbously striated with bright greens and yellows.

The woman braced her hands on her hips as she eyed the animal print on Blythe's face with a grimace. "You must be Phink's little friend."

Blythe couldn't help but stare. The woman's suit was of the highest quality, but it was far too small for her. The jacket strained over her torso, and the pant legs barely hit her ankles. The material itself was a soft, gleaming material unlike anything Blythe had seen. Its movements were hypnotic as its wearer glided under the lights.

"Blythe Ramos," she said, offering her hand as she pretended not to notice the buttons threatening to pop off over the woman's round chest.

They did not shake hands.

"Elitia Kenwood." The blonde set her manicured hands on her hips and smirked down her nose at Blythe. "I'm the manager of Tanya's Place."

"Assistant Manager," said the man at the bar.

Elitia smiled, and while it was a sweet, embarrassed smile, it had no impact on those snake eyes. "Yes, of course. Phink is in charge now."

There was something unpleasant in the way Elitia looked at Phink then. Her words and tone were polite enough, and no one commented on it, but Blythe recognized the nasty undertones behind her words.

Blythe raised a concerned eyebrow toward Phink, but he either didn't notice or didn't care to address it. Phink caught her by the elbow and redirected her toward the unfamiliar man as he abandoned his drink on the counter and spun on his stool to face her.

As remarkable a sight as Elitia Kenwood made, the guy beside her was anything but. His appearance was utterly humanoid, not a single hint of fur or scales in sight, and he had the perfect symmetry and proportions of a classically handsome man.

"Blythe," Phink said, giving her a pointed nudge, "I'd like you to meet Master Leopold Troy."

Blythe did a double take. Her spine straightened as her eyes darted to Elitia's impressive form then back to that perfect male face.

"Oh!"

Blythe gaped at the unassuming vampire; his lack of animal attributes was starting to make sense. Unlike Blythe and her fellow humans, the Nocturni were born with impeccable splicing abilities. Their designer metabolisms let them pick and choose their side effects.

Blythe's face flushed with the unfairness of it all. She'd been splicing with a laundry list of creature genomes since childhood, first fortifying herself as most everyone else, and then so she could reap the athletic benefits of choice species. Few vamps would give themselves jaguar spots when they could just as easily enjoy the superior speed and flexibility without the visible evidence.

This vamp looked more human than she did.

"Wait," Blythe gave an incredulous laugh. "*Master Troy*? As in . . . ?"

She glanced at Phink for confirmation, and he nodded. "He's the current head of the Troy Harem. Our very own local celebrity."

From the sidelines, Blythe detected a short, derisive huff from Elitia. Neither Phink nor Troy seemed to notice, but it was possible neither of them had her enhanced hearing; Blythe's splicing side effects weren't limited to a few unsightly cat markings.

"Celebrity is not the term I would use," the vampire drawled. He reached back to collect his ruby-red drink from the bar, and she caught sight of a fashionably small fang as he raised it to his lips.

With a nervous chuckle, Blythe nudged Phink back, aiming for his ribs. "Nice. So, what's a non-celebrity Nocturnus doing here during my audition?"

"He's here *for* your audition," Phink corrected as he blocked her elbow with a hard smile. "Master Troy has to approve all new hires."

"Huh. That's . . ." Blythe's brow furrowed with confusion, ". . . not normal."

"Well, Tanya's is not a normal HEPP House," Elitia sniped.

Blythe met the woman's glower with a wary stare. She noted the flush on Elitia's face as much as the defensive set of her fist on her hip, but no one else paid her any mind.

"Indeed," the vampire said with an air of impatience. He never so much as glanced in Elitia's direction.

With her jaw slightly unhinged, Blythe watched Master Troy drain his drink. Back at Centrism, she bumped into loner vamps and some belonging to the minor Harems, but the Troys were one of The Nine Bloodlines. What in the cosmos did the equivalent of Nocturni Royalty have to do with a shithole of a human-run establishment?

Her bafflement must have been obvious because Elitia snapped her pudgy fingers directly in front of her face.

"As I was saying," the big blonde said with a prideful harumph, "Tanya's is unique among HEPP's properties. We have a long-standing relationship with the Troy Harem. It gives them"—she hesitated as she cast an unreadable look at the vampire—"a certain influence over House prospects."

Master Troy set down his drink with a loud clink before gliding onto his feet. Without looking at her, he said, "Congratulations, Ms. Ramos. You're hired."

As Blythe blinked in incomprehension, Phink gave a strangled laugh. "Don't you want to see her dance first?"

Master Troy gave her a cursory once-over on his way toward the exit. "I trust your judgment, Mr. Phink."

There was a sharp clack of heels as Elitia took a halting step after him. "You're certain, sire? I hardly think another obviously spliced body is going to draw in more customers."

"The only thing I'm certain of is that I have more important matters to attend to than micromanaging HEPP's charity business for them."

Elitia reared back with righteous affront. "We're no charity!"

Master Troy reached the door and cast an unimpressed look over his shoulder at the lot of them. "The last time anyone from my family stepped through your door with any sort of pleasure, your parents hadn't yet been conceived." He opened the door with a dismissive wave. "My presence here is nothing but an illusion of cooperation between my Harem and your species. I'm content to let Mr. Phink attempt to salvage what he can from it."

As the door swung shut behind the vampire, Blythe compared Phink's stunned stupor to Elitia's red face.

Elitia glared at her. There was no fire behind it, but something else. It was something dark and cold that sent shivers of alarm down Blythe's back.

Blythe eyed the door. "Maybe this isn't such a great idea, Phink."

Without comment, Elitia spun on her heel and stomped off through a door marked "employees only." She seemed to suck all the air out of the room as she went, and the door slammed shut behind her with a note of finality.

Blythe's eyes went wide as she peered at Phink. "Seriously, Phinkster?"

He scowled. "Don't call me that."

"You want me to work for *her*?" Blythe flapped her hand in Elitia's direction.

"No." He rolled his eyes. "You'll work for me, just like you did at Centrism."

"Did you get hit in the head?" She seethed under her breath. "Because you must have amnesia. No other way you forgot why I grouped up with Tilla in the first place—"

"Let's not be melodramatic—"

"You're not painting another target on my back, Phink!"

Phink shut his mouth. He took a full step back, biting his lips into a thin line as he glared anywhere but at her.

Blythe's insides shriveled up, and she slumped. "I didn't mean it like that."

"You did. And that's fair."

For a long moment, neither of them spoke.

"There's no way you blame me worse than I do," he said at long last.

Blythe cringed, shaking her head to disperse the stinging at the corners of her eyes. "I don't blame you."

"You should." He sighed. "But that's ancient history. Humans First is a problem for Earth, and you left that all behind for good reasons."

Blythe couldn't quite meet his eye as she sniffled and nodded. "Yeah. I really did."

"This isn't Centrism."

She snorted.

"And this isn't Earth," he continued, undeterred. "We're as removed from that shitstorm as it's possible to get, and you're not the only one who needs to get on with their life."

Blythe stayed silent as she considered his words. She weighed them against the sad smile on Tilla's face as they parted ways in front of their damaged ship. She tested the idea of returning to the stage against her resolve to remain with the crew and the possibility she might feel like part of it someday.

Underneath it all, she thought about the thin veneer of unwarranted hatred she felt emanating from Elitia Kenwood. She thought about it hard, and she couldn't help but compare it to the insurmountable distance and relative safety she found aboard The Zephyr.

Then, for one glorious heart-stopping moment, she wondered if that was enough to compete with the opportunity to dance again. Safety was one thing, but what about boredom? Was it worth trading in for the heat of a spotlight on her skin and the adrenaline rush of applause? What about the regular vitality of well-used muscles and the satisfying exhaustion of using her body the way it craved most?

It might just be worth her while. If only she wasn't so afraid.

"This could be a golden opportunity for us," Phink said, taking her hand in his and squeezing tight. "You and me, we can do this thing right, like we used to, but better. Please, Blythe? I can't do this alone."

Blythe groaned. "That might work on Sly, Phinkerton, but not me. I'm more selfish than that."

She tried to tug free, but Phink held fast. It was possible she didn't put much effort into the attempt.

"Give me two weeks!" Phink shook her for emphasis. "Come on, Blythe! Together, we can whip this place into shape, garner a following, and as soon as we can prove ourselves to Troy, I swear, we can kick Elitia out on her ass."

Blythe rolled her eyes as she stopped trying to get away. "You don't know that."

He countered with a knowing smirk, "I have more than a strong inkling!"

Blythe folded her arms over her chest and cocked her hip. Expectant, she waited for him to keep talking.

Phink did not disappoint her.

EARTH WAS DYING, AND EVERYONE KNEW IT. THE PLANET WASN'T inhabitable beyond the environmental protections of the few remaining ports, but that hadn't stopped humankind from trying their damnedest to outlast the planet. The earliest splicing experiments didn't result in giving humans super durability though; they resulted in Homo nocturni.

Vampires.

The nine people who were both rich and desperate enough to subject themselves to experimentation gave birth to the species. By the time Mars and the moon were colonized, there were many more families besides them, but the descendants of the original nine persisted as de facto royalty. The Troy Harem was one of those Bloodlines, and it was the most notorious of all the Lunar-based Harems.

The prestigious lineage was only partially responsible for the notoriety.

"Let me get this straight," Blythe said as she held up a hand to interrupt Phink's prattle. "HEPP's entertainment business on Lunar-5 was responsible for one of the only documented cases of a Nocturni child abduction, and you expect me to believe the Harem —who just happens to be one of the most powerful in existence— didn't wipe the place clear off the face of the moon?"

"Yep." Phink raised his latest beer in a toast before taking a long draw from the bottle.

Blythe laughed in his face. It wasn't funny, but it was unbelievable.

"Far as anyone knows," Phink continued the tale, "Tanya Troy is the only Heir from The Nine to ever go missing. The last place she was seen alive was right here." He knocked his knuckles on the bar.

Blythe sobered as she inspected the barren establishment anew. "What was a kid doing here, anyway?"

Phink snorted into his drink. "She was a Nocturna. You know anyone with the guts to ask a child-sized apex predator how old she is?"

Blythe winced, her smile going sheepish. She may have grown up on Earth, but her years on Centrism's stage had taught her plenty about vampires. They aged much slower than their human counterparts, and it was usually impossible and always unwise to make such a judgment based on their appearance. Depending on their diet, lifestyle and preferences, a vampire could appear decades older or younger than a human of the same age.

Trying to redeem herself, Blythe sat up straight and affected an air of nonchalance as she told Phink, "Rookie mistake. I know better than that."

"You better," Phink chuckled.

As the talk subsided to the sounds of sloshing alcohol, Blythe reconsidered the calligraphy letters hanging above the bar. Tanya's Place.

"I don't get it," Blythe admitted between sips of beer, still studying the sign. "She wasn't just another vampire. How does the intended leader of any Harem disappear from a crowded bar? Stars above, and why would the Harem advertise the loss? That can't be good for business."

She didn't realize how loud she was getting until the Employees Only door popped open and Elitia graced them with a smarmy smile. "Would you mind lowering your voice, dear? I have work to concentrate on."

Blythe's stomach gave a nasty turn as she gave the woman a nod of acknowledgment. Elitia disappeared behind the door, muttering under her breath something about untrained animals and shitty business decisions.

Phink didn't hear the snide commentary though. For all his splicing, he never adopted Blythe's fickle hearing.

"I really don't like her," Blythe commented as she refocused on her drink.

"I don't blame you." After another swig, Phink jerked his chin toward the back door with a knowing look. "So, about her . . . I'm not saying play nice, but ignore her. For now, she's an unavoidable fixture." He gave her one of his wannabe paternal smiles. "Technically speaking, Elitia's not employed by HEPP. She's the third generation of her family indentured into serving the place."

Blythe choked on her drink.

It wasn't the first time she'd heard about an indenture contract. HEPP used them in conjunction with law enforcement to ensure fair punishment without unnecessary loss. Nonetheless, Blythe could count the number of indentured souls she'd met on the fingers of one hand.

"Elitia's great-grandfather was managing the House back when Tanya Troy went missing," Phink explained, his voice heavy and his shoulders slumping. "The Harem blamed him. They couldn't prove he was directly responsible, but they said his negligence cost them not just a family member, but a generation's worth of hopes and investments."

Blythe gave a sympathetic hum. "Yeah, it's not like vampires reproduce that often."

"Exactly."

Grievances between humans and Nocturni were a touchy matter. It wasn't HEPP's job to mitigate interspecies conflicts—that's what The Guard was for—but the continuation of human existence was HEPP's ultimate mission. Indentured work was the acceptable alternative to letting vampires steamroll their less-evolved cousins.

"From what I've heard," Phink continued, "Tanya's parents wanted to crucify old Kenwood and have a bloodbath in his staff's remains. The Guard intervened enough to stop a massacre, but HEPP had their hands full keeping it that way. They signed a good percentage of all the House's future proceeds over to the Harem, but the money wasn't enough for the vampires."

Blythe sighed and slumped in her stool, nodding along. "Ergo, a multi-generational indenture."

Phink shrugged with a vague agreement. "Elitia's great-great-grandchildren will be the last generation forced to work for the Troy Harem."

Blythe held up her fingers as she tried to count the generations.

Seven? "Damn." Blythe almost pitied Elitia. Almost. The idea made her skin crawl.

"Yep," Phink agreed. "Now, I don't think Elitia's consciously trying to tank the business out of spite—"

Blythe made a dubious noise.

"—but I wouldn't put it past earlier generations. The Harem's just about written the place off, but I'd love to see Master Troy's reaction if I managed to make it viable again."

As he spoke, Phink's voice grew stronger, surer. Blythe knew what was coming, but the sobering tale of the Troys and the Kenwoods was a heavy load to sit tall under.

"We could make this place great, Blythe," Phink said, undaunted by her inattention. "And honestly, it would do you some good. Sly left you a small fortune, and you've barely touched it. You got a free ride off Earth and decided to bypass all of Luna's opportunity to fly around on a rusty merchant bucket."

Blythe pouted at him. "It's not rusty."

But it *was* scratched. She didn't tell him that. He didn't need the extra ammunition against her anyway. Phink hitched up his trousers as he faced her head-on. Then he made his final argument.

"You're not the only one who needs this chance, Blythe. I'm trying to make up for everything you went through because of my recklessness."

With a pathetic whine, Blythe dropped her forehead onto the bar. She didn't want to look at him if he was going to play dirty and guilt her into this half-baked scheme.

"I never should have suggested you market yourself as pure and un-spliced. If I hadn't pushed for it so hard, you would have listened to Sly the first time he warned you off."

Blythe squeezed her eyes shut against a flash flood of waterworks. She didn't need to see him; the genuine grief in his voice was audible, even without her feline senses activating.

Phink sighed and set a featherlight hand on her head. "I know I couldn't stop those bigots from torching your apartment on Earth, but even I can manage to stop Elitia-fucking-Kenwood from stabbing you in the back with her cattiness, right?"

Blythe laughed, choking a bit on the lump in her throat. She shouldn't have, not if she knew what the future held in store for her, but she did.

CHAPTER 3

Blythe liked to imagine herself as a strong and independent woman, but that public image was a lot easier to pull off when she had someone like Sylvester Spurgeon holding her up. As two of the handful of humans born on Earth in their generation, they'd been inseparable for the longest time, from snot-nosed kids to the highest-paid showrunners at Centrism, the sole HEPP House in the American Port. She was there for him when his mother died, and he returned the favor when her parents took off.

They weren't family; in many ways, they were more than that. It hadn't hurt when her parents left—Blythe saw it coming years in advance—but Sly? That gutted her.

"I love this idea!" Sly cheered from her couch's armrest.

The furniture was less a couch and more an oversized chair, but it filled the living space of her apartment to the max. Her comms unit was perched on the plush armrest across from her while she sat sideways, her back pressed to the opposite arm with her knees tucked to her chest. The device gave off a delicate glow, and Sly's projected image floated above it in real time.

Much like her idea of a proper couch, Sly wasn't there. Not really.

If he were, she might be done fixing the chaos growing out of her head already.

"I always knew you'd be a fancy-schmancy Moon Diva, someday," Sly teased.

Blythe responded with a noncommittal hum and kept the majority of her attention on the mirror propped up on her thighs. She made a disgruntled face as she watched her reflection work the pintail of a comb into the fraying end of the latest loc. A mere fraction of her head was freed from the twists, and she couldn't stop herself from wishing she had an extra pair of hands to speed up the process.

In typical Sly fashion, her best friend was prattling on in the background without seeming to notice her ordeal.

"I'm sure tagging along with Tilla was a nice change of pace, but we all know your heart belongs to the stage!"

Over the edge of her mirror, Blythe spied him lifting his chin and tossing up a hand for dramatic flair. She rewarded his exuberance with a giggle, and the hair beneath her fingers seemed to unravel with the slightest more ease.

Sly's face grew larger as he loomed into his comms, and the graphics on her current device were so detailed that she almost believed he was looking right at her, as if there weren't so many lightyears between them. His pointed features and reddish hair were a comforting sight, but her breath caught in her throat when she noticed the pinprick spots covering his nose.

Blythe dropped her comb.

"Have Phink record your first show at Tanya's," Sly ordered with a cheeky grin. "I want to see—"

"Stars above," Blythe murmured, "you have *freckles* now?"

Sly blinked. He went cross-eyed in the attempt to focus on his own nose. "Oh, hey! Look at that!"

As he folded over with peals of laughter, Blythe tried to smile. She wasn't very successful, considering how her thoughts were stuck circling ideas of sun damage and change.

They were Earthlings. They didn't have freckles. They just . . . didn't.

"Shit." Sly refocused on her. "Didn't I tell you? Of course not. You've been so busy. Right! I did a thing! It only took me the better part of a year, but I did it!"

Blythe's jaw dropped as she realized what he'd done. Blinking rapidly, she diverted her stare from the comms and started a blind search for her errant comb.

"I went outside!" he crowed, "without cover!"

She didn't find the comb, but she did knock over the water and conditioner she was using to soak each loc. She watched the bottle roll away with a peculiar ringing in her ears. It sounded an awful lot like Sly's voice.

"I mean, I used some sunscreen," he said, "I'm not a complete idiot, but still! I didn't panic! Look at this little Earthling go!"

His sudden silence cued her to respond, but Blythe thought the wayward water bottle was a safer place to rest her gaze.

"Blythe?"

Blythe cleared her throat and slid to the floor to reclaim her tools. "That's amazing, Sly. Didn't know you had the balls for it."

"You only say that because you're jealous."

"Of your potential skin cancer?"

"Of my substantially larger balls!"

Blythe snorted and managed to catch her breath. She found her comb underneath the couch. "No thanks. I've had enough of those interfering with my life."

He laughed at her. Blythe perked up at the sound and found him cackling at her with his head thrown back and mouth gaping. Careless. Relaxed. Happy.

And freckled.

He wasn't the boy she knew. The thought crashed into her brain with the visceral force of a blow to her chest. She swayed.

Sly's mirth subsided into a soft smile. "I miss you."

"Yeah," she said, climbing back onto the couch. "Me too."

"Phink's probably right, you know." He avoided her gaze as he shrugged. "You've been on that ship long enough. It's been years, Blythe. I doubt the Humans First crowd even remembers your name."

Blythe's fist tightened on the comb till the bristles bit into her fingers. In that moment, the distance she put between herself and their homeworld amounted to nothing but a substantial chill racing down her spine.

It was an uncommonly strong reaction, granted, but it wasn't unwarranted.

She used to think Humans First was nothing but a bunch of fetishists with a wistful romanticism for authentic, un-spliced humanity. In a time period where genetic modifications and nonhuman phenotypes were the norm, Blythe once managed a bit of sympathy for them.

She wasn't that naïve anymore.

Blythe heaved a sigh and patted around for the partially removed loc. "I want to tell you Humans First hasn't crossed my mind in a while, but you know me too well to believe that particular lie."

Sly snorted, but he didn't disagree.

"There's a part of me that can't wait to dance again," she admitted, "but it feels small. Insignificant."

She found the twist and rolled it between her fingers. It was a hefty piece, but it felt somehow diminished since she last touched it, as if the turn in conversation made the very hair on her head lesser.

Blythe gave a short, dark laugh and tossed the loc back over her shoulder. "Then there's the part of me that's convinced any spotlight will turn into a neon bullseye on the back of my head."

Sly didn't join in her sardonic laughter. He bit his lip and fidgeted. "No lie, Blythe? Leaving Earth and lying low was a smart idea. Smarter and a lot more extreme than I thought you were ready for."

"Thanks, Sly," Blythe said without inflection as she slumped in her seat. "You say the nicest things."

He rolled his eyes. "I don't mean it like that. I just know this wasn't the life you imagined for yourself. Your life on Earth was nothing like mine—your needs were met! You never had a vested interest in getting off the planet, until the choice was taken away from you."

They lapsed into a tense silence. Blythe couldn't bring herself to look toward the comms. She had the unnerving feeling that Sly was looking at her with too much understanding.

He was always annoyingly insightful like that. Of the two of them, Sly was the clever one. He always had a plan, usually more than one, and if he didn't have a ready solution to any given problem, he had an uncanny ability to make something up in the moment. He was adaptable in ways Blythe envied.

Blythe said, "I need to let you go."

"But—"

"Moon Divas don't walk around with their head half-done," she said, scooping the comms up in one hand. "I want my hair done before hitting that stage, and you're distracting me."

She shut off the device before he could argue.

Phink was right. Sly was right. It was time to move on with her life and let the past stay where she left it.

ALL SASS AND JOKING ASIDE, BLYTHE'S EXPERIENCE AT THE LUNAR House was a far cry from what she or Sly had known on Earth. From her first day on the payroll, she recognized the differences.

For starters, Tanya's Place was not currently open to the public. Phink convinced Master Troy and HEPP that the establishment would benefit from a couple weeks of polishing, both of the venue and its employees.

The bar and stage were nothing like the separated lounges and showrooms Blythe was used to at Centrism. There wasn't enough space to expand or designate separate rooms out of the open floor plan, but Phink was determined to brighten the place up with fresh paint. He was careful to keep the elaborate bar top the same, and the geodes within it seemed to sparkle in appreciation of the new lighting fixtures.

Before long, Tanya's Place would be a cozy lounge that Blythe might be proud to perform at.

It wasn't quite there yet.

"This was a mistake," Blythe muttered as she sidled up to Phink's side to start her first day on the job.

They stood within arm's reach of the stage, watching two of Tanya's other self-professed talents practice. Blythe didn't recognize either of the young women, and the longer she watched them try to shimmy in sync with each other and their muted music, the gladder she was of it.

"Too late now," Phink said as he frowned at the so-called performers. "You told Tilla you were jumping ship?"

Blythe shrugged. "Not exactly. I'm on leave till the next time they're in port."

With greater symmetry than the two practicing dancers, Blythe and Phink tilted their heads to follow an attempted cartwheel. Only one of the girls landed on her feet, and not where she ought to have been.

"This is what I have to work with," Phink muttered. "Kind of makes Elitia seem like the least of my concerns."

Blythe blew out a breath. "You're in trouble, Phink."

"No shit." Without another word, Phink grappled for the comms on his wrist, and the music stopped. "Take a break, ladies. Let's give Blythe the floor for a bit, yeah?"

Within seconds, they had the bar to themselves.

"It's impressive how quick they move when they're not performing," Blythe said.

"They don't have the same spirit as the lot at Centrism, that's for sure." Phink sighed as he massaged his temples. "Most Earthlings are motivated to charm their way off planet. Here, working for HEPP is just a dead-end job as a glorified trick pony."

Blythe dropped her bag on the edge of the stage and turned to face him with a heap of disheartened expectation dragging her shoulders back. "All your staff are like that?"

He shrugged. "The barkeeps know what they're doing."

Blythe hung her head. "I remember you asking me to help. You never mentioned a one-woman show."

"You can catch them up to speed."

"Don't you dare put that on me, Phink."

He responded by slipping the comms from his wrist and forcing it into her hand. "All you have to do is what you do best. Dance. Enjoy yourself. Show them how it's done, and once you've galvanized them into putting in a decent effort, you can buy me a drink with your first round of tips."

"You're an asshole."

"That's why we get along."

Despite herself, Blythe was smiling as she slipped the comms onto her wrist.

IN THE ENSUING DAYS, IT BECAME CLEAR THAT PHINK HAD misjudged Tanya's assorted performers.

Blythe didn't take any cues from her peers about minimizing the music; if she was using the stage for rehearsal, she was blasting the beat till it reverberated off the walls. The only person who seemed to notice was Elitia.

"Do you mind?" the blonde wailed every time she stuck her nose out of the Employees Only door. "Some of us are trying to work!"

Blythe didn't bother issuing another reminder that the back rooms were decently soundproofed from the public areas. Instead, she fell into a deep back bend. The routine didn't ask for it, but it felt right in the moment; she couldn't think of a movement better suited to telling someone they were being ignored.

Elitia slammed the door shut as she ran back to her office.

No one else intruded on her rehearsal time. For the third day in a row, Blythe took her time stretching between runs of her preferred routine, and she tacked on a few random exercises and spins for the fun of it. It took her well over the time block Phink allotted her on the schedule, but still no one approached her.

Like every other day so far, one or two of the other performers revealed themselves for no apparent reason than to ogle her sweaty form and grab something from behind the bar. She had yet to see any of them show the slightest interest in climbing on stage.

Blythe wasn't sure if she was impressed or disgusted. Back on Earth, people begged for this kind of opportunity. She tried not to dwell on it too long and instead threw herself back into practice.

She was careful with herself, checking her form and reevaluating the feel of each muscle after every turn to make sure she wasn't overdoing it. She wasn't as strong as she once was, and the last thing she needed was to injure herself when Phink needed her most.

That didn't mean she was forced to take it slow.

The years of splicing worked in her favor. Before long, she was back to wiping sweat off the jaguar markings, and she discovered she rather liked the metallic sheen it left behind on the yellow areas. Her body definition was returning with a vengeance, along with the stamina and prowess of ancient Earth's wildest cats.

The House and its staff weren't celebrating her return to artistry, but her body sure seemed to be.

The exhilaration of putting herself through the paces almost made up for the necessary evil that was Elitia Kenwood.

She blamed Elitia for the staff's general attitude. She told Phink as much, and according to him, she wasn't the only one.

Blythe was cooling down with her arms stretched high above her and her eyes lazily closed when her music cut off. Blinking herself to greater awareness, Blythe lowered her arms as she stared down at Elitia from the stage.

"Oh, good!" Elitia chirped with cloying sweetness as she set Phink's master comms back on top of Blythe's workout bag with a nasty, self-satisfied smirk. "You're done for the day, right?"

"No, actually."

Blythe's fatigued muscles and sweaty clothes told another story, but Blythe wasn't about to say so.

Elitia pretended not to hear her. She snapped her fingers at Blythe while flapping her other hand toward the public toilets.

"Go grab supplies from the back. I need you to clean up the restrooms before you leave."

Blythe glared down at her from the stage as she blew an impatient sigh. "I'm not a custodian, Elitia."

"I beg your pardon?" Elitia did a double take, gaping between Blythe and the vacant spread of the room.

Except the lounge wasn't quite so vacant as she previously thought. No less than three of the nameless faces she was supposed to be sharing rehearsal time with were clustered at the far end of the bar, not far from the door leading to the back rooms. They were watching Elitia and Blythe like a pack of hungry scavengers waiting to pick their bones clean.

What in the cosmos had Elitia been saying to them?

Blythe hopped down from the stage and pulled her arms back in another cool-down stretch. Now on even flooring, she had to crane her neck back to meet the other woman's gaze, but she did so comfortably.

"I'm not cleaning crew," Blythe said, her words short and crisp but professionally polite. "I'm a performer."

The layers of dark makeup on Elitia's lashes seemed to bounce off her cheeks as she blinked down at Blythe. "You are an employee, Ms. Ramos. My employee, no less, which means you do what I say and address me with respect." She smiled, her lips closed tight and wickedness glinting in her eyes. "And you'll address me as Ms. Kenwood from now on, yes?"

Elitia stomped her heel as she turned away. Blythe wasn't sure if she was trying to be comically dramatic, but she was.

As a result, Blythe forgot to be wary.

"You aren't the one who hired me, Elitia."

Elitia froze mid-step. The shameless snoops by the bar erupted into excited twitters too garbled to be deciphered. One of them scampered for the Employees Only door with a resolute shake of her head.

"Since cleaning duties weren't included in the job description, I think I'm good to go."

"You two"—Elitia pointed at the remaining staff at the bar one at a time—"go clean the bathrooms. I need to have a chat here with our resident Earthling."

Blythe frowned. "They don't need to do that. They're performers too. Technically."

With her back still turned to Blythe, the angry flush creeping up the back of Elitia's neck was obvious and immensely satisfying.

"Also," Blythe added as she scooped up her bag, "if it's respect you're wanting, you might want to start practicing first."

Elitia spun around. Her mouth was set in a hard line, and her face was an interesting shade of red teetering toward purple.

"Excuse me?" she spat, her teeth clenched behind her smile. "I'm not sure about the flea-infested port you came from, but here on Lunar-5, we have certain standards to uphold. If you expect to keep working here, you'll get over yourself and do as you're told."

The Assistant Manager stomped out of the room, with Blythe and her plus two staring after her.

That was when Blythe's baffled humor finally turned the corner into indignation.

"Don't touch those bathrooms," she advised the other performers as she copied Elitia's exit in the other direction.

BLYTHE WALKED THROUGH TANYA'S DOOR THE NEXT DAY HALF expecting to find the big blonde lying in wait to fire her. Instead, she found seven wannabe entertainers huddled around the table closest to the stage and snickering among themselves.

One of them spotted Blythe and began hushing the others. Blythe stalled out in the entryway and watched the commotion gradually peter off into quiet. It took a while.

Blythe made a vague gesture toward their table. "What's all this?"

One of the previous day's witnesses to her little tiff with Elitia piped up, "Mr. Phink said—"

"Don't call him that!" Blythe interrupted with genuine alarm. "It's just Phink. No 'Mister' allowed."

"Yeah, well, he said you could help us fix up our acts."

Blythe wasn't sure what happened after that. The rest of the day passed in a whirlwind of aggravating conversations with amateurs and a headache born from attempting to learn names and sequences she didn't care about. The next time she had a chance to check a clock, nine hours had passed, and she spent none of it on her own act.

More surprising still, Blythe realized there hadn't been a hint of Elitia in all that time.

She went home that night shaking her head in bafflement, too exhausted to realize she'd made an enemy.

THE DAYS FLEW BY, AND BLYTHE WAS BEGINNING TO HOPE SHE AND Phink had a chance at saving Tanya's Place after all. None of the staff were on Blythe's level, but they weren't embarrassing themselves.

There was a boy who couldn't keep time to save his life, but with the proper guidance, he made an amusing sort of contortionist. The two girls were finally on beat and completing their turns more often than not, but it was fortunate for everyone that dancing was not the core element in their performance; they turned out to be decent singers. There were other nuggets of talent hidden away in Tanya's undisciplined lineup, but none as promising.

"I say cut the others loose and focus on them," Blythe suggested to Phink sometime during her week. "They won't be drawing in crowds any time soon, but give them enough props and effects, and get on their asses about practicing, and they can probably keep you up and running."

Phink studied her from across the bar until the weight of his gaze made her fidget. "You say that like you won't be involved."

Blythe shrugged and started playing with the smooth wave of hair falling over her shoulder. It felt good to slide her fingers through all the sleekness, and if focusing on it happened to help her ignore the heavy expectation in Phink's face, so much the better.

"At this rate, The Zephyr will be back well before you're ready to reopen," she said without looking at him.

He scoffed. "Bullshit. I saw you twirling around up there yesterday. You're not giving it up again. No way."

She tried to fend off the smile but failed. "Yeah, I don't think I have it in me to do it again."

"And with any luck, you'll never have to."

Without missing a beat, Phink produced two bottles from beneath the bar and offered her one. She uncapped it in time to meet his raised beverage with a cheery clink of glass.

He cheered, "To a bright and inevitable future!"

For the first time in years, Blythe let the idea of such a thing warm her soul. She was close to giddy from the prospect, so she tilted her head back to drain the alcohol like it was water after a grueling workout.

It was the absolute worst moment for Master Leopold Troy to show up unannounced.

"You certainly look comfortable here, Ms. Ramos."

"Shit!" Blythe squeaked as Phink choked on his drink. They each jumped out of their skins as they spun toward the vampire.

Master Troy stood in the entryway in a suit every bit as rich as the last one she'd seen him in, but more casual—with an open collar and absent of any necktie. With his mouth closed over his fangs and the sharp points of his ears hidden behind his hair, Blythe almost mistook him for a pure-blooded human.

While Phink bent behind the counter to finish coughing up his drink, Blythe greeted the vampire with a strained smile.

"Yeah! I'm comfy." She cleared her throat and tried for a semblance of professionalism. "What brings you here tonight, Master Troy?"

He didn't answer right away. His face remained bland and unenthused as he took in the partially remodeled bar. The vampire waited for a red-faced Phink to catch his breath and reemerge from behind the bar before giving her any sign of acknowledgment.

"I came to bring you this."

Master Troy lifted a hand to his heart and slipped his fingertips inside the opening of his shirt. He retrieved a thin silver chain.

Dangling from his lax grip was an oval pendant, smooth and polished but without embellishment.

Blythe eyed it as she fought the urge to fidget. She and Phink traded baffled glances.

"That's . . ." Phink hesitated. ". . . lovely?"

The vampire shrugged one lean shoulder. "I suppose."

With a swipe of his thumb along the oval's edge, a bright white line began to glow across its front. Blythe ducked her head, blinking fast as the shine intensified. When the glow leveled out and her eyes adjusted enough to raise her head, Blythe found a face of amber and sepia tones projected onto the counter.

It was a lovely face, a dark-haired female with a slender neck and shoulders supporting cheeks that were round and flush with youth. Like Master Troy, she might have passed for human if it weren't for the pearly fangs beaming from her carefree smile. The diamond-studded necklace around her throat was another giveaway —Blythe had never met a human who could afford rocks like that, not on Earth or Luna.

"This was Tanya," Master Troy said without inflection, as if conducting a chore. "My cousin."

"Ah." Phink's shoulders sagged as his voice grew soft. "Yes, Elitia told me about her."

"We're sorry for your loss," Blythe murmured as she picked at her drink's label.

"Don't be. It was a long time ago." The portrait disappeared as the vampire tucked the keepsake into his palm, testing its weight with borderline disinterest. "Truth be told, I only met her once. If she hadn't disappeared, I would be sipping blood-wine in Lunar-2 right now."

Blythe offered an uneasy smile before trading flummoxed glances with Phink. She saw no answers in his perturbed expression, but it was amusing to see the flash of panic in his widening eyes the second before the locket came flying at his nose.

Phink fumbled the catch, but he managed to save the vampire's keepsake from breaking on the floor.

"Personally, I don't care what you do with this place," Master Troy persisted with his blasé tone, "and as the scion of my Harem, my expectations are low. It's nothing personal, you understand."

Phink blinked down at the jewelry cradled in his palm without comprehension.

"With that said," the vampire continued, "my father and uncle have a request. They want to see Tanya's portrait incorporated in a memorial of some sort."

Phink jerked his head up, gaping at the vampire.

Blythe leaned over the bar to poke him into action.

He swatted her away with one hand while the other offered the locket back to the vampire. "I'm sorry, Master Troy, but this establishment is for entertainment purposes . . ."

Phink trailed off when the vampire made no move to reclaim the trinket. In a bid for a solution, he turned his wide beseeching eyes on Blythe.

"Yeah." Blythe cleared her throat and saved the locket from his outstretched hand. "A memorial would be a mood killer—"

"In the best-case scenario," Phink added. "Most likely, it'll be a deterrent."

"Depressing," Blythe tacked on with a helpful nod.

"Exactly!" Phink said, jumping on the lifeline she provided. "People come to HEPP Houses to revel in human life, not to be reminded of the dead."

Master Troy sighed but didn't otherwise react.

Phink shot Blythe another alarmed look. If he was hoping she would come up with something brilliant to get him out of this situation, he was in for disappointment. Sly was the witty one, not her. She was the blunt one, so she turned to the powerful vampire she'd had the honor to meet and told him: "Do you really think this is appropriate?"

"Stars above, Blythe," Phink muttered before smacking the back of her head and yanking the locket from her hand.

Master Troy was unmoved, though. He heard her, certainly, but he didn't seem to care about what she said.

"My parents are sentimental optimists," Master Troy explained with a touch of derision. "They've been spreading rumors among Luna's Nocturni about your hopes of making this little club worthy of association with our Harem, but you and I know that's unlikely. Accommodating my father's whims really ought to be a non-issue, all things considered."

"Right," Phink agreed, and the resignation in his voice made Blythe cringe.

"I don't care where you put it, or what form it takes," the vampire said, "just don't let Kenwood turn it into a cheap joke. Tanya was the intended leader of our Harem, and any memorial should show the respect she deserves."

When he'd entered the bar, Master Troy had made no noise—no approaching footsteps or clearing of his posh throat—and the snap of the door closing on his way out was disproportionately harsh.

Together, Blythe and Phink peered at the locket like criminals reading their death sentence.

Blythe deflated onto her barstool and muttered, "Guess that inevitable future isn't looking so bright after all."

AS THEIR ANCESTORS ONCE SAID, THE SHOW MUST GO ON.

Phink wasn't giving up on Tanya's Place just yet, and Blythe wasn't giving up her dancing again at the first sign of trouble. While Phink dedicated himself to coming up with a cleverly understated way to appease the Troy Harem, Blythe found herself the unofficial taskmaster, in charge of keeping the other performers on track for reopening.

Elitia seemed content with this arrangement, provided Blythe appeared to respect the sanctity of her office. It wasn't a hardship for Blythe; she had zero interest in ever venturing into Elitia's lair.

It took a Herculean amount of patience, but Blythe managed to carve out a couple hours of stage time for herself before Phink made Tanya's Place unavailable for a few days. A team of painters was scheduled to overhaul the place, and Blythe's unexpected posse of students utilized every last minute they could before they were kicked out for the duration.

Blythe didn't blame them. By the time she and Phink managed to chase them all out the door, she felt ready to dropkick any one of them if it got her ten minutes of solitude with the performance space at her disposal.

"Don't stay too late," Phink warned on his way out. "Elitia's managing inventory, so she'll lock up when she leaves. You better be done by then, or I wouldn't put it past her to lock you in overnight."

Phink chuckled under his breath, and Blythe didn't have the heart to tell him the little joke was probably a legitimate concern.

"I'll leave the moment she shows her face," Blythe promised.

Once he was gone, Blythe had a moment to gather her thoughts and enjoy the stillness before stripping down to her sweatpants and crop top. Then she focused on selecting some music to warm up to.

Phink carried out the House's master comms unit when he left, so she couldn't play her chosen toons from the stage speakers. It wouldn't be as loud as she liked, but that was just as well. She didn't need to get into another spat with Elitia so late at night when there were no witnesses.

It seemed the thought had occurred to Elitia as well. Blythe was still considering her audio options when the rear door creaked open and that blonde head popped into the lounge.

"Phink's gone already?"

"Yeah. Did you need him for—"

Blythe stopped talking when Elitia sucked her head back through the doorway and put a solid barrier between them.

"Rude much?" Blythe sneered at the door before refocusing on her comms.

She wasn't about to waste her solo rehearsal time on Elitia's passive-aggressive bullshit, though. With a shrug, Blythe selected a familiar beat and got to work.

It was nothing like practicing used to be. She didn't have a dedicated studio space to herself, and the bar's after-hours darkness would have been an issue if she didn't have a touch of feline night vision helping her out. Despite it all, Blythe was glad for the poor lighting; it successfully camouflaged the empty tables and ample standing room.

Tanya's Place was boring compared to her memories of Centrism. Blythe used to dance her ass off each night to an ever-revolving door of appreciative gazes. She was more than entertainment there; she was a fantasy brought to life, a reminder of the humanity from which they all came from. Her audiences used to be an eclectic mix of humans and vamps alike, and regardless of their species, they admired her furless skin and lithe form with envy as much as desire. She was human, an exotic specimen of a bygone era when natural fragility was the norm instead of a vanishingly rare luxury.

That was before one splice too many painted yellow-and-black spots on her skin.

A good number of those vivid markings were on full display to the vacant room as she swung her leg out for a rapid spin. The eager strain of her limbs and tendons made her feel alive, bringing warmth to the surface of her skin and sending a ticklish pooling of sweat down her back and into her cleavage. It was the good and useful ache of activity, and she reveled in it.

It turned out to be a major distraction.

Blythe planted her feet to interrupt the spin when she realized she was being watched. Elitia was glaring at her from another doorway, but the wrong one. In the poor lighting of the public entrance, the larger woman almost dissolved into the shadows. Blythe only caught her when the dim practice light reflected off the sickly neon green of Elitia's eyes.

"You're done with inventory already?" Blythe called across the open floor plan as she crossed her arms over her heaving chest.

Elitia's reptilian eyes kept glaring. In the long seconds it took her to answer, the sweat dripping down Blythe's back went cold.

"There's a bit left to do."

Blythe nodded and unfolded her arms to swing them in concentrated circles designed to regain her sense of momentum.

In the corner of her eye, Elitia never moved.

Blythe was no stranger to being watched, but she didn't like the prickle of the woman's relentless attention. She dropped her arms and gave up any pretense of resuming the routine.

"Can I help you?"

"You've done more than enough of that, thanks."

Blythe felt the muscles of her shoulders and back turn to solid rock without her conscious permission. Her jaw was tight enough to hurt as she stepped to the front lip of the stage.

"How about you move away from the door, Elitia?"

"No thanks."

Blythe's eyes narrowed. "Why not?"

Elitia shrugged, and the motion made the streetlights play over the silken silver of her favored suit jacket in hypnotic swirls. "I'm waiting for my cousin. He's bringing me dinner."

As far as excuses went, her words seemed reasonable. That said nothing for the elusive quality in Elitia's voice that had Blythe's baby hairs standing on end.

Blythe raised her wrist to check her comms. "A bit late for dinner, isn't it?"

Again, the woman shrugged. Blythe's night vision wasn't so

good that she could tell for sure, but she thought she caught sight of a vicious smirk.

"Whatever," Blythe huffed as she leaped off the stage. "I'm done anyway."

"Looks like it."

Blythe snatched her bag from a table and scoffed a sharp "fuck you" under her breath. No matter what she'd privately told herself when Phink took off earlier, Blythe didn't truly think the other woman would leave her stranded in the bar overnight. Until that moment. Blythe wasn't going to give her a chance to pull it off.

Elitia didn't hear her cussing. At least, she didn't react as Blythe put on her shoes and made a direct line toward the door. She was almost toe-to-toe with Elitia when the blonde sidestepped into her path with one of her disgustingly self-satisfied smiles.

"You should stick around for a minute and meet my cousin."

"No thanks."

"He's just like you, an Earthling with an overinflated ego and splicing addiction."

"Aren't you hilarious."

Blythe stepped backward to keep eye contact, and while she wasn't about to admit anything to Elitia's face, the action zapped her in the gut with a fission of fear. Elitia had a solid foot of height and unknown weight on Blythe.

"Get out of my way, Elitia. I'm leaving."

"A shame."

Elitia gave a sigh of phony disappointment and turned to the side to reach for the front door. She held it wide open for Blythe.

"I think he'd be just your type."

"Doubtful," Blythe griped as she squeezed past Elitia's bulk to get out. She took a deep breath of Lunar-5's wider atmosphere and turned to give the other woman a smart-assed wave as she swung her bag over her shoulder. "If he's related to you and he has a dick, he's definitely not my type."

A masculine laugh sounded nearby. "Is that so?"

Blythe jumped. Her bag hit the ground as she turned to see three human men traipsing toward them.

They were all spliced to varying degrees, and while their inhuman attributes were obvious, they could be called conservative by Earthling standards. Two of them had slitted cat's eyes, one of whom had the faint fuzz of tiger stripes on his arms, though the fur was thin enough to leave the pinup girl tattooed on his skin visible. They looked similar enough that they could have been brothers, or maybe they were simply spliced with the same regiment of cocktails.

The third was the one who laughed at her. He had slitted eyes as well, but Blythe wasn't so confident about the species it was derived from, given the thick rolls of dark-brown scales splotching the pasty-white skin of his neck and one hand. The scales didn't have the right consistency for a snake, but it might have been alligator or something more obscure. Maybe it was the reptilian attributes or the prideful jut of his jaw, but Blythe found him instantly familiar.

"So, you're the cousin?" Blythe huffed as she bent to retrieve her fallen bag.

He raised his arms with a cocky smirk, as if putting himself on display for her. Blythe wiped the expression off his face when she didn't give him a second glance.

She told Elitia, "There you go, I met him. Bye now."

"Hold on, now," the cousin said, jogging a few paces to catch Blythe while she was still in Elitia's vicinity. "Let me at least buy you a drink."

"Do I know you?" Blythe huffed as she got a better look at his face.

Scales aside, he looked nothing like Elitia. Yet the longer she stared, the stronger her certainty became. She'd seen him before.

The man flushed and shot his cousin a nervous glance as his friends snickered at his expense.

"Never mind," Blythe scoffed and turned to leave.

She must have seen him at Lunar-5's splicing center, the one and only time she'd gone in for a checkup. The yellow hues embedded in her skin seemed to brighten as a side effect of that visit, and she hadn't been back since, but the moon was a small rock. Coincidences happened.

The guy didn't take the hint. He hustled over to fall into step beside her. "Just one drink—"

"I said no." Blythe lengthened her stride and waved him toward his friends. "I'm spent. You guys have a good night, though."

"Oh, we will," the guy with the tiger stripes grinned at her.

"It'd be better with you joining us."

As he spoke, a hand sporting patches of armored skin darted out to grope her arm. Her skin got pinched by the scales.

Blythe yelped and slapped him clear across the face. Her palm connected with a resounding crack that sent echoes of ache reverberating up her arm. It was a solid hit. Satisfying.

His head snapped to the side, and he stumbled backward.

"Piss off," Blythe warned as she readied to run.

She took a step, and the ground shifted underneath her. Her ankle rolled. She stumbled. Her breath hitched, and the dark spots weren't just on her skin, but popping into thin air, obscuring her vision.

"I'm surprised you turned me down," the guy's disembodied voice whispered in her ear with haunting familiarity. "Dick never seemed like a turnoff for you on Earth. Then again, you weren't a splicing piece of shit then either."

Blythe swayed backward into his scaled arms and slurred, "Fucking hypocrite."

"No." As the world faded to black, dry lips brushed her

forehead, and he whispered, "You were always supposed to be better than me. That was part of the appeal."

Her hearing sharpened in desperation as her vision darkened. She caught Elitia tutting under her breath, "I thought you said she wouldn't recognize you?"

Then the world turned black.

$\mathcal{A}$t the behest of a visiting Martian vamp with deep pockets, Phink once set up a cage on one of Centrism's central stages. As the most prolific dancer in the joint, Blythe got first dibs at trying it out during practice. The experience put a bad taste in her mouth, and she handed it over to another artist without a backward glance. The thing disappeared without conversation a few days later.

That cage was a luxury suite compared to the steel-barred box she awoke in. This one had a lock.

It didn't stop her from trying to yank the gate open. For what must have been the hundredth time since she woke to find herself alone in a cage, the chain rattled and shrieked in protest. It was the only thing she could hear over the thundering of her pulse and panting breaths.

She breathed hard from the futile exertion against the unforgiving metal. She wasn't hyperventilating or crying herself useless. She wasn't screaming for help. Not anymore.

How long had she been trapped? Where was she?

Blythe fell limp with her back against the bars, legs folded under her as she watched the disturbed lock settle, its swing slowing faster than her heartbeat. She sat there and breathed, fully appreciating the insurmountable weight of her body. She wished she could stretch out her legs while sitting, but the cage was too cramped. The top of the prison wasn't quite high enough for her to stand up straight either, but at least it let her shake the stiffness from her lower limbs on occasion.

She must have been here for hours. Surely.

With a groan that treaded the line between dramatic disgust and genuine horror, Blythe spread her knees and grabbed at the crotch of her sweatpants. The fabric was dry but stiff and itchy. Fuck. No wonder her bladder wasn't screaming at her.

Had it been a matter of hours? Had it been *days*?

She was still dressed, thank the stars. She still wore the familiar crop top, the one that supported her breasts well enough to forgo a bra while letting her skin breathe the way she liked during hours of exercise. Right now, so long and far from the healthy flush of a recent dance, the outfit left her shivering and smelly. The brown waves of her straightened hair were stiff, tangled, and crunchy from sweat and stage products that sat too long.

Her reliable comms unit was missing too. Her wrist felt cold.

Stars above. Did Phink know she was missing yet?

The empty room beyond the cage was insultingly vast. It might have been a storage room at some point, before Elitia-fucking-Kenwood's douchebag of a cousin turned it into a giant human trafficking crate. There was a single door, blank and solid like the rest of the surroundings. The walls were smooth, though streaked with years of grime, with shelves built in along two-thirds of the perimeter. There was nothing on those shelves now. No clocks. No parcels of food. No jugs of water. There wasn't even a window. There was nothing.

Blythe's chest and throat constricted all over again as she stared through the bars. Her lungs burned, her heart ached, and the disheartening sight of her slate-gray surroundings blurred as her eyes summoned fresh tears.

All that existed was her and the cage. Nothing else.

CHAPTER 5

Blythe was on the cusp of admitting defeat and curling up into a ball to die. It'd been days of isolation, all without food or water. She was parched, her lips cracked and bled, and the muscle mass she'd just begun building back up on Phink's behalf was withering fast. Before long, she would be skinnier than Sly; that mental image threatened to make her cry again, so she forced herself to stop thinking about Sly—or Phink, for that matter.

She didn't have the moisture to spare for tears.

The door opened with a soft click. The minor sound cracked the still air of the makeshift prison with the force of a gunshot.

Blythe leaped to her feet and smacked her skull on the overhead bars.

"Fuck!" She crouched back down with both hands clamped over her head.

Elitia's asshat cousin snickered as he closed the door behind him. Blythe rubbed her sore head and glared at him as he approached the cage with a paper bundle in hand. The bastard caught her staring and began tossing the item between his palms.

His brow lifted, as if he were challenging her to a friendly ball game.

The feline DNA in Blythe's veins was stronger than even she knew. In that moment, it went beyond the black-and-gold markings on her skin and the inhuman edge to her speed and flexibility; even the occasional sensitivity of her nose and ears didn't compare to the feral manifestation of her disgust and fear. Staring down her kidnapper through the bars, she discovered a new catlike attribute.

Her back arched, and the fine hair at the back of her neck stood up. Before she realized what she was doing, Blythe bared her teeth and hissed.

The asshole gaped at her, blinking those slitted eyes twice in quick succession before he tossed his head back with laughter.

Blythe shimmied out of the animalistic crouch and gripped the bars with one white-knuckled hand. Her brain raced for something to say, something cutting and smart that would wipe the grin off his face. What would Sly say in this situation?

The thought caught her off guard, and she flinched. Sly would never be in this situation in the first place. He'd been the one to warn her about welcoming the Humans First crowd into her parlor, after all. She wizened up too late.

The sorry excuse for a human being knelt just beyond arm's reach of the cage. He was smiling.

"Crazy how things turn out, huh?"

"Yeah," Blythe sniped, "real crazy."

"It's a small universe, Blythe. I'm not going to stroke your ego and claim I was hunting you down all this time, but I admit, it was nice hearing your name dropped on the table at the latest family reunion." He wagged his fingers playfully as he said those last few words, his smile sick and wide.

"Two long years, and you still perk up at the slightest mention of my name? I'm flattered," Blythe said in a dry tone that made his smile frost over. "I never bothered to learn yours."

His face warped with a dissatisfied sneer. Now that she was looking at him up close, it was easy to recall his face. He was notable back then, without visible scales or slitted eyes, and his humanness sometimes caught her eye from Centrism's stage. It was no wonder she couldn't place him earlier; there was nothing remarkable about him now. He was just another spliced man in a galaxy that routinely renounced the mortal purity he was so obsessed with.

Fucking Humans First.

He sneered as he unwrapped the bundle he was carrying, yanking the paper free. He tossed his handful of items onto the floor with an angry jerk of his hand. "I was trying to be nice, for old time's sake, but if you're going to be such a bitch, here."

A meager sandwich flopped onto the floor, bread and cheese scattering. He fished a bottle of water out of his pocket and smashed it down onto the bread before letting it topple and roll away.

"Breakfast is served," he announced as he stood tall and stomped toward the door. "Since you like animals so much, you can eat off the floor like one."

Blythe eyed the pitiful food as she hugged her knees to her chest. The bread had the look of the freeze-dried stuff Tilla kept in stock on The Zephyr, with all the appeal of moldy cardboard. The cheese was no better, just a stiff brick of solid orange that was recognizably artificial. Blythe's empty stomach rolled till she stopped looking at it.

Her eyes landed on the water bottle.

She glared at the closed door. She muttered a vicious "sack of shit," under her breath, but it did nothing to make her feel better.

Jaw clenched tight, Blythe turned in a full circle to inspect the room again. There was still nothing to see besides a spilt sandwich and a wayward water bottle. At least there was nowhere for a camera to hide.

Blythe glanced at the bottle again.

She sighed and hung her head. "This is a mistake," she told herself aloud, "but I'm doing it anyway."

She slipped the sweatpants off her legs, and the action released a puff of stale ammonia into the air. Blythe gagged. She was grateful that her spliced senses had the decency to spare her in that moment. A human's limited nose was bad enough.

Careful to breathe through her mouth instead, Blythe scooted to the cage's edge and threaded her soiled pants through the bars. Her arms were next. She made a half-hearted attempt to reach for the nearest slice of bread on the floor before accepting it wasn't going to happen. The bastard had dropped it less than a hand's span from her outstretched fingertips.

The water bottle was farther away.

"Fuck me," she groaned as she gathered the cuffs of the sweatpants in one hand.

She tried to aim for the bottle, flinging the waistband out like a whip. The limp fabric didn't travel well through the air.

"Fuck!" she groaned, loud and careless and bordering on hysterics.

Her mouth was so dry. She couldn't resist the urge to lick her lips, and her skin was turning ashy. She needed that damn water.

She needed the bottle too. She wasn't going to piss herself again, not while fully conscious. She refused.

Not much later, her arms were weak with exhaustion, and she had nothing to show for it. One hand gripped onto cold steel, and the other went limp where it stretched beyond the cage, the pant legs barely contained in her fingers. Her face was jammed between two bars till the skin on her cheeks and jaw stretched with the sort of burning pain that suggested something might rip soon, if she wasn't careful.

It did no good. The water bottle remained out of reach.

The door clicked open again.

Blythe sat up straight and reeled in the useless sweatpants.

There was nothing she could do about the smell or the telling ache to the skin on her face, but she wouldn't give the fucker the satisfaction of seeing her slumped over in a futile attempt to hydrate herself.

Blythe glared toward the door, and her resolve faltered.

The man who crept toward her was not Elitia-fucking-Kenwood's cousin.

His advanced age was startling. It wasn't the number of years that did it, but the decades' worth of wear and tear so obvious in his sagging skin and rheumatic eyes. He had a balding head crowned by stringy gray wisps that fell past his shoulders, with the greatest concentration of whitened hairs growing from his overlong eyebrows and short-cropped beard. He was hunched over, as if the weight of such a long existence were too much for his thin shoulders.

He was a marvel that didn't make any sense. Humans only survived in the greater universe thanks to modern technologies, but this man looked like an ancient ancestor brought back to life. He was human, un-spliced and untouched by the medicines and innovations that could ease his old age.

"Good evening, Ms. Ramos."

Blythe winced. His voice was as rough and cragged as his wizened skin. Despite the posh accent of a Lunar native, it was gross and grating to her ears.

Though his steps were short and slow, he seemed to be walking under his own power as he slowed to a stop before the fallen water bottle. Blythe bit her tongue as she watched him inspect the mess on the floor.

"I see," he said with a calm disappointment that sent chills down Blythe's spine.

He didn't bend to pick it up, instead choosing to nudge the bottle forward with his foot. At least, Blythe assumed it was his foot; she couldn't see through the many folds of fabric pooling on the cement floor around him. He was draped in a silvery robe made of a fabric that moved like a mirage of flowing metals.

She'd seen its like only once before.

As he toed the water into her reach, the skin on Blythe's arms pebbled. The moment it was possible to do so, her hand darted out to snatch it up.

The old man didn't flinch or startle. He didn't react at all. He just watched her, rubbing the arthritic knolls of his knuckles with the liver spot-marked fingers of his other hand as she guzzled.

Blythe drank with her eyes open, watching him back. His silence was as unnerving as his rheumy gaze. He didn't make a sound as she drained the water, replaced the cap, and cradled the empty container in her lap. Clad in that otherworldly robe, she was half convinced he was a ghost.

Throat tight, Blythe nodded at the garment. "Nice dress."

"Thank you." His smile was small and warm, almost genuine. She might've found it reassuring if it weren't for the cold bars against her palm and the nauseating stiffness of her underwear. "My apologies for the unfortunate accommodations, Ms. Ramos."

Blythe snorted. She immediately clapped a hand over her mouth in horror, but the old man didn't seem to mind.

"I will have a talk with Andy concerning his poor treatment of you. No matter your failings, you are still a human woman, and you should be treated as such."

"Sure." Blythe nodded along and tried to ignore the disgust turning her stomach. "And you are? What? The Grand Master of the local Humans First faction?"

He tilted his chin in a small bow. "Of course. But you may call me Gregoire."

Blythe jerked away from the bars as if burned.

He chuckled, small and quiet like an easily amused grandpa.

From one second to the next, Blythe could no longer hear him over the force of her panicked breaths. Icey fear rushed up from her gut and squeezed her throat. It was already too surreal to accept a random Humans First lackey with a grudge had chanced upon her the moment she stepped off Tilla's ship; she couldn't believe a whole chapter had conspired against her, at the behest of an actual Grand Master.

Blythe's breath caught in horror; there wasn't supposed to be any organized collectives of Humans First on Luna. She checked long before ever renting a place on Lunar-5.

She couldn't look at him as she hugged her knees to her chest, the plastic bottle crunching between her thighs and torso. Voice shaking, she said, "I thought Humans First was an Earthly group?"

Gregoire's smile was bright and sympathetic. "We are from Earth, just as all life in the universe is. Without us, the parasites would not exist, and Earth's beasts would never survive. This world, like all colonized worlds, is as much our right as anyone else's."

Blythe's stomach churned. Numb, she mumbled, "If you say so."

"I do." He sidestepped the soiled sandwich and gave her cage a wide berth as he inched around the perimeter of the room. "It is not merely my say-so, but my purpose. The Human Existence and Preservation Project claims to ensure humanity's existence alongside our false cousins, the Nocturni, but it is the good men and women like myself who champion the human spirit!"

Blythe didn't like the quiet roar of validation in his voice when he said "human spirit." It sent chills up and down her spine and flooded her mouth with the taste of bile.

"That very same spirit," the old man stressed, "that same humanity, is something we share, you and I. The Nocturni lost theirs millennia ago, and the poor beasts used in splicing experiments know no better, but you and I have it in our veins."

He raised a gnarled fist and shook it at her for emphasis.

"It is in our bodies and souls, and that humanity must be preserved and nurtured! It is our birthright, and our greatest honor!"

Blythe's eyes stung, but no tears were trickling down her face. Not yet. He was behind her, having rounded the cage as he spoke, and she didn't raise her head to look at him as she croaked the words burning at the tip of her tongue:

"Is this what you call humanity?"

He paused. His footsteps went silent, and she could feel his presence behind her.

"No, my dear."

Blythe squeezed her eyes shut against the sad resignation in his voice.

"This is what we call an unfortunate necessity."

She laughed. It was low, weak, and short, but a laugh, nonetheless.

"There are always consequences to every action, Ms. Ramos," he said, ignoring her outburst. "While your splicing habit is regrettable, it isn't surprising. I can sympathize with you on that point. But lying to your fellow man about your purity? I do not know if that can be so easily forgiven, my dear."

Something hot and noxious flared from the pit of her stomach, and Blythe's whole body warmed. She was shaking as she twisted around and gripped the bars.

"Fuck you!"

His expression fell. With a gentle shake of his head, he turned to leave.

"Fuck! You!" she yelled after him.

He paused in the open doorway to glance back at her. "All human life is precious, Ms. Ramos, yours as much as mine. I hope you learn that during your time with us, but for now, I will have Andy bring you a proper meal and a bucket to relieve yourself with some dignity. I suspect you'll be here a while."

~

AS PROMISED, SHE WAS PROVIDED A BUCKET AND A MARGINALLY more substantial sandwich that wasn't served on a dirty floor. A package of bottled waters accompanied the meal, set outside her cage within easy reach through the bars. Elitia's cousin Andy delivered it all with a sneer and plenty of grumbling.

"By the way," he said as he retreated backward so he could smirk at her, "congratulations! You have officially lasted a full forty-eight hours in Humans First custody, and guess what? No one's come looking for you yet!"

Blythe balled up her soiled sweatpants and threw them at him.

He stopped laughing as he scurried out of range. His nose wrinkled as he glared at the pants where they landed on the floor between them. "Bitch."

"Takes one to know one."

He slammed the door on his way out.

Once he was gone, Blythe downed some more water and allowed herself another good cry. It was supposed to be a ten-minute pity party, or so she told herself, but time was meaningless and unmeasurable in the bland confines of her prison.

Forty-eight hours. She'd been missing for two lousy days, but it felt like it had been weeks already. The worst part was that she knew he was right: no one was looking for her. Not yet.

What would happen when Phink showed up to a freshly painted bar and no Blythe? What would Elitia tell him?

If she had any luck at all, Phink would be combing the galaxy for her within a few days. Tilla would be leading the hunt from The Zephyr's control room, and if they didn't find her soon, Sly would be notified, and then the Nocturni would get involved.

Yes, she told herself. Yes. She would be found. Rescue would come. Yes. Somehow.

The cage did nothing to distract her from the whirlwind of wild thoughts. Gregoire and Andy left her with nothing to do but replay conjectures and suppositions until she was dizzy with anxiety. She tried to be realistic as she envisioned what her rescue might look like, but it kept turning the corner into disbelief.

Luna's Human Services Department would officially spearhead the search for her, but they were a public service with limited resources and jurisdiction. HEPP might show an interest in her recovery, but she hadn't been a high-earning employee of theirs in years, and she had a history of refusing to participate in reproduction programs; most likely, HEPP wouldn't invest much in finding her.

With such facts in mind, Blythe inevitably tired of drawing circles around the same conclusion.

Her best chances lay with the Nocturni.

She wasn't fool enough to believe any vampires might already be involved in searching for her. She was nothing to them, barely established at a HEPP House that owed a particular bloodline a substantial debt. Phink might make a case about her being the Troy Harem's responsibility, but it wouldn't go anywhere. Not on its own.

She needed Sly.

If no one else had the resources to spare for her sorry Earthling ass, the Vauqeulin Harem did. Sly's vampire did. Kahled was alive and well thanks to Sly, and Sly did all he did with her support. She'd been there, at his side, rushing to the Harem's aide when they needed it. Yes. That logic was sound.

Sly could pay a ransom if it came down to it. He would rescue her, smooth over her mistakes, and make everything better, like he always did. Even if he had to rope his vampire into the debacle, he would. It was inevitable. She might not know Kahled personally, but she had no doubt he would crush entire planets to dust if Sly asked him to.

Yes, she repeated to herself over, and over, and over. Sly would save her. He always did.

She just had to survive long enough to give him the chance.

ANDY CAME AND WENT SIX MORE TIMES, EITHER TO EMPTY HER bucket or drop something edible alongside her water supply. The first few times, they traded insults and as-yet-unsubstantiated threats. When he started wearing a gas mask to avoid her stench, Blythe stopped engaging in the verbal sparring sessions. She wasted a water bottle trying to get her underwear and private bits clean, but there wasn't any soap, and she had no way to anticipate Andy's appearances; the last thing she wanted was him catching her naked.

She didn't know how many days had passed. Were they feeding her once a day? Every other day? She didn't know. She was struggling to make herself care.

"Grub time," Andy announced at some point.

Blythe ignored him. She sat curled up in a ball in the corner of the cage farthest from the door with her forehead on her knee and hair obscuring her face. The once-sleek tresses were matted and frizzy from the days of neglect, but it made an effective shield.

Andy kicked the cage till the room filled with the jarring sound of rattling metal. "Here, kitty, kitty."

She ignored him.

"Eat up, pussy."

Blythe didn't react. She bit the inside of her cheek till it bled, but she did *not* react.

He gave a satisfied laugh, and she heard something flop onto the floor. It was startlingly loud, and she almost lifted her head. Blythe took a cautious breath to calm her nerves and kept still. She couldn't smell anything over the reek of body odor and the bucket's fumes, but her ears were beginning to thrum with heightened sensitivity, the audio sharpening the longer she kept her eyes closed.

No matter what dirtbags like Andy said, the animal genetics in her system did not actually turn her into a cat. Her hypersensitivity was neither consistent nor controllable, but the feline edge to her hearing wasn't new either. She couldn't predict when the heightened hearing would go into effect, but she knew how to use it when it did.

She minded his footsteps and the sound of his breath. He didn't have the lung capacity she did, which could come in handy if she ever got a chance to run away. She heard the door handle turn, heard the lock begin to slide. She heard him pause and the excited hitch in his breath. He let go of the doorknob and stepped back toward the cage.

Blythe tensed, but she gave no outward sign of noticing him.

"You were hot shit back on Earth," he said, voice dripping with disbelief. "Now look at you. Locked up just like the animals you've been fucking with for stars only know how long."

Under the clumping, filthy curtain of her hair, behind the shield of her limbs wrapped around her, Blythe squeezed her eyes shut. She ignored him.

"I used to dream about sweeping you off your feet and carrying you off that stage," he said in a wistful tone. "I would watch you dance, flaunting what I thought was raw human flesh in front of constant crowds of sinful mortals and overgrown parasites, and you know what I thought?"

She didn't answer him. She ignored him. If it was the last thing she did, she would ignore him.

"I thought you were too good for all of them." His voice cracked with old grief. "I thought you were too good for me. You were supposed to be pure. You had everybody fooled, and I wasted my money and time on this fantasy that you were untouchable."

She pretended she couldn't hear the accusation in his voice. She tried not to notice as it blended into something hateful and viciously proud. She told herself his delusions had nothing to do with her and strived to unravel the nauseating knot in her gut that tightened with his every word.

"I wanted to save you so badly," he whispered. "The only reason I didn't was because I didn't want to soil you with my tainted hands."

There was a soft chime as he wrapped a hand around a bar, a nearly inaudible thud as he leaned against the barrier.

"You don't know what it did to me when I heard about your spots. I never bought the lies that it was a side effect of your first foray into splicing. I doubt anyone did. Damn, but you and the animal-fuckers at HEPP must really think people are stupid, if you thought that was a decent cover story."

Blythe couldn't keep still any longer. She shifted enough to press her eye sockets into her knees, hoping the pressure would stem the tears stinging along her lash line. He was right about one thing; she was stupid. She and Phink never should have marketed her as pure-blooded. They never should have welcomed a bunch of unhinged douchebags into her audiences.

"You know," he continued with a mean smugness, "armadillos are seriously ugly creatures, but they're tough. I've got all the elasticity of normal skin, with a good amount of armor built right in that can stop a vamp's fangs in their tracks. I guess my parents thought they were doing me a favor by giving me these."

She heard the click of his nail tapping the bony plates decorating the side of his throat.

"I was a dumb kid the first time I noticed the scales. Believe it or not, I first thought they were pretty cool, back when they were easy to hide. I was young, stupid. I didn't appreciate the damage that splicing was doing to my humanity. But you? You were a grown-ass adult, knowingly contaminating yourself over and over again. Do you know how fucked up that is?"

Without raising her head, Blythe muttered, "Tell someone who cares."

Her ears rang as he rattled the bars and shouted, "*You* should care!"

Blythe breathed through the pain in her head before deigning to lift her gaze. She glared at the ceiling rather than him. "And you should really invest in a therapist."

He didn't like that. She could hear it in the hissing of his breath through his teeth, the incensed pounding of his heart. She could feel it emanating off him in a stream of boiling, unspent violence.

For the first time, Blythe was glad for the cage.

His scales clashed with the steel in a jarring smack. Blythe's ears stung as the noise reverberated through her head, and she closed her eyes to let it pass.

"You're no better than me!"

Blythe shrugged her shoulders and curled back into her protective ball. She didn't know how good an armadillo's senses were, but she was willing to bet he couldn't hear the frightened skip in her heartbeat or smell the anxiety seeping from her pores.

She heard him stand and felt the swish of his leg and the rattle of the cage as he kicked it. "Bitch!"

She went back to ignoring him.

"You should be begging me for help!" Andy's voice grew louder, whinier. "I know what the Grand Master has planned for you! You think this is as bad as it gets? Stupid bitch, you don't have a clue!"

Every muscle in Blythe's body clenched hard. Somehow, she didn't think he was creative enough to bluff.

CHAPTER 6

There was no way of knowing how long they kept her in the cage. It could have been hours or days. It continued for long enough that she slept twice and scarfed down another meal, but there was no other indicator to judge the time by.

It wasn't long enough for Andy's threat to fade from the foreground of her thoughts.

The next time she saw Gregoire, he was dressed in the same molten silver robe as before, but this time, he leaned on a cane with every laborious step. It was ornately carved from a dark material, and from the distinctive tick of its point hitting the floor, Blythe suspected it was actual stained wood. It wasn't an ancient artifact from Earth though. It had the polished gleam of newness.

Where in the universe did these guys find living trees to make a trinket? Blythe knew there were Nocturni Harems who cultivated extraterrestrial forests, but they were a jealously guarded resource. Blythe had to wait decades for Sly to stumble into a Companionship before she got the opportunity to bite into a real-life, unprocessed apple, but Gregoire was walking around with a wooden masterpiece that was younger than she was.

He rounded the side of the cage and paused to consider the lock and chain, with his hands lightly folded over the bulbed handle of the cane.

"What vampire did you steal that from?"

He responded with a secretive little smile. "I didn't steal it. I made it."

Blythe's brow rose in suspicion, but she didn't call him a liar out loud. Andy's threat was too fresh, and Gregoire's affectation of grandfatherly thoughtfulness were making the baby hairs at the base of her skull stand on end.

The lock on her cage jingled as the old man lifted it in his palm. Studying it, he asked, "I suspect you'd appreciate a bath, wouldn't you, Ms. Ramos?"

Blythe's gorge rose. "Depends. What's it going to cost me?"

He made a soft wheezing sound; it took Blythe a moment to realize he was laughing.

"Something funny?" she said with more snap than was probably wise.

He glanced up at her as he fiddled with the lock. "I've already told you; you're a woman, not an animal. Basic hygiene ought to be a human right."

Blythe stared straight at him as she voiced a dry, "Wow."

"I can appreciate your suspicion, unnecessary as it may be."

She never spied a key, never saw him input a passcode. The lock released with a gentle cinch and slipped from the bars into his hand. The hinges of the cage's door turned, free and noiseless, as he opened it and held it aside for her. He made a genteel gesture with the cane.

"Come, my dear."

Blythe's skin crawled at the sound of his voice issuing the endearment. His expectant smile was the very picture of encouragement, but it made her want to scream.

She couldn't stay in the cage though, languishing in her own filth and self-pity. She wouldn't. As she uncurled from a crouch in the center of the prison, she told herself it was her decision. Her choice to comply. Her bare feet touched down on the cold cement of the floor beyond the bars, and she reassured herself that she was one step closer to escape.

It felt like a lie.

GREGOIRE LED HER DOWN A FEW BLAND HALLWAYS WITH A PAIR OF stoic and dutiful minions. She didn't recognize either of them, not like she did Andy, but both men had a good half-foot of height and close to a hundred pounds on her. They never touched her, but their presence was enough to dissuade her from doing something stupid like making a run for it.

Blythe half expected to be thrown in a stall and hosed down. Instead, Gregoire paused before one of the many unremarkable doors and indicated a basket on the floor where she found a clean pair of pants and a T-shirt. They were cut and sized for a man twice her size, but Blythe didn't need a cat's nose to notice the fresh citrus infused into the fabric; the pleasantness of it felt like a subtle snub to the stink permeating her person.

There was no visible lock on the door, but when Gregoire set his fingers around the handle, Blythe's ears caught the whirring of electronics and the mechanical shifting of a bolt. It was disturbingly quiet, nearly inaudible to her spliced senses, yet Gregoire paused for only a moment before opening the door, like he could hear it.

Maybe he had too much practice.

A seal hissed open, and Blythe jerked away with her hands over her ears as she was assaulted by the noise of pounding water.

Gregoire chuckled again. When Blythe's senses adjusted to the sudden change in auditory stimulation, she saw him wave her forward without a sign that he planned to follow.

"You'll find soap and towels along the wall near the pool. I'll give you twenty minutes." His kindly smile faltered as he eyed her and added, in complete seriousness, "It seems you could use a bit of a soak."

Blythe's face warmed as she fought the impulse to cuss him out. Hugging the basket of laundered clothes to her chest, Blythe scurried past him without comment. Her jaw was clenched tight enough to hurt.

It popped loose a second later when she got a look at the washroom.

It was beautiful.

There were countless shades of greens and blues, in textures and constructions she didn't immediately recognize. The space was huge. The ceiling was several stories high and bright as daytime on a hospitable planet.

It was amazing and confounding. Blythe's breath sped up as she took in more details.

The forceful water wasn't coming from a shower, but a fabricated waterfall built into the far corner. It flowed into an elongated pool of a blue-green, glistening liquid. The polished stones along the pool's edge receded into a green carpet unlike any other Blythe knew of; it was soft and compressed in some areas, yet prickly and crisp in others. Stars above, but there were flowers—literal, living flowers and plants—cleverly planted into concealed soil beds, and while there were no trees, there were countless vines and nets of foliage reaching up to the towering ceiling.

"It's a forest," Blythe whispered in awe.

She dropped the basket and reached for one of the hanging nets of greenery. She made a noise of disappointment when she recognized the material at her fingertips. The leaf was plastic.

"What is this?"

She was shaking as she crouched near a handful of brightly colored flowers. She prodded at the roots and her heart stuttered in her chest as she realized the soil was organic, moist and soft. She stroked a petal and uttered a trembling moan at the foreign sensation of raw nature against her skin.

Where was she? How did a human terrorist organization manage to grow their own plants? Even with the subsidized elements, it was a convincing attempt at mimicking ancient Earth at the height of its glory. It was more convincing than the animal enclosures at Luna's wildcat conservatory.

It stole the breath from Blythe's lungs, the strength from her legs. She collapsed onto the odd carpet and came to the thought-stopping conclusion that she was sitting on grass.

"My stars," she whinnied as she crawled toward the water's edge.

It was real, mostly. The closer she got to the pool, the more artificial the blades of grass began to feel. The sections up against the rocks where water lapped onto the greenery didn't feel as plastic as the hanging leaves, but it didn't have the authenticity of the flower petals either.

It was confounding.

She couldn't remember the last time she watched a film or glanced at a picture depicting grass. She never expected to learn what fresh greenery smelled and felt like, even after being forced to leave Earth. She hadn't sought out any such experiences, instead having chosen to tour the stars while aboard The Zephyr.

She was supposed to be safe on that ship.

Blythe felt more than a little dizzy as she sat on her ass. Given her circumstances, she figured she was justified.

An unfamiliar whisper echoed throughout the room: "You're losing time."

Blythe jolted upright onto her knees, twisting to glare about the fantastical space around her. There was no one there. All she could see was green and blue and inanimate objects. She cast about for a speaker or surveillance system, but there was nothing.

She wasn't surprised. The voice hadn't carried like a projection. It was soft and intimate.

It was the voice of a young woman.

"Hello?" Blythe stood, hands over her chest to stifle the frantic thrumming inside it. "Who's there?"

The response was slow to come, but it was the same disembodied voice that echoed throughout the orchestrated foliage. "You need to get clean."

Blythe huffed a small, stunned laugh. "Yeah? So you can enjoy a free show?"

Silence.

"Hello?"

The voice continued with a slight waiver that made Blythe think of a blushing child. "I won't watch. Promise."

Hesitant, Blythe tiptoed back to the abandoned basket of clothing. As she gathered it in her arms, she kept a wary eye out for any sign of movement. Besides the constant splash of the waterfall, there was none. Blythe's gaze continued circling the room, gleaning nothing as she crept toward the pool.

"Who are you?"

No one answered.

Blythe glanced down as she dipped her toes in the water. It was lukewarm at best, but fresh. Reassured that the water was just as it appeared, Blythe turned in a wide circle and said, "I'd feel a lot better about getting naked if I knew where you were."

"Please," the voice continued with a thin edge of impatience. "Wash. If not for my sake, then do it for yours."

Blythe's stomach turned as she set the basket at the pool's edge. "What do you mean?"

There was another long pause, then the voice continued in a strained whisper that was too soft to echo as it had before, "You might not get this chance again."

Blythe's head whipped around, convinced she detected a

direction from the voice. It was wishful thinking; after the startling noise of the waterfall, her hearing had eased back to the realms of mundanity. Her ears told her nothing more than her eyes.

There was green, so much green, and after shifting her weight to adjust her vantage point, Blythe concluded there were too many layers of faux-forest between herself and anyone else. Blythe didn't have a hope of seeing through the greenery; hopefully, the same was true of the stranger.

With hesitant and jerky movements, Blythe stripped and slid into the water. She went slow, heart in her throat, until she found the pool's floor. Thank the stars, but it wasn't too deep. Blythe dropped her whole body in and crouched till the water covered her breasts. She tried not to freak out over the realization that the pool was big enough to swim in.

Once she was safely obscured by ripples and reflections, Blythe turned to keep her eye on the deepest shadows in the foliage. "I'm cleaning. Happy?"

No one answered her.

Toes gripping the pool's beveled floor, Blythe inched over to the far side of the waterfall where she spotted a shelf built into the fake rocks. She discovered a series of uniform jars, sponges, and a small stack of folded towels.

"So . . ." Blythe called over the din of the water, "which of these is soap?"

There was no answer.

"Fine," Blythe muttered to herself, "be that way."

She didn't turn her back to the room at large, but she redirected the bulk of her attention to the jars. She opened each and took a good sniff. None of it smelled familiar, but she recognized the textures enough to make an educated guess.

She grabbed a sponge and started scrubbing, primed to react to any sign of another person. The soap was mild enough on her skin and did the job, but no matter which jar she tried, the products proved ineffective at detangling her hair. The unlabeled jars cleared out the worst of the stale stage products from her last practice, but none of them were conditioned well enough for easy finger combing. She did the best she could with the mysterious jars and shaky fingers. At least there was enough clean water to soak the curls back into existence.

Despite the setback, she got clean in record time. Her skin was still wet as she yanked the oversized pants up her legs, and she was perversely glad to find the shirt covering so much more of her jaguar spots. Dressed in clean clothes and a shred of decency, Blythe shoved her foul underwear and crop top into the basket and waved it in the air.

She called out, "What should I do with this?"

The only answer she got was silence.

Blythe dropped the basket. "Are you still there?"

She didn't see anything, but she heard movement. Whoever the stranger was, she was well beyond the first layer of greenery.

Blythe pushed a dripping curl behind her ear and insisted, "What's this all about? Are you here to keep an eye on me, or what? Are you trapped here too?"

She waited, but there was no answer.

Blythe reconsidered the beautiful setup with the sensation of a heavy mantle settling on her shoulders. The first time Tilla brought her to Lunar-5, they had taken her to HEPP's conservation property where they housed and sustained the few feline species that had been granted sanctuary on the moon. It was the first time Blythe ever saw a cat in the flesh, and she'd been in awe. There were tigers and jaguars, lions, and lynxes, even a frightfully skinny pair of jaguars the appointed tour guide called "cheetahs." Each and every one of them was pampered with fake trees and cleverly decorated enclosures.

Blythe wondered if the great big cats ever enjoyed as much true, living nature as she was witnessing in that moment.

Her shoulders drooped. There was a terrible quiver to her voice when she spoke. "Gregoire said I was still human, and I deserved to be treated as one."

At long last, there was a response, a choked, keening whine. It wasn't a direct reply; there were no words, and it was nearly too quiet for Blythe's human senses to discern. It was a response, nonetheless.

Blythe craned her neck back to peer up at the towering ceiling. It was painted a cheerful baby-blue, like a sky. A fake sky.

"Is this what they'll do to me?" Blythe asked as her knees threatened to give way. "If I don't buy into their supremacist crap? They'll spin some bullshit about how mixing my humanity with creature genes means I deserve to be treated like an animal?"

Another whine, louder and, dare she believe it, more sympathetic.

Blythe nodded up at the false sky. Her eyes burned, but she was too furious to let the tears fall. Her hands clenched into fists at her sides, and her nails bit into her palms, but she relished the sensation.

At least the pain felt real.

It was possible Gregoire sensed her flaring ire when he and his minions collected her from the pretend forest. Instead of leading her straight down the hall to her storage room-turned-prison, he chose to take the scenic route.

Blythe counted one left turn, then a right, then a dead end that melted away as they neared it. Her attempts to cultivate a mental map for escape came to an immediate end.

"Where are we?"

"Luna, of course." Gregoire beamed, his gaze fond as it surveyed the stretch of monstrously thick glass in front of them. "In our more melodramatic moments, we like to call it 'the dark side of the moon.'"

It was a window. Instead of a wall, inches-thick glass stood as the lone barrier between them and the moon's raw atmosphere. There were no domes of hospitable air and no sign of any other building. They were on ground level; the cool gray of the moon's surface sat mere feet away.

No dome. No other structures. No pedestrians. There was no Lunar Port in sight.

As Gregoire stepped closer to admire the star-speckled abyss, Blythe stayed on the edge of the hall's original dead end. She could see more than enough from there.

"As you can see, Ms. Ramos, there is nowhere to go, no one for you to rely on but your fellow men." Gregoire surveyed the chilling horizon with his chin held high. "Humanity lost its way when we created Homo nocturni. Now, so far down the path we set for ourselves, it's no surprise the parasites consider Luna and her colonies vampire territory. The true horror is not their financial and social domination though."

He paused and turned to look at her. There was a slight uptick to his lip and an expectancy on his face that made her stomach roll.

"The real horror," he said with gravity, "the real *evil* is how they've brainwashed the majority of surviving humans into complacency. You do not yet appreciate how blessed you are, Ms. Ramos, but you are standing in the only exclusively human settlement beyond Earth's exosphere."

Blythe gaped at him as she swayed on her feet. He couldn't be serious, but he was. Before she could gather her wits and reconcile the undeniable urge to smack an old man, he was at her side. He took her elbow to steer her back the way they'd come, like a doting elder guiding a youngster.

"I'm afraid the only way out of here is with an interstellar spacecraft, Ms. Ramos. Even the most devout Humans First supporters can't get near one without the Grand Master's blessing. Before we continue this conversation, I'd like you to think on that for a bit."

$\sim$

THE CAGE WAS CLEANED IN HER ABSENCE, THE WASTE BUCKET refreshed, the water restocked, and a threadbare blanket left in a heap in the corner. Blythe was grateful, and she hated it with a viciousness that tied her stomach into nasty knots.

From then on, every time Andy entered the room, Blythe pulled the blanket over her head. She didn't care that the rough material rubbed deplorable amounts of frizz from her hair and turned the curls into a knotted mess, or that it filled her nose with the scent of moths and neglect. She stayed like that, huddled into a ball and refusing to interact with anyone. Time passed, and countless meals were left on the floor beside the bars, but Blythe saw no one. Not Andy, not the other woman being held captive and treated like a beast. She never even saw Gregoire. She pretended the world in its entirety ended at the flimsy border of her blanket-shield.

"How are you faring, Ms. Ramos?"

The old man gave a gentle tap to the bars with his cane, but Blythe remained swaddled and out of view. He did this often, stopping by for minutes at a time, trying to get her to talk. She had yet to respond to him. She didn't know what he wanted, only that she had no interest in giving it to him.

He sighed, and she knew he was about to give up and go back to whatever bigoted nonsense he filled his days with.

Except that's not what happened.

She wasn't ready for the cinch of the lock releasing. She tensed, not daring to expose herself as she listened to the lock clattering away. She felt the air move as the cage door opened without a sound.

"I had such high hopes for you," Gregoire lamented. "But this isn't getting us anywhere, is it?"

She heard him shuffle away. With her plain and human ears, she heard him abandon the open cage and open the door beyond it.

"It seems we'll have to find another use for Ms. Ramos after all. What a shame."

As if her body were trying to warn her, Blythe's ears and nose switched into overdrive. Despite the cloying blanket over her head, she had the sudden awareness of heavy-set boots treading toward her, along with the distinct musk of sweat, dirt, and the reek of jet fuel.

She didn't know what was happening. She didn't want to know. She knew the doors were open, the locks unlocked, but she was frozen beneath her blanket, petrified.

The footsteps reached the cage.

She couldn't move. She couldn't breathe. Perhaps she'd suffocate, stifled by the flimsy barrier, by the only thing remaining between her and them.

She felt them enter the cage with her, and bile filled her mouth.

"Enough of this," an unfamiliar voice grumbled.

A hand landed on her shoulder.

It was like he jabbed her with a taser. Blythe tossed the blanket with a piercing shriek, kicking and punching with all her might at anything that came near. She didn't see them. There was too much movement, too much terror, too much hair in her face. She couldn't see, but she felt an impact with her bare foot, a sharp pain in her knuckles, and the spray of hot blood as her fist connected. She heard a man grunt and another cussing her out, but she didn't see them.

She couldn't tell if Andy was one of the men who dragged her from the cage. She screamed and fought as they forced her down the hall. She could feel the bruises forming on her biceps where they held her too tight, but it didn't stop her struggles.

The air was knocked from her lungs when they threw her through a doorway. Her knees skidded on strange flooring, and she cried out as her face crashed into something covered in jagged points—grass.

A heavy door slammed shut and someone barked, "Feeding time, Doll Face!"

Blythe scrambled to her knees as she shoved curls and grass from her eyes. Panting and twitching like cornered prey, she frantically searched the would-be forest for an approaching enemy. The sound of running water was jarringly absent, and Blythe reeled as she recognized the washroom without the active waterfall.

"Come on, Doll!"

A fist caught her by the hair, and Blythe screamed as she was yanked off-balance. She scratched and pushed at the unyielding grip, only to get shaken like a used rag till her scalp felt like it was on fire.

Blythe stopped fighting when she felt the edge of a blade on her throat.

"Yeah," Andy said from the sidelines, voice cloying with sadistic glee, "look who's ready to be a good girl now."

The man holding Blythe by the hair scoffed, "Shut up. You're embarrassing."

"So, we *do* agree on something," Blythe muttered before rational thought could catch up with her mouth.

Everyone went still.

After a beat, the hand in her hair tightened, tugging as the knife pressed harder to her skin. "Are you serious right now?"

She answered honestly, "I don't know. Maybe?"

Blythe knew there was a deadly weapon at her neck, but she was having a hard time believing it was real. She was on her knees in the grass, for fuck's sake. How was any of it real?

Andy sputtered as he stomped past her and her handler. He was red-faced with indignation, yes, but also with the blood leaking from his busted nose.

"Oh, thank fuck," Blythe whispered aloud. She'd never broken another person's bones before, but she was strangely relieved to know he was her first.

That was the point Blythe thought she might be insane. Or in shock.

"Dolly!" Andy screamed as he stomped his foot on a battered patch of grass. "Get out here, Dolly! You get your ass out here right now, or we're letting this bitch's blood go to waste all over your fucking lawn!"

Blythe felt numb and weightless, like she would float straight out of her body at any moment. All she could hear was Andy screeching about blood. All she could see was the false forest fit for a kept animal. All she could feel was the cold rush of reality crashing over her.

"I mean it, Doll!" Andy hollered as he stormed back over to Blythe.

Blythe was too stunned to stop him from grabbing her upper arm and yanking her from the other man's hold. The sting of the blade slicing beneath her ear barely registered.

"I don't want to hear any of your shit!" Andy yelled as he shoved Blythe face-first into the greenery. "We're doing you a favor, bringing you this blood bag, you damn vamp! You better appreciate it!"

Vamp. Blythe's mind ran that solitary word on a loop while the shouting dragged on.

Stars above. The other captive wasn't a woman. She was a Nocturna.

"You mention the word 'consent' one more time, and I swear, this'll be your last chance to bite into certified human meat!"

A Humans First faction that shouldn't exist was imprisoning a vampire.

"Now, Dolly!"

It wasn't possible.

"You bleed her, or I will!"

A fucking Nocturna! Blythe screamed inside the safety of her skull. How did no one know about this? Vampires were social creatures who rarely strayed far from their Harems. Why wasn't hers looking for her? Was she a loner?

Blythe's heart gave a loud pang as it continued racing.

Andy continued raging, uninterrupted and uncaring as Blythe tried to uncurl from a fetal position at his feet. Closing her eyes, Blythe hoped that the vampire's ears were half as sharp as her own.

She whispered, "It's okay."

But it wasn't okay at all. Andy's tantrum was probably loud enough to mask her voice from the sharpest ears, Nocturni or not. She tried anyway.

"You can do it," she whispered. "Bite me. Even if it hurts, it'll be better than whatever they do to me."

White-hot pain burst along her side, and Blythe screamed as she fell over.

"I'm not fucking around, Doll!"

She saw his boot swing this time. She didn't understand what it was doing, but the dumb animal part of her reacted anyway. Before Andy could kick her a second time and break a rib, Blythe rolled away. She didn't consciously flow onto her feet like she would during a dance, but her movements were swift and well-executed just the same. The combination of muscle memory and instinct got her past the pool and the first nature-disguised net.

She forgot that the forest was fake, that there was nowhere to go. It didn't matter, because at that moment, she was free. She was getting away!

She forgot about the second man.

He caught her by the back of her shirt. The collar pulled taut over her throat, choking her for one heart-stopping moment before she was yanked off her feet again. She landed hard on her shoulder with a disturbing pop, and pain whipped all other thoughts from her mind.

She heard Andy laugh, the sound high and revolting with disdain.

Wrong. Her arm felt all wrong, and she couldn't move it. Wrong. Wrong. Wrong.

Andy snarled, "You stupid bitch."

Blythe knew she was about to die then. She heard it in his voice. She could feel it in the intensity of his stare. When he crouched over her, she saw the intent carved into his sneer and glinting off the blade in his hand.

She almost laughed. It was a fucking pocketknife. A cheap one.

"I want her!"

The viciousness washed off Andy's expression as he paled. He looked away from Blythe with widening eyes, and the next moment, he disappeared. Blythe didn't know what happened to him. She hoped he hit a wall and cracked his head open, but she couldn't be bothered to check.

She was distracted.

"I heard you," the vampire murmured as she loomed over Blythe. "I'm sorry. I'm so sorry. I'll do what I can."

"Oh . . ." Blythe gaped up at her, more than a little dizzy and breathless with pain and shock. "Aren't you gorgeous . . ."

Big electric-blue eyes framed in the longest lashes blinked down at her. A curtain of pale, shimmering hair hung over one slender shoulder in a sleek curtain. She seemed young and otherworldly. Blythe couldn't be sure, but she thought she might be dying, and this was her guardian angel come to deliver her to safety.

The vampire's lips did a funny sort of squirm, as if she were frowning and laughing at the same time. A soft, feminine hand cupped the back of her neck, and another circled her waist to lift her from the grass. Blythe's head spun.

"Am I dying?"

"Um . . . I don't think so?"

The unnamed man barked, "Get on with it, bloodsucker! Before I lose patience!"

That fair head bent close to her, and pink lips brushed her ear. "I'm sorry."

"Me too," Blythe murmured.

The bite didn't hurt. Blythe thought it probably should, but all she could feel was the trembling in the arms that held her and the tears leaking onto the side of her neck. Blythe wanted to reassure her, but over the vampire's shoulder, she saw Andy glowering at them as he pinched his bloodied shirt to his nose.

Serves him right, Blythe thought, but the satisfaction was superficial and hollow. She didn't give a damn about Elitia-fucking-Kenwood's dirtbag cousin or his crooked nose. All she cared about was the unknown female at her neck issuing pitiful little whimpers with every reluctant sip. Blythe had never imagined a vampire could be so frail.

She never thought a vampire could be so broken.

CHAPTER 7

One sleep and zero meals later, and Blythe's shock had finally run its course. It got her through the unmedicated setting of her shoulder and dulled her memory of the trek back to her cage. When the last of it faded, she was left with nothing but pain and anger.

The pain wasn't so consuming now that the dislocation had been reduced. Andy's brutish friend hadn't bothered to provide her a sling after popping the joint into place with a speed and agony that made Blythe's sight white-out for long, harrowing seconds. She had to rip up the edges of her blanket with her teeth and functioning arm to make the sling herself. The throbbing persisted down into her bicep and across her clavicle, but the longer she sat in isolation, the easier it became to ignore. It hurt, but it was manageable.

The rage was not.

She was sick with it. Every time she tried to think about something—anything—besides what went down in the vampire's enclosure, she ended up on her hand and knees, dry heaving till her abdomen screamed at her to stop. If they bothered to bring her food, she had no doubt it would come spewing out of her coated in stomach acid that boiled from the force of her anger.

They left her alone with her rage. They brought her no food, no water. Andy never showed to make a nasty remark or check if her bucket needed to be refreshed. No one bothered her.

That was fine. She could sit and ferment in the insane fury swarming her heart and mind, and when the time was right, she would use it. She wouldn't run or make any attempt at escape. She already tried that, and it got her nowhere. No. Next time, she would go down fighting. She would give them the wildcat they imagined she was becoming.

She waited and fumed. As the uninterrupted solitude dragged on, she adjusted her expectations. She was still ready for a fight, mentally at least, but she began to doubt if she'd get the chance. Maybe they hadn't left her to stew in her misery; maybe they were done with her. They might have tossed her aside to spoil, hoping she would die on her own since the vampire hadn't done the job for them.

She was wrong.

Hours or days passed before the storage room's door finally creaked open. Gregoire inched his way toward her with his unnamed brute of a lackey shadowing him. They carried no water. No food.

"It pains me that things have come to this, my dear," the old man said, voice heavy with bereavement.

Blythe snorted but gave no other acknowledgment.

He crept toward the cage with a somber shake of his head. "I wish you could come to appreciate your role, Ms. Ramos. Your sacrifice means the betterment of your fellow man."

As the cage's lock clicked open, Blythe's muscles went tense and ready.

"Come along," Gregoire encouraged with a kind gesture of his cane, without pushing the barred door open. "Dolly's been asking for you."

Those words caught her off guard. The expectant energy gathering in her limbs dissipated, and without any conscious effort to comply, Blythe was on her feet and pushing her way past the bars.

She stood a few feet in front of the Grand Master, nothing between them but air, and all her righteous rage had twisted sideways like a knife in her side preparing to gut her.

"Why?" she asked.

The man gave her a small sad smile. "I dare say, it seems concerned about your well-being. The creature appears rather taken with you."

The lackey guffawed. "Guess you make a better chew toy than a woman."

Teeth clenched, Blythe did her best to ignore him as he shoved her toward the door.

Nothing more was said as they escorted her out of the storage room and down the hall. No one held her arms this time. No threats were made. No one stopped her from looking every which way and taking note of each door and passage they passed. None of them were labeled, and she suspected they didn't plan to let her live long anyway, but it still seemed careless.

Blythe's ears weren't augmented like a cat's at the time, but she thought she caught the sound of hissing airlocks and a thrumming engine coming from one of the halls. She hoped so.

The men walked her right up to the forest's door. While his underling set an anticipatory hand on the handle, Gregoire set a fragile, wrinkled one on her good shoulder.

"You should know," he said, "I have owned Dolly for longer than you have been alive."

Blythe's stomach rolled, and she shrugged his hand off her with a viciousness that made her injury shriek. Her jaw was clenched too tight for speech as she glared at him.

He was unfazed. "It likes to pretend otherwise, but its kind is dependent on us. Like any proper owner, I try to appease it and maintain its health. You're not the first misguided human I've gifted to the beast."

A noise of disgust escaped from her tight throat.

Gregoire clucked with stale amusement as his eyes lowered to the scabs on her throat. "You are the first it's accepted though. The only one it's bitten. Did you know that?"

"You're sick," Blythe spat.

"No." He shook his head as if disappointed and gestured to his minion. "You're the one with a splicing addiction. I am pure humanity, my dear."

Oh, how Blythe wanted to hurt him. She made a move to do just that, but before she could raise her nails to chest height, she was manhandled out of range. Her shoulder spasmed with fresh pain as her back hit the wall, the brute's hand solid at the base of her throat.

"I wonder what it sees in you," Gregoire spoke casually as he studied her. "Won't you ask it about that for me?"

"Fuck off."

The old man sighed and walked away in slow, achy steps without giving her another glance.

Blythe screamed after him, "If this is what you call humanity, you can keep it and shove it up your ass!"

It wasn't particularly clever or cutting, as far as dramatic farewells went, but it was heartfelt. It left her panting in the lackey's hold.

She was paid back for the remark with a shove into the false wilderness. The door slammed shut behind her and locked just as fast. No one followed her in.

Blythe breathed hard. Her chest heaved too much to keep her makeshift sling comfortably in place. She glared daggers at the sealed door and tried to lengthen her inhales, tried to regain her composure. She really tried.

She was so preoccupied with containing her useless rage that she never heard the vampire approach.

"You're alive?"

"Fuck!" Blythe shouted as she spun on her heel, her fist swinging without thought. The momentum carried her too far, and she stumbled till her upper back tumbled into the door. Streaks of pain shot down her injured arm, and dark spots popped in and out of her sight as she slid to the floor gasping.

It became a waiting game then. She sat there, shaking worse than the phony leaves and struggling to breathe. All the while, she waited for her fury to abate, for her thoughts to slow into something understandable. She waited for her heart and nerves to stop trying to escape straight out of her rib cage.

She wasn't the only one waiting.

The vampire crouched in the grass, well beyond reach. They stared at each other with wide terrified eyes, each of them visibly vibrating with tension.

The Nocturna was as gorgeous as Blythe's panicked brain originally thought. She was clad in nothing but loose tresses and the fairest skin. Her hair wasn't a pale blonde after all; it was the palest of grays, nearly white, and silken. It flowed like mild waves down to her exposed navel. A section on the side of her scalp had been shaved at some point in the recent past; the fresh growth was no less shiny than the rest, but it seemed sharper and jarringly inelegant.

Her fangs were tiny, almost undetectable, and only the pointed ear on the shaved side was visible through all the hair.

Anywhere else in the universe, she would pass for human.

And they called her a doll.

A fresh wave of anger flooded Blythe's cheeks with warmth. She gritted her teeth without thinking and loosed a low hiss.

The vampire bit her lip and frowned. She crouched lower, the grass crinkling under her knees, and the way she shied away from continued eye contact made her look impossibly young.

"I'm so sorry," Blythe said.

Then she was waiting not only on her nerves to calm, but for the vampire to respond.

It never happened, nothing verbal at least. As silence descended, the Nocturna began to uncoil from her crouch. She moved slow, but with the ease and modesty of too much practice using her hair as a shield. She settled in a cross-legged position, hair covering her small breasts like a shawl and pooling in her lap to hide her groin. Her hands rested on her knees, and her head tilted forward as her blue eyes lost focus.

She was stiller than still. Statuesque, even.

It should have been unnerving, but Blythe found it sobering. The longer she surveyed the Nocturna in her calm suspension, the slower Blythe's breath and pulse became.

Gradually, Blythe began to see past the elfin features and eye-catching hair. The vampire was frightfully thin, with faint circles bruising her eyes and a grayness to her skin that was more common on corpses. The observation sat on Blythe's chest like a leaden anchor, bringing her nerves back down to solid ground.

Clearing her throat, Blythe pushed off the door and scooted forward.

The Nocturna's eyes brightened as her attention narrowed on Blythe's face. Her body didn't move, not an inch, only her eyes.

Blythe left a good distance between them as she knelt before the vampire. She felt small under her gaze, like a bereaved supplicant before a fabled deity brought to life.

"I'm so—" Blythe stopped the useless repetition in its track and searched for something more to say. "I'm Blythe. What's your name?"

She felt stupid as the words left her tongue. Her cheeks burned hotter than ever as silence screamed between them.

Blythe sat back on her heels and began reestablishing her sling. Her hands shook, one with pain, the other with persisting fears and worries.

She gasped when a second pair of hands latched on to the blanket's rags.

"Let me," the Nocturna said, her voice soft and sweet.

Wordless, Blythe nodded and let her take over. The vampire adjusted the sling with speed and grace, bringing far less pain and better results than Blythe could manage on her own. When it was done, her slender hands were reluctant to leave Blythe's arm. She didn't restore the distance.

"How long has it been since you touched someone?" Blythe whispered as she stretched out her good arm for the Nocturna's hand.

The Nocturna was slow to turn her hand over to reciprocate, but her grip was tight enough to betray her need.

"How long have you been here?" Blythe pressed, still hushed. "What's your name?"

The Nocturna's eyes made a wary lap around the greenery before she whispered, "I'm Dolly."

"Bullshit. What's your real name?"

She never got an answer.

The Nocturna was on her feet before Blythe recognized the sound of the door bursting open. Blythe spun on her ass to face the entry and her breath caught.

Andy stood in the doorway with a malicious grin stretched across his face. He had Gregoire's fancy walking stick in one hand and an artifact of a gun in the other.

"I fucking knew it!" Andy said as he waved the gun in their direction. "I told him you wouldn't put the bitch out of her misery, and I was right!"

A deep male voice roared from the hall, "Kenwood! What the fuck are you doing?!"

"I knew they beat the fight out of you too long ago," Andy sneered at the Nocturna. "I didn't realize they defanged you too. What use is a kept mutt if it can't even bite on command?"

He angled the gun straight at Blythe.

"Stupid bitches, the both of you."

Blythe tapped the Nocturna's ankle as Andy pulled the trigger and breathed, "The door!"

What happened next was a mess of movement, searing pain, and screaming. Blythe couldn't make heads or tails of any of it, and with her shoulder and arm burning as if caught in a ray of sunfire, she didn't want to. Blythe felt her throat tear and go hoarse with the force of her cries, but every gasping breath forced her quiet enough to hear gunshots and a man's furious shrieking.

The fury didn't last long. The shrieking did. It turned desperate and pleading as Blythe's shock ran unchecked. By the time she gathered her wits and pulled herself off the floor, the screams were done. The gunshots were distant.

She was alone.

The forest was caked in red.

"Stars above!"

Blythe gaped at the body in the open doorway. It wasn't the first corpse she'd seen, not even her first time witnessing the results of an unhinged vampire attack, but it was the first time she could recognize the deceased from memories of a living being. His intestines looked like anyone else's, she was sure, and the ugly hatred carved into his face above his partial decapitation warped his features into something grotesque, but he was recognizable.

Andy Kenwood was dead. In a daze, Blythe noticed the severed halves of Gregoire's cane in each of his fists, while the gun lay in a pool of blood.

Stars above, but the bullet missed her. The recent dislocation throbbed, but she was otherwise unharmed—

Another gunshot sounded in the distance.

She startled, her hand smacking over her mouth to stifle an inaudible shriek. The silence that followed was gross and exciting.

Blythe trembled as she crawled toward the door. By the time she reached the body, she had the mind to get to her feet. She accessed the hall more or less upright but shaking. She stepped into the brighter light of the hall and slipped on the combination of smooth flooring and slick blood before catching herself against a wall.

"Woah," Blythe commented aloud for the reassurance of her own voice. "Messy."

She swayed as she stared at the second body but found her equilibrium with the next deep breath. Gregoire's nameless thug wasn't half as imposing with his throat ripped out.

"Blythe?"

Blythe looked up.

The Nocturna stood at the end of the hall, bare chest heaving as she drew a path of bloody footprints back toward Blythe. Her eyes were bright, electrifying against so much crimson. From her perfect lips down to her toes, the vampire was drenched in the color.

Blythe froze. She couldn't make her feet move forward if she wanted to. Did she want to? Did she want to turn tail and run? Such complicated questions were beyond her at that moment.

"You killed them? All of them?"

". . . I think so?"

The vampire slowed on her approach. Her fierce expression crumbled with each step, worse and worse until the blood became meaningless next to the innocent terror filling those electric-blue eyes. She came to a halt, and despite the length of hallway between them, Blythe could see her shaking as she hugged herself. The tears fell thick enough to draw streaks in the gore splattering her cheeks.

Blythe's feet came unglued, and she rushed forward as fast as mortal adrenaline allowed. It didn't feel fast enough.

The vampire's knees hit the floor with a crack.

"I've got you!" Blythe vowed as she flung an arm around her.

The Nocturna shuddered with brutal sobs. Thin arms circled Blythe's waist, holding on with bruising force as a wet face pressed to Blythe's chest. Her shirt was soaked in seconds.

"Come on!" Blythe tugged at her, using her grip as much as her body weight to urge the vampire to rise. "We need to get out of here while we have a chance. Do you know where we can find a ship?"

The vampire struggled to catch the air necessary for speech. "I — I don't— I'm— I can't—!"

Through blubbering distress and disjointed words, Blythe pieced together the point. "You can't pilot a craft?"

The Nocturna nodded frantically through gut-wrenching wails.

"Well, I can."

Without wasting any more time, Blythe shoved her good shoulder under the other female's armpit and lifted them off the filthy floor.

"I knew I would die here."

"Don't say that," Blythe said as she tried to open yet another locked door.

They'd been wandering the utilitarian halls for hours. The building was filled with nothing but bland white sealed doors. There was an industrial kitchen left exposed, but the cabinets were all locked by the same invisible mechanisms as the doors. Blythe's anxiety jumped through the roof each time they discovered a hallway consisting of glass and a vast spacescape where a wall ought to be. There were a few, and each view was as impressive and terrifyingly barren as the last.

There was nothing else to see. Not unless they ventured back toward the vampire enclosure, where the door was jammed open by body parts.

Blythe counted a total of five corpses, all of them young men.

"That old fart got out of here somehow," Blythe grumbled as she returned to the vampire's side.

Said vampire was right where Blythe left her, sitting on the floor in front of the glass wall overlooking the lifeless moon. She wore a torn and bloodied shirt from one of the fallen men, and she hugged her knees to her chest, tucked beneath the soiled cloth like a makeshift cocoon.

Blythe knelt next to her and brushed the fine hair back over a slender shoulder. "I don't know what they've been feeding you, but could you try imbuing yourself with a sensitive nose or something that could help us find a way out of here?"

The Nocturna stopped stargazing long enough to shoot her an incredulous look. "That's not how it works."

Blythe hung her head as she sighed. "Okay. Any other ideas we could try?"

The Nocturna shook her head, mute as her eyes returned to the stars.

With a frustrated groan, Blythe stood and resumed hunting for an exit. At this point, she'd be happy to find a toilet, or any room that wasn't welded shut.

Instead, she just found another body.

"For fuck's sake."

Hands on her hips, Blythe stared down at the guy. He wasn't one she recognized, though he was more or less intact. Blythe wasn't surprised; this far from her forestry prison, whatever bloodlust that had control of the vampire had waned. This goon was spared with the quick death of a broken neck. Blythe was no expert, but the backward positioning of his head seemed pretty telling.

The lack of bloodshed wasn't the only difference between this body and the others.

"Thank the stars," Blythe said with a relieved laugh as she knelt and reached for the dead man's wrist.

The device she found there wasn't a comms. It was better.

∽

More time passed, and because Humans First didn't seem to believe in clocks any more than they did any real sense of morality, Blythe didn't have a clue how long it'd been. Even the commandeered device didn't want to give her anything useful in that regard. It was a significant chunk of time, though; she sailed straight through the period where her stomach ached as it ate itself. Eventually her body made a few other time-sensitive demands, and she trekked back to the useless kitchen so she could take a shit on Humans First's dining table.

In the off chance Gregoire or his people ever came back, she wanted to leave a poignant message, and they hadn't been considerate enough to leave her any writing supplies.

The time passed quicker when she had a goal to focus on.

"Okay!"

Blythe clapped her hands as she wandered back to the vampire. It had been a while since she last checked in on her companion, but the female hadn't moved an inch. She barely flinched when Blythe clapped a second time next to her ear.

"Okay," Blythe repeated, a touch snippy as she crouched beside the Nocturna. "I have good and bad news. Which do you want first?"

The Nocturna blinked, face still directed at the stars. Her head tilted ever-so-slightly in Blythe's direction. "You can tell me something good?"

Blythe's heart threatened to break at the dull resignation in the other's voice, but she choked it back. Summoning her inner-Sly, she forced a little excess pep into her voice when she answered.

"I think I found a ship."

The Nocturna faced her with fair brows raised high.

Blythe grinned and wiggled her fingers as she held up her uninjured arm. From wrist to elbow, her limb was encased in a flexible metal bracer with all sorts of buttons and markings carved into it.

The Nocturna frowned, quirking her head to the side as she studied it. Hesitant, she asked, "What is it?"

"A captain's bracer," Blythe said. She rolled back her shoulder and bent her arm so she could tap the fingers of her bandaged arm along the controls. The device buzzed to life. "See? It's fully charged and functioning. If you look at this display—"

"What display?"

"The glowing one. This!" Blythe raised her arm in front of the Nocturna's confused face and indicated the green backlit script on the device's screen with a jab of her nose.

The Nocturna's eyes darted from Blythe's to the bracer and back again. The furrow of her brow and tension in her shoulders seemed to leak away as she did so. When her gaze settled on Blythe's face, she seemed almost relaxed. Then she smiled.

"You can use it?" she asked with a sweetness that made Blythe feel weepy. "You can get us out of here?"

Blushing, Blythe lowered her arm to cradle the bracer in her lap. "Maybe, but . . ."

"But . . . ?"

"I'm pretty sure the ship's behind a locked door."

The Nocturna's face fell. Her shoulders drooped.

"So, I was thinking," Blythe shifted, unable to hold her gaze as she mumbled, "if you have the strength to rip a guy in half, maybe you could break down the door?"

The Nocturna pursed her lips and turned back to the window. Blythe couldn't help but stare as the vampire's ears burned a bright pink.

Blythe prodded her shoulder, her touch careful and light. "Well?"

"I don't know how I did that," she said without looking at

Blythe. "I've never done something like that before. I don't . . ." She bit her lip. "I'm not . . . like that. I'm not strong."

Blythe snorted. "Uh-huh. Sure."

The pink in the Nocturna's ears spread to her face and turned a distinct red. "It's true."

"Maybe, but where does that leave us then?"

Without waiting for a response, Blythe twisted her torso so her good arm could move freely, if awkwardly, to grab the vampire's pointed chin. No matter what the Nocturna said, Blythe expected she wouldn't budge even if Blythe put her full weight into making her turn her head. To her surprise, Blythe didn't have to apply more than the barest pressure before their eyes met.

"We're one stupid door away from freedom," Blythe whispered, her mouth going dry. "What do you have left to lose?"

IT DIDN'T TAKE LONG FOR THEM TO APPRECIATE THAT HUMAN BODIES were much frailer than solid doors. In the end, the Nocturna was panting and sweating through the dead man's shirt, nursing a bruised fist.

"Stop." Blythe was calm as she urged the vampire away from the door. It was dented, but barely so. "You're going to break your wrist if you haven't already."

The Nocturna's lower lip trembled as she frowned at the floor.

"Hey." Blythe went to cup that lovely face in her hands and nearly smacked herself with the resistance from her sling. She was quick to course correct and wrap her good arm around the Nocturna's shoulders. "It's okay. At least you tried, right?"

Blythe didn't tug or step closer. She did nothing but offer a half-hug. When the vampire curled into her side and buried her face in the side of Blythe's neck, she wasn't prepared for it. She stumbled.

Before Blythe could anticipate the fall, it was stopped by the Nocturna's arms catching her around the waist.

A cold nose sniffled against her throat. "I'm sorry."

Once Blythe realized she was being nuzzled and not about to crack her head on the floor, she relaxed a little into the embrace. She leaned her cheek against the Nocturna's shaved head and lied, "It's okay."

The body against hers was so slight and cold with malnourishment. Blythe felt her shiver from head to toe. In a terrified whisper, the Nocturna asked, "What do we do?"

Blythe tightened her arm around the Nocturna and pretended to think it over. She didn't need to, she just needed a minute to shore up her resolve.

While the Nocturna was busy wailing on the door, Blythe did her best to familiarize herself with the device on her arm. She made a few valuable discoveries, but try as she might, she couldn't find a good way of turning them into a solid escape plan.

Stars above, but she needed Sly.

The stolen captain's bracer was getting heavier and heavier with every second.

"Blythe? Is this it? Are we . . . done?"

Blythe began slow, trying to imbue her voice with a confidence she didn't feel, "I don't suppose you know if there's an airlocked hangar beyond this door, do you?"

The Nocturna raised her head enough to blink up at her, a cute frown creasing the skin above her watery eyes. "I don't know. Maybe." She pulled away, rubbing her arm as she avoided Blythe's eye. "I don't have many memories from when they first brought me here. It's been a while."

Blythe took her by the arm and pressed, "If you had to guess? As if your life depended on it; not to put too much pressure on you, Hun, but I'm pretty sure it does."

Those electric eyes darted from side to side, frantic and pleading. "Yes? Maybe? I don't know!"

"Okay!"

The word left Blythe's mouth without her permission and with all the snap of the panic she'd been pretending not to feel. The Nocturna flinched at the noise, and Blythe felt despicable.

"Okay," she repeated, soft and gentle as she gave a bolstering squeeze to the vampire's shoulder. "Fine. We'll just have to take a risk."

"Okay."

The vampire latched on to Blythe's wrist with both hands. Of the two of them, she was the taller by a few inches, but she looked up at Blythe through wet eyelashes, as if the human was her only hope for survival. She was still caked in the dried blood of her captors, but the expression on her face was helpless.

In a spike of desperation and anxiety, Blythe whirled away and began walking.

The vampire caught her fingers and held fast. She followed.

Blythe led her back to the kitchens without speaking. The Nocturna gave a small laugh of disbelief when she caught scent of the present Blythe left for Gregoire on the table, but there was no comment as Blythe pulled her to the farthest corner of the food-prep area.

"This should be far enough."

"For what?"

Blythe leaned back against the wall, crouching down behind a long stainless-steel counter. As the Nocturna took her lead and knelt beside her, Blythe slipped her arm from the sling with a grimace. Her shoulder protested with warning streaks of pain shooting into her arm and collar, but she needed a free hand. The vampire watched her struggle to unstrap the bracer for only a moment before stepping up to help.

"Thanks," Blythe murmured as the metal slipped off and left her forearm chilled. "I need it on my other arm, so I can maneuver the controls."

Instead of handing the device back, the Nocturna took the wrist of Blythe's damaged arm and slid it into place. There was no pain, only the quiet click of the device closing on her arm. Before Blythe could offer more gratitude, the Nocturna refitted the sling so Blythe's arm was strapped close to her chest, but with a decent pocket of space for her free hand to access the controls.

"What's the plan?"

Blythe tapped at the bracer till she found the right settings, then she showed her the screen.

The vampire's lips moved soundlessly as she read. Then, eyes wide, she read it out loud, "Laser cannon?"

"Yep."

According to the captain's bracer, the ship it belonged to was a personal transport with half a tank of fuel and a few questionable customizations. Blythe wasn't sure how a random Humans First flunky got outfitted with militaristic weapons, and she didn't have the faintest idea how much power was behind a Ratheon RL-2000 laser cannon, but it was all she had to work with.

She hoped it was enough.

"I can't fly the ship remotely, but I can control its defenses," Blythe explained as she tapped on the bracer's screen. A small red indicator light started flashing. "We can either stay here and probably starve to death or be killed when reinforcements show up, or we can blast a new exit into existence and crawl through to the getaway ship."

Blythe hesitated, and the vampire leaned into her with a wealth of hopeful expectation on her face.

Fuck. The pretty little bloodsucker was going to make her say it.

"There's also the possibility we'll end up blowing a hole through a perimeter wall and getting ourselves killed much faster."

At first, there was no reaction. Then, after a long moment, the vampire's stunned face smoothed into an unreadable expression. She gave a short, curt nod.

"All right then." Blythe rolled her head from side to side as she took a deep, bracing breath. "Let's hope we're not about to destroy any oxygen barriers. I'd rather not suffocate to death."

"We won't," the Nocturna murmured, her voice dull and distracted. "Luna's atmosphere reacts the same way as the vacuum of space. We'd explode first."

". . . Oh."

The vampire made an aborted attempt to retake Blythe's hand, as if she momentarily forgot why they needed that hand unencumbered. With a heavy, resigned sigh, she shifted against Blythe's side, mimicking her posture tucked flat against the wall. They pressed together from shoulder to elbow hard enough to make Blythe's injury throb, but not hard enough to demand renewed distance.

Without further ado, Blythe swiped over the bracer's flashing red light.

CHAPTER 8

When the dust settled, they were alive. It was a nice change in the general trajectory of Blythe's life of late, but she didn't let the surprise get ahead of her. She knew better than to get her hopes up.

Those hopes took a hard hit when they got a good look at the conveyance waiting for them beyond the fresh demolition.

"Is this real?"

"I think so," Blythe murmured. She was having a hard time breathing on account of her heart pounding away in the vicinity of her throat.

The vampire's grip on Blythe's fingers was bruising as they stared at the skinny hulk of metal comprising the private vehicle. It was a sleek little transport, designed for air and land travel but not much else. It was large enough for the pilot and a passenger, but only for a brief stint where legroom could be safely sacrificed. If its pristine cherry-red paint job wasn't indicative enough, the thickness of its hull made it clear the craft was never intended for the outer limits of Luna's atmosphere.

It wouldn't get them far, to the nearest colony, maybe, but no farther.

Its size was only part of the disappointment. The ship was decorated with the sort of intricate cartoon that no one would expose to the harsh realities of outer space. It was a pinup girl, done up in an ancient and prestigious style. Maybe Blythe was being biased, but she thought the illustration was almost painfully human in its depiction. From her rounded ears and waifish frame, to her rosy cheeks and seductive grin filled with sparkling, blunt teeth, the alluring caricature of a mortal woman was as human as it could be.

It was well done, but something about the design was insulting.

"You can fly this, right?" the vampire asked as she studied the artwork with dismay.

"Probably."

Blythe's confidence wavered as she slipped into the cockpit. She paired the bracer to the control panel, and the ship's console flashed awake.

"This is not The Zephyr," she muttered.

"What's The Zephyr?"

"Don't worry about it."

As the vampire crawled over her to cram herself behind the pilot's seat, Blythe took inventory and tried not to panic all over again. Blythe wasn't much mechanically minded, but she picked up enough knowledge from Tilla to recognize the main features of most modern transports. She could activate the life support features in her sleep, as any amateur spacefarer might. She could even launch and steer it. She was not so sure about the navigation. Or the landing procedure.

Somehow, Blythe doubted that was the ideal moment to tell the traumatized vampire breathing down her neck that she'd never landed a ship on her own before.

Stars above, but where was Sly when she needed him? Sly's flight experience was limited to back seat driving Kahled

Vauqeulin's chauffeur, but she would have appreciated him slapping some calm and sense into her just then. He was good at that.

Instead, Blythe felt two feminine hands land on her shoulders. "Are we really doing this?"

Blythe's lips were too tightly pressed to form a response. After a beat, she nodded and sealed them in the cabin.

THEY GOT OFF THE GROUND WITHOUT INCIDENT, AND BLYTHE started up a distress signal the moment they hit the dust cloud.

It wasn't a cloud in the Earthling sense of the word. White, puffy clouds hadn't existed on Earth in centuries, but Blythe was more than familiar with the concept. By the time she was born, noxious gray and orange plumes were the trademark of the dying planet.

Blythe usually preferred Luna's clouds by far. Luna's atmosphere was minuscule compared to their planet of origin, and the sky acted accordingly; the layer of moondust and space particulates that swarmed above the moon's surface was thin enough to leave ample opportunity for stargazing from the ground, and it conveniently marked the height necessary to broadcast the widest signal. It wasn't as good for receiving signals, though. The ship was meant for low-altitude flight, and the dust cloud meddled with several sensors and message reception.

It was a toss-up whether the cloud would help or hinder their escape.

"We don't have a determined heading," Blythe said as she released the controls to rest her hand in her lap. "Bastard must have scrubbed his flight log and itinerary every time he landed. He left nothing for me to work with. No coordinates. No time stamps. Nothing."

From behind came a half-hearted, "Okay."

The craft was set to cruise, so they were safe for the moment. Blythe had no worries about taking her eyes off the view to peer at the vampire huddled behind her.

The Nocturna was curled into a ball, hugging her knees and making herself small as she craned her head back to stare through the cockpit's shield to the endless cosmos. The passing stars reflected in her blue eyes in a startling way that summoned fantasies of ancient Earth's clearest skies. It almost made Blythe smile.

Resting her cheek against the pilot's headrest, Blythe asked in a soft, unintrusive tone, "What's your name, Hun?"

Those pale eyes darted to her face before refocusing overhead. "It doesn't matter."

Blythe leaned into the seat with a loud sigh. "I'm not calling you Doll, Dolly, or Doll Face."

She expected the Nocturna to flinch, but the complete lack of reaction was somehow worse. The poor creature reverted to her statuesque stillness, and it only seemed to highlight the blood smears staining her skin. There was something red and gelatinous caught in the short, uneven hairs on the side of her skull.

Blythe's mouth tasted sour.

They said nothing for a long moment. As the vampire watched the heavens, Blythe watched the vampire. A whole lot of watching was going on.

Eventually, Blythe gave up and turned back around. She tried to relax, telling herself she needed to preserve her energy and rest in preparation for the inevitable landing she'd have to muddle her way through. The internal pep talk did no good.

She tried to imagine what Sly would do in this situation. She tried to recall his comms info from the recesses of her exhausted brain.

"I'm not her anymore."

Blythe startled to full alertness. She turned, hugging the headrest as she stared at the vampire.

The vampire stared back. Her face pinkened as the corners of her mouth shrugged down. "I've been gone for a while. Some days, I barely remember what it's like to be a part of a Harem. To be Nocturni."

Blythe disliked the subtle curve of tragedy along that pale brow. Without thinking it through, Blythe reached out to smooth back the furrowed skin between the vampire's brows. Dried blood flaked away under her touch, but Blythe flicked it off and went back for more, combing the silvery hair from that angelic face.

Said face leaned into her touch, accompanied by the slightest sigh of relief.

"What's your name?" Blythe asked.

"Meaningless," she answered, voice quiet and cracking as she nuzzled Blythe's palm. "Even if I could remember who I used to be, I can never be that again. I've been a beast kept in a cage for too long."

"Not anymore though."

The vampire met and held Blythe's gaze, the slightest, weakest upward twitch to her lips. "No. Not anymore. I guess I get to be something else now."

"Some*one*," Blythe corrected, rolling her eyes as she picked gore from the Nocturna's silver hair.

THEY WERE LOST. IT WAS OBVIOUS. BLYTHE WAS STILL DISTURBED when she stopped dozing an hour later to discover an unfamiliar landscape of gray rock in every direction.

"Maybe we're going in the wrong direction?"

"No way to know," Blythe muttered as she fiddled with the comms built into the dashboard.

The distress signal was still flashing away with undaunted rhythm, and Blythe was still hoping to make a connection with a nearby colony or passing transport. She needed a lifeline, be it an official rescue or an inconvenienced star surfer. Anything would do. A part of her kept expecting to see The Zephyr emerge over the horizon, lights flashing like a beacon, but that thinking was wistful and dangerously immature.

"I'll try to remember Phink's contact info again," Blythe suggested for the umpteenth time as she steered them out of the dust cloud.

It was no more fruitful than the last time.

~

"How about . . . Amanda?"

"No, thank you."

"Britney?"

"Absolutely not."

"Candace!"

"Ew. No."

"Daphne?"

Silence answered her.

Blythe sat up straight in the pilot's chair and spun around, her eyes and grin wide. "Darcy!"

The Nocturna glowered at her, but Blythe was tempted to think she was fighting a smile. "No. Not Darcy."

Blythe slumped till her backside bumped the control panel. "Whatever. I'm still not calling you Doll."

~

The hours stretched on, and they took turns napping and monitoring the comms.

"Maybe we should turn around."

Blythe snorted. "You want to return to the Humans First

compound? Because that's about as far as this fuel tank might take us."

"How about Isabelle?"

"No."

"Jane?"

"Seriously?"

"No, not really."

"Thank the cosmos."

"I know! Ready? Here it is: Katrina!"

"Wait. Are you just spouting off the first name you can think of in order of the popular alphabet?"

". . . It took you this long to figure that out?"

". . . No comment . . ."

Blythe studied the Nocturna's reflection in the cockpit's overhead glass and wondered how the dried blood didn't detract from the female's ethereal beauty. Her features were pointed, but while superimposed over a swirling galaxy, they seemed less sharp and inhumane and more delicate. Otherworldly. The long hair flowing past one cheek looked like a silken pillow designed to cushion such a fair head.

The shorn area on the other side of her face was a rough, ugly landscape matted with dark, drying fluids. Blythe was overcome with the inane urge to scrub the area clean.

"Did you do that yourself?" Blythe asked instead.

The Nocturna's answering expression was more pout than frown. "Do what?"

Blythe gestured toward her own temple. "The undercut. It would be cute if you got it done professionally."

In the unintended mirror of the glass, the vampire's frown smoothed into a stark blankness. It was so quick, so harsh, that it made Blythe shudder.

"Never mind—"

"I didn't do it myself."

Blythe bit her lips shut and tore her gaze from the overhead image of that beautiful face. It remained gorgeous—but unsettling —as the youthful flesh went stone cold and still.

Mournful silence reigned. It ended only when the Nocturna offered an unprompted remark.

"Gregoire's grandmother was the one who started it."

Blythe didn't ask for more detail. She wasn't sure she wanted to hear more if the Nocturna was going to keep speaking in such a deadened tone, so quiet and dangerous with a depth of emotion that wasn't possible to express in words.

"She said I was an animal. That I deserved to be used for my resources like any other beast."

"You never tried to escape?" Blythe asked in a nerve-shot bid to lead the conversation in another direction.

"Once or twice."

They left it at that.

THE SHIP JOSTLED AS THEY DESCENDED BELOW THE DUST CLOUD IN a hurry.

"What's happening?"

"I remembered Phink's comms code!" Blythe announced, breathless with excitement. "Maybe not his current one, but it's definitely a working sequence. Fuck me, but if we make it through this alive, I'm never inputting anything into my comms without memorizing it first."

"You won't have to. If we make it through this alive," the Nocturna said, "I'll get you the most secure comms available."

As the ship leveled out, Blythe jabbed at the comms display, and the vampire hung off her good shoulder. Her cheek pressed so close to Blythe's, the woman could feel the motion of her lips as she spoke.

"There won't be a man alive capable of taking it off you."

Blythe laughed, and by unspoken agreement, they ignored the high-pitched edge of hysteria in the sound.

The call went through, but it wasn't Phink on the other end.

"You have contacted a privatized and highly secure line, from an unrecognized source," a crisp European voice snapped from the speaker. "Speak your name and purpose, else I alert the authorities. The Harems do not accept solicitation nor—"

"Blythe Ramos!" Blythe crowed over him as her stunned brain pieced things together. It wasn't Phink's contact she remembered after all.

"Beg your pardon?"

"My name is Blythe Ramos! I got this number from Sylvester Spurgeon!"

As the Nocturna whined a soft "who?" in her ear, the man on the comms went quiet.

"Hello?" Blythe pressed closer to the display, her knuckles pale around the controls. "Fuck! You know what—mayday!"

The Nocturna jerked back with a gasp as Blythe started shouting.

"Mayday! Mayday!"

"Excuse me?" the man wailed in indignant alarm. "What in the good cosmos is this about?"

"May-fucking-day!" Blythe shrieked as she shook the controls. "We have an emergency, and we need help!"

He spluttered back, "Now, wait a moment—"

"No!" Blythe cut him off with a venomous snap to her words. "I will *not* wait. I'm stranded in the middle of nowhere thanks to an extremist bag of colossal dicks, with an eighth of a tank of fuel and no civilization in sight. I haven't eaten or peed in hours, and official channels aren't responding to my distress signal!"

She stopped shouting long enough to catch her breath and let the Nocturna wipe the anxious sweat from her brow.

"Goodness," the man whispered from the speaker. "If this is any sort of jest—"

Blythe stiffened, but before she could start yelling again, a pale hand slipped over her mouth.

"You have two options," the Nocturna said in a clear, strong voice that didn't match the terrified tremor of the arms holding Blythe in check, "either alert emergency services and save our lives, or you can explain to Mr. Spurgeon why you left his friend for dead on the dark side of the moon."

"Ah . . . All right. What are your coordinates again?"

The hand slid from Blythe's mouth and patted her on the shoulder. With a tearful huff of laughter, Blythe began reading off their location from the dashboard display.

"First thing I'm going to do is take a long, hot bath," Blythe said with a wistful moan. "With bubbles."

A soft chuckle came from the rear of the cockpit. "Doubtful."

"Oh, just you watch."

"Technically, I've already done that."

They dissolved into giggles that made zero sense.

The distress signal was still going strong. The fuel gauge was creeping closer and closer to empty. Mister Uppity of the Vauqeulin Harem's employ disconnected from comms over an hour ago and of the two attempts they'd made to regain contact, one was unsuccessful, and the other reached an automated messaging system.

Yet here they were. Giggling.

When Blythe managed to get control of herself, she was crying. From the relieved gasps sounding behind her, she wasn't the only one.

"I figured it out, by the way," Blythe said as she slumped in her seat.

"What did you figure out, Blythe?"

"Your name."

"Oh?"

"Yeah." Blythe heaved a breath as she stared up at the stars. "Your name is Polaris."

Silence. Blythe thought the Nocturna might have been holding her breath.

"You're Polaris," Blythe said, as if it were a fact etched in stone. "After the North Star."

"Pretty," the Nocturna said, quiet and shy. "I'm not familiar with it."

Eyes still trained on the sky, Blythe nodded to herself. The name felt right. She sank lower in the seat and spoke as her eyes glazed over, the vivid stars blurring, as if they, too, were softening to the idea.

"On Earth, you can't see the sky. There's a whole universe beyond this nasty atmosphere, but from the ground, you can't see it through the smog."

"That sounds terrible."

"I guess so," Blythe shrugged. "Sly would agree with you. He was full of hopes and dreams, full of stories and songs about these stars we'd never seen. I never had the imagination for it, but I could listen to him talk for hours. He was the one who told me about Polaris."

"You miss him."

Blythe sighed. "Yeah."

"He was your lover?"

"No!" Blythe laughed. "He's . . . my person. Like family, but more than that."

The Nocturna made a short, confused whine. "More than family?"

Blythe took the time to roll the idea around in her head before responding. "Yeah. He was there for me when no one else was. Even my parents. He was like my personal hero."

They lapsed into silence, and all Blythe could see was a cold, endless galaxy stretching out above them. She didn't have the energy to tense up or cry, but she felt smaller than ever. Smaller than she'd been in the cage, smaller than she'd been under Andy Kenwood's vengeful scorn. She was no more or less insignificant than she had been then, but now she was . . . untethered. Directionless. Lost.

"Polaris was part of some constellation," Blythe said. "I don't remember which one, though I bet Sly would. It doesn't matter."

She shook herself.

"Polaris used to be the brightest star visible in the sky from the ground. There was no other like it, not just as bright but none as steady. It was this dependable plot point in the sky, and over time, I guess it became synonymous with hope and guidance."

The seat creaked as the Nocturna pulled herself over it. As she loomed over Blythe, her hair fell around them, screening the starlight till they were enveloped in a glorious curtain of gleaming silver. Upside down from Blythe's perspective, the Nocturna's smile was no less breathtaking.

Holding her bluest of blue gaze, Blythe cleared her throat and said, "Polaris pointed toward freedom."

"I love it," Polaris whispered, eyes wet and smile tremulous.

~

THEIR RELIEVING OPTIMISM DIDN'T LAST MUCH LONGER.

Another half-hour passed and the console lit up with warnings. They were running out of fuel. Soon, all auxiliary power would have to be allocated to the ship's life support features. There was still no sign of civilization, no blip on the radar to indicate an approaching rescue.

"We should land," Polaris suggested, her voice monotonous and quiet.

Blythe sighed. She closed her eyes against the ache in her shoulder as she slipped her arm free of the sling. Whether it did them any good or not, she wanted both hands on the controls.

When Blythe's silence dragged on too long without any change to the ship's trajectory, Polaris reached over the pilot's chair and brushed the frizzing curls back from her face. The gesture should have been comforting, but it was too shaky and the hair too matted. Blythe wasn't comforted at all.

"This ship isn't going to make it to a colony," Polaris breathed into her ear. "The best we can do now is stay put, conserve power, and wait for help."

Blythe gnawed on her lip as she frowned at the dashboard. "I probably should have mentioned this before, but I only have the barest idea how to land this thing in one piece."

There was no reaction to her words. The slender fingers stroking her hair never faltered.

Without turning to look at the other female, Blythe reached up with her good hand and gripped Polaris's fingers tight. "Get ready for a rough landing then."

CHAPTER 9

The next thing Blythe knew was total darkness. Her nose twitched with a flash of feline sensitivity that stung her nostrils with antiseptic and air so cold, it burned her throat when she inhaled too fast. She heard beeping. Voices.

"—no favors like this."

"No."

"Please, Miss. You need rest."

"I'm not leaving her side. Not until she wakes up."

This announcement was met with a heavy sigh of aggrieved resignation. The speaker was European and female. Something about it tickled the edges of Blythe's memory. She didn't recognize the voice, not exactly, but the inkling of confused alarm that had woken her receded at the sound. Was this person familiar? Not quite?

Someone lifted her hand, encasing it in the warm, silken skin of another's palms. "Blythe?"

Her eyelids were heavy. They weren't as heavy as her limbs, but she struggled to lift them anyway.

At first, she didn't recognize the pale, lovely face frowning down at her. When her brain finally scrounged up the right info, it came in sluggish, incomplete blurbs.

"Polaris?"

She was answered with a breathtaking smile and the hopeful widening of eyes so blue, it hurt Blythe's heart to stare into them.

"Welcome back, Ms. Ramos."

Blythe tilted her head to the side and spied a woman standing behind the Nocturna's shoulder. She was elderly with peach skin that was lined and creased, though well maintained, and a tightness around her mouth that spoke to decades of undaunted authority. She was thin and tall, with the stiff, upright bearing of someone important. The coiffed hair on her head was whiter than the last time Blythe met her.

Blythe gaped up at the old woman. "Madam Walters?"

Emmeline Walters offered a polite smile, and Blythe choked on the relief that crashed over her.

"Oh, Blythe!" Polaris whined as her pretty face crowded Blythe's view. "You don't need to cry! We're safe! You did it!"

"Hush, now," Walters scolded the vampire gently as she pulled her back by the shoulders. "Give her space. There are times when a good cry is all we can manage. I daresay she's earned it."

Polaris was reluctant to let go of her hand. When she did, Blythe's arm flopped onto the mattress at her side like a leaden weight.

"Oh! I'm sorry!" Polaris gasped, jerking in Walters's grip in a bid to get back to Blythe's side.

Walters spun them around and neatly redirected the vampire toward the door. "There, she's awake, and you owe me a thorough cleansing in a proper bath. Off you go."

Blythe watched Polaris inch toward the door of a very white and blurry room with wet eyes. Infusing her voice with every ounce of the fantastical peace weighing her down, Blythe told her, "It's okay, Hun. Go take care of yourself."

Polaris was slow to leave, and Blythe felt her gaze like a laser on the side of her face the whole while. Blythe tried not to blush under the attention as she wiped her eyes dry and surveyed the room.

The impression of whiteness was accurate, yet insufficient. She was in a bedroom, and a very clean and sophisticated one at that. The bed she lay in was dressed in thick off-white linens with delicate patterns embroidered on the blanket. The walls were white, not due to paint, but due to striated swirls of grays and pearls; she might have expected the design to mimic wood grain, but considering whose House she was in, it was possible the room was lined in actual wood panels. The bureau spanning the wall opposite her was a deep mahogany that was even more convincing, with its darkness artfully interrupted with a white-and-gold runner lying atop it. In the corner was a matching chair large enough to fit two adult humans; its cushions were as light and pristine as the rest of the room.

There was also a window, only one, and it wasn't large, but the gossamer curtains framing it did nothing to detract from the view. Earth wasn't visible, but two pinpoints of brilliant blue-white glittered in a sea of gold-and-pink star streams.

"Alpha Centauri," the old woman explained as she followed Blythe's gaze. "They're the stars closest to Luna, save for the Milky Way's sun."

"How—?" Blythe's voice cracked with unfathomable relief. "Where are we?"

"The Vauqeulin Harem's Lunar residence. The Heir's vacation home, if you will."

Blythe laughed in amazement, still staring around the luxuriant room. "What happened?"

The old woman sighed and shifted closer to Blythe's bedside. Before speaking, she folded her hands together in front of her hips and frowned at them in thought.

"I'm not entirely sure how you came to be stranded so far from any of the colonies, Ms. Ramos, but you managed to drop your vehicle a few hours from my doorstep. You were fortunate. By the time Reese reached you, you were unconscious and"—one of Walters's thin brows arched high in bewilderment before she formed the name—"Miss Polaris was slurring her words. Poor Reese was beside himself. I don't think he ever appreciated how mortal the Nocturni are before that moment."

Blythe's arms didn't want to cooperate as she tried to lift them to rub the lingering wetness from her eyes. She discovered her dislocated shoulder was fully immobilized with professional bandages, but the hand seemed unencumbered. The only other bandage she noticed was the minuscule strip covering the bite mark on her throat.

Blythe frowned. "Did we crash?"

"No. Why?"

Blythe would have shrugged if her body had the energy for movement. She settled for a noncommittal groan and let her head flop back into the pillow.

"If there was no crash, why was I unconscious? Why am I so weak?"

Why did it sound like she was speaking with a mouthful of cotton clogging her words? Why couldn't she lift her arm? She wasn't paralyzed, she could tell that much.

"Ah. Yes." Walters nodded to herself as she launched into explanation, saying, "Your ship went dark some time before you were found. Life support was the last thing to go, as it does in these situations."

Blythe's head lulled to the side as she squinted up at Walters. "I suffocated?"

Walters gave her a subdued smile. "A touch of cerebral hypoxia, I'm afraid. The Harem doctors assure me you'll make a full recovery."

With a deep, cleansing breath, Blythe closed her eyes. "Thank the stars."

"Indeed."

She did it. She escaped and made it to safety. She made it.

They made it.

A wave of soul-deep exhaustion washed over Blythe. If she'd been standing, she had no doubt she would have dropped with all the finesse and immediacy of an anchor. The sensation was unspeakable, like she'd been given permission to let go of all the stress and fright of the recent past, to the point where she was floating up and away from her own body.

Stars above, but she was going to have such a good sleep.

Halfway there already, Blythe managed one more all-important question, "Sly?"

"I notified Master Kahled personally," Walters said. "I have no doubt he passed the message along."

Blythe wanted to give an expectant grin and say something pointed like "he better have" or "damn right," but her desire proved no match for the deep solace swarming her person. The only knowledge that truly mattered in that moment was that she and the Nocturna were alive and well, free and clear.

They made it. Her and Polaris.

FEW NOCTURNI HAREMS HAD THE MEANS TO BUILD AND MAINTAIN a private property so removed from any port city, be it on the moon or elsewhere. Fortunately, the Vauqeulins were not just any Harem. They were among the elite, descended from the original nine vampires, and they had the wealth and legacy to prove it. More than that, an argument could be made that they were the most prestigious and vital bloodline of the entire species.

Being the forerunners of modern evolution had that effect. Nosferatu's Curse, of all things, did have that effect.

"I can't afford this," Blythe said as Walters set a food tray over her lap stacked with fresh fruits and steaming baked goods.

Walters ignored her.

"Seriously," Blythe stressed. "The money Sly left me is barely going to cover the cost of all this elite medical care, and I have no idea if I even have a job waiting—"

"Don't be absurd," Walters huffed in offense as she forced an honest silver utensil into Blythe's unbandaged hand. "We're not charging you."

Blythe stared after her as the old woman strutted out of the room, as if treating a random Earthling like a visiting princess was no more remarkable than any other task on her to-do list.

Blythe couldn't imagine being so accustomed to having Harem resources at her disposal. She could barely comprehend the easy graciousness being shown to her.

Her personal exposure to vampires had set her expectations low. Earthly Ports weren't strictly segregated, but she never properly interacted with vampires until she was shaking her ass for them on Centrism's stage. The experience never brought her harm—not from the Nocturni anyway—but it didn't do much to convince her they were any less sleezy or entitled than her upbringing suggested.

She wasn't prepared for the full force of the Vauqeulin Harem's goodwill being aimed at her.

It started small and reasonable.

"Write everything you remember on here," Walters instructed as she settled a large handheld comms in her lap.

The screen was open to a detailed and official-looking page. Blythe's heart did a funny little lurch against her ribcage as she read the prompts before each section. It was a grievance report.

"For now, this will serve as your statement on the whole ordeal, so include everything from the day leading to your abduction to the moment you contacted us. I'll send this directly to Human Services on your behalf, and the investigation will be well underway by the time your shoulder fully heals."

Walters remained at her side with a sympathetic ear and guiding voice the entire evening while Blythe finished the harrowing paperwork. She only left to answer the door and accept several tea trays and to answer her staff's pressing concerns.

Once the Head of Household finally took her leave, things started to seem a little less reasonable.

Hesitant and full of dread, Blythe asked a different staff member —a cute chubby girl with orange eyes and fur like peach-fuzz coating half her skin—about the cost for her top-tier accommodations.

"Don't worry about it," she said. "Master Vauqeulin will take care of it, I'm sure."

This was far from a solitary occurrence.

At one point, a middle-aged man dressed in voluminous green robes that heightened the reds in the fur patches along his forearm breezed into her room without knocking. He forwent any introduction and proceeded to talk her ear off about his position as the Harem's preferred Lunar stylist kept on retainer. In the handful of hours he spent unknotting, cutting, and coaxing her hair into healthy ringlets, he managed to distract her with inane fashion commentary and repeated scoldings to take greater care with her curls. She never caught his name.

Not long after, a group of three servants clad in unofficial uniforms of black and white brought her presents. The first set a wooden tray containing a feast fit for royalty over her lap. The second one rolled in a metal stand with multiple garment bags swinging from it, along with assurances that her "soiled garments" had been appropriately confiscated and forwarded to Human Services for processing.

The third staff member handed her a sparkling new comms unit.

"I can't take all this," Blythe insisted, trying to hand it back.

"Nonsense," said one as she unfolded Blythe's napkin and laid it over her lap.

"Master Vauqeulin would expect nothing less for a friend of the Harem," said another as he began stripping the bags from the hanging outfits. "Consider it a get well soon gift."

"Okay, but this is too much—"

"It's yours nevertheless," the third staff member said as he nudged her hand holding the comms back toward her. "The Harem is nothing if not gracious to their own."

"But I'm not—"

"Nonsense!" the first one stressed again.

"There's not a human on this property who doesn't know your name, Ms. Ramos," the second man said, smirking down at her as his female coworker began fussing with the tray over her lap. "Word is out how you helped save Master Kahled's life."

Blythe blanched.

Until recently, a diagnosis of Nosferatu's Curse was a death sentence for the Nocturni. The Nocturni tended to quietly ship off their diseased kin to less populated areas where they would be destined to lose their minds and control of their splicing abilities, until such a time where the vampire posed too great a threat to be allowed to live.

Blythe first thought that was the best way to handle the Curse, too, when she found herself walking over a pile of corpses in Sly's wake. She was as surprised as everyone else when Sly managed to bring Kahled back to sanity and subsequently restore a measure of the vampire's control over his innate splicing abilities.

"I had nothing to do with that!'" Blythe insisted, "That was Sly! I just happened to be there for moral support—"

"And here you are again," the man cheered over her, "miraculously alive after rescuing yet another of the Nocturni!"

Blythe's eyes grew painfully huge as she shook her head at him. "It's not like that."

They had no interest in her denials.

HER PROTESTS MEANT NOTHING LATER THAT NIGHT WHEN IT WAS just her and Polaris in the white room. They sat together side by side against the headboard, staring at the comms cradled in Blythe's hands. Unlike her former device, this one was gold. Despite herself, Blythe liked the way its amber gleam complimented the yellows in her jaguar spots.

Polaris sat cross-legged beside her. She was dressed in a day robe of deep-blue silk with gold embroidery. It hung off her shoulders and draped over her body like a cape, barely cinched closed at her waist. Her bare knee poked out from the folds, and from the way the fabric settled over her chest, Blythe suspected the Nocturna wore nothing underneath.

Blythe was trying not to think about that. From what she gathered from Walters and her staff, they'd had a rough time finding anything Polaris was willing to wear. After years of dressing in nothing but her skin, Polaris's sense of modesty seemed close to nonexistent.

Fortunately, Blythe had a ready-made distraction in her lap.

The Nocturna's face was neutral, but her soft voice gave her away as she asked, "Do you want me to go?"

"No." Blythe gave Polaris's exposed knee a reassuring pat, then her fingers were breezing over the comms.

Sly answered in record time. "Blythe? Stars above, Blythe! You're okay?"

Blythe's throat felt tight, and her eyes ached as she nodded at his projection. She couldn't speak, even if she could decide on something to say.

Sly stared back at her, just as tearful. "I'm on my way," he promised.

"Oh, no, Sly—" Her voice broke on a sob.

"You're okay," he insisted. "You're going to be just fine. I'll be there in a few days, a week, max."

She shook her head in denial, but he talked over her with his usual frenetic determination.

"I'm already off the ground and en route. Kahled's not happy about it, but he'll be fine without me for a bit. He's got a stockpile of my blood in storage."

Blythe dropped her skull back against the headboard as she switched off her visual transmissions. Sly didn't need to see her ugly cry, and she wasn't so sure she could handle the sight of him anyway. The anxious crease to his brow and unhappy jut of his jaw made her feel pathetic.

"I'm coming," he stressed.

The connection cut off before Blythe could reply. Most likely, Sly's transport entered a pocket of space weather too dense to sustain a signal. As the comms dimmed to plain old metal, Blythe's body shuddered with a deluge of grief.

Sly was needed elsewhere, on the distant dwarf planet the Vauqeulins had transformed into a mini paradise over the centuries. Ethos was supposed to be no more than a place to stash the bloodline while it died out as a result of Nosferatu's Curse, but the disease had gone largely dormant, and the Harem flourished. Sly wasn't the first pure-blooded human to be used as treatment for Nosferatu's Curse, but as far as the known universe was concerned, he was the first to help it evolve into something else.

He was more valuable to the Nocturni race as Kahled's blood donor than he could ever be as Blythe's friend. It was no wonder he never came to her rescue.

"I'm an idiot," Blythe murmured.

"No," Polaris whispered back as she snuggled into Blythe's side.

Blythe wanted to be the strong, independent woman she needed to be. She'd invested years into proving she was that person, the one Sly needed her to be, so he could go live his life.

But she wasn't. He said he was coming, and Blythe didn't argue.

Smooth and graceful, Polaris slipped an arm behind Blythe's back and hugged her waist. That fair head settled on Blythe's shoulder in silent support, and she squeezed. She held Blythe tight, held her together as it felt like she was shattering apart. It was so little, and at the same time so very much.

Blythe didn't have the strength to return the embrace, but she buried her face in Polaris's mane. They stayed that way for longer than Blythe could track and fell asleep with their heads pressed together.

Blythe was bedridden for several days while Walters insisted she rest and let her shoulder heal. The dislocation's rough reset during her captivity nearly caused further damage. According to the medics in residence, the injury might have repaired already if she'd been seen to by a professional and given adequate medicines in the first place. As things were, she would need to wear the sling for another week.

With few exceptions, Polaris refused to leave her side for the duration of the healing.

One such instance saw Walters bullying the Nocturna into getting some fresh air, and moments later, a sharp knock sounded on Blythe's door. It opened without her acknowledgment, and Blythe startled upright in the bed. She promptly stopped stirring the lukewarm tea in her lap.

"I owe you an apology."

A young man stood in the doorway. He was tall and slender, with a rigidity to him that seemed equally due to nerves as much as posture. Light, sandy brown hair fell below his cleft chin, and his magenta dress left his shoulders exposed. Much like his nose, they were covered in distinct freckles.

Blythe scanned the room as if expecting to discover someone else he was speaking to. "What?"

"My apology," the young man said as he clasped his hands together behind his back and rocked onto his heels. "When you first contacted the Harem, I should have taken you seriously. I thought you were having me on."

Blythe leaned forward in bed, squinting at him. "And you are . . . ?"

His cheeks pinkened, and his mouth tightened into a thin line. "Reese. I was monitoring comms when you reached out to us."

"Ah!" Blythe slapped her thigh as she threw her shoulders back into the pillows. "Mr. Uppity! Yeah, now I remember cussing you out."

His blush deepened as he nodded. "Yes. You certainly did."

They stared at each other.

After a moment, Blythe fiddled with her teaspoon and offered him a smile. "Apology accepted."

He nodded again and turned to leave, his hands still locked together behind him. He made it two steps out the door before he stopped and about-faced with his chin held high.

"I want you to know," he said, "I admire you greatly for what you've done—"

"I don't do men anymore."

He blinked at her. "That's . . . quite nice for you?"

An inkling of tension leaked from Blythe's shoulders. Her upper back relaxed, and she snorted into her teacup.

Reese shook himself and started over. "I simply wish you to

know that I was unaware of your contributions to the Harem or your recent ordeals when we last spoke. I know better now."

Blythe smirked at him as she lowered her drink. "That's quite nice for you."

Blush flaring bright, he attempted a smile as he backed out of the room. "Yes. Well. I've things to attend to, so . . . good night."

Blythe raised her good hand to wiggle her fingers at him. "Bye!"

She was still shaking her head and snickering ten minutes later when the door popped open again.

Polaris rushed into the room in a flurry of silver hair and skidded to the edge of the bed. Her eyes were impossibly wide, and her pallor was ghostly gray as she braced both hands on the bed and whined in Blythe's face.

Blythe reached for her without a second thought. "What's wrong, Hun?"

Polaris's gaze was piercing as she peered at Blythe. After a second, the color returned to her face, and her eyes narrowed with a frown.

"You're okay? You're not upset?"

Blythe gave an awkward chuckle as she swept a wisp of silver behind the delicate point of the Nocturna's ear. There was no longer blood clotting the strands, and the hair felt incredible, silken and strong, yet flexible and oh-so-soft. It was so much healthier than the rest of her.

"Polaris, Hun . . ." Blythe let a small laugh suffuse her sighs as she said, "Look at where we are. What could I possibly be upset about?"

Polaris deflated and plopped down on the bed. "Reese suggested you were upset."

Blythe snickered. She hastened to contain it when Polaris pouted at her.

"I thought he did something to upset you." The Nocturna glared at the wall as she crossed her arms tight over her chest. "I wanted to be sure before I made him regret it."

"My hero." Blythe giggled as she petted Polaris's arm.

That was how she discovered that Polaris had the prettiest blush to ever grace the moon.

It took longer than she cared to admit for Blythe to call Phink. She waited till morning, after the manor's interior lighting adjusted to mimic daytime and the staff had stuffed her and Polaris full of fresh fruit, hot crepes, and eggs.

"Blythe!" Phink whisper-wailed from the comms the moment he got a look at her face.

"Don't start crying," she warned him with a grouchy lift of her chin. "If you start, I'll start, and I'm pretty sure my tear ducts should be out of commission for the foreseeable future after the week I've had."

"Week?" He choked. "Shit, girl, you've been gone for the better part of a month!"

Blythe's heart stuttered.

On the other side of the guest room, Polaris made a quiet noise. She didn't move from her place by the window, nor shift her gaze from the stars to look at Blythe.

With a dizzying sensation, Blythe looked from the half-starved vampire to herself. She glanced over the projection of Phink's fuzzy face to eye the unfamiliar comms unit decorating her wrist. It fit her, but barely. Her old device once sat flush against her arm, making the warm-brown of her skin seem much darker than it was against the metal. This one hung off her wrist with room to spare.

Had it really been that long? Had she truly lasted a month in that fucking cage?

"Never mind all that." Phink waved the subject away with a

split-second sneer and wrinkled his nose. "You're safe now. The dirtbags who took you are dead, and Human Services is breathing down Elitia's neck for what she did to you. Everything's going to be fine."

Phink's tone was confident, but Blythe had a hard time focusing on him. She was distracted by the comparison between her skinny arm and the even skinnier vampire curled into a ball in the chair nearby.

"Blythe," Phink snapped, "you hear me, girl? You're going to be fine, dammit."

"Yeah," Blythe agreed, but it felt wrong.

Polaris must have heard the lie in her voice. The Nocturna stiffened and sat forward in her chair, uncurling as she focused on Blythe.

Through Phink's hologram, Blythe caught her eye with the intention of sharing a reassuring smile. Her lips didn't curve like she wanted though; her face was frozen into blankness. Blythe didn't need a mirror to guess how disheartened her expression must seem; she could feel it well enough.

More than that, she could see its reflection in Polaris's super-blue eyes.

This wasn't over yet. Not for either of them.

CHAPTER 10

"You lead a blessed life, Madam Walters," Blythe said one day as Polaris guided her onto a padded chair beside the old woman. "This is incredible."

It was true. They were outside on the mansion's back terrace with a glorious view of the Milky Way Galaxy swirling overhead. The stars Alpha Centauri A and B were no longer visible, instead giving way for what was left of Earth to go on display. The planet was a giant orb in the distant sky, swirling with fiery reds and smokey grays.

Such a view wasn't possible from Earth. It wasn't quite the same from any of the Lunar colonies either. Here, the barrier protecting them from the moon's natural atmosphere wasn't as obvious and bulbous as the domes that incubated the colonies. It was more expensive—crystal clear and subtle enough to give them the illusion of outdoor exposure.

If Blythe was being honest, it was a little terrifying.

"I wouldn't call myself blessed, Ms. Ramos." Walters adjusted the heavy shawl on her thin shoulders and shot an unreadable look at Blythe and Polaris. "I've worked hard for my position, and I continue working to deserve it."

"I know," Blythe assured her. "You're amazing like that."

Walters gave a long-suffering sigh as she refocused on the sky, but Blythe noticed the slight smile tugging at her lips.

Blythe had yet to meet another human who could command a room with ease the way Emmeline Walters does. Despite her relative fragility, she was capable of ordering full-grown vampires to do her bidding. It wasn't like the Harem leader had named her his proxy or anything like that; it was a simple matter of Walters expecting things to go her way and willing the necessary players into compliance. No one could convince Blythe otherwise.

The first and only other time Blythe met Emmeline Walters, there was blood painting the walls and more than one crazed vampire roaming the building. In the aftermath of Kahled's frenzy, Blythe had the privilege of watching Walters scold him and the present leader of the Harem, as if they were a pair of schoolboys caught with their hands in a cookie jar. Walters was unfazed by their fangs and superhuman strength then, and Blythe suspected the same would be true now.

After all, Polaris showed up covered in blood and guts, and no one else had the nerve to verbally smack the Nocturna into cooperation.

As if the old woman could read her mind, Walters lowered her gaze from the view and focused on Polaris. Blythe shifted around so she could follow the other woman's line of sight to where the Nocturna stood beside her.

Polaris was a vision. She stood tall with her eyes closed and face lifted to the heavens. Starlight rained down on her fair skin and gleaming hair, and for a moment, she almost seemed to glow with it. The thin straps of her dress weren't visible given the angle, but Blythe was happy to admire the fit anyway; the loose article spilled over her unbound breasts and down to her knees in pink folds that paled to near white under the stars. She remained barefoot.

The vampire must have felt their stares. Eyes still closed, she whispered, "I missed this."

"Stargazing?" Blythe asked, reaching for Polaris's hand.

"Yes." The vampire wove their fingers together like it was second nature, like they'd been doing it for decades.

Walters leaned an elbow on her chair's armrest, so she could peer around Blythe. "Did your Harem have a garden, Polaris?"

Polaris sighed and opened her eyes. They stayed fixated on the sky as she answered in a cool, monotonous tone, "Not on Luna."

Walters hummed in acceptance, but her gaze was sharp as it lingered on Polaris.

Blythe tightened her grip on the Nocturna's hand and tried not to tense up. Walters had been direct but gentle in every inquiry she'd made of Blythe since she woke up in the guest room. Somehow, Blythe doubted the careful approach would work on Polaris. It hadn't yet, and Blythe had been trying to get her to talk for longer than Walters had known Polaris existed.

They still didn't know her real name.

When the lull in conversation stretched a little too long, Walters made another adjustment to her shawl and ventured again, "Who has the better garden, Polaris? Your Harem or mine? The truth, now. I won't have you sugarcoating your opinions."

Blythe gave a small, encouraging chuckle. Her palm was still snug in Polaris's grip, so she gave it a squeeze.

The Nocturna was slow to answer. She lowered her eyes to ground level and took a few moments to observe the expanse of moonrock beneath the oxygenated barrier.

The area designating the patio had been chiseled smooth and the perimeter lined with crystalized meteorites that would sell for a fortune on Earth. Beyond that space, the garden consisted of similarly bordered segments housing different flora from across the known universe. Most of it was jewel-like or a collection of muted colors, and all of it was unfamiliar to Blythe. It was pretty and subtle in its extravagance. Serene.

Blythe found it boring.

There was no grass or manufactured waterfalls, and Blythe found it a chilling comparison to the colorful enclosure Polaris would be familiar with.

"Mine was better," Polaris said, surprising Blythe with no mention of Humans First's phony forest. "Brighter. We had more color."

Blythe squeezed her hand hard. "Did you grow flowers?"

"Yes."

"It sounds beautiful."

Blythe tugged on their joined hands, and Polaris knelt beside her chair. Blythe cupped that lovely face in her palm, and the vampire closed her eyes as she leaned into the touch.

"*You* are beautiful," Blythe amended, "and you're free. If you want flowers, you can have flowers. Just name where you could grow them, and we'll get you there."

Polaris began to smile, but she was quick to hide it by nuzzling into Blythe's touch. It only lasted a moment, then the Nocturna pulled away and rose to her feet. Blythe couldn't be sure, but she thought she saw a hint of wetness in Polaris's eyes before she headed back toward the manor. "I'll go get you some tea."

Blythe cringed. "You don't need to—"

"It's good for you."

Blythe watched the Nocturna run back inside with a lump in her throat.

"Give her time," Walters advised.

Blythe faced forward and resettled in the chair, pretending she didn't feel the old woman's attention. She still caught a shrewd look crossing Walters's face, like she was piecing together a puzzle.

"You really don't know who she is?"

"Do you?" Blythe glowered back at her, but she didn't have the energy to put any fire behind it.

"I have my suspicions."

By unspoken agreement, they turned their sights on the stars. Blythe wasn't naïve enough to think Walters summoned the resident invalid to the garden for some leisurely stargazing, but she wasn't about to force whatever conversation they were about to have.

Eventually, Walters cleared her throat and said, "The Zephyr touched down on Lunar-5 this morning. Soon, they'll be on their way to collect you, with Phink in tow."

Blythe sat on that information for a moment, mulling it over. The news was nothing she hadn't expected. It should have made her smile, happy to be that much closer to her people and home. Instead, she just felt numb.

"Sylvester will arrive first," Walters said with enviable nonchalance. "Kahled gifted him a star cruiser for his birthday, and he left Ethos not long after your disappearance became interplanetary news. He should be here within the week. I suspect The Zephyr will take a few days longer."

"Probably," Blythe commented, her voice dry and uninvested. "They should be on a job right now."

Walters hummed in acknowledgment. Before Blythe could think up something more to say, Walters was staring at her again. Her tone was grave when she next spoke.

"The port authorities have been in contact as well."

Easier than breathing, Blythe tossed aside her confounding reaction to her proposed return home. The change in topic was much simpler; she already knew how she felt about it.

"Who?" she demanded. "The Guard?"

"Not exactly."

Blythe's jaw clenched.

"The investigation is early yet. I don't know how The Guard is handling the situation," Walters said. "I told Human Services when we first found you; they were shocked to hear a Nocturna was involved and promised they would notify The Guard, but I haven't heard from them yet."

Blythe shifted, sitting up straighter in her chair. "Phink said Human Services hasn't arrested Kenwood. Is this why? They're letting The Guard deal with her?"

"I don't know. In either case, she claims no knowledge of any abducted Nocturna."

"She's lying."

"I don't think she is." Walters turned away, dropping her gaze. "What little Polaris has said is telling. I'm certain she's older than Kahled, and he doesn't recognize her. She may have been in captivity his entire life."

"Bullshit," Blythe spat.

"With no connection between Polaris and Kenwood, The Guard has no justification for keeping hold of the woman. She's been released into Master Troy's custody and is already back at the HEPP House."

"You're fucking with me."

"I'm afraid not."

Blythe lurched forward in her chair. The pain meds and quality bandages did nothing to stop the twinges in her shoulder, but she ignored it.

"That bitch sold me out to a terrorist," she hissed.

"I believe you," Walters said immediately, "but conflicts between humans are for Human Services to deal with, not The Guard. If you want to press charges against—"

"If?" Blythe sputtered. "Like I'm not a victim here, too?"

Walters closed her eyes and rubbed her bottom lip. She said nothing for a long while.

Blythe's flaring temper waned beneath her confusion. "I don't understand."

"Strictly speaking," Walters huffed, dissatisfied, "from Human

Services's perspective, the situation is effectively stuck in a stalemate. They have no evidence to go on beside your word versus Kenwood's."

Blythe tossed her head back and screamed through her teeth. She gestured at herself, and despite using her good arm, the movement was jerky enough to send throbs of fresh pain through her opposing shoulder.

"I am right here! Polaris is here! You saw us when we first escaped. What more evidence do they need?"

"Human Services has neither the funding nor manpower to send their investigators beyond the port boundaries," Walters said with strained patience, like she was delivering an explanation she didn't agree with. "I sent ahead your statement, along with the clothing you arrived in, but it has yet to be processed. Once yourself and the escape craft are delivered to the port, I'm sure this matter will be swiftly settled."

"But that makes no sense!" Blythe scowled as she began pacing. "I don't have to be there to identify her cousin by name on Tanya's security footage."

"Apparently, Tanya's Place hasn't been outfitted with functional surveillance in some time."

Blythe released a loud, ugly laugh.

Walters waited for her to quiet down. "It was the first thing Mr. Phink looked into after you disappeared."

Blythe clenched her teeth and stood there, shaking. She wasn't lightheaded, not like she'd been every time she got up to use the restroom over the past week, but she was unsteady as she resumed pacing. Her heart was pounding, her body vibrating with a silent, boiling rage. She kept moving anyhow, and her steps proved too heavy and awkward for her liking.

"Fuck!"

"Calm yourself."

Blythe hissed at the old woman.

Walters took an audible, measured breath before gaining her feet. She stepped into Blythe's path and forced her to stop with a raised hand.

"There is nothing you can do about it right this moment. Take a breath. Control yourself."

It was difficult to argue with Walters's cool assurance staring her in the face. Blythe opened her mouth to give it a shot anyway. "They can't—"

"You cannot control the actions of others," Walters countered with her iron-hard composure. "You can only control yourself and prepare yourself and those you trust for the right opportunity."

Blythe scoffed in her face. "I'm not waiting around for my supervisor to have me abducted again."

"Naturally."

"And I'm sick of putting my life on hold because Humans First has a stick up their ass!"

"That's fair."

Blythe jabbed her finger in the old woman's face. "Then don't tell me to calm the fuck down!"

Walters swatted her hand away. It was quick and sharp, but harmless and damn effective. Blythe shut up.

"If letting you loose in my garden to vent your rage would be beneficial, I would let you," Walters said as she folded her hands together with an unimpressed frown creasing her brow and tightening her mouth. "You are still recovering and liable to reinjury. Scream and cry if you wish, but please sit down. If you can't calm yourself, I will call for a sedative."

Blythe scoffed and backstepped. "You are not going to sedate me."

"I wonder if Sylvester would share your confidence."

Blythe eyed the other woman with a mixture of wariness and reluctant amusement. As admirable and fierce as Blythe imagined her to be, her knowledge and experience with Walters was limited.

Sly lived with her for the better part of a year, though, and Blythe always had the impression he was the slightest bit scared of the old woman.

"According to our doctor, you shouldn't be left alone until we can be certain your strength and coordination have returned," Walters explained as she adjusted her shawl and retook her seat. "I will sit with you until Polaris returns."

Blythe frowned as she dumped herself back into the neighboring chair. She was still shaking from interrupted rage and, most likely, lingering weakness.

"Please," Walters said with infuriating calm, "do stop pouting. The screaming was at least tolerable."

"I'm not pouting," Blythe sneered.

"No? My mistake."

Blythe slumped in her chair, glaring everywhere that wasn't Walters's direction. True to her word, Walters sat with her as she stewed in useless fury and the initial bubbling bursts of shame.

She wasn't a child throwing a tantrum. The fact that she felt like one wasn't Walters's fault.

"I'm sorry," she grumbled after some time. "I shouldn't be taking this out on you."

Walters nodded and shot her a small, but genuine smile. "Apology accepted."

Instead of letting the silence resume to fester like an open and agitated wound, Blythe sat up straight in her chair and fiddled with the edge of her sling as she stole glances at the other woman.

"What did you mean," she asked, "about preparing myself and the people I trust?"

Walters didn't reply immediately. Instead, she chose to mull over her words for a long, agonizing moment that threatened to ignite the hot lump in Blythe's chest into a fresh fit. When she finally deigned to speak, her words were deliberate.

"I may not have lived as long as the Nocturni, but I've lived a long life. I've witnessed much and heard speak of more. Your descriptions of this Humans First compound existing unnoticed on Luna troubles me."

The cool resignation in her voice trickled over Blythe like something tangible. She shifted in her seat and looked up in time to catch Walters's eye. The intense focus she saw there was both exhilarating and unfathomable. Blythe began to think Sly might've been onto something all those times he fretted that Walters was spliced with a powerful bird of prey.

"I've heard as much as I like to, from both you and Polaris," Walters continued. "From your accounts of that place and its leader, this . . . Gregoire . . ." She trailed off with a sneer of distaste.

Blythe watched her expression go pinched and worrisome as Walters turned toward the stars. She didn't know the old woman well, but she didn't like the look of her, of the dark thoughts swimming behind her eyes and the ramrod stiffness in her posture.

"I don't know," Walters admitted with a sigh. "Whatever The Guard finds, whatever they do next . . . I doubt this will be the last we've heard of this man and his fanatics."

CHAPTER 11

*B*lythe's fortitude returned with a vengeance in the ensuing days. She was ready to get moving long before her arm was.

"You should be resting," Polaris fretted as she shadowed Blythe through the manor halls.

"I'm fine," Blythe argued, her voice monotonous from repeating the sentiment. "If I rest any longer, I'm going to start ripping my hair out."

Behind her, Polaris made a low noise of distress, and Blythe winced.

A full week of freedom, and Blythe was still learning how to communicate effectively with the Nocturna. Raising her voice was likely to turn the poor female into a preternaturally silent and trembling mess, regardless of the root cause. There were times where the sound of Blythe's excitement seemed as damning as the barest hint of her anger. She was growing to hate the way Polaris shrank away at the first sign of any extreme emotion.

Blythe blew out a hard breath as she slowed to a stop in the middle of a hallway. She turned around to find Polaris jerking to a standstill several inches behind.

"Thank you," Blythe said with all the sincerity she could muster. "You're right, I should probably be resting, but I've got more than physical needs to deal with. I need to get out of my own head. You can understand that, right?"

Polaris flushed. It wasn't the splotchy burst of color that belied her shame like it had during their escape; it was a healthy infusion of rose throughout her skin. Blythe hoped it wasn't indicative of embarrassment.

Blythe took hold of her hand just to be safe. "I'm not mad at you. I just don't like being . . ."

As her voice trailed off, Blythe went cold. There was no tactful way to say what she wanted to say.

Polaris knew anyway, and she took pity on her. With a small smile, she suggested, "Caged?"

Blythe's answering grin felt painful. "Something like that. I was going to say 'cooped up.'"

"A little less on the nose," Polaris agreed with a nod.

"Yeah."

Blythe watched the smile fade from Polaris's face as those brilliant blue eyes dropped toward the floor. It made her wish Andy were still alive just so she could have something appropriate to take her frustration out on.

The two of them were about the same height, but it felt wrong to have to duck down to catch the vampire's eye or to grip her chin to raise her face. Vampires were usually so much larger than their human counterparts. Blythe didn't let the weirdness stop her.

Their eyes locked and Blythe said, "We're safe."

The blue in Polaris's eyes brightened. It wasn't a trick of the lighting. They were standing close enough together for Blythe to see pale streaks dart out from her pupils. The effect was nothing short of magical.

"Wow," Blythe whispered without meaning to.

"We're safe," Polaris repeated back to her in a subdued, quivering voice. She didn't say it as a question, but it wasn't quite a statement either.

Blythe's hand slid down from the Nocturna's chin, trailing down her arm till she could give her hand a soft tug. "Come with me?"

She didn't need to ask, but it felt important to try anyway.

Since their arrival at the Vauqeulin mansion, Polaris stuck to her side like an industrial adhesive. Granted, Blythe was confined to bed for most of that time, but Polaris escorted her on each of the few forays she made to the garden and the dining room. More than once, Blythe had the unsettling thought that the Nocturna's behavior had more in common with a loyal dog than a person.

Of course she was coming with Blythe.

Polaris didn't answer with words, but her smile was quick and open as she tucked her hand into Blythe's and got them walking again.

It took Blythe a rough minute to recall Walters's directions to the library, but Polaris didn't rush her. When Blythe took them down the wrong hallway and had to double back, the Nocturna didn't comment, only gave her hand a gentle squeeze. She never spoke, never complained, and she followed Blythe's whims with a slight smile that never faltered. It was as if the Nocturna didn't care where they were heading or when they would get there; she seemed content to simply be in Blythe's presence.

It was a strange, understated sort of spotlight that Blythe wasn't familiar with.

Blythe didn't need enhanced senses to hear the commotion in the library well before she saw it. She could hear Reese's posh accent ordering people around, and his voice worked like a beacon.

"No, no! You can't put that there. Does this look like a Melvillian Catalog to you?"

Reese's ire and impatience became more pronounced with every step they took. Other voices were barely discernible as they responded to him, and they only seemed to stir Reese into greater fervor.

"Ugh. Just give it to me. I'll take care of it myself. Where's the rest of it?"

Blythe turned a corner and spotted the library door. It was propped open by no less than three large metal crates. A staff member scrambled into the hall with his hair and collar askew, but he took no notice of Blythe or Polaris as he hastened to dig through the topmost container.

Steps slowing, Blythe nudged Polaris and asked out of the corner of her mouth. "We could find somewhere less crowded, if you like."

The servant grunted as he heaved an armful of books from the crate. One of them slipped and fell back inside with a hollow thud. The container began to slide. Blythe gasped a useless warning as the crate upended, certain it was going to break the poor man's foot. From the shrill sound of his scream, he thought so too.

It never happened.

One moment, Polaris was beside her, holding her hand, and the next, Blythe and the servant were left gaping as the Nocturna righted the container with a single hand. Delicate fingers still gripping the metal, the vampire glanced toward the library then around the obstructed hallway. She never grunted or strained as she tugged the crate off the pile, and she seamlessly repositioned it on the floor against the wall several steps away.

Polaris rubbed her hands on the thin blue skirt covering her thighs and turned to Blythe with a cautious cast to her eyes. "Maybe they could use some help?"

Over the Nocturna's shoulder, the staff member gave Blythe a frantic nod.

"Stars have mercy, but there is a system here for a reason!"

Reese wailed from within the library. "Why won't you people use it?"

Polaris held out her arms for the servant's book load. "May I?"

"Please do, Miss."

He dropped the mountain of hardback tomes into her hands with a strained grimace. As he did so, Polaris started shooting wide-eyed looks at Blythe.

Blythe glanced back over each shoulder, but there was no one else behind her. "What?"

Polaris's eyes went impossibly larger, and she jerked her head toward the servant she was helping. The guy was almost sweating as he hurried to convey more books from the crate to Polaris's arms.

"What?" Blythe gave her a bemused look of incomprehension and started toward the open crate. "Should I help?"

"No!" Polaris and the servant cried in unison.

The man hugged the current volume to his chest, as if he expected Blythe to try to take it from him. "You mustn't bother yourself, Ms. Ramos. You're still recovering."

"I can do it," Polaris insisted, as if anyone doubted her ability.

Blythe threw up her unslung hand in defeat and stepped out of their way. She leaned against the wall and watched the staff member load Polaris up till his brow was shiny with sweat and the books towered above the Nocturna's head, but she didn't try to help. In return, Polaris didn't try to send her any more unspoken signals.

The first crate was emptied, and Polaris carted the last of its goods into the room before anyone bothered addressing her again.

"Ms. Ramos?" Reese frowned at her from the library doorway. He was wearing trousers for once, but the top was long, leaving the pant leg exposed only from the knee down, plus a narrow slit up one thigh.

Blythe thought aloud, "Do the Vauqeulins always dress their human staff in the finest threads, or are we just special?"

"We're special," he replied without hesitation as he leaned on the doorframe. "What are you doing out here?"

Blythe shrugged her good shoulder as she thought back to a time when a slitted dress like that would have made her muscular legs look epic under show lights. She was never able to afford the artful Lunar fabric Reese's was made from, though.

Reese's frown deepened with concern. "Ms. Ramos?"

"Sorry." She shook herself into the present. "I'm waiting for Polaris."

He glanced behind him, scowled, then backed up through the doorway as he beckoned her. "Come on, then. At the very least, you can wait in a chair."

He vanished into the library before she could refute the offer. With a resigned sigh that was mostly for show, Blythe pushed off the wall and headed inside.

It wasn't a bad decision, all things considered.

Blythe didn't have any plans for the day. The initial idea to track down the library was half-formed and based on the nerve-rattling combination of cabin fever and too-recent nightmares. She just wanted to get out of the guest room.

She was successful. Clearly.

"Here you are," Reese announced as he patted the headrest of a carved wooden chair padded in thick magenta cushions. "I'll send for some tea, shall I?"

"That's not necessary," Blythe said as she sank into the chair. The seat sank several inches beneath her weight and surprised a moan out of her. "Oh! Wow. That's *really* comfy."

No one ever claimed Blythe had a talent with words.

Once she was settled in the corner, comfortable and out of the way, Reese and the handful of staff milling about the library seemed to forget all about her. Blythe had an unobstructed view and spent the next hour snacking on pastries and pretending to sip tea as she watched them reorganize the collection with Polaris's help. She couldn't complain.

The view from her chair was very, *very* good.

The room itself was like a page from a history book brought to life. The ceiling was high, and every inch of wall hosted a built-in shelf with at least two rolling ladders built in. There were two levels to the floor, with Blythe's chair and side table perched on the upper, but the floor folded down three steps to the lower one. There were more bookshelves down there, but they were short and almost decorative next to luxurious seating accommodations and the carved mahogany coffee table at the center of the room. Blythe didn't know much about libraries, but she knew this one must be beautiful and grand by anyone's standards.

Polaris put it all to shame.

The Nocturna was slender, but the sanctuary and sudden influx of a healthy diet were already making an impact on her body. Her arms were thicker, her curves fuller and more noticeable than they'd been when they were covered in nothing but hair. Substance was returning to her form in a rush that was beyond human possibility.

She looked good—healthy—and she moved like it.

No matter how many books or bulky furnishings were handed to her, Polaris traipsed around the room like an easy breeze, complete with the flutter of pale-blue skirts dancing around her legs. The blue dress she wore that day was as loose-fitting as everything else she had decided to wear, and it folded around her body in a way that left little to the imagination. She had the effortless ease of a predator blended with the casual disregard of someone young and untested.

Polaris made a pretty picture, even if it didn't make much sense with what little Blythe knew about the Nocturna.

Polaris's dress strap slipped off her shoulder as she set a line of books on a shelf, and the neckline dropped lower across one pale breast. Coincidentally or not, Blythe noticed her sling and borrowed clothing growing too hot and constrictive for comfort.

"She's recovering well," said Reese.

Blythe jerked upright in her chair, uttering a low hiss as cold tea spilled down her front.

Reese's hand appeared in front of her face waving a handkerchief. Glancing up, she saw him standing by her shoulder, one elbow braced on the high back ridge of her chair. His expression was smug and somewhat expectant. It was by far the most casual she'd seen him yet.

"Where did you come from?" Blythe scowled as she snatched the linen and began scrubbing at her blouse.

"I've been standing here for five minutes, waiting to see if you were going to drink that," he countered, amused. "You didn't notice?"

Blushing, Blythe glared down at the delicate R.W. embroidered into the handkerchief. "No."

He hummed, still smirking as he turned to survey the room.

Blythe threw her head and shoulders back into the chair's cushions with a huff and followed his gaze. They watched Polaris as she knelt on the lower level and began arranging books along a bottom shelf. The thin skirt fanned out around her in a near perfect arch, covering her legs and feet, yet laying on her skin in a way that made her shape discernible. Blythe wondered if the Nocturna knew what she looked like and if it was intentional.

"She really is lovely," Reese said with obvious appreciation in his tone. "Even among Nocturni, she'd stand out."

Blythe shot him a narrowed sideways glance. "She's had enough of strange men ogling her, I imagine. Stop it."

"You first."

Blythe bristled, sliding to the edge of her seat as she straightened. "She likes me looking at her."

"She said as much, did she?"

His humor cooled as he refocused on Blythe. There was

something heavy and sympathetic in his expression, and she wasn't sure she was ready to deal with it. Probably not.

"I've lived my entire life in close contact with vampires, Ms. Ramos. Polaris is not like most. She's damaged. A victim."

"Zip it," Blythe snapped under her breath as she rose from the seat. "She can hear you."

"I'm not saying anything she doesn't already know," he said, not unkindly. "But what about you? Have you spoken to her about what happened to her? To yourself?"

Blythe's free hand curled into a fist at her side. "That's none of your business."

She turned her back on him with every intention of making a dramatic and well-deserved exit. She took two steps before stalling out the moment she realized something had changed.

Polaris was nowhere to be seen. She'd left the library.

Blythe's stomach dropped at the same time her heart lurched into her throat. Her airway already felt tight, and the rush of internal pressure seemed to cut off her oxygen supply.

Reese yanked her out of it with a solid hand on her shoulder. "Calm down, she hasn't gone far."

As Blythe spun to face him, she forced her lungs to work slower and pretended she was fine. "I don't want to talk to you right now."

"That's fine." He nodded once and stepped back as he folded his hands behind him. He held her gaze as he insisted, "Don't talk to me, but consider talking to Polaris. You're the only one she'll engage with for anything meaningful, and I suspect it might do you both some good."

Blythe answered with a croak of laughter. "You're a doctor? And here I was thinking you were housekeeping."

The cautious sympathy on his face bled away to make room for an exasperation that felt far more familiar than it should. "I'm not a housekeeper. I," he stressed, pride seeping through gritted teeth, "am the manor's chief librarian."

"Still not a doctor, then."

He scowled at her with an arched brow. Something in his posture or lack of amusement struck Blythe as notable. Familiar. It was . . . known.

She frowned as the inkling of déjà vu crescendoed into a scream inside her head. "Have we met before?"

His expression cleared as he blinked at her. "Excuse me?"

"Before," Blythe stressed, taking a step forward as she squinted at him. "Before I dropped a stolen aircraft and two escaped abductees on your porch. Did we ever meet?"

He shuffled backward, frowning. "Of course not."

"You're sure about that?"

But Blythe wasn't listening to whatever he had to say. She stared at him without really seeing him. His sandy hair and rich outfit filled her field of vision, but she couldn't describe them to save her life. Her mind was racing, spinning in circles around the last time she'd found a man so vaguely familiar.

"Ms. Ramos? Take a breath."

"Yeah." Blythe's voice shook as she stumbled away from him. "I know you. Don't I?"

"No. You're confused."

She'd been confused when she first saw Andy at Tanya's Place too. She hadn't recognized him for what he was, not until it was too late.

"Ms. Ramos? You need to breathe. Please. Take a breath."

"No." Blythe shook her head at dizzying speeds, her functional hand raised as if to ward him off. "I just . . . I need a minute."

Before she could clear her head or bully her guts into settling down, her ears started ringing. Sifting through the noise was next to impossible, but she thought she could make out Andy's voice whispering "Here, kitty, kitty." She swayed on her feet, and as Reese's freckled hands reached to catch her, all she could feel was another man's arms around her, telling her how she was supposed to be better than him.

Stars above, but she couldn't breathe. She couldn't feel the floor under her feet, couldn't recognize the high ceiling above her with its crown molding.

"You're okay. You're safe."

Safe? No. No. No. She was alive, but she wasn't safe.

In the distance, she heard Polaris scream her name. She sensed a commotion. She felt the shift as the world rearranged around her. She was awake, but she couldn't track what was happening. All she could focus on was Gregoire's saccharine-sick tone as he preached his perverse concepts of humanity.

Blythe felt her knees give out. She felt the way her body folded to the floor. It was a hard, smooth wood surface but cool. It wasn't as cold as cement or unforgiving as metal bars, but close enough that for a moment, Blythe second-guessed where she was.

The line between sense memory and the present blurred further when she felt the blood. That was when she realized the screams weren't only in her head.

CHAPTER 12

*R*eese's blood was under her fingernails, and Blythe couldn't figure out how it got there.

"You're all right," Walters murmured as she cleaned the red from the crevices on Blythe's hands with a cloth.

The evidence of violence turned the creamy-ocher fabric a nasty brown, and Blythe found herself flinching away in disgust. It did her no good; the earthy pigment suffused the rest of the main bathroom in the guest wing, and Blythe turned away only to spot more drops of damning crimson soiling the lush surroundings.

The marble countertop Blythe sat on was inlaid with a mosaic of creams and browns and golds, with a deep sink by her hip. Walters kept dipping her cloth into said sink as the bloody mess saturated it anew.

Polaris was nowhere in sight.

Blythe whispered, "This was my fault."

"No." Walters set the cloth in the sink with a forceful splash before twirling away in a flurry of skirts. "If you need to blame someone, blame Humans First. They did this, not you."

As she strode away from Blythe, Walters was haloed in the

magnificent browns and ambers of the stone archway set behind the clawfoot tub. She watched the Head of House bend to turn the taps and fill the basin with enough steaming water to soak the most robust of Nocturni; Walters with her towering height could probably lay down in it without touching the sides.

It was a bath meant for beings far greater than Blythe Ramos.

"Humans First isn't here," Blythe reminded Walters in a deadened tone. "I am."

"Nonsense," Walters sniped as she passed from the grand bath to a cabinet, and all but threw its door open. "You're traumatized, Ms. Ramos. Both of you."

Blythe bit her tongue to withhold another useless apology.

The old woman's movements continued with a notable snap and jerk as she gathered hygiene items and transported them to the antique toiletry table beside the tub. "It's not your fault you succumbed to a panic attack," she said, "and it's not Polaris's fault for reacting so—"

The unflappable woman stalled out, words failing her as her movements ceased. Blythe opened her mouth to ask if everything was all right, but then Walters resumed her self-appointed task.

"Polaris thought she was defending you, I'm sure," Walters added with a note of finality.

Blythe stared at the old woman's hands as they laid out soaps and creams and steel manicure tools Blythe couldn't begin to name. She could see what Walters was doing; it was happening right in front of her, as clear as the garden's view of the stars. Blythe couldn't feel the unforgiving marble under her ass and hear the water trebling away in the background. She was there for the experience, but it didn't feel real.

It was like her mind was floating away, close by but disconnected from her body.

For the love of the moon, but she was exhausted.

"I thought . . ." Blythe cut herself off. She had to clear her throat twice before she could control her mouth enough for words. "I thought I knew him. I was so sure."

"Who?"

Blythe tried to say that she didn't know, but her lips parted on a strangled breath. She shook her head as she choked on a sob.

AFTER WALTERS GENTLY BULLIED HER IN AND OUT OF THE BATH, she demanded Blythe take a medicinally encouraged sleep and be looked over by the on-site doctors once or twice more. The old woman made no further mention of Polaris or the library incident. Blythe was so wrapped up in her own untethered mindset that she didn't think to ask about the aftermath.

Such questions pressed down on her with a vengeful urgency the moment she woke in the whited-out guest room.

"Don't fret, Miss," one of the many servants told her as he bustled her back into bed with one hand and held her breakfast tray aloft with the other. "Accommodations have been made for the lady Nocturna's recovery, much like your own. I have no answers for you now, but try to be patient. These things take time."

"What's that even supposed to mean?!" Blythe wailed after him.

He ran off without giving her an answer. With no energy and marginally more awareness of the property's layout, Blythe couldn't muster up the nerve to chase after him. She was stuck in the room, laid up like an invalid and far from being on the mend as she had been the previous day; all she could do was wait.

She was still picking at the fruit and crumpets laid over her lap when the flamboyant stylist returned in an array of chaotic and vibrant robes. As he set about spritzing and combing her hair on his own accord, Blythe pushed him for answers.

"I wouldn't worry your pretty little head on it," the stylist chattered. "It's not like anyone died."

"That's nice to know." She scowled over her shoulder at him.

He smacked her cheek back in the right direction with the comb and prattled on, "A little blood loss is like a rite of passage when you work for the Harems. The librarian will be fine, why, I'll wager he regains consciousness before the specialist Walters called for arrives from Mars!"

Blythe's scalp burned as she tried to jerk out of his grasp. "Specialist? What specialist?"

"Stars above, did no one tell you? The Harem's sending a psychologist to evaluate our mysterious little Nocturna. Walters can't very well risk the staff over an unstable loner."

The implication stunned Blythe into complacency. As the stylist hauled her back into an accessible position, her thoughts turned cartwheels trying to connect this latest information with the reassurances her frail heart so desperately needed.

Surely Polaris wasn't crazy? Walters wouldn't really turn her out, would she? Would the Nocturna continue to deny any connections to a Harem even when faced with tantamount exile?

While her thoughts circled the same worrisome idea, the stylist continued his incessant chatting. He freshened up her hair and left her head smelling like shea butter and surrounded by bouncing curls, but filled with nothing but questions.

"I have good news and bad news," Walters announced as she came through the guest room door one evening.

Blythe rolled from her back to her side to peer at her. "Hit me with the good shit first."

"Reese is stable."

Blythe closed her eyes at the first sign of relieved tears. "Thank the stars."

No matter what the staff said in the past few hours since the library incident, Blythe kept waiting to hear that he was dead. She wished it was an anxiety born from being a decent human being with concern for an innocent man who'd been kind to her, but she didn't have the energy to lie to herself. Reese was an acquaintance. She didn't know enough about him to be too invested in his welfare.

She dreaded whatever his murder would mean for Polaris though. Stars above, never mind the logistical ramifications, but how would the poor Nocturna live with herself if the worst should happen?

Blythe braced herself and opened her eyes. "What's the bad news?"

"Polaris won't feed. I've brought her several blood donations from myself and willing staff with each meal, but she'll have none of it."

Blythe squeezed her eyes shut again and hid her face in a pillow. The cushion did little to muffle her scream. Walters waited for her to finish and lift her head before speaking again.

"The psychologist is still a couple days out, but I don't need him to tell me she's punishing herself. Would you speak to her?"

Blythe sighed and rubbed her temple. "Am I allowed?"

It had been days since she last saw Polaris, and no one seemed inclined to speak about her at length. It resulted in a lot of avoided eye contact and silent services to her room, since the vampire was all Blythe wanted to talk about. Walters had decided at some point that Blythe needed space and rest apart from her fellow escapee, and the staff seemed to take her word as law.

"I don't think you realize the gravity of the situation," Walters said with a sharpness that made Blythe feel small. "When Reese wakes up, he will be fully within his rights to contact The Guard."

A harsh squeak of alarm escaped Blythe before she muffled it with her hand.

She didn't have the vaguest idea what The Guard would do in this situation. The Harem had yet to hear from the appropriate authorities in regard to Polaris's involvement with Luna's hitherto unknown Humans First problem. Even if that investigation was going nowhere, there was no telling what The Guard might do if Polaris was labeled an aggressor before they ever met with her as a victim.

Walters's shoulders relaxed the slightest bit. For the first time, Blythe thought she looked her age.

"I don't want to see her incarcerated any more than you do, Ms. Ramos. I can't say if your attachment to each other is healthy or not, and I wouldn't normally fret over a vampire abstaining from blood for a few nights, but this is not a normal situation, is it."

It wasn't a question.

Blythe heaved herself upright and out of bed under Walters's stern watch and followed her out without another word.

Polaris shared Blythe's room from the moment they were rescued. She slept beside Blythe with layers of bedclothes between them, or she slept curled into a ball in the chair in the corner. Once, Blythe woke from a nightmare to discover the Nocturna sprawled on the carpet beneath the window. At the time, Blythe simply tossed an extra pillow onto the floor and waited for the vampire to cuddle into it before resettling herself. She never thought anything more about the arrangement.

Did Walters ever assign Polaris a guest room of her own? Was it Polaris's idea to make them roommates while Blythe was unconscious? Was this ever a conversation topic at all?

These questions were left unanswered. Walters didn't lead her to another guest room.

The door was larger than average, with a carved wooden plaque set into its face, the words detailed in gold. That gold calligraphy assigned the room beyond as *The Scion's Office*.

Blythe bulked as Walters reached for the small screen built into the wall beside the door.

"Polaris is in here?"

Walters paused, frowning. "This property wasn't built for the containment of violent Nocturni. It was either this or the token holding cell in the basement."

With a sigh, the older woman began tapping away at the screen. Blythe heard the invisible locks on the door release with a cheerful click.

"Polaris is no criminal," Walters said with an air of finality that piqued Blythe's interest. "I won't treat her as such, and besides that, I can't say with any confidence if the basement room could hold a matured vampire for long anyway."

Before Blythe could press for more information, Walters pushed the door open.

"Blythe? Oh, Blythe!"

Polaris was sitting on the windowsill of an enormous half-oval window on the far side of the room. Blythe saw a grandiose desk of dark wood filling the space below the window and a pile of cream linens atop a mattress tucked along the left-hand wall, but she never got the chance to admire more details. She gleaned a strong impression of intricate and warm-hued décor right before her vision was obscured by silver.

Polaris's hair smacked into Blythe's face as the Nocturna rushed her. Walters took a sharp, startled breath, but she didn't intrude as Polaris hugged her like their lives depended on it.

Blythe shivered as lips rubbed over her cheek with a mewling whimper. "You're okay? Truly?"

"Yeah, Hun."

Blythe looped her arm around Polaris's waist and turned to catch Walters frowning at them. Blythe's face heated with foolishness as she made a subtle shift of her head and mouthed the words, *"Can I offer her my vein?"*

Walters gave a short shake of her head. Her lips seemed to vanish with how tightly she pressed them together.

Polaris sniffled against her cheek and pulled back so they could look at each other properly. Blythe noticed the blue dress was gone, leaving Polaris in baggy gym shorts and an oversized shirt that would have suited someone like Tilla much better. Dressed like that, the Nocturna looked small and fragile, almost childish.

Blythe's smile wilted as quickly as it appeared.

No matter what she looked like, Blythe had watched her shed human blood twice now. Right or wrong, Blythe was partially responsible both times. Before Blythe came along, had Polaris ever harmed a soul?

Blythe brushed the short hairs of the undercut back from Polaris's face, tucking the strands behind a pointed ear before dragging her fingertips over the awkward area. The undercut was growing faster in the past week. Polaris was lovely with the asymmetry, but Blythe's heartbeat sped up when she imagined how ethereal the Nocturna would look when it grew even with the rest of her hair.

"How are you, Hun?" Blythe murmured.

Polaris shrugged as she cradled Blythe's good hand and began tracing the creases in her palm with a diligent fingertip. She didn't look at Blythe but became intent on their joined hands.

"They tell me you won't feed," Blythe coaxed. "Why aren't you taking care of yourself, Polaris?"

The Nocturna didn't lift her head. She didn't speak, didn't move. Blythe felt a chill spread along the skin that touched hers. Stars, but she went so eerily, perfectly still, just as she'd done the first time they met face-to-face.

"Don't do that," Blythe whispered. "You've come this far with me already. We have just a little farther to go. Stay with me."

Still, Polaris didn't move.

Blythe gave their hands a jarring shake. "Stay with me?"

She held her breath as she waited for the vampire to respond. Polaris dipped her chin in a nod before Blythe's lungs could start screaming for relief.

Blythe bent her knees to try and catch Polaris's eye. She would have been successful too, if the Nocturna hadn't dropped her hand and twirled away.

"Promise me you'll feed?" Blythe pleaded.

Her jaw clenched tighter and tighter as she watched Polaris brace her hands on the massive desk. Each palm landed a decent distance from her body, leaving her bent over with her arms straight, almost overextended. Her head dropped forward.

Blythe's skin crawled with the wrongness of it.

"Polaris?"

She didn't like it. The pose, the body language. There was nothing wrong with it, logically. The weariness it suggested was more than reasonable, given the circumstances. Blythe hated it anyway.

It didn't feel like Polaris. It felt like looking at a stranger.

Blythe straightened. Irritation and a fresh spark of concern streaked up her spine like a flashfire. No matter how careful she was to keep soft and quiet, there was no disguising the upset in her voice.

"I'm not leaving till you promise me you'll start taking care of yourself. Eat. Feed. All that shit."

She was ready for a fight. The tension in her shoulders and the knot in her gut warned her as much. It wasn't like she expected the Nocturna to spin around and growl at her or tell her to fuck off, but a tiny, desperate part of Blythe almost hoped she would.

Instead, Polaris kept her back to her and said, "I promise."

Blythe stumbled back into Walters. It was as if a physical line connecting them had been unceremoniously cut, and without the pull on the other end, Blythe found herself thrown off-balance.

Out of the corner of her eye, she could tell Walters was staring back and forth between them, as if she were trying to piece together a puzzle.

"Go now," Polaris said, her voice dull and quiet. "Please."

~

BLYTHE'S SLING WAS REMOVED THE NEXT DAY WITH INSTRUCTION TO make a slow return to normal activity in the following days. No matter how loud or vehemently Blythe argued that she felt fine, everyone from the medics to the maids seemed inclined to treat her like an invalid. When the doctor said "No heavy lifting for another week," the staff interpreted that recommendation as an order to keep her from lifting a finger.

She might have found the coddling amusing once upon a time. Now? Not so much.

"Let me take it!" Blythe hissed at the nameless servant as she tried to yank the food tray from his hands.

He held firm. "Absolutely not! I will accompany—"

"I don't need a fucking escort!"

He flinched, turning his face in mild disgust to avoid her spittle.

"Stars above!" Blythe released the tray to toss her hands in the air, her face burning. She took a breath, but it did little to cool her down. "I am perfectly capable of carrying a plate."

His eyes narrowed on her face. "Should I remind you that you're not permitted to be alone with her?"

She made a dismissive gesture. "Polaris won't hurt me. You want her to eat, don't you?"

The previous day's conversation yielded unimpressive results. According to Walters, Polaris accepted a pint of freshly donated blood within the hour of Blythe's return to her guest room, but she hadn't touched the plate of food that came with it. That morning, she hadn't acknowledged the staff members at all when they brought her breakfast.

"You don't know the passcode to the office."

Hands on her hips, Blythe glowered at the unhelpful servant. "I would if you gave it to me."

He raised the tray with a pointed look. "This is a metal platter, heavy with a midday meal. You, Ms. Ramos, are our guest. Even if you weren't still recovering from a recent injury, I would have to insist—"

He was cut off by a sharp clap of impatient hands.

"Enough dawdling," Walters said, her words as clipped as her heels on the polished floor of the hallway as she strode toward them. Neat and swift, she stepped between them and divested the man of his burden. "I will see to Polaris. If you would be so kind as to escort Ms. Ramos—"

Blythe blustered with indignation. "I don't need a—"

She bit her tongue when Walters turned that no-nonsense look on her. "I have neither the time nor inclination to let you get lost trying to find your way to the receiving lounge. I will have you safely delivered there, and then you are welcome to direct your attitude at Sylvester instead of my staff."

Blythe gaped at the older woman. "Sly's here?"

Walters lifted her chin back the way she'd come from. There was a minuscule curl of amusement to her mouth. "Go. Let him be your problem for the moment."

She needed no further encouragement. With a pop to her step, Blythe gestured for the infuriating staff member to lead the way, then they were heading down the hall. Behind her, the clicks of Walters's heels faded fast and barely gave her pause.

But there was a pause. It was brief, hardly more than a stumble, really, but it happened.

Blythe recovered her stride as she told herself Polaris would be fine. Walters would convince her to eat, and Blythe would be free to lose herself in her best friend's presence. The prospect wasn't quite as enticing as it should have been.

The Vauqeulin's Lunar mansion was unnecessarily large for a vacation home. Blythe was a beat away from jogging to keep up with her guide, yet it still took forever to traverse the property. She was preparing to make a snide remark about the Vauqeulins' apparent need to overcompensate when their pace finally slowed.

Her guide pried open one-half of an undecorated set of doors and held it open for her. "Ms. Ramos," he said with a slight bow.

Blythe passed by him with a snort of dry laughter.

The lounge was much like the rest of the manor, from what Blythe had seen. A thick cream carpet was offset by warm-brown walls and similarly shaded leather couches arranged in a wide u-shape in the middle of the room. The bookshelves along the rear wall showcased a few books and a multitude of artifacts, while the wall immediately right of the doors was eclipsed by a single sheet of clear, reinforced glass. The window was framed in thick burgundy curtains that echoed the accent colors in the couch cushions and brought out the red undertones in the wooden furnishings. A fully stocked bar that hosted more crystal than Tanya's Place and Centrism combined stood behind the largest couch.

The space was impressive and empty. At first glance, anyway.

One of the love seats was positioned with its back to the door. A pair of feet stuck out over the armrest. Said feet were crossed at the ankles and clad in shiny black dress shoes with silken laces.

Blythe crept closer. "Sly?"

The dress shoes shot into the air in a flurry of movement and a squeal of her name. "Blythe!"

She didn't get a great look at him as he flailed over the back of the loveseat and came careening into her arms. Despite his exuberance, he managed to catch her around the waist without causing any pain to her shoulder. His dark hair was redder than ever as she buried her face in it. He was still thin, but when she hugged him, he felt firmer, more solid than she'd anticipated.

He leaned back to see her face without unlocking his arms from her waist. He was a tad taller than he should have been. The fancy shoes on his feet had a bit of heel. More than that, he'd learned to stand up straight since the last time she saw him.

And now he had freckles. So many freckles.

Blythe shrugged her arms from the embrace to hold his face in her hands. "You're really here?"

There were unshed tears in his eyes as he nodded. "Why in the cosmos would I be anywhere else right now?"

She didn't answer. She couldn't. She had no control and no cares as she folded into him and pressed her face against his shoulder. It was a thicker, less-bony shoulder than she planned for, but it was warm with familiar undercurrents in the scent.

A shockwave of emotion raced through her.

There was no telling which of them started crying first. Blythe's knees were the first to give out, but they dropped to the carpet in a tangle of trembling, needy limbs. She clung to him with all her strength—her friend, her brother, her person—and he clung back.

Safe. She was safe, and it was finally starting to feel real.

SHE DIDN'T MEAN TO GET DISTRACTED. SOMEHOW, THE DAY managed to pass her by without noticing.

Sly let her cry and talk and cry some more before he gave her a tour of his top-of-the-line star cruiser. It was the brightest vehicle in the whole hangar bay, all sleek chromes and fine details. It wasn't the needlessly large indulgence of her imagination, but the ship could accommodate a six-person crew along with three or four passengers. Blythe wanted to fly it, but Sly's chauffeur wouldn't let them in the control room on account of some mysterious occurrence from the last time Sly was allowed on the steering deck.

No one would divulge further details, no matter how much she begged.

She stopped when Sly insisted she reciprocate with a tour of the manor. The bizarre fact that *he* should have been the one to show *her* around his Harem's property was left hanging over their heads like a neon cloud of harmless yet odorous gas; no one addressed it, but they all knew it was there.

It didn't help that Blythe's knowledge of the manor was so limited. Between a dozen random staffers and Blythe's incomplete mental map, she managed to bring them from the hangar to the guest wing. She let him stick his nose in her temporary bedroom, then dragged him to the dining room, then they were both introduced to the nearby kitchen.

After that, they checked out the garden. They weren't out there long. Despite Blythe's lingering awe at the seamless view, Sly must have gotten used to the galactic light show while living on Ethos. He was appreciative and plenty vocal as he surveyed the outdoor set up, but his interest waned in record time.

Blythe tried to ignore the sour ball that spontaneously appeared in the pit of her stomach as she followed him back inside.

At that point, the only place left to show him was the library. It wasn't until she threw open the door with a dramatic flourish and saw the look on his face that she remembered what happened there.

Stars above, but the blood pool was larger than she thought.

One section of the upper level was still sectioned off with neon-orange tape. The massive stain was still visible from the doorway, dark and damning. It seemed the current staff didn't have the biohazard cleaning experience one might expect from the hired help of a vampire abode.

"What happened here?"

Blythe winced with her entire body, leaning back and sidestepping as he entered the room ahead of her. "There was an accident."

He shot her an incredulous look.

She couldn't hold his gaze as her stomach churned and the skin on her arms pebbled. "It might have been— No. It *was* my fault."

His voice went soft as he returned to her side to rub her arm. "Blythe? Can you tell me about it?"

Blythe yanked away from him, as if he'd slapped her. "Stop that."

He frowned. "Stop what?"

"*Tell me about it, Blythe?*" she mocked. "Seriously, Sly? I'm not a fucking kid!"

"Woah." He raised his hands to ward her off, his frown deepening. "Calm down, Blythe. I didn't mean—"

"You never do!" she screamed at him through gritted teeth. "You never mean to be condescending, you're only ever trying to help me. But it's not— You can't— You're not— You always just . . ."

She didn't know where the words or the temper were coming from. It didn't come from her, not consciously anyway. She didn't know where her tongue was heading until the words were already in the air, and by that point, it was too late. The damage was done, and there was no way to piece herself back together.

"It's not fair!" She screamed as her vision grew blurry and dark. "You're always there! Always! But then I needed you, and you weren't! You were gone!"

"I'm here now!"

"All our lives," she cried over him, "you let me lean on you like you were some infallible knight in shining armor, but then you just . . . left!"

Sly's voice broke, "Oh, Blythe—"

She batted him away when he reached for her. "I needed you, and you weren't there!"

"I know."

She ignored his miserable whisper. She was moving and couldn't stop. It didn't matter that she couldn't see straight, that the motion only made her knotted stomach that much more likely to upheave; she had to keep moving. Wild gestures accompanied every screeching word from her mouth.

"I kept waiting for you to save me, and you never did! You left me to deal with this bullshit universe alone, and the moment I stood still long enough, it fucked me over! Where were you, Sly?"

She was still shrieking at him when help arrived. Someone tried to steer her from the library.

"Where were you?!"

Adding insult to injury, her sense of smell spiked with sensitivity. Blinded by sobs, Blythe's nose went into overdrive, and she caught the homey comfort of Sly's base scent and the salt of his tears. She registered the musk of so many books and the stale copper tinge of dried blood.

"Where . . . were . . . you?!"

Somehow, some way, Sly got to her again. His fingers pushed the ringlets back from her forehead as he pleaded, "You're safe, Blythe! You're safe, and I'm right here!"

Blythe wanted to believe him. But she didn't.

MUCH LATER, AFTER WALTERS ONCE AGAIN THREATENED HER WITH a sedative and Sly had to play peacekeeper, Blythe said, "I'm sorry."

Her voice was hoarse from all the strain. It was ugly. It grated her ears as much as the inside of her skull, but she'd long since run out of the energy necessary to care. Her body felt like a lump of iron, cold and lifeless and insurmountably heavy; she half expected to drop through the cloud-like mattress of the guest bed and keep on going till she crashed through the floor and popped a new crater on the moon.

"You have nothing to apologize for," said Sly. He kept a firm hold on her hand as he scrubbed at the tear tracks on his cheek.

"I'm sorry anyway."

He didn't comment. They sat in silence for a long moment, but Blythe knew he wouldn't leave it at that. Sly always had to have the last word, and usually it worked in her favor and left her smiling. She didn't expect any miracles from him right then.

It was a lesson years in the making. It was about time she learned it.

"Hey," he whispered, scooting to the edge of his chair so he could rest his chin on her shoulder.

Blythe didn't react. She'd done enough of that lately.

"Phink and Tilla are only a few days out," he said, his breath puffing against her throat. "How would you feel about them checking in for a day or two, then returning to the colony without you? You could come back to Ethos with me, or you can stay here as long as you need. Take some time. Rest."

She didn't respond. She waited for the suggestion to evoke some kind of emotion, but it didn't. It just . . . didn't.

"I talked to Walters." Sly's voice stayed hushed, his words crawling along as if wary of startling a cornered animal. "That doctor is going to be here tomorrow. The psychologist."

Blythe snorted under her breath.

"We think it'd be good for you to spend some time with him. Give yourself a few weeks to recover."

"You're probably right," she admitted. "You usually are."

"Not always."

Her eyes ached, so she closed them, warding off the hurt as much as the sight of his concerned face. It did little to trap the renewed moisture gathering behind her lash line.

"I should have listened to you."

Even as a teen, Sly knew better than to tangle with Humans First sympathizers. He'd warned her over and over again. He warned her before she ever agreed to let Phink promote her as a pure-blooded human on Centrism's stage. He kept warning her afterward too, but she never listened. Why didn't she listen?

At some point in recent years, Sly must have developed enough tact not to say *I told you so*. Without his characteristic commentary, he left his chair and climbed onto the bed beside her. He kept hold of her hand even as he settled on top of her perfectly white blanket, his chin digging into her collar.

He said nothing, but his uncharacteristic silence sat awkward and stiff. It was so unlike the reassuring warmth of Polaris's presence at her side; it threatened to reignite her anger.

When did she stop expecting Sly to save her and begin expecting to find Polaris lurking nearby every time she turned around? When had she traded one crutch for another, and why hadn't she noticed?

CHAPTER 13

Dr. Balint arrived on schedule, but it took an additional three days before Blythe got a chance to meet him. She didn't blame the psychologist though. Polaris was still skipping meals and feedings, despite the promise she made to Blythe; the vampire needed the doctor's attention more than she did.

Reese had yet to wake up. Walters assured Blythe that he was recovering well enough to move from the medical suite to his own bed, but it wasn't enough to convince Blythe's lungs to draw a full breath with ease.

Blythe doubted the doctor was prepared to be greeted by a violent Nocturna. Traumatized, yes, but not potentially homicidal.

"I thought he was supposed to be here for you," Sly grumbled as he picked at his lunch.

"He's here for both of us," Blythe reminded him for the third time that day. "Polaris is as much a victim as I am. Arguably more so."

She would repeat that sentiment as often as necessary. No matter what happened when Reese awoke, Blythe wouldn't see the Nocturna returned to a cage if she could help it.

Sly didn't disagree, but he also didn't share her priorities. He huffed and resumed stabbing at his food without argument.

It was a sore spot for them right now. On the one hand, Blythe could appreciate Sly's unofficial position as her advocate. Humans were rarely prioritized over Nocturni for any number of reasons, ranging from safety concerns regarding the species, to the financial clout of the associated Harem. Sly was here for her, and he held an unusually important position for a human Companion on account of his rare and pure blood; to him, it wouldn't seem right to him that Blythe should be left to struggle alone while efforts were focused on the mystery vampire next door. Blythe imagined she'd be just as irritated if their positions were reversed.

On the other hand, Sly didn't know Polaris. Not like Blythe did.

She watched Sly glower at the pasta in front of him without attempting to raise the fork to his mouth. They were the only people in the dining room, and the scrape of his utensil on the plate echoed in a way that promised to give her a headache if it continued much longer.

"What do you think they'll do to her?"

Sly froze, fork suspended over his plate. He glanced sideways at her without turning his head. "What do you mean?"

She responded with a disapproving glower. "You know what I mean."

"I really don't."

Blythe folded her arms and leaned over the table toward him, gaze sharp and expectant. "You know exactly what the Nocturni do to uncontrollable vamps."

Sly shoved away from the table, sending his chair legs screeching across the polished floor. "Polaris isn't the same as Kahled. He's sick—"

"So is she!" Blythe slid to the edge of her seat, palms flat on the table as she tried to make up for the sudden distance he'd put between them. "She might not be Cursed, but her lack of control isn't her fault."

He gave a vehement nod that did nothing to assuage the defensiveness in his tone. "No one's saying she's a bad person, I just don't think you can compare her to Kahled. Their situations are completely different."

A hard, hot lump was forming in her throat. "Can't you just tell me they're not going to hurt her?"

Sly's hands dug into his hair, and he released a groan through clenched teeth. "I don't know!"

"Make your best guess, then!"

He deflated, sinking down in his seat. It took too long for him to meet her eye. "She nearly murdered an innocent man, Blythe."

"She thought she was protecting me," Blythe argued. "The only difference between her and your Nocturnus is that she wasn't a successful killer."

Sly flinched. "That's not quite true."

Blythe scoffed. "Right, so Polaris maims a random guy, and her life is forfeit, but Kahled gets to slaughter his own kin during a Cursed episode, and no one minds because he happens to be the former leader of one of The Nine—"

"Kahled never attacked a human. The Guard was never involve—"

"Sure," Blythe snarked, turning away from him, "that makes it so much fairer."

Sly sighed as he reached for her wrist and gave it a squeeze. "I don't know what they'll do with her, but I hear you. She needs help. Specifically, she needs the kind of help her Harem should be giving her."

Blythe recoiled.

In the few weeks since they dropped out of the sky into Walters's lap, Polaris never once mentioned her Harem. She never alluded to her birth name nor any affiliations.

"Vampires don't go missing every day," Sly said with a note of warning.

"It's a big universe," Blythe muttered. "The Nocturni live long lives."

There were a handful of possible identities Polaris could claim, and confirming it would be a simple matter of a DNA test.

All of that meant nothing if Polaris refused to cooperate.

"She needs her Harem, Blythe."

Blythe bowed her head. "I was afraid you were going to say that."

BLYTHE MET WITH DR. BALINT THAT EVENING IN THE GARDEN. HE was waiting for her in one of Walters's padded wicker chairs, a bulky comms screen balanced on his knee. Her heart sank at the sight of him.

He wasn't much to look at. As she settled in the seat across from him, the word 'bland' came to mind. From the frayed edges of his gray suit to the dull brown of his skin, he gave off an impression of meek weariness. The exhaustion combined with a lifetime of access to Luna's top-tier resources made his age unknowable; he could have been ten or forty years older than herself, and Blythe wouldn't be surprised. His hair reached his chin in brown sheets a shade or two darker than his skin, and while it was clean and combed, it was in dire need of a trim. His short beard was patchy and might have been better described as out of control stubble.

The only reason she didn't turn around and walk away was because he came with the Vauqeulin Harem's recommendation. She wouldn't put it past a nameless vampire to pawn her off on the most convenient healthcare professional, but Sly trusted his Harem. They wouldn't shortchange him like that.

"Dr. Balint?" Blythe asked as she sat across from him and offered her hand.

He was short; he had to part from the chair to reach her. "Please. Call me Lyall."

He didn't quite have the proper lilt of a Lunar accent, but there was a familiar quality in his soft tenor. Looks aside, he at least had the soothing voice someone might hope for in a psychologist.

Like a consummate professional, he didn't let the staring contest go on for long.

"I've heard quite a bit about you, Blythe."

The flow of his words was as mild and unassuming as his face. It made her smile despite herself. "I can't say the same, but I'm guessing you've dealt with similar . . ." she hesitated, "situations?"

He nodded. "Unfortunately, you're not the first human I've counseled after a run-in with Humans First."

Blythe tried to ignore the shiver that raced up her spine. Dr. Balint didn't react, so maybe she managed to hide it. Clearing her throat, she asked, "What about Polaris?"

His gaze went distant, sailing straight past her as he thought. "I've worked with Nocturni patients before. None quite like her, though."

"Can you help her?"

Dr. Balint answered with a patient smile that didn't reach his eyes. "We're not here to talk about Polaris's treatment."

Blythe barked a cutting laugh. "I'll be honest, Doc, I don't see this working out for me—or her—without a shit-ton of overlap."

Before she was done, Dr. Balint began nodding along. "I'm not about to ignore your shared experiences, Blythe, but we're not there yet. Right now, I want to focus on you. We don't know each other, and that needs to change if you want to trust me with your truth."

"Pretty," Blythe admitted, and it felt like all the substance in her spine blew out of her mouth with the word. "Very pretty words, Doc."

"Words are only a fraction of the equation," he said as his focus switched to the device in his hands. "What happened to you isn't something most people can talk their way through. Maybe you'll be the exception, maybe not. Either way, I'm here to help."

Blythe didn't say anything, not right away. She thought it over —his words, the situation, everything. He let her take her time, but she felt his attention all the same when he finished with his comms. After a minute, Blythe sighed and leaned toward him, her hands hanging between her knees with a white-knuckled grip holding her palms together.

"You know," she said, words almost as heavy as her heart, "you'd be doing me a lot of help just by telling me she won't be punished for what she did to Reese. Just tell me you can help her, that it's at least an option."

He didn't respond right away. Maybe he knew she wouldn't believe him if he did.

Dr. Balint stood and placed his comms on the vacated seat. He crouched in front of Blythe and gestured toward her hands in a wordless question.

Frowning, Blythe loosened her grip and nodded.

His skin was cool and dry when he took her hands in his, but his touch was featherlight and calm. He caught her eye and held it.

"I will never lie to you, Blythe. Do you believe that?"

His eyes were dark, much darker than the rest of his coloring prepared her for. They were bottomless and genuine, the exact opposite of Gregoire's judgmental gaze.

Eyes watering for no good reason, Blythe nodded.

"I can promise I'll do all that I can, for you and Polaris, but I can't control what the Nocturni or The Guard decide to do, and I can't predict the future. We are only human, you and I."

She nodded and said in a monotone, "We're limited."

"Yes." He gave her hands a subtle but solid shake. "But limits can be pushed. The trick is to do it without breaking beyond hope of repair."

BLYTHE DIDN'T KNOW IF SHE WAS RELIEVED OR UNDERWHELMED BY Dr. Balint. As the week progressed, she began to warm to him, despite herself. He had this guileful way of steering her away from Polaris as a subject of conversation, and redirecting her thoughts toward herself. He eased her into talking about certain aspects of her abduction and subsequent captivity in a way that let her speak about it without devolving into an incomprehensible mess. He seemed to have a sixth sense regarding her threshold for any given topic, and she was surprised any time he changed direction or ended a session early right as the horrid taste of the words leaving her tongue started backing up to make her feel ill.

She wondered if he was always so careful with his clients.

As it turned out, Dr. Balint's approach wasn't half as forgiving when they somehow wandered far from the subject of her ordeals with Humans First.

"Madam Walters tells me we're expecting company tomorrow," the doctor mentioned during a quiet moment in their latest meeting.

Blythe shot him a curious frown. "Yeah, my old crew is flying in."

"Along with Mr. Phink, yes?"

"Yeah, I guess so."

He scrawled something on his comms screen with his finger, and Blythe was tempted to ask what, despite his consistent refusal to share his notes with her.

Blythe's eyes narrowed further as she leaned forward in her favored garden seat. "Why?"

"I find it interesting that you haven't mentioned him to me, is all."

Blythe sat back in her chair and crossed her arms. "Was I supposed to?"

"Not necessarily." Balint shrugged as he met her eye with a tempered smile. "It's natural to surround ourselves with trusted friends and family in times like this, though. We may not need a support system in quite the same way the Nocturni need their Harems, for example, but we still have that need."

Blythe hunched her shoulders, jaw tense as she nodded back. "Yeah. I'll be happy to see him."

And she was. It was simple as that, and there wasn't much else to say about it.

Except Balint didn't see it that way. In that unending mellow tone of his, he said, "Most people in your position would be more enthusiastic about reuniting with their chosen father figure."

A bark of laughter leaped from her throat before she could stop it. It rolled out of her with the force of air leaving a popped balloon. Blythe just about spilled out of her chair as she cackled.

"Phink's not my parent! Who in the cosmos gave you that idea?"

"No one." He dabbed at his screen with a small chuckle. "I drew my own conclusions from a look through your records and a two minute conversation with Sly Spurgeon."

Blythe's laughter subsided to a nervous giggle. "Sly's got a big mouth."

Balint made a noncommittal noise, but he didn't take pity on her. The stare he leveled on her was expectant.

At least Blythe knew where this conversation was going now.

"Phink and Sly are my friends," she posited after clearing her throat, "the only two I still have from Earth, actually."

Balint hummed. "Quite some friends you have there. They're the only recurring figures in your HEPP file since your parents left you."

Blythe cut him off with a derisive snort. "You're supposed to be helping me sift through my trauma, not digging through my childhood boo-boos."

He quirked an unamused brow at her as he set his comms beside him on the chair's arm. "Trauma comes in many forms, Blythe."

Blythe hopped to her feet with a huff. "That's an old injury, doc. Let's leave the scar as it is and deal with the open wound I'm working with now, okay?"

She loomed over him with her hands on her hips, waiting to see the insistent glint in his eye fade away.

It didn't. He opened his mouth to speak, and Blythe spun on her heel to end the session herself.

The door to the mansion opened before she took a full step. A female servant with a short, round figure bustled through the portal, wide eyes aimed at the doctor.

"I hate to intrude, Doctor, but it's an emergency. It's Reese! He's awake and not doing so well."

BLYTHE DIDN'T MEET WITH THE PSYCHOLOGIST AGAIN THAT NIGHT. She wandered the halls for a bit, steering clear of the hubbub coming in and out of the staff's quarters, but that grew old fast. Sly eventually tracked her down for dinner, but he was only two bites into his shepherd's pie when he was summoned away to answer Kahled's routine call.

With nothing to do but wonder how Reese was and what his status might mean, Blythe tracked down Walters to ask if she could speak to Polaris. She was given an immediate and resounding no.

"It's no use arguing with me," Walters said as she directed Blythe back down the hall, away from the scion's office. "Even if I wanted to, I wouldn't let you in there right now. Polaris has requested solitude, so she can process Reese's reaction on her own—"

Blythe balked. "She talked to him already?"

"Absolutely not," Walters scoffed, as if Blythe were being absurd, "but she was notified when he awoke, and in what state."

"State?" Blythe shrieked, "I didn't hear Reese was in a *state*?"

"Indeed, because the last thing we need right now is his panic or Polaris's anxiety spreading to you."

Blythe squawked in alarm and two wiry, wrinkled hands grasped her by the shoulders to hold her steady. She found Walters's piercing eyes much too close to her own.

"The best you can do at this moment is keep control of yourself," Walters said. "Stop fretting and jumping to conclusions when we don't yet know if Reese is even interested in pressing charges."

Blythe bit her lower lip the moment she felt it trembling. She wanted to say something—anything—to respond to Walters's impossibly level-headed determination, but she couldn't find the words or air to do it. Eyes burning, she shook her head.

The grip on one of her shoulders released so Walters could sweep the errant curls from her face.

"Enough of this," the woman said, cool but kind. "Difficult as it may be, we must hold ourselves together and be prepared for whatever may happen. Polaris and Reese can't do it right now, so the least we can do is keep calm in their stead. Do you hear me, Ms. Ramos?"

Inhaling hard through her nose, Blythe nodded.

DESPITE WALTERS INSTRUCTIONS, KEEPING HERSELF FROM screaming and pummeling the walls to vent her frustration was no easy feat for Blythe. She spent the night tossing and turning, only to abandon the bed a couple hours before the manor's breakfast spread would be set out.

She was startled to find a flurry of activity sweeping the halls. Blythe scurried out of the way of several harried staff members on her way to the kitchens, where she discovered Sly dressed in silken sleepwear and stuffing his cheeks with a pastry straight from a lightly steaming pan.

"Oh, good! You're up!" he greeted through his mouthful. "Waking you was the next thing on my to-do list. Want some?"

Blythe nudged his hand away when he offered her a spoonful of something puffy and sweet. "What's going on?"

Sly twirled the spoon around toward his maw as he shrugged. "The Zephyr's pulling in early. All the commotion is Walters's way of welcoming new visitors. I think they're putting together a feast?"

Locating the hangar bay took longer than Blythe cared to admit. Between her lack of sleep and poor sense of direction, she was bound to have a tough time to begin with; it didn't help that she had to compete with the pan of streusel-topped goodness for Sly's attention either. Nevertheless, the two of them managed to skid into The Zephyr's shadow beside Balint and Walters in time to see the gangway lower to the ground.

Phink's bulbous belly was the first thing they saw exiting the craft, a split second before the rest of him came jogging straight at them.

"Dammit," Blythe hissed under her breath as her eyes flooded over.

Sly nudged her, snickering as his own tear ducts activated.

Phink barreled toward them in his usual business attire, but Blythe noticed there were liquid stains on his shirtfront and an unusual abundance of creases. The scant skin visible beneath his fur was splotchy and red, his undereye bruised.

He looked terrible, and Blythe wasn't prepared for the wealth of emotion the sight of him inspired. It damn near choked her as her arms reached for him on their own accord.

Phink didn't slow down till he crashed into her. For all he was short and rotund, he was plenty strong enough to lift her off the floor. Wordless and sniffling, he hugged her till her ribs creaked in warning. Then Sly's skinny arms joined in, and Blythe was smothered anew as she sobbed.

She wasn't the only one.

Blythe couldn't track what was happening as Tilla came charging off the ship to join the group hug. The rest of the crew were not far behind, and there were countless hands patting her back and endless voices cheering her name.

It was a lot.

"Captain, if you don't mind?" Walters raised her voice above the din. "Breakfast is awaiting you and yours in the dining hall!"

"Yes ma'am." Tilla drew themselves together with a huff as they wiped their eyes. They turned to address the throng of celebrating spacefarers and roared, "Chow time! Rein it in, kids!"

They were gone as quickly as they came, in a whirlwind of chattering voices and needy touches as they passed Blythe. The Zephyr was modest with a suitably sized crew, and Blythe was able to note each familiar face as they stole one-armed hugs and grazed her arm on their way out of the hangar; in that moment, it didn't seem to matter that she'd only been a coworker and acquaintance to most of them. For two years, she was one of them. Maybe they didn't know her *well*, but they still knew her.

It was possible none of them expected to see her alive again, and wasn't that a sobering thought?

"I'll keep the horde occupied and give you some space to acclimate," Tilla murmured in her ear at the tail end of the crowd. One big golden hand tucked a curl behind her ear before Tilla stepped away with a stiff grin. "You don't know how good it is to see you again."

"I might have some idea," Blythe said as she leaned into Phink and Sly's joint embrace. Tears threatened to overwhelm her again as she said, "Thank you for coming for me."

"Anytime."

As the captain marched after their crew, Blythe let her legs give out. As one, she, Sly, and Phink stumbled backward two or three paces and fell off-kilter before Phink managed to recover his footing and keep them upright.

Blythe barked a boisterous laugh to stem further crying. It was futile.

They collapsed together on the concrete floor, and the limbs crowding her held on tighter than ever. No matter Phink's space travel stink or the impact of Sly's new luxurious lifestyle, Blythe felt immersed in the reassuring scents of home. It wasn't the same as feeling safe, but it was close; it was grounding, the exact same sensation as finding a solid surface underfoot after too long drifting in zero-gravity.

A part of her wanted to languish in the moment forever.

It came to a natural end with the screech of a second gangway hitting the hangar floor.

Blythe sat up from the tangle of limbs with a start. "What was that?"

"Easy, girl," Phink grumbled as he tugged her back into his arms. "Don't worry about him. We can deal with Lugh later."

"Who's Lugh?"

Blythe traded a wide-eyed stare with Sly, but there was no reassurance in his baffled expression.

As the noise of Tilla's crew faded into the distance, Blythe's ears tuned in to the slow and steady clack of heavy boots descending a metal pathway. She couldn't see the second ship around The Zephyr's girth, but she could hear its lone passenger with the clarity of any cornered jaguar.

"Now, don't freak out," Phink murmured.

"Wow, Phinkly," Sly sassed, "could you be less ominous?"

Phink ignored him with practiced ease and gave Blythe a bracing squeeze. "We crossed flight paths with him hours ago, but

Tilla wasn't sure he was heading here until they were signaling to land."

Blythe stopped listening to Phink then. As those foreign footsteps met the hangar's concrete, a cold cascade rushed over Blythe, and her gut twisted.

A dark, willowy figure emerged from behind The Zephyr. His clothes were as black as his skin, from the hood of his duster coat to his ragged boots, and while his height made him appear too thin, the span of his shoulders was considerable and solid.

He wasn't wearing a uniform, but she recognized the deliberate way he carried himself, how he scanned the room in an endless yet subtle loop. How many times had she seen Sly's dad do the same thing, or noticed such a person failing to blend into Centrism's crowd?

"Ezra Lugh," he said in a deep purr as Walters approached. "The Guard sent me. I hear you're harboring a vampire I should meet."

CHAPTER 14

By wordless and unanimous decision, Blythe did not meet Ezra Lugh directly that first day. Walters took charge of the Guard and held him at bay while Phink and Sly frog-marched her out of the hangar and proceeded with an impromptu campaign of distraction.

It almost worked, but no amount of good food and traipsing down memory lane with friends could keep her nightmares at bay. Blythe woke the next morning in a cold sweat by a harsh rapping on her guest room door. She gripped the doorknob with a nauseating certainty that Walters was waiting on the other side, ready to tell her Polaris had been arrested and taken away while she slept.

In truth, Walters *was* waiting for her just beyond the threshold, but Sly was with her. He wore a maniacal grin and kept bouncing on the balls of his feet while the old woman stood stern and composed at his side.

Blythe blinked at them as she rubbed the confusion from her face. "What's going on?"

"Someone wants to see you," Sly chirped. "Get dressed, lazy bones. It's about time you introduce me to your vampire."

Blythe's weary brain skidded to a sluggish halt. It took a long moment for her to figure out what he meant, then she turned wide hopeful eyes on Walters.

"You're letting me see her again?"

Walters's eye twitched like she was forcing back the urge to roll her eyes. "Dr. Balint has determined she's no risk to you. So long as that remains the case, neither of us see much point in keeping you apart."

Blythe slammed the door in their faces and rushed to get dressed. She grabbed the first complete outfit she could find from the rake of get well gifts, then she was bounding down the hall in a deep-purple jumpsuit that managed to cover every inch of her skin save for her head, shoulders, and hands. It was suspiciously well-fitted to her frame, but she didn't have time to dwell over the fact.

She didn't second-guess the ensemble until Walters let her into the scion's office. Polaris took one look at her and clapped both hands over her mouth, her eyes bulging as she dragged them over Blythe's frame.

Blythe stalled out in the middle of the office with her arms half-raised in greeting. She might've stood there like an idiot forever if Sly didn't pop up behind her.

"Hi! You must be Polaris. I'm Sly!"

The Nocturna recoiled. Her eyes narrowed on his face as her hands lowered, and her expression was wary as it flickered between Blythe and Sly.

Blythe jabbed her elbow into Sly's side as she aimed an oversized smile at Polaris. "Hey, Hun. I missed you. By the way, this is Sly. I told you about him."

Sly took a giant backstep and tucked his hands in his back pockets without losing his grin. "Whatever she's told you, it's probably true, but in my defense, she's known since infancy."

The room seemed to hold its breath as they waited for Polaris to respond. In the doorway, Blythe could feel Walters shifting as if to intervene.

Taking a slow, deliberate breath, Polaris shimmied her shoulders and relaxed. Instead of laying limp against the pink skirt of her dress, her fingers curled into fistfuls of wavey fabric. With another breath, Polaris stepped in Blythe's direction, but she wasn't direct about it. Stars above, but the Nocturna had about as much tact as Sly did; she gave him a wide berth as she eased into Blythe's shadow and tucked herself into the woman's side.

Blythe slid her arm around Polaris's pale shoulders without a second thought.

What had happened since the last time they spoke? What had Polaris revealed to Dr. Balint in the past week or more? Was she as raw on the inside as Blythe felt at times? All the time?

While her morbid thoughts kept Blythe silent, Sly didn't seem to have that problem. He kept his distance as he leaned sideways to catch Polaris's eye. Once he did, he smiled. It wasn't a smile Blythe recognized; there was a softness there that didn't fit her mental image of him.

He said, "Thank you, Polaris."

Blythe's brow rose as the Nocturna turn to solid rock in her arms. Without looking at Polaris's face, she was certain Sly had the Nocturna's complete attention.

"I heard you helped Blythe escape," he said, his voice infused with that unnerving gentleness. "I owe you. Anything you need, Kahled and I will help you out. No questions asked."

Polaris's rigidity didn't thaw in the slightest, but she shifted. More of her weight leaned into Blythe's side as the Nocturna gave Sly the slightest shake of her head. When she spoke, it was with a formality Blythe didn't expect.

"You needn't thank me."

The Nocturna laid her head in the crook of Blythe's shoulder, and despite the tension pervading her slender form, Polaris's cheek was comfortable against her throat. The vampire's body was stiff with unnamed anxieties, but her warmth was real and infusive. Blythe imagined her worries would melt away if she stayed close long enough.

It was a tempting fantasy. It ensnared her almost to the point she missed the rest of the conversation.

"You brought my best friend back to me. Of course I'm going to thank you."

"You're wrong."

Polaris's dainty nose snuffled against Blythe's collar, and she relaxed the slightest bit more. In the next breath, Blythe's body followed her lead.

"It was the other way around," Polaris said. "Blythe rescued us. I never dreamed of making it out of there alive before her."

Blythe's heart cracked in response. She could feel the splintering as it cut a jagged line straight through the core of her. It hurt much like a sudden collision, the sharp and immediate ache dulled by surprise, only to make way for waves of debilitating pain. As if she could hear the damage happening in real time, Polaris wound her arms around Blythe's waist and began applying the pressure necessary to keep her in one piece.

For her ears only, Polaris whispered, "You saved us."

Blythe buried her face in those silvery locks with such force that her curls got tangled in it. She hugged Polaris as tight as she dared, till her catlike hearing activated, and she picked up the subtle gasp of air being squeezed from the vampire's lungs.

"Blythe?" Sly asked. "Are you okay?"

He was right there, not even a stone's throw away. It didn't matter; his voice reached her as if coming from an insurmountable distance. No matter the nearness, he was still worlds away.

Polaris, though? Slight and shaken as she was, she felt real. Undeniable.

For the love of the cosmos, but she wouldn't survive it if The Guard tried to take her vampire away.

"Shit. Um . . . okay," Sly said as he began inching out of the room. "Do you two need a moment? You look like you need a moment."

It didn't make sense. Polaris was still an enigma, question marks crossing over her past and sinister shadows obscuring her present. She was made of equal parts bloodshed and sweetness, from unspeakable horrors and fantastical hopes. There was so much Blythe didn't know about her, but what she did know was paramount to any of Blythe's concepts of reality.

"I'll just step out for a bit then. 'Kay, Blythe? Okay, then."

Wrapped up in Polaris's arms and moved beyond tears, Blythe hardly noticed when Sly slipped from the room.

Her universe had never felt more out of control, and she was desperate for an anchor, for anything, anyone to keep her grounded. It should have been Sly, with his lifelong support and unfailing humor. But it wasn't. Not anymore.

NEITHER BLYTHE NOR POLARIS SAID MUCH ONCE SLY LEFT THEM alone that morning. They didn't need to. There was no point in stammering words when each other's presence was all the comfort they could want. They ate breakfast and lunch when it was delivered, and when necessary, Blythe disentangled herself from Polaris long enough to utilize the private toilet attached to the office. When Walters and two of her staff intruded under the guise of cleaning the room, the two females removed themselves to the insulated garden.

That was where Dr. Balint found them that evening.

"I thought I might find you here."

As the doctor settled into the same lounger he tended to prefer,

Blythe didn't budge. She was perched on the corner of a gray velveteen loveseat requisitioned from an indoor parlor. Polaris was snuggled under Blythe's arm with her legs curled up on the cushion. Blythe suspected the Nocturna was sleeping, but her body tensed up moments before Blythe's human hearing caught the sound of Balint's approach.

Balint chuckled when neither female acknowledged him. "I'll admit, ladies, this is the most at ease I've seen either of you yet."

Blythe realized the doctor had a point; she wasn't weak with relief or raw and vulnerable from the reunion with the vampire. It was more like she felt . . . settled. Balanced.

Polaris seemed similarly affected. She lifted her head to give a slight nod in Balint's direction before resettling her cheek against Blythe's shoulder.

Blythe rubbed the Nocturna's arm in reassurance while she gave the doctor a tight smile. "I had a feeling we'd see you sooner or later, Doc."

"Good thing I didn't disappoint you then."

A soft, casual silence descended as Balint studied them, his stare pausing for the longest moments on Polaris. Blythe returned his regard with a strange mix of exhaustion and resolve, keeping her body limp and her breathing even. She didn't know what he would say or if she'd like it, but with Polaris's warmth seeping into her side, Blythe couldn't care less.

Still staring and thinking, the doctor began nodding to himself. He wasn't smiling.

Blythe sighed. "What?"

He shrugged one thin shoulder. "I have concerns. That's all."

Polaris shivered. Blythe felt the movement since they were pressed so close together, but she doubted Balint could see it.

Blythe tightened her arm around the Nocturna as she gave Balint a half-hearted glare. "That's all?"

One of those sympathetic smiles lit up his eyes as they darted to

Polaris, as if to say his concerns had nothing to do with the human half of their twosome.

Blythe's jumpsuit covered the base of her throat, but the exposed shoulder where Polaris rested her head was keen to the movement of the Nocturna's lips. Polaris's whisper glided over Blythe's jaguar spots and seemed to sneak under the fabric along her collar, tickling her neck.

"I'm sorry," Polaris murmured.

Blythe blinked down at the vampire. "For what?"

Without lifting her head to meet Blythe's bemused stare, Polaris said, "Lyall worries I'm using you."

"That's not what I said," Balint interjected, his tone mild as ever.

Blythe shot him an expectant look. "What did you say, then?"

His attention continued to waver between them as he thought. He took his time formulating his answer before he eased back into his chair. "I cannot truly appreciate what the two of you went through, but I make my living from understanding mental and emotional damage. I've learned there's sometimes a fine, but distinct line between coping mechanisms and crutches."

Blythe's ears prickled with a flash of sensitivity, and she heard Polaris's monotone mutter, "He thinks we're codependent."

Balint didn't hear the vampire's explanation. Blythe never had the chance to tense up with burgeoning defensiveness before his ongoing words caught up to her.

"You're both understandably raw right now, Blythe," he said. "I'll tell you the same thing I told Polaris: we can approach your healing the same way an orthopedic surgeon would address a broken bone; we can use bandages and aids for as long as needed, but only up until the point that they are useful. When those tools start to hinder your progress instead of improving it, it's time to set them aside and let your weight back on the injured limb. Do you understand what I'm saying here?"

Blythe frowned. Her face was still aimed at the doctor, but every iota of her attention was trained on the female at her side.

Across from them, Balint remained calm and unassuming in his seat. "It's like you said during one of our previous sessions, Blythe; there is a degree of inescapable overlap between the two of you, but that in no way negates the eventual need for you to learn to deal with your issues under your own power. That goes for both of you."

Neither of them responded.

For her part, Blythe was busy replaying every interaction she'd had with Polaris so far. The immediate empathy she'd felt the first time she heard the Nocturna's voice. The ease with which she encouraged the vampire to take her blood. The nonsensical acceptance she had of Polaris's violent actions.

Was that normal? Was it unhealthy? Would she still find Polaris's beauty so ethereal and absolute if they'd met on more commonplace terms? Was there any possible way to know an answer to that question?

"I'm sorry," Polaris repeated.

"You don't need to be." Blythe hugged her tight. It wasn't solely for Polaris's sake; it felt like the pressure might vanquish the unsettling numbness creeping over her own nerves.

"I want to be clear," Balint said, and it was a minor miracle that the loudness of his voice didn't startle Blythe straight off the couch, "I am by no means saying your relationship is codependent. It's simply something to watch out for."

"Sure," Blythe sniped. "It's just something you're *concerned* about. No big deal."

Blythe bit her tongue and went quiet, not recognizing the bite in her sarcastic tone. It felt wrong, like the phantom of a previous self darting out of the shadows to startle her. The sassy, careless Blythe who existed back on Earth was a different entity, altogether removed from the person she was now.

No one else seemed to appreciate the jarring effect.

"Nocturni and humans are inherently social creatures," Balint said with the cadence of a cautious lecturer. "We need interaction with others. It's not mere desire or impulse, but a very real necessity. For a brief and intense period, the two of you existed in a bubble where you had no one else you could turn to. It's understandable that such instincts would persist now that you're free—"

Blythe listened as he kept talking. Judging from the eerie stillness of the body next to hers, Polaris seemed to be doing the same. Maybe the Nocturna was just zoning out in that supernaturally meditative state she sometimes fell into. There was no way to tell.

Well. There was almost no way to tell.

Blythe nudged Polaris off her with slow but determined movements. Balint's voice faltered into quiet as she put half an arm's span of distance between herself and the Nocturna.

Meeting those shockingly blue eyes straight on, Blythe asked, "What do you think? Do you feel like you need me?"

Polaris's face was unreadable. Her fine brows crunched low, shadowing those striking blue orbs. She waited a heartbeat before answering. "Maybe? I don't know."

Pale fingers brushed a curl from Blythe's face, stroking over the black-and-gold spots at her temple. Blythe closed her eyes and began to lean into the touch before considering what that might look like to Dr. Balint. She blinked open her eyes and pulled back to meet Polaris's watery stare instead.

"I know I want you," Polaris said, soft but sure. She didn't try to close the distance between them again, but her fingertip landed on Blythe's knee, trembling. "I know I care about you, about your well-being and your happiness. Your future. I can't imagine not being part of it."

Blythe nodded, her throat too dry and her jaw too tight for words.

"Maybe Lyall's right," Polaris said with a sad smile. "I don't have the means or ability to make it happen, but I would find a way to give you the moon if you asked for it."

"You don't even know me."

Polaris shrugged and her fingers curled into a firm fist where they pressed against Blythe's knee. "I can't tell you how long I spent in that place. How many times they provided me blood I didn't want. You weren't the first human they tried to make me drink from."

She paused, then in a swaying motion too quick for Blythe to track, Polaris slipped close for a fleeting kiss to the woman's cheek. She was there and gone again before Blythe could react.

"I promise you, Blythe," Polaris said in earnest, "you were the only one I ever touched. In all the time I spent there, you were the only one who wasn't frightened or disgusted by my existence."

Sniffling, Blythe snickered. "How could anyone be disgusted by you?"

Polaris smiled. It was so tearful and lovely that Blythe could forgive herself for forgetting they weren't alone. The Nocturna unfurled her fingers to grip Blythe's thigh and pressed their foreheads together.

With a conspiratorial whisper, the vampire said, "You reminded me of my humanity. You saved me."

"No." A shuddering breath burst from Blythe's lips as she reached for Polaris with both hands. "It was all you. You were the one who fought them off and cleared the way."

But Polaris was shaking her head long before Blythe finished the sentence. "I didn't even notice the door was open till you pointed it out—"

"I wouldn't have made it out alone—"

"I'd given up on escaping so long ago—"

"But you—"

"It was you!"

Their voices clashed, one over the other, till all details of speech were lost. It didn't matter. The floodgates had been battered down between one lamentation and the next, and before long, they were left sobbing into each other's hair. They clung to one another's arms and shuddered with their combined tears. It was messy and gut-wrenching, yes, but it was wonderful.

Each teardrop carried off a load of fears. Blythe didn't know if the cleansing wash was coming from Polaris or herself, and she ultimately didn't care. Together, they had stumbled into a pocket of reality bursting with relief and comfort, and it was deep and honest enough to lose herself in.

Maybe there was danger in it. In the quagmire of emotion and physical sensation, Blythe could see how tempting it would be to stay put, lost and reliant on Polaris's embrace. The sound of the Nocturna's sobs in her ear were loud and ensnaring, not unlike a siren's call. It would be easy, so very, very easy, to give up all her cares in favor of making Polaris the center of her universe.

It wouldn't end well, but it would certainly be easy.

Dr. Balint escorted them back to Blythe's room instead of pressuring them to join everyone else for dinner.

"You're going to be all right," he said as he patted Polaris's shoulder in the doorway. "Keep supporting each other and prioritizing your individual journeys in turn. Things may not go smoothly, but progress rarely does."

"A tad cryptic there, Doc," Blythe cautioned, "but thanks for the advice anyway."

He bid them good night with an encouraging smile and a promise to send food along in a bit, then they were left alone. At last.

Blythe cast a wary glance at the closed door. "What are the chances of Walters busting down the door to drag you back to the office if you try to stay here tonight?"

Graceful and sinuous as any cat, Polaris brushed up against her to nuzzle Blythe's cheek. "I don't care."

A spark of warmth lighted in Blythe's belly at the gentle touch. In another time, in a different place, under different circumstances, Blythe wouldn't hesitate to glide her hands over Polaris's hips, or even lower. Given the current situation, though, Blythe shelved the urge in favor of kissing the tip of the vampire's nose.

"They told you about the Guard?"

Polaris gave a slight nod. "Lyall warned me. He didn't know about Reese until he got here."

Blythe cupped the Nocturna's face in her palms and vowed, "I won't let him take you from me."

"We might not have a choice," Polaris wept.

Blythe hushed her with a kiss. It was closed-mouthed and sweet but drawn out and insistent. It was powerful.

Polaris retreated a half step with a shaky inhale. "Wait. I have to tell you something."

"Oh. Okay. What?"

Polaris leaned into Blythe a bit more, trusting the entire weight of her head into Blythe's reverent hands. Her lashes did an uncertain flutter before she seemed to find her resolve and squeezed her eyes closed. As the Nocturna took a breath, Blythe felt hands slide around her waist with the barest hint of pressure.

"I never fed from them. Gregoire's other prisoners."

Blythe's heart lurched. "It wouldn't matter to me if you did."

"Yes, but it matters to me."

Polaris dragged her featherlight touch from Blythe's waist to take her wrists in a firmer grip. She opened her eyes and stole Blythe's breath away. They were blue, still, but not their usual shade; there was a brightness to them, striations of shocking white that turned her eyes magical.

"No matter how hard I tried," Polaris said in a fervent whisper, "I never had the strength to fight them, to give back even a portion of the awfulness they showed me. Then there you were."

Blythe interrupted with another quiet kiss. "It took both of us."

"It took *you*," Polaris stressed, voice still hushed. "The only human blood I've had over the decades amounted to a mouthful siphoned off from reluctant veins, but then you came to me."

She pried Blythe's hands from her face and firmed her grip, shaking the woman as if trying to will Blythe into believing her words.

"You let me have my fill of human blood—your blood—and it gave me back the strength I never noticed I lost."

She darted forward to plant a hard kiss on Blythe's lips. If her words hadn't already struck Blythe speechless, the unbridled emotion in that kiss would have. When they parted, it took a long moment before Blythe could lace together a coherent thought.

Against all reason, there was only one thought floating to the surface of her mind.

"Polaris?"

"Yes, Blythe?"

"What's your real name?"

The Nocturna sucked in a racking breath that sounded pained, and Blythe knew she wasn't ready to provide an answer. For now, that shuddering gasp would have to be answer enough.

Blythe wrapped her fingers in that silver hair with utmost care and deliberation. She didn't pull, but she used the tresses as a guide to tilt the Nocturna's head. This time, when their mouths met, there was nothing quick or sweet about it. No. This time, Blythe parted her lips and poured every ounce of pent-up emotion from the past few weeks into a single all-consuming kiss.

Polaris matched her intensity without hesitation. Her fingers dug into Blythe's back with thrilling strength that crushed their bodies together. Through the snug confines of her own clothing, Blythe could feel the flow of the Nocturna's flimsy dress and the pleasant give of her breasts. For all her fearsome strength, the Nocturna's body was soft and inviting with ample curves.

It was a stark comparison to herself. Blythe might have lost muscle mass in the years since she danced at Centrism, but she would always have a solid build. She was compact and lean, her curves and lines hard-won and trained.

She was rough next to Polaris. Polaris, who was small and light, nearly as insubstantial as her clothing—but in that moment, she encompassed the entire universe.

"I want you," Polaris breathed as she backstepped toward the bed.

She shucked the pink dress from her shoulders, and Blythe stared openly as the fabric dropped into a puddle around her nimble feet.

"I knew it," Blythe hissed under her breath, already reaching for her. All suspicions that the vampire didn't wear a bra were confirmed; the tight peaks of her nipples were a darker pink than the dress, and they were a sight almost capable of distracting from the strip of pale silk across her hips.

They moved in tandem, the space between them disappearing as they neared the bed. With one handful of flowing metallic locks and the other around a plump breast, Blythe fell onto the mattress. She crawled on top of Polaris and found herself cradled in welcoming curves and heated skin.

Time lost all meaning after that.

They lost themselves in aimless kisses. They traded touches and moans and exchanged feverish instructions whenever they had the breath to spare. They petted and rolled around till the bedding was shoved to the floor, till Blythe sweated halfway out of her clothes and Polaris's skin was flush with arousal. They explored each other without rush, but with every sense of indulgence.

Polaris responded to Blythe's touch like it was magic. Her eyes glowed with that unprecedented light as she arched under Blythe's hands and moaned into her mouth. It took next to no effort to get her out of the silk underwear, and by the time Blythe's mouth found her core, she was a wet, shivering mess. Polaris mewled in eager pleasure at the first swipe of Blythe's tongue over her clit and subsequently ceased any attempts to reign in her noises.

The Nocturna was magnificent. She was unapologetic and relentless in her desire, and Blythe got swept up in it like a sheet caught in a storm. By the time Polaris reached her end, Blythe's tongue ached from straining and her scalp itched from Polaris's zealous grasp.

Blythe left her stretched out on her back as she recovered. In the meantime, Blythe rolled off the side of the mattress and began wriggling her lower half out of the jumpsuit. It was practically plastered to her legs from sweat and slick, but she was determined. While she struggled with the fabric, she admired the body splayed on her bed.

Though far from innocent-looking, Polaris remained as angelically lovely as ever. As she lay panting, the full-body blush painted her in fetching shades of rose. The warmth infusing her skin was even more eye-catching against the cool tones of her metallic hair and illuminated eyes.

Blythe tossed the last of her clothing over her shoulder and gave a little extra sway to her hips as she reapproached the bed. The white in Polaris's eyes seemed to eclipse the blue entirely as they tracked the motion.

"Have your eyes always done that?"

"Done what?" Polaris asked as she squirmed into an upright position against the headboard. She held out a hand, fingers flexing greedily.

"Your eyes." Blythe chuckled and gave the vampire her hand so Polaris could reel her in the rest of the way. "They're glowing, you know."

"Are they?" Polaris giggled, then she distracted them both with a lengthy kiss.

Naked together for the first time, they relaxed against the pillows while ensuring as much skin-to-skin contact as possible. Blythe had the wild thought that the hard line of her hip bone might leave a permanent indentation on Polaris's pliant flesh.

It was a nonsensical thought but amusing nonetheless; whether they spent moments together or decades, Blythe would never leave a permanent mark on the vampire's skin. If Blythe was lucky, she might earn one for herself. Two neat little scars on her throat would be insignificant among all the jaguar spots dotting her person, but she rather liked the sneakiness of carrying around such a subtle reminder of their love affair.

Blythe had no doubt that this was love. As Polaris's hand slid between her legs and two long fingers delved between her folds, Blythe nearly admitted it out loud. She didn't though. She bit back the words and replaced them with a guttural moan, determined to keep them to herself for a more appropriate moment.

Sex and love were not the same thing, as Blythe knew well. Someday, when they were both ready for it, Blythe would tell Polaris how she was the first lover she had ever truly cared for. Maybe it would be sometime soon, maybe not for another year, but Blythe knew when she said those fateful words, it would happen when they were not only safe, but whole and well.

Yes, she decided as she gasped into Polaris's mouth. She would tell Polaris she loved her when they were far beyond the shitty events that brought them together. They would put the past behind them—all of it—and this time, Blythe really would move on, because this time, she wouldn't be doing it alone.

It was a glittering moment of sappy optimism born from a

desperately needed orgasm. Blythe should have known better than to trust it.

"If I can't tell you, I doubt I'll ever tell anyone."

Polaris's whisper reached her through a dense fog of afterglow. Blythe was more than half asleep and well on her way to dreaming. Truly. She might have dreamed it.

"My name is Tanya."

CHAPTER 15

By the following morning, Blythe convinced herself any whispered confessions were delirium-induced imaginings. It was easy to do while Polaris lay in her bed, haloed in silver hair and plush white bedding as she slept with the most peaceful, subtle smile on her face. Blythe didn't have the heart to wake her.

Besides, she didn't need Polaris for this next part. Their little break from reality was over. It did its job, though, and now Blythe had the presence of mind to do something proactive.

She was leaving the guest wing when she bumped into Sly.

"What are you doing up so early?" she asked, frowning at him.

Sly pursed his lips and turned pink, and she knew he hadn't intended to run into her. Even so, he shook off his discontent and raised his occupied hands with a stiff grin. "Would you believe I was bringing myself breakfast in bed?"

Blythe eyed the heaping stack of pancakes in his one hand and the artfully wrapped silverware in his other. "Nope."

He scrunched his nose in thought, but Blythe didn't have the patience for whatever half-cocked excuse he was struggling to form.

He was awake and dressed for the day, she had no qualms about stealing the pancakes from his grasp.

"Woah! Where are you going?"

"I'm bringing Reese breakfast," she said over her shoulder as she continued toward the staff's dormitories.

"Those are mine!"

"Bullshit. You already ate, I can tell. You can either go back to the kitchens for a new plate, or you tell me what it is you're up to, skulking around before anyone else is up. Didn't Walters insist you take the master bedroom, anyway? Last I checked, you're not exactly her guest."

Sly grumbled something unflattering under his breath, but a moment later, she felt him hurry along behind her.

"Reese is the guy Polaris gutted, right?"

"It was a misunderstanding."

"Does he know you're bringing him breakfast at . . ."—he paused, making a show of checking the comms on his wrist—"four in the morning?"

"Good question. What about you?"

They were each saved from answering when they turned into the residential wing of the manor and almost slipped past the door Blythe needed. The polished wood plaque on its front read *Reese W.*

"How convenient," Sly simpered. "We're here!"

Blythe shot him a dark look as she knocked on the door. Given the hour and the last-minute decision to visit, Blythe was prepared to knock multiple times, and louder if need be.

Instead, a faint "come in" answered her first knock.

Blythe hesitated. Reese was up and about already? Was he expecting someone?

She didn't know what she would find on the other side of the door. In theory, Reese would be lying in bed, pale and bandaged, but alive and on the mend. Since the moment Balint was called on to attend him, no one saw fit to tell Blythe how or what the young man was doing. Blythe spent the trek from her room to his telling herself that it would be fine, so long as he wasn't still bleeding and panicked, but when the moment came, she had no idea what to expect.

As luck would have it, Reese was bleeding. He had a papercut.

Blythe balked as she held the door open. "What are you doing?"

Reese popped his sliced finger from his mouth and lifted his gaze from the book in his hands so he could frown at her. "Shouldn't I be the one asking that?"

Blythe jabbed her finger at the made-up bed in the corner, and her bafflement made her voice snap harsher than warranted. "You should be resting!"

Reese shrugged and returned to his book. "I can rest and read at the same time."

She stared at him. From the way he craned over her shoulder, Sly was doing likewise. The cutlery in his hand dug into the small of her back for a second before she bumped her hips backward to clue him in.

At least Reese wasn't panicking, blood notwithstanding. He stood before a bookshelf, one massive tome balanced on his forearm as he perused its pages. He was pale, and his throat was obviously bandaged, but his rigid stance and alert expression made it clear he felt fine.

He was reading, yes, but he certainly wasn't resting.

He might as well have been back at work. The bedroom was like an extension of the library. The walls may have been white and the bookshelves freestanding, but the atmosphere was the same. The gold-and-burgundy bedspread would have been at home in the more formal setting, and the desk in the corner looked like the humbled cousin of the one she spied in the scion's office.

Reese showed his book more consideration than the intruders in his doorway.

"Uh, hi?" Sly chirped while Blythe gaped. "We brought

breakfast. Pretty sure that's something you're supposed to have days after being exsanguinated."

"You can put it over there." Reese flapped his hand toward his desk without prying his eyes from the book, and he promptly stuck his nicked finger back in his mouth.

As Sly wiggled around her and snagged the pancakes from her hand, Blythe eased over to the other man's side. "So," she hesitated, "you're looking well."

He pulled his finger from his mouth and said "Thank you" as he inspected the cut. Satisfied he was no longer leaking, he flipped his book closed and focused on her. He skimmed over her from head to toe twice, his gaze shrewd and expression unreadable.

Blythe stiffened under such regard.

Before she could speak, Reese said, "Yes. You seem better as well. That's . . ." His jaw flexed as he searched for the right word, before finally settling on: ". . . fortunate."

Blythe gave a nervous laugh. "You got your artery severed, but you were worried about me?"

He frowned, blinking at her as if perplexed. "You weren't exactly in top form at the time either."

Blythe gave him a strained smile. "You're not wrong. I'm sorry about that."

"Don't be." He hefted the book higher against his torso and glided off toward the desk, seemingly at ease. He whisked the napkin off the silverware and peered down at the pancakes with a narrowing of his eyes. "I don't suppose you know whatever it was that triggered you so badly?"

Blythe shifted her weight from foot to foot, turning away to stare—unseeing—at the nearest bookcase. "It wasn't personal."

"I didn't think it was."

"Polaris didn't—"

Everyone froze. Blythe's mouth went dry as she watched

Reese's shoulders lift with tension, and nearby, Sly yanked his curious fingers away from the papers on the desk to stare at her.

Slow and deliberate, Sly shook his head at her. "Maybe not now—"

"She didn't know what I was reacting to," Blythe said over him. "She just thought she was protecting me. She understands better now, and she feels terrible about what she did—"

"If it's all the same to you, Ms. Ramos, I'd rather hear it from her."

As he turned around, Reese lifted his chin and stared down at her with utter stoicism.

Blythe's heart filled her throat with a hopeful pang. "You'll speak with her? Before you talk to The Guard?"

Reese blinked. He blinked twice more, then frowned. "Come again?"

"The Guard—a Guard—arrived yesterday," Blythe explained as Sly made a distressed noise on the sidelines. "I wanted . . . that is, I was hoping to talk to you before you—if you—decided to press charges—"

"Oh! Because Polaris assaulted me?"

Blythe's eyes widened as she nodded. "Obviously."

"Stars above, is that why The Guard's here?" Reese's face flushed pink with weak alarm. "Oh no. No, no, I never reported the incident— Well, I thought about it, at first, but not since—"

"Wait." Blythe stopped him with a hand on his arm. "You don't blame her?"

"Of course not!" His expression wavered, and he looked away from her. "Not rationally, at any rate."

"So, you won't tell The Guard about what she did?" Blythe pressed.

"Now, hold on. I'm not about to lie to the authorities, just to be clear—"

"Oh, my stars!" Sly gasped, drawing their attention.

Blythe and Reese turned to watch Sly scoop up a thin stack of papers from the desk with a gaping maw and the general attitude of someone holding a precious treasure. He stared at Reese with a wicked smirk creeping across his face.

"Your last name is Walters?"

Blythe turned on Reese. "Bullshit."

"You're *related* to Emmeline Walters?" Sly said with mirthful accusation as he pointed at the name printed on the topmost page.

Considering his recent blood loss, Reese turned an impressive shade of fuchsia. He leaped forward to yank the papers from Sly's hand. "She's my grandmother, if you must know."

Blythe slapped her hands over her gaping mouth. "No! That's why you seemed so familiar!"

"I did?"

"I'm still getting over the fact Walters ever had a baby," Sly interjected.

Reese puffed up his chest as he began correcting any assumptions Sly might be jumping to regarding Walters's maternal instinct. "Birthing my father was her assumed duty to HEPP before she became a Companion— Wait. Why am I telling you this?"

"Because I have one of those trustworthy and charismatic faces?"

Sly beamed as Reese's frown intensified. The librarian glared down his nose at Sly, as if he'd only just realized a stranger was riffling through his bedroom and prying into his personal life.

Sly wiggled his fingers at Reese with an unrepentant grin. "Nice to meet you. Call me Sly."

Reese gaped. "Sly Spurgeon? Master Kahled's Companion? Truly?"

Sly's grin went brittle with surprise.

"I can't believe it!" Reese tossed his book on the desk with a resounding clatter of cutlery. He grabbed Sly's hand with both of his and gave it a vigorous shake. "Sylvester Spurgeon, in the flesh! It is an absolutely honor."

Sly's freckles seemed darker than ever as he paled and his jaw dropped. Blythe stared; she couldn't remember ever seeing him struck speechless before. And then she thought back over what Reese had said.

In that moment, the universe was comically small. Andy was Elitia's cousin, Reese was Walters's grandson, and Sly's infamy was reaching intergalactic proportions, so much so, it forced even Walters's own kin to trip over his own words. It was all so ridiculous and unreal. She had to react.

With a burst of laughter, Blythe doubled over. She laughed hard and loud as she clutched her gut. The amusement burst out of her with a vengeance, as if every chuckle or snicker she hadn't uttered in the past month or more was suddenly being summoned straight from her soul.

In the midst of it all was the awareness that Polaris was safe. No one was actively trying to return her to a cage.

The relief was transcendent. It swept Blythe off her feet, and she descended into lunacy in the middle of the room, blocking the door and effectively holding Sly and Reese captive. Each man was too silly on his own, yet alone put together, and perfectly framed by the unbelievability of the situation, so she laughed. They were staring at her, but she couldn't catch her breath long enough to explain.

She tried. She nearly got it under control too.

Then Sly snorted.

Blythe's knees went weak with renewed mirth, and as a ring of his familiar laughter rent the air, she stumbled toward a bookcase to catch her weight on a shelf. They laughed and laughed with no end in sight. At some point, Sly dug his fingers into Reese's shoulder to keep himself upright, and the sight sent Blythe reeling into another bout of cackling.

It was a good—no, it was a great laugh. It was the full-bellied rumble of pent-up stress and overwhelming relief and a spiking joy that was unadulterated by wrongs or fears. It rolled through Blythe like a force of nature, and the echo of it in Sly's voice thrummed at the edges of her personal whirlwind.

Eventually, with sore stomachs and dry throats, they calmed down to find poor Reese staring at them with round, earnest eyes.

With genuine concern, Reese asked, "What is wrong with you people?"

It was the wrong thing to say, and Reese was left to deal with two nonsensical Earthlings rolling on his floor with inexplicable laughter.

IT WAS EASIER TO FACE DR. BALINT WHEN THEY MET LATER THAT morning. He sat in the corner chair in her guest room with that patient smile on his face as he listened to her chortle over the morning's laughing fit. He made casual comments to keep her talking, but nothing that delved too deep. Before she knew it, the words flying out of her mouth were miles away from the topic of pancakes and fussy librarians.

Somehow, some inconceivable way, she ended up focusing on Sly and Centrism.

"He never had much interest in show business," Blythe said with a nostalgic chuckle, "but the money was good, and having me around all night, every night was the best."

"It sounds like you miss it."

Blythe's lingering humor cooled. "Yeah. I really do."

"Are you looking forward to performing again?" Dr. Balint asked, tapping away at the comms tablet in his lap.

"Sure," Blythe said, "but it wouldn't be the same."

"No, but should it be? From the way you and Sly talk about it, Centrism—"

"You talked to Sly?"

"Twice now."

Blythe frowned and bit back a probing comment about what might traumatize Sly of all people.

Balint saw the inkling on her face anyway. "We're only talking about Sly as he pertains to you and your story, Blythe. As I was saying, Centrism seemed like an extension of your childhood in a way, the two of you joking around on the job with few concerns beyond immediate comfort and distant dreams. It sounds wonderful, but fleeting."

Blythe didn't respond. Her throat felt clogged, her lungs compressed. Her brain couldn't decide which hole to dig. Did she want to know why Sly was seeking Balint out that morning, or was she ready to admit the golden years of her life were over? Neither option sounded appealing.

She wasn't feeling so talkative anymore.

"Maybe that part of your life is done," Balint said, choosing for her. "Would that be so bad?"

She heard him shifting in the chair, but she didn't turn her head to look at him. She was lying on her back across the middle of the bed, and the ceiling felt like a safer place to settle her gaze.

"I'm talking about moving on, Blythe."

A shiver of something not quite like fear trilled up her spine. Out loud, she murmured, "I thought I already had."

"With the merchant ship?" Dr. Balint's voice dragged as he skimmed his notes. "The Zephyr?"

"Maybe?"

Blythe's jaw began to ache from prolonged clenching. She closed her eyes and took a deep breath, trying to will herself to relax. Instead, she felt a wave of exhaustion wash over her.

"No," she admitted. "I think I was close but not quite there. Tilla knew. They wanted me to . . . I don't know." She raised a hand in a flippant gesture to indicate the universe and present situation at large. "Maybe you're right. Maybe I should have worked harder, committed to the crew and left the stage good and far behind me, then none of this would've happened."

"Maybe," Dr. Balint said without inflection, "or maybe Andrew Kenwood would have recognized you on the street the next time you landed in Lunar-5. Maybe—now, bear with me here—but *maybe* you don't need to take responsibility for his actions."

Slow and soft, Blythe said, "Maybe."

That single word drained her of whatever energy she had left. It floated from her tongue with an unnecessarily long exhale that squeezed her lungs to the point of collapse. It felt like she was folding in on herself, shrinking away from the dulcet tone of Dr. Balint's voice and the carefully laid path he'd carved out for her. As easy as this conversation had been overall, she was beyond ready for it to end.

"You don't have to let recent experiences stop you from creating a fulfilling future," Balint said in a voice that was smooth and warm, as if he knew she was fading away and his chance to make an impact was fleeting. "I want you to think about what that might look like. The Zephyr is restocking as we speak, but Tilla's willing to sit put for a few more days. You have some time to decide if you want to return to the ship."

She didn't respond, but he didn't leave her be.

"Or not. You could try accepting that there's no going back, that the best way to deal with all that's happened is to push onward. It sounds like Phink has a stage ready and waiting for you. Does that still interest you?"

Blythe raised herself up on her elbows so she could shoot him a deadpan glower. "In your professional opinion, Doc, do you think working under Elitia-fucking-Kenwood again is a smart idea for me?"

"I didn't say that." His answering smile was tight but widening in encouragement. "But that investigation is still open, last I heard. What do you think about that?"

Chewing her tongue in thought, Blythe rolled onto her front and started picking at the pearlescent stitching of the quilt. While she did, the doctor waited in easy silence.

"I think"—her breath hitched for a moment—"I think I'll kill her if I ever see her again."

She shook with the cold hard truth of it. The words expelled from her mouth to make room for a feverish anger.

Eyes burning with tears, Blythe said, "I think I get why Polaris went at Reese the way she did."

"Anger is a vital component in the healing process, for humans and Nocturni alike."

She took another breath, but it did nothing to ease her tension. With a groan, Blythe dropped her forehead onto the bedding. "Does it ever end?"

"Eventually." He joined her then, and the mattress sagged by her shoulder as he sat down and rested a hand on her upper back. "It may be scary, but the anger you feel now is justified and useful. For now, maybe it's nothing more than a means for survival, but some day, when you're ready, you can use it as a tool to move beyond the darkness."

Blythe kept her scoff to herself. She didn't have the energy to spare anyway—not for making noise, and certainly not for entertaining Balint's optimism. He couldn't feel the tumultuous mass writhing in her gut or the way it consumed her reserves till there was nothing left.

"I can't take the anger away, Blythe," he said, rubbing her back, "but I can help you direct it some."

Blythe spat out a small, doubtful laugh. "What do you have in mind, Doc?"

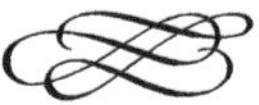

CHAPTER 16

Days later, Blythe still hadn't warmed up to Balint's suggested "direction."

"You can't keep avoiding him," Phink griped.

Between the fuzzy guy's ballooning belly and the way he stood shoulder to shoulder with Tilla's solid muscle, the open hallway became a dead end. Blythe had no hope of worming her way past them and making it to the kitchen undaunted on her own.

Polaris stood a half step behind her, evidently uninterested or unwilling to clear the way. Blythe could feel the Nocturna's fingers curling into the loose blouse at the small of Blythe's back with a nervous tremble.

With a sigh of defeat, Blythe asked, "What are my chances of putting this off until after lunch?"

Tilla crossed their burly arms with a determined huff.

Beside the captain, Phink's frown drooped further. "Ezra Lugh isn't a saint, and you can't expect him to have the patience of one. You're not going anywhere until you talk to him, and if this goes on much longer, it's going to cost us a free ride back to Lunar-5."

"I have jobs lined up," Tilla grumbled when Phink gave a pointed tilt of his head toward them.

"Great." Blythe snatched up Polaris's hand and smiled so wide and false that it hurt. "We'll come with you. When do we leave? Tomorrow?"

"Not funny," Tilla and Phink deadpanned.

At the same time, Polaris pressed into Blythe's side with a cautioning whimper. It was soft enough to almost escape Blythe's notice. Almost.

Phink made a disgruntled noise, and Blythe wasn't quick enough to stop him from launching into his version of the speech Walters and Balint had already delivered. His wasn't as polite or heartening as the other two, not by half.

"What's the hang-up here, Blythe? Lugh's already talked to Reese, and he's clearly not here for whatever went down with him. For the love of the cosmos, Blythe, he deals exclusively with Humans First cases! You should *want* to talk to him! Both of you!"

"Well, we don't!" Blythe hissed in his face. "Forgive me for not wanting to air out all my filthy baggage with a stranger!"

Phink flinched, but there was no other reaction to her outburst. To varying degrees, Blythe was sure each of them knew her refusal to speak with Lugh was only in part due to her unwillingness to divulge details of her captivity.

The name Troy was floating around the manor like a sinister ghost. It was spoken in whispers off the lips of everyone, from Sly to the most unassuming servant. Blythe wasn't sure how or why, and she didn't care to know. All she cared about were the implications.

The Troy Harem belonged to The Nine Bloodlines. What would happen if they learned their Heir had been abducted and kept like an exotic pet by Humans First?

No one wanted the moon exploding into a racial war, and Blythe didn't want Leopold Troy swooping in and stealing her vampire away like a prized treasure.

It was better for everyone if they didn't talk to Lugh and The Guard. Surely.

As if Tilla could read her mind, they stepped in front of Phink and spoke for her ears only, "Ezra Lugh is the closest The Guard has to a detective, Blythe. Even if I wanted to, he won't let me take off with Polaris on board."

"You don't know—"

"He's been very clear about it."

"Fuck," Blythe hissed under her breath.

Polaris squeezed her hand. "It's fine."

Blythe turned to meet those ever-blue eyes. They were as cold and clear as crystals—and maybe harder.

Polaris squeezed her hand tight. "You're not alone in this."

It felt like a hot gnarled coal was scratching its way up her throat, but Blythe croaked out a few words anyway, "We'll talk to him together?"

In a small tired voice, Polaris agreed, "Together."

Then they were flush together, clinging to each other in the middle of the hall. Since her release from the scion's office, Polaris made it a point not to crowd Blythe's every motion, but she never seemed to miss an opportunity to touch. Blythe couldn't usually tell whether such contact was a show of solidarity or possession, but it was obvious in that moment; Blythe strained a little as she held the Nocturna upright as much as herself.

Nearby, Tilla made a soft noise of understanding and began to retreat down the hall.

"I'll set up the meeting then," Phink murmured as he gave them space.

Once they were alone, Blythe stepped back and raised her arm. She meant the motion to be slow and measured, but her hand shook as she brushed the hair back from Polaris's face and combed it down the length of her pale arm.

The hair was fluid and lukewarm to the touch, the texture as smooth and pristine as the precious metal look of it. Nuzzling into Blythe's touch as she was, the jaggedness of the involuntary undercut was totally disguised.

"I have an idea," Blythe said as she kept caressing the vampire's arm.

"Hmm?"

"I think you should do something for you," Blythe said with the sense that her tongue was tripping over itself. "I think it would be good for you to make your own decision about your appearance. Maybe get your hair cut?"

"No."

The promptness of the reply startled Blythe's touch to stillness before she noticed the iron-hard tension flooding the vampire's body. It wasn't the same discomfited rigidity from moments ago, but the indomitable donning of a shield.

"Okay." With deliberate calm, Blythe continued petting Polaris's arm. When the vampire's bicep began to soften, she suggested, "What about dying it?"

Polaris shot her an unimpressed glare, but the stiffness didn't rush back. "I'm a Nocturna, Blythe, not a chameleon. It takes months of tailored dieting and attentiveness to alter my appearance so drastically. At minimum."

Blythe frowned as she watched Polaris pick up a few strands of silvery hair and dangle them between them with a resigned sigh.

"At this point, it'll probably take me years to change this."

Blythe mulled that comment over for a moment, weighing it alongside what little she knew about the control Humans First might have exerted over Polaris's person. Try as she might, she couldn't quite choke back the sass from her next comment.

"So, vampires don't believe in artificial hair dye then?"

Polaris turned wide incensed eyes at her.

Blythe met the stare with an arched eyebrow. "Do they?"

They locked gazes, one incredulous, the other expectant. The eye contact lasted a mere moment before they dissolved into a chorus of weak, cautious giggles. Polaris stifled her bubble of humor by burying her face in Blythe's shoulder. Her arms locked around Blythe's waist a tad too tightly, and if the discordant notes of hysteria bled into her voice, it went unacknowledged. In return, Blythe returned the embrace threefold and sniffed back a tear.

That was how Walters found them when she rounded the corner.

"I hate to interrupt . . ." Walters spoke with a vague disapproval, her shrewd gaze darting between them, as if she'd caught them fornicating in the passageway.

Blythe's waist felt cold as Polaris pulled away. She turned to find the Nocturna hugging herself and casting wary glances toward the kitchen, as if she was considering running away. For her part, Blythe found the pink creeping across the Nocturna's face most endearing.

Blythe retook the vampire's wrist and held fast as she turned to Walters. "You're not interrupting. We were just heading to lunch—"

She cut herself short as she caught Polaris's uneasy shift in her periphery.

"—but I lost my appetite," she finished, and the way Polaris melted at her side felt like a breath of fresh air entering her own lungs.

As one, the two females sidestepped to allow Walters through. Instead of doing just that, the older woman clasped her hands and gave them an assessing stare.

"Very well," she decided, dropping her hands to her sides. "I'll leave you to yourselves for now, but I must speak with Mr. Phink, if you happen to know where he is?"

Blythe opened her mouth to ask what the matter was, but Polaris's raised arm crossed Blythe's chest to direct Walters down the hall. Without further comment, the Head of House strode off in that direction like a woman on a mission.

REGARDLESS OF WHAT WAS SAID TO PHINK, IT SEEMED POLARIS WAS not quite ready to face the imposing Guard. They skipped lunch, cloistered away together in a secluded corner of the garden, and only once Blythe's stomach started roaring did they venture back inside. It was pure happenstance that they encountered Sly being harassed by the dramatically dressed stylist on retainer, but the run-in seemed to light a fire in the Nocturna's eyes that Blythe couldn't make heads or tails of.

It made sense later, when Blythe carried a substantial case of precious metals and jewels from the stylist's studio to the guest wing's bathroom. She opened the door to find Polaris looming over the marbled counter with a flick of fire dancing between the fingers of her gloved hands.

"You're sure about this?" Sly asked as he watched on with a pinched expression on his face. He was seated on the counter a full arm's length away from where the vampire lingered by the sink.

Blythe paused in the doorway, wondering what might have happened between the two in her absence.

"You needn't worry," Polaris said as she blew out the flame and snapped off her gloves. Her freed hands went directly to her head and began twisting all that silver hair in a braid.

Blythe leaned on the doorframe and watched her lover's fingers weave an intricate braid without hesitation. Blythe could manage a simplified version on her own head while blindfolded, but the way Polaris worked the sleek strands into a seamless design was mesmerizing, almost like a dance. Despite the complexity, Polaris's motions held the fluidity of muscle memory.

That memory halted in its tracks when Polaris reached the end of her braid and reached for something to tie it off. She reached to the left side of the sink, where there was nothing but bronze and gold marbling. Polaris's hand froze then quivered.

"I got it," Blythe said as she entered the room fully.

She set her armload by Sly's hip and stepped behind Polaris as she plucked a hair tie from a bathroom drawer. Blythe had no occasion to use half the beauty products and tools within the guest wing's stockpile, but it hadn't stopped the fawning housekeepers from showing her where everything was kept.

Blythe got distracted from thoughts of the staff the moment she got her hands in all those glorious strands. It should have taken seconds to tie off the braid, but the texture begged for Blythe's touch to linger.

Polaris's hair was abundant and thick, nothing short of luxurious. There were no dead ends, no frizz of any kind. Whatever natural oils the Nocturna produced seemed to be unhindered by the limited diet Polaris was subjected to for so long. No matter how much Blythe pulled and tugged at it, be it for styling or in the heat of a satisfying moment, the hair remained strong and full, immune to damage in ways any human would envy.

Polaris didn't seem to mind the delay. She was keeping busy with the assortment of metal tools and pieces laid out on a cloth in front of her. Blythe was careful to breathe through her mouth to avoid the strong stench of antiseptic as the Nocturna cleaned the items with practiced fingers.

Even Sly found the stench bothersome. He kept rubbing beneath his nose and squirming around, repositioning his gangly limbs every few seconds as he shot dubious glances at the materials in Polaris's hands.

The Nocturna must have felt his uneasy attention. She tilted her face in his general direction and asked, "You don't like needles?"

"Nope!" He snorted. "Apparently, you do."

Polaris shrugged. "I've lived through worse."

In the giant mirror spanning the countertop, Blythe caught sight of her best friend flushing as he looked away. Blythe gave him a subtle shake of her head to stop him from floundering through an unhelpful apology. He acknowledged her advice with a quick gesture, and Blythe was sure the moment would pass them by without consequence.

She was wrong.

"I had my ears pierced before," Polaris said, unprompted and without inflection. "Long ago. Before . . . everything."

Blythe's heart gave a poignant lurch into her throat. Her feline hearing kicked in, so she could hear the stutter in Sly's breath and the eerie calm in Polaris's heartbeat. She wanted nothing more than to soothe them both, but only one of them was beyond her arm's reach.

Flinging her arms around the Nocturna's shoulders, Blythe kissed the crown of her head and rested her cheek there as she shared a sad smile with Sly.

After a mournful beat of silence, Sly asked, "Did you pierce them yourself last time too?"

Blythe expected Polaris to hedge around the question or end the conversation outright. Instead, she made a subtle chuffing noise in the back of her throat as she slipped the gloves back on. "No. My mother did it. Right here."

When Polaris raised a hand to her earlobe, Blythe considered pulling back to get a better view of the spot in question, but she was comfortable where she was. Or she *was* too comfortable to move up until the coppery scent of blood flooded her nose.

Blythe jerked back with a start, only to discover Polaris had already wiped the minimal smear away. The Nocturna slipped away to retrieve the jewelry case, then returned to her original position as she threaded a silver hoop through the new hole without fuss.

Blythe scowled and crossed her arms over her chest. "A little warning would have been nice."

"Apparently, it's no big deal," Sly snarked, but he had a pinched expression on his face as he watched Polaris reach for the hollow needle again.

"It's not," Blythe said in Polaris's defense, "but I would have appreciated a second to brace myself for fresh bloodshed."

Polaris laughed. It was short and quiet, but a laugh nonetheless.

It did little to delay the tendril of shame twisting around Blythe's throat. All jokes aside, Blythe was hyperaware of the fact that her most recent experiences with blood had all been executed by Polaris's hands.

"I didn't think this would qualify for such dramatic language, Blythe," the vampire said as she tossed a red dotted tissue into the disposal bin. Despite the teasing edge to her voice, it was quick to turn wistful and heavy. "Relax. Vampires don't bleed as freely as humans."

No known words could describe how Blythe's heart ached then. Biting her inner cheek, Blythe reinforced her resolve not to ask Polaris questions neither of them were ready to address. Polaris's real name burned in the back of her mind like a branding iron.

They must have been on the same mental wavelength, because Polaris shimmied her shoulders like she was shedding the shroud of seriousness. She glanced over her shoulder to give Blythe a strained smile. "See? It's already healed."

Blythe leaned close to inspect the piercing and took the liberty to comb Polaris's baby hairs back from the ear in question. There was no sign of injury, no blood, no swelling. If she hadn't known better, she would have thought the puncture was created years ago instead of seconds.

Sly snorted a laugh. "Fucking vampires."

Polaris beamed at him as she selected another piece of jewelry. "Mama did my first pair," she said, and if her casual speech was forced, it was still convincing and bright. "She talked me through the second set. She said I needed to know how to do it cleanly for the inevitable day when I forgot to replace my earrings and they healed shut."

Blythe watched with studious attention as Polaris executed the matching hole on the other ear. This one barely bled; Polaris didn't bother with a tissue, but dabbed the red away with a gloved finger.

"Like I said," Sly interjected, "fucking vamps."

While Blythe shot him a dark look for using the slur, Polaris held up her needle and gave him a grin. "Would you like a turn?"

"No!" He hopped off the counter and backed away with his hands up. "Don't get me wrong, I'd love to, but I'm contractually obligated to only let one vampire spill my blood under very specific circumstances."

Polaris picked up another earring as her gaze darted between the two humans. "Vauqeulin's Companion, right?"

"Yep." Blythe watched Polaris's face as she ventured to ask, "Have you ever met him?"

Polaris blanched as she became engrossed with the jewelry. "Polaris?"

The Nocturna lowered her head farther as she mumbled, "Him? I thought . . . Is Tahliah Vauqeulin not your lover?"

Blythe's stomach dropped. Feeling slightly nauseous, she turned wide expectant eyes on Sly.

The way he gnawed on his lip as he stared at Polaris didn't bode well. He noticed Blythe's attention and flushed.

"Tahliah was Kahled's mother and Heir before him." He winced as his eyes trailed back to Polaris. "I didn't realize you knew her—"

"Don't worry over it," Polaris interjected without looking up. "We met, but we weren't especially close."

Sly turned a flabbergasted expression on Blythe. She wished she didn't know him so well; there could be no mistaking the conclusions he was jumping to.

Blythe's heart sank. She went a little lightheaded with the suddenness.

Sly was smart and well connected. He wasn't listening at her keyhole the night Polaris whispered her name in Blythe's drowsy ear, but the damage was done just the same. The Vauqeulins didn't mingle with just any random Harem. As Kahled's Companion, Sly was likely to have Polaris's birth name lighting up his brain like fireworks within minutes.

It was almost comical how visible the understanding was on his face.

Blythe shook her head, begging him with her eyes not to say anything.

"What happened to her?"

Both humans clamped their mouths shut, staring at each other with chilling realization. Would Polaris—Tanya—know the former Vauqeulin Heir well enough to mourn her?

"What happened to Tahliah?" Polaris asked. "Why isn't she leading her Harem?"

"Um . . ." Blythe sent Sly a beseeching stare.

Sly gave a full-bodied shrug as if resigning himself to jumping headfirst off a cliff. "She developed Nosferatu's Curse."

Polaris dropped an earring. She made no immediate move to recover it.

Blythe wanted to scream as Sly asked, "You're familiar with the disease?"

"Yes."

Blythe reached for Polaris's shoulder, a lame warning drying up on her lips. Her fingertips halted centimeters from Polaris's skin. The damage was done.

Polaris slid to one knee in a fluid motion that almost disguised the sorrow in her body language. Her hand shook as she retrieved the earring. She reached for the antiseptic to clean it before regaining her full height.

"It's supposed to be rare, but most Harems have their stories," Polaris lied.

Nosferatu's Curse was not common knowledge, even among the Harems. The only confirmed cases in all Nocturni history occurred within nine specific families. Blythe only knew about it because of Sly.

Polaris took a deep breath, and Blythe watched her hands tremble to stillness. "In theory, it's possible for all Nocturni to develop it. Our born splicing abilities could fail any of us and turn us into monsters."

Blythe clapped a hand on the vampire's arm with more firmness than comfort. "Not everyone needs a genetic disease to feel bloodthirsty. I would know."

The room turned into a tableau then—not just the occupants, but the very air seemed to go still and expectant.

Eventually, Polaris gave a single nod and resumed cleaning the jewelry. Blythe let her touch fall aside with the dreadful sensation that her lover was worlds away instead of inches.

It was obvious the Nocturna was done talking. Blythe and Sly might have melted into the floor for all the attention she gave them. Polaris's movements were sharp and quick as she began picking through the flashy pieces in the case and punching fresh holes through her flesh. She never slowed till there were two diamond piercings in each lobe and several helix hoops climbing the outer rim of both ears.

Blythe set a few featherlight fingers on the vampire's shoulder. "Did you have this many before?"

"No." Polaris hesitated as she caught Blythe's gaze in the mirror. The hand cleaning the needle stilled. Staring into Blythe's concerned reflection, the Nocturna lowered her hands to the counter and raised her chin as if bracing herself for a formal debate. The posturing made her seem older, or at least more mature than the smooth, unlined skin of her face suggested.

Blythe frowned and removed her hand from Polaris's shoulder.

"I always wanted more than I was allowed," Polaris admitted in a monotone. Her voice was cool and disconnected, like a stone statue moved to speech. "Before Humans First, it was my Harem dictating my appearance; before Gregoire and his family, it was my own."

Nearby, Sly made a low, angry noise. Without looking, Blythe knew his shoulders were slumping as he scowled at no one. She'd seen it often enough to know.

She wasn't so familiar with the cool regard Polaris used on her as she said, "Is this still my decision, Blythe?"

Blythe might have been more comfortable with sharp icicles dragging down her back.

"Of course it is, Hun."

With a weak smile and a sickened heart, Blythe picked up the piercing needle and began disinfecting it in imitation of Polaris's technique. When she presented it to Polaris seconds later, it was accepted with a strained uptick of her lips, and Blythe knew the present hurt hadn't been intentional. It was real and unfortunate, but it wasn't a weapon, and Polaris would never use it as one.

The air in the bathroom was oppressive as Blythe wordlessly assisted the vampire. The assortment of jewelry within the case shrank as the pile of soiled tissue in the trash grew. Blythe kept her lips sealed, while her eyes spoke volumes every time Polaris stared at her between piercings.

It wasn't a happy thing, whatever it was passing between them. In the shadowy corners of her mind, Blythe knew it was necessary all the same.

Polaris hesitated with one last studded emerald caught between her thumb and finger. She bit her lip as she looked up at Blythe through her lashes.

"It's your call," Blythe said before giving her a long, chaste kiss. "You're beautiful either way."

Polaris smiled wide and unhindered, unlike any smile she'd worn before. That smile made Blythe's heartbeat stutter in her chest, and it never faded, even as Polaris leaned toward the mirror and brought the needle to the side of her nose.

For once in his life, Sly kept quiet too. Possibly, he'd excused himself, but Blythe couldn't be bothered to check.

All she knew was Polaris.

The Nocturna freed her hair from the braid and shook out the silver tresses. Between the glorious hair and the minor fortune's worth of jewelry gleaming from her ears and face, Polaris seemed more ethereal than ever. Blythe watched her admire her reflection with a subtle shift of stance and lift to her chin, and it was like watching her lover transform. She was evolving before Blythe's eyes.

Blythe realized then what the jewelry meant to Polaris. She was arming herself for battle.

CHAPTER 17

Much to Blythe's surprise, it took several more days before Ezra Lugh was available to speak with her and Polaris. What he was doing in that time was anyone's guess, since Blythe's inquiries among the staff were met with so few answers. She didn't like how much time the Guard was spending in the manor library, or that he'd been spotted deep in hushed conversations with both Madam Walters and Doctor Balint on multiple occasions. Even Sly was caught in the Guard's snares from time to time, but he was uncharacteristically tight-lipped about the topics they discussed. At least he wasn't talking to Reese, but Blythe would feel a lot better if she knew exactly what he was sniffing after.

There was no doubt that the Guard was sniffing about for something, perhaps literally.

Blythe didn't notice the splicing side effects until she got a close look at Lugh's face, but his wide nose flared as she and Polaris entered the room. He drew an audible breath, and Blythe had no doubt his sense of smell was significantly better than her own.

They were meeting in the lounge where Blythe found Sly his

first day on the premises. The carpet was just as creamy and plush, the décor as warm and inviting as ever. None of it could pull a soul's attention from the intimidating figure Ezra Lugh made.

He stood before the grand window with its celestial view with his bald head and ebony skin on full display. The hooded duster lay slung over the back of the leather couch, and the heather gray of his shirt was striking against his darkness, accentuating the grays in his goatee. His eyes were shrewd and the color of absinthe, with pupils like narrow slits.

He watched them enter the room with a polite stoicism that pulled his generous lips together in a harsh line. He could have been reining in a smile or just as easily controlling a frown. Blythe wished she knew which.

Polaris fell a half step behind her as they crossed to his side of the room, so Blythe rolled back her shoulders and took the lead. "You're looking into Humans First?"

The skin around his eyes tightened at her tone, but he showed no other reaction as he inclined his head. "Ms. Ramos." He spoke in a deep accent Blythe didn't recognize. When he focused on the Nocturna, the stern set of his jaw seemed to soften. "Ms. Polaris?"

The vampire pressed harder into Blythe's side, and her silver head bobbed against Blythe's shoulder as she returned his nod.

"Let's get this over with," Blythe said with persistent attitude. "You have questions for us?"

"I do," he said, his eyes gliding between the two females. "Are you aware we located the Humans First compound and the handful of bodies you left there?"

His gaze narrowed on Polaris's slender form, and Blythe released her grip on the Nocturna's hand to plant herself in his way. Arms crossed and hip cocked, Blythe felt the all too familiar tension creep up her jaw anew as she glowered at him. Something cold and bloodthirsty bloomed in her gut.

"You found Andy Kenwood's body?"

Lugh nodded. "What was left of him."

Blythe scoffed. "And yet, his cousin is still roaming around Tanya's Place like she owns it."

Polaris flinched. It was only then that Blythe realized the Nocturna wouldn't know about the HEPP House's current moniker.

Lugh's gaze slid to Polaris to note the reaction.

Blythe jumped forward without thought and got in his face as she hissed, "If you have half a brain in that big head of yours, you know Elitia Kenwood is part of this."

"Yes." His sharp eyes flashed back to hers. He wasn't amused, not angry either, but infuriatingly cool and collected. "I was hoping you could provide me with proof."

Blythe's nose nearly brushed the shirt buttons on his chest, but she could feel Polaris still shying away behind her. Most likely, the Nocturna didn't see the way Lugh's gaze flickered in her direction. The pointed look was all for Blythe's benefit.

Blythe's flaring temper cooled in a rush. "You're not talking to her alone."

"According to you?"

"According to *us*."

Without breaking eye contact, Blythe unwound her defensive posture and reached back for Polaris's hand. She lifted their interlocked fingers like she was brandishing a trophy. If the action pulled Polaris against her, safe and snug, so much the better.

Lugh's eyes flashed black. One blink later, his irises were green again.

Blythe peered closer at his face. He wasn't quite bald; he was covered in an ultra-fine sheet of black hairs. "What are you spliced with? Cat?"

"Several." He smiled, and she was hard-pressed to tell if it was genuine or not as he eyed the spots on her face. "You?"

She snorted. "Obviously."

Yes, she decided; it was slight, but there was honest amusement in his smile. He gave her a considerate once-over, and all but dismissed her as he peered around her at Polaris. "I would very much like to speak with you in private, Ms. Polaris."

Instead of replying with words, Polaris pressed tighter to Blythe's back and dropped her head onto the woman's shoulder.

Blythe had no way of knowing what expression was on Polaris's face, but Lugh's teeth were blinding as he grinned. "Understood."

With the ease of a consummate host at a dinner party, he stepped away and headed toward the bar stationed behind the couch. As he rounded the sitting area, he pocketed one hand and used the other to gesture for them to be seated.

"Here is what I propose," he said as he tilted a bottle to study its label, "I will tell you what I know, and you, Ms. Ramos, will tell me all you know. If our lady vampire wishes to interject, she is welcome to it, but I shall keep my hopes to a minimum."

He made a selection and hefted an unopened liquor bottle to his chest. He caught Blythe's eye as he began picking at the seal.

"If that talk goes well," he continued, and his accent seemed to thicken as his speech picked up speed, "perhaps we might share our unsubstantiated suspicions with one another, yes?"

Blythe didn't answer. Sure, it sounded more than fair, but she didn't trust for a moment that this strange Guard was content to let Polaris's silence stand.

"Blythe?" Polaris whispered in her ear. "Why don't we sit?"

"You should know," Lugh commented as he seemed to concentrate on his drink, "I have an uncommonly keen ear."

"Noted," Blythe grumbled.

She threw an arm around Polaris's waist and all but dragged her vampire to the leather loveseat adjacent to the couch and bar. They sat together, each of them stiff as stone. With an inaudible huff, Blythe rolled her head from ear to ear and tried to will her body into a semblance of calm.

Lugh raised a pair of crystal glasses in one hand toward her. "Whiskey?"

"No thanks." She frowned. "Are you supposed to be drinking on the job?"

He shrugged as he poured the deep amber liquid into a glass. "Would you consider this a formal interrogation?"

"No," Polaris chimed in. As solid as her volume was, she still managed to sound meek. Her hand settled on Blythe's thigh and tightened as if in warning.

Blythe made a mental note to remind Polaris that wordless messages were not their strong suit.

Lugh rounded the bar and sat himself in the corner of the couch farthest from them. He seemed at ease as he crossed one ankle over the other knee and balanced the glass on his raised calf, but Blythe was almost certain the motions were calculated. She could practically hear Sly calling her paranoid from across the manor, and Balint's voice was warning her about jumping to conclusions. As the Guard stretched an arm over the back of the couch like he was socializing with an old friend, Blythe told her conscience to go eat shit.

"Here is the situation," Lugh said conversationally as he studied the liquid in his glass. "I have an as of yet unidentified vampire and an unprecedented presence of human terrorists jumping to the top of my priority list. Adjacent to that, we have the disappearance of a Lunar-based Earthling after getting involved with a family that is deeply indentured to a most prestigious Harem."

He paused for a sip of his drink, and Blythe reconsidered her wariness. He wasn't reassuring; he was an asshole. She was about to stomp out of the room when he lowered the drink with a subtle smack of his lips.

"Whatever happened between the Kenwood woman and yourself does not fall within The Guard's purview," he said.

"Officially, I can direct you to the Human Services Department if you wish to press charges against her."

Something in his not-quite-smirk said he didn't expect that to satisfy her, and he was right. Blythe leaned forward in her seat. "And unofficially?"

"I could see you becoming a valuable character witness if and when I find cause to contest the Kenwood family's indenture contract."

Bold as possible, Lugh dragged his gaze over to Polaris and sipped his whiskey.

"Of course, Andrew Kenwood's body and the circumstances surrounding it are only small pieces of that puzzle. I'll need irrefutable evidence that the Kenwoods have caused and continue to cause harm to the Nocturni."

Polaris buried her face in Blythe's neck, and Blythe's insides went cold. Even her vocal cords seemed too frozen to utter the threatening growl building in her chest.

Lugh knew who Polaris was. Why didn't he come right out and say it?

In response to their joint silence, Lugh sighed and began reciting choice facts.

"The HEPP House known as Tanya's Place has barely managed to stay in business under the conservatorship of Ms. Kenwood," he rattled off smoothly. "She has a reputation for greeting Nocturni clientele with a cold shoulder, and she has quite the drunken tendency toward thinly veiled insults regarding overt splicing side effects in humans."

He paused to take a long draw from his drink. His eyes remained on Blythe's face the whole time.

Blythe fumed in silence and listened. Her hands curled into fists so tight that her nails threatened to break the skin on her palms.

Lugh lowered his glass. "Approximately two months ago, Ms. Kenwood was demoted to make room for Mr. Phink. He brought you on, proved her incompetent, and began making moves to have her removed from House management and replaced by yourself."

Blythe snorted back a startled gasp and spat, "Bullshit."

He ignored her outburst. "He submitted a formal request to Master Leopold Troy, suggesting he sell the indenture back to HEPP and place you in the position with a more traditional salary."

While Blythe gaped at him, he took another drink. Then he continued the debrief in the same casual and succinct tone he began with.

"Three days later," he said, "you mysteriously disappeared."

Blythe was breathless as she braced her elbows on her knees. "You're not stupid enough to think that's a coincidence."

"Of course not." He drained the alcohol in a final toss of the glass before reaching over the couch back to deposit it on the bar. "And it's no less coincidental that Andrew John Kenwood III is currently residing in Lunar-2's human mortuary awaiting my visit before being crushed into space dust and released into the ether."

Blythe perked up at that. She wasn't the only one.

"You haven't been to Gregoire's compound yourself?" Polaris stared at the Guard with a strange gleam in her eyes.

Lugh nodded. "An associate of mine managed to reverse engineer a flight path after Reese Walters provided us data from your escape vehicle. The Guard located the unmanned property and launched a raid, but I was off-world at the time."

Polaris inched forward to the edge of her seat. "Where?"

He held her gaze. "Kepler."

The Nocturna's spine snapped straight.

Slow and deliberate, Lugh raised his empty glass in a mockery of a toast.

"Congratulations, ladies. In one go, you managed to not only save yourselves, but you confirmed the presence of a terrorist organization that has successfully hidden on Luna for the bulk of a century. Have you any idea of the uproar this is causing among the Harems?"

A chill stole down Blythe's back, as if the very blood in her veins were running cold. Polaris's hand slid off her thigh, and the sensation flooded into her legs unhindered.

Lugh spoke to the Nocturna directly with a mildness he hadn't used with Blythe. "No matter your fears, I can guarantee your Harem will rest at nothing to track down those who hurt you."

Polaris said nothing.

"You need only give them the chance."

Blythe lurched to her feet as she grabbed Polaris's hand. "We're done here."

She didn't get far, jerking to a halt when Polaris remained seated. Blythe couldn't bring herself to look at her lover.

"Thanks to you," Lugh said, all his attention on Polaris, "we now have control of a facility we didn't know existed, a name for the presumed leader of Humans First's local chapter, and a pile of partially identifiable bodies that will lead us neatly to their constituents."

"Impressive," Polaris said without inflection.

"We also have a golden opportunity," Lugh said, honey infusing his voice. "For the better part of twenty years, I have analyzed Humans First rhetoric and charted their movements in and out of Lunar ports. They've been here longer than I've been alive, yet only now will the intergalactic Guard recognize they are no longer an Earth-bound problem. With you emerging at the heart of it all, the Nocturni will cooperate like never before."

As he spoke, Polaris seemed to shrink. She yanked her hand from Blythe's so she could hug herself, and Blythe's heartstrings snapped.

"You're not using her like that," she said.

Lugh met her eye with a sudden sharpness that made Blythe's breath catch. "That is not your choice to make."

Blythe turned her back on him and knelt in front of Polaris. She gripped the vampire's knees as she begged, "Tell him to fuck off, Hun. You owe him nothing more than a statement, if that."

But Polaris paid her no mind. Her gaze was locked on Lugh.

"You know what your well-being means to the Nocturni, don't you?" His voice grew more heated with every word. "A full-fledged Nocturna, bested and held captive by human extremists. When I first joined The Guard, such an idea would have been laughable."

Blythe squeezed Polaris's knees and shook her. "Let's just leave."

Lugh spoke over her, "Your continued existence garners a degree of interest and allocation of resources the Lunar Guard doesn't usually have at their disposal."

"Then go run a fundraiser!" Blythe sniped.

"One word from you, Polaris, and we can make one unfortunate Harem whole again. More than that, we'll be so much closer to bringing your abductors to justice."

Blythe shoved off Polaris's leg and spun to face him. She slammed her palm onto the coffee table; the wood didn't buckle, but it gave a satisfying creak that echoed the stinging pain suffusing her hand.

"Stop it," she snarled. "Can't you see her? She's been through enough."

Lugh's verdant eyes darted from Blythe to Polaris on a frenzied loop. Blythe recognized the eager glint she saw in them. It was more than a desire to finish a job or a mere hunger for justice. He looked possessed by the same furious flame that tried to burn Blythe up every time she closed her eyes and saw Gregoire's face.

Stars above, but she was tempted to follow him down that dark, steep path. All that stopped her from jumping ahead was the equally compelling image of Polaris's grief-stricken face.

"She doesn't want to go back," Blythe hissed.

There was no sympathy in his expression as he refocused on

Polaris. "What we want and what we need are not always the same thing. This is so much bigger than that."

Blythe wanted to slap him. She didn't though. He had Polaris's attention, and Blythe was desperate to know what the Nocturna would do with it.

"You pulled back a curtain on a very real threat to your entire species," he implored. "I've seen for myself how those who would abduct you could harm us all."

Polaris didn't respond. Blythe shifted to get a good look at her lover's face, but it was no use. Polaris had adopted her stony exterior. Only the rough glaze to her eyes showed she was still present.

Lugh inched forward and braced himself on the table with both ebony hands splayed. "I have been fighting them with one hand tied and no support, but you? Polaris, you could rally the Harems. Force them into action."

"You can't put that on her," Blythe muttered.

"Just look at how quickly we responded and how easily we found that compound!" Lugh said in a hushed fervor, as if he hadn't heard Blythe at all. "With cooperation from the Harems, we might run Humans First off the face of the moon completely."

No, Blythe thought with all her might. *No, don't go. Don't leave me.*

"You could stop them from spreading to the rest of the galaxy. Bar them from reaching Mars. Kepler. Anywhere else." Lugh spoke in a fervent hush, but it rang in Blythe's ears all the same. "All you have to do is go home."

This was too much for Polaris. Between one blink and the next, the vampire morphed from a stone-faced fixture to an explosion of movement. She said nothing and looked to no one as she vanished through the doorway.

The door slammed shut behind her, and Blythe was left behind.

Shaking and breathless, Blythe climbed to her feet. Staring at the closed door, she said, "You can't force her to do anything."

"I don't have to," he said from behind her. "If she turns out to be descended from The Nine, then the mere fact she exists will have a lasting impact on what the Harems do next. Up to now, the only vampires counted among The Guard are loners, but the Vauqeulin Harem has already reached out to me with a list of Harem-supported applicants."

Blythe didn't know what to say to that. She bit her lip and said nothing.

"Believe me," he said, stern and grave, "I would love nothing more than to see her sail off into the starlight without fuss. But you should know, her own kind will never let that happen. They are already on their way."

Blythe didn't stick around to hear any more. She couldn't.

SHE EXPECTED THE UPSET TO PETER OUT OR WAN, BUT IT WOULDN'T. The longer Lugh's words ate at her, the nastier she felt. The way he went after Polaris and the disregard he showed to Elitia's involvement waged war on her sensibilities. It was warping her, mutating her in ways splicing could never hope to.

For the first time, she sought Balint out on her own.

When she barged through the door, she noticed his guest room was a bluer version of her own. Fortunately for her, Balint was more than capable of taking her disruption in stride.

"Just tell me this is normal?" she begged, sick to her stomach with insurmountable fury. "Tell me this is temporary. That there's something I can do to make it go away."

She was on her knees, crouched in front of the doctor where he sat at the foot of his bed. The dark skin over her knuckles turned ashen with the tightness of her grip on his pant leg.

"Oh, Blythe." He pried her hand off him with steady fingers and held tight. "There are no hard and fast rules here. Grief never travels in a straight line, and it rarely retraces its path exactly. I wish I could give you guarantees, truly, but I can't."

He joined her on the floor and gathered her other hand as well. Blythe returned his grip tenfold; she heard his bones creak from it.

"I don't have a magical solution for you," he said, hushed and heartfelt, "but I can support you through this storm. Your rage is real and terrifying, but it won't scare me away. Polaris, Phink, and Sly—it's the same with them."

Blythe was trembling all over as she leaned in. Her forehead nearly touched his when she uttered a nasty whisper, "You don't understand. I want to kill them."

In that moment, she didn't know who she was talking about. Gregoire and Kenwood, sure. Lugh. Maybe even Leopold Troy.

Balint closed the distance, his head set against hers as he shook her hands in earnest. "This will pass. Trust me. We'll get through this."

"I wish I could go back there," she pressed on in that deadly, quiet voice she didn't recognize, "I want to find Gregoire and rip him to pieces. Maybe take a bath in Elitia-fucking-Kenwood's guts."

"I know."

"I don't think I could stop myself if I saw them again," she admitted through gritted teeth. "I don't even want to try."

What she really wanted to do was hunt Gregoire down and serve his head on a pike to Polaris and maybe frame Ezra Lugh for the murder so he would get off their backs. She couldn't find a way to translate this urge into comprehensible words though. She did the best she could, and the things that left her mouth were bad enough on their own.

Balint let her talk. He held her fast and remained close, welcoming her words and touch as she spouted all sorts of vileness and hatred. He never faltered. He let her go off without interruption or judgment.

She ran out of steam in her own time. She was shaking hard enough to hear her teeth chattering, her breath ragged and a clammy sweat trailing down her back and soaking the fine hairs at her temples. There were no tears streaming down her face, but her eyes burned with suffocating emotion all the same.

"This isn't me," she said at long last, once the anger had cooled into numbness.

He gave her a hug. She was too exhausted to reciprocate, but she gave him her weight all the same.

"This isn't me," she repeated.

"Maybe not." His calm, melodic voice washed over her like a balm. "Or maybe it is, and you're finally meeting a part of yourself you never needed to face before."

The thought made her shudder.

lythe's debilitating anger must have had a stronger impact on the good doctor than she thought. She didn't catch sight of Lugh for the rest of the week, and it didn't take long for her to learn that Balint was running interference on her behalf.

He wasn't the only one who provided a buffer between Blythe and looming reality, but that was about to change.

"You're sure about this?" Sly asked from his perch on the bottom lip of The Zephyr's gangway.

"No," Blythe admitted.

"There's still time to change your mind," he suggested. "Not much, but some."

Blythe ignored him in favor of perusing The Zephyr's front corner. Where she once left an ugly scratch was a smooth sheet of metal. It wasn't new, but it was far less dinged and burned than the rest of the ship's hull. Blythe was glad, and it took a long moment for her to recognize the small puff of relief suffusing her chest at the sight.

The hangar around them was filled with the cacophony of the merchant crew. They were hard at work, bustling about with the help of the manor staff as they restocked provisions and topped off their fuel. Phink was nearby bickering with Madam Walters in a quiet and grouchy manner. Even Reese was there, urging a bemused crewmember to take one of his books along for the journey.

Blythe didn't want to deal with any of them, but the ship's imminent departure was forcing her hand.

"You lot go ahead," Tilla said as they approached with a gaggle of star surfers. "I need to speak with Blythe."

"Here we go," Sly sang under his breath as he hopped to his feet. He positioned himself at Blythe's side like a skinny kid pretending to be a stern sentry.

"We had a plan," Tilla said as they came to a stop in front of them. "You and Phink would join us for a delivery in Lunar-2, then I cleared the schedule to make sure you got home safe and sound."

Blythe's heart sank at the depleted tone in Tilla's voice.

"If you gave that Guard your statement like you were supposed to, that would still be happening," Tilla sighed.

The downward slope of Blythe's heart leveled out in a rush. For the love of the cosmos, but she couldn't recall who had decided on that plan. She had no memory of agreeing to return to Lunar-5. She didn't remember asking Tilla and Phink to come get her either.

"Even if he let me go, I'm not sure I would," Blythe admitted.

Tilla ducked their head with a somber nod. "Polaris."

"Polaris," Blythe agreed.

In the cool cavern of the garage, Blythe fought against an unnamed pressure. It was hard to breathe, extraordinarily difficult to think, and impossible to feel the solid floor beneath her feet. She wasn't dizzy, not quite, but her equilibrium was shot. She stayed on her feet while her outward composure divorced from the emotional storm brewing inside her.

Whatever epiphany was threatening to break through her mind was delayed as Tilla almost knocked her over with a pat to her shoulder.

"I can wait another hour, if you want to go give him your statement now."

With a weak laugh, Blythe shrugged away from the captain's reach. She craned her neck to stare at The Zephyr's familiar bulk. Try as she might, she couldn't see herself slipping inside and trotting off to her bunk again like the past few months never happened.

"I think we both know your time with us has run its course," Tilla said.

Blythe's knees threatened to give out, but Sly caught her before she could waver.

"That's fine," Sly said after placing a peck on her head. "You have options. Here's a good place to lay low and plan your next move, and rumor has it, Walters would be thrilled to hire you on. Well, her version of thrilled, anyway."

Blythe chuckled, and Tilla's deep huff and Sly's smooth tenor accompanied her like a tease of a faded memory.

Nearby, metal and tools clanged, and excited voices clashed as shipmates got carried away with their duties. The crew was busy doing preflight checks and routine maintenance. It was a disconcerting, mundane backdrop to such a heavyhearted moment. Blythe closed her eyes and listened to the goings-on, as if there was a hidden meaning waiting to be deciphered from it all.

Instead of clarity, she got a powerful hand settling on her arm.

"For what it's worth, I don't think going back to that HEPP House would do you any favors, either," Tilla said. "After everything you've been through, Blythe, you deserve better. You deserve to be happy."

Blythe choked on her dying laughter. "Somehow, I don't think that's where I'm headed."

She wasn't sure when her base concept of happiness became tangled up in startling blue eyes and deceptively angelic features, but it was too late to change it now.

∽

IF SHE DIDN'T KNOW BETTER, BLYTHE MIGHT HAVE SAID LUGH found the captain intimidating. It seemed a little too coincidental that the moment The Zephyr moved beyond the horizon, The Guard reappeared for the first time since their disastrous meeting.

Blythe caught him watching her from a lounge doorway, and she sneered. She made a quick start in the opposite direction, but Phink caught her by the arm.

He jerked his furry head toward Lugh. "Let's talk to him. Together."

Blythe grimaced.

"You don't have to get into the later shit, but between the two of us, we could at least give Elitia a decent character assassination."

"Now there's an idea," Sly agreed as he sidled up to her side. The three of them effectively blocked the hall.

Blythe cringed as she reminded them, "Not his jurisdiction, guys."

Phink snorted. "If your vampire is who we think she is, it's only a matter of time before The Guard gets their hands on Elitia. You can give Lugh your statement, and Tilla can swing back around after hitting Lunar-2—"

"Let's not go there," Sly interjected. "No one says she absolutely has to go back to Lunar-5—"

"I am!" Phink blustered, "She's got an apartment to clear out, at the very least. Not to mention a lucrative job prospect—"

"She could just as easily find that here! Or on Ethos—"

"Bah! Blythe doesn't want to go to Ethos."

"How would you know—"

As the two men devolved into a mesh of noise, Blythe wiggled out from between them and took off down the hall. Neither Sly nor Phink seemed to notice, but she felt Ezra Lugh's gaze burning holes into her back right up till she turned the corner.

The lingering discomfort that chased her back to the guest wing was like a phantom of his attention. It was no surprise his name was the first thing to leave her mouth when she barged into Balint's room without knocking.

"Ezra Lugh," Blythe grumbled as she dropped onto the foot of his bed, right next to Polaris.

She didn't know the Nocturna would be with the doctor when she realized her feet were leading her in that direction. In the split second of stunned quiet that greeted her intrusion, Blythe's face went warm with embarrassment. She looked from where Polaris sat, legs crossed like a well-bred lady, to where Balint stood at the standard guest room dresser with a tea bag hanging from his fingers.

"Sorry. I should go—"

As Blythe's backside left the mattress, Polaris caught her wrist and yanked her back down.

"Tell us," the Nocturna demanded with the faintest note of desperation. "The Guard. What did he do?"

"Nothing." Blythe deflated, staring from Polaris to Balint, as if the air between them would tell her what they were talking about before she barged in. "He just bothers me."

"Ah," Balint set his tea bag in a cup and lifted a dainty ceramic pot from the same tray. "Yes, I gathered the first interview with Ezra didn't sit well with either of you."

Blythe watched him prepare his tea with narrowed eyes. "Ezra, is it?"

He ignored the probing suspicion in her tone and appeared absorbed with the tea as he asked, "I know why Polaris dislikes him. Would you like to tell me your reasons, Blythe?"

"He's a pushy jerk."

"I already told him that," Polaris provided.

"Tilla's barely taken off, and he's already enlisted Phink to rope me back into another interrogation!"

Polaris bristled as she took Blythe's hand in solidarity.

Blythe wasn't sure where to go next, not with the conversation or anything else. She leaned into Polaris's shoulder, realized how easy it would be to lose herself in the vampire's warmth, and forced herself to sit upright again.

"I don't think any of them get it," Blythe said, her words taking her by surprise as she said them. "Lugh, Phink, even Sly. They talk like this isn't something we're recovering from, like we're still in the middle of it, fighting to survive."

"In many ways, you are."

As one, both females' attentions zeroed in on the doctor.

Balint met their wide eyes with a calm quiet that seemed to demand they calm down and collect their thoughts. He stirred sweetener into his cup and gave them a moment to stare and think.

Damn him, but it did something. Blythe's eyes stung for reasons she didn't want to look at, and she felt Polaris snuffle into her curls. A gentle kiss was laid beside her ear, and Blythe twitched away from the tickle of it.

Polaris eased back as if scolded. Blythe started to reach for her on autopilot, but froze when she realized Polaris wasn't retreating. The Nocturna sat tall and squared her shoulders as she leveled a weighty look on Balint.

Polaris said, "You're right."

Blythe flinched.

"This isn't over," Polaris continued, composed and without inflection. "Gregoire's still out there."

"Don't." Blythe took her lover's wrists, and though her grip was tight enough to bruise a human, Polaris didn't react.

"I wish I could tell you this experience won't always affect you, but that wouldn't be honest," Balint said. "Certain events and people . . . they have a way of altering the course of our lives."

"Haven't we done enough?" Blythe swallowed the lump in her throat as she avoided all eye contact. "Would it be so horrible of us if we didn't help Lugh?"

Polaris pried one hand free so she could stroke it down Blythe's spine. Stars above, but Blythe wished she knew what was going through the vampire's mind. The Nocturna stayed silent and expectant without answering Blythe's questions.

Balint took his time forming a response.

"I know it may not feel this way to either of you right now," he said, "but there's always a chance you have a piece of information that could accelerate The Guard's investigation. It may be tempting to let the raw injury scab over as quickly as you can, but the freshness of the memories could mean a wealth of difference."

Neither female spoke as they considered his statement.

Blythe slid her hand onto Polaris's thigh and clutched at her like the muscle was a stress ball. Polaris let her—encouraged it even—with another glacial caress down Blythe's back.

"It could mean preventing this from happening to anyone else," Balint added, "and swifter justice for yourselves."

Justice. Blythe turned the concept over and over in her head like she was contemplating a fine wine on her tongue. She didn't know shit about wine that wasn't bottom-of-the-barrel brands served up to ignorant Earthlings back at Centrism.

Stars above, but things were so much simpler back then. Her and Sly. Her and Phink. Her and the stage. There used to be an order to the universe.

"It's not fair to ask it of you," Balint said with endless sympathy, "but I truly believe you are strong enough to rise to the challenge. That goes for both of you."

Blythe wanted to believe him, but she didn't.

Did Balint know that Blythe's concerns began and ended with the female seated beside her? Did he know Polaris's real name? Had the Nocturna confessed, or had he worked it out on his own? Did he know the scope of expectations and hurdles she might be shouldered with if they gave Lugh what he wanted?

Regardless of the answers, Blythe was certain the doctor didn't appreciate the position he was putting either of them in. Blythe couldn't assume what Polaris thought, but for herself, it came down to a choice between a sliver of peace and an uphill battle with no end in sight.

∾

THERE WAS NO ESCAPING THE INEVITABLE. BLYTHE KNEW THAT WITH the same bone-deep certainty that warned her not to leave The Zephyr or else Humans First would catch up to her—which was exactly what happened.

Blythe tossed and turned a few more nights and evaded all signs of Lugh or Phink during the daytime hours. Polaris spent that time by her side whenever she wasn't sequestered with Balint, but she didn't speak much, certainly not to assuage Blythe's worries about their tenuous future.

In the end, the practice in avoidance did no one any good.

Blythe sat up late one night waiting for Polaris to wrap up her hours-long session with Dr. Balint, and she found herself with nothing but time and her own thoughts to occupy her. All the opinions and advice of people around her coalesced into a maelstrom of pressure and expectation. Blythe spent long seconds focusing on her breath and waiting for her body or soul to break under the strain. The only reason it didn't was because she found an anchoring point in the chaos of thought.

She didn't want Humans First to do what they did to her and Polaris to anyone else. That wasn't a question worth asking. She couldn't decide if that was enough to revisit the experience.

Out loud. In detail. To a stranger.

Then again . . . maybe, just maybe, if Lugh heard Blythe's story, he wouldn't need one from Polaris.

Blythe abandoned her cold bed and started tapping on the other doors lining the guest wing. She skipped over Balint's in a hurry when her feline hearing decided to perk up at the muffled sobs leaking past the door. None of the other rooms showed signs of occupancy.

It seemed the Guard was no sleepier than herself. She found him seated on the lower level of the library, sprawling in one of the upholstered recliners with an embossed tome open and balanced on one thigh.

As Blythe entered the room, she noticed the high-backed chair she once sat in had been repositioned. It was now hiding a bloodstain. She pretended not to notice and was soon sitting across from Lugh, keeping to the edge of the cushion for fear it might lull her into a dangerous realm of relaxation.

"What a pleasant surprise." Lugh glanced up at her without raising his face from the book. "Good evening, Ms. Ramos."

Blythe nodded at him as she chewed on her tongue and reconsidered what she wanted to say to him.

The Guard closed his book with a hefty thud and set it on his armrest. He gave her his undivided attention as he crossed one ankle over the opposing knee.

Blythe found his manner irritating.

"So . . ." Blythe began with a barely contained sneer, "when I wouldn't play your game, you went after Phink instead, huh?"

Lugh hummed a short, lazy sound of amusement. "I wouldn't call it a game, but, yes, we spoke. If he's the reason you've sought me out tonight, perhaps I should send him a gift basket?"

Blythe slouched forward to brace her elbows on her knees and glowered harder. "You're not funny."

"I never claimed to be," he said as he mirrored her posture.

They stared each other down in wary silence.

Blythe took the moment to study him. He was tall and lean, with the sort of musculature that was deceptive when stretched over such a long frame. She watched the way the shadows blended with his dark fur and darker skin, and a flash of hot anger crept up her neck. Lugh was easily as heavily spliced as she was, but she had no doubt Andy and his pals wouldn't dare paint a target on his back.

Not as he was now, at any rate.

"You've been in The Guard all this time," she said, "and you've always been focused on Humans First?"

She didn't know what answer she was hoping for. Would she feel better knowing Lugh was personally invested in the steaming pile of shit she was caught up in? What if she was just another victim in a long list of people he'd spoken to in pursuit of his own demons?

Lugh's answer, when it came, was so direct that it answered her question without telling her a damn thing she really wanted to know.

"Humans First has been around centuries longer than you or I," he said with a small shrug. "They will doubtless be around long after we're dead. My life's goal is to simply make that hard for them."

"Ah. You're an optimist."

He huffed an inaudible laugh. "I like you, Ms. Ramos."

"That's nice."

"May I call you Blythe?"

"If you want."

"Very well, Blythe." He scooted forward an eager inch or two without changing his posture. "I already told you all I know about the events leading to your intersection with our mystery vampire. Would you like to add anything?"

Blythe nodded and jumped to the first thing that came to her mind. "You mentioned Andrew."

Lugh peered into her face with a growing intensity lighting up his verdant eyes. Blythe wasn't sure how she knew, but in that moment, they were both done tiptoeing around the issue at hand.

As Lugh's casual attitude dropped away, he let gravity infuse his words, "Say the word, we'll pause everything, and I'll summon your doctor."

She believed him. The burning need to chase answers was still evident in his sharp gaze, but it was tempered with a consideration and self-control that hadn't been there the last time they spoke. She wondered if Walters had spoken to him, wondered if the old woman's poise and mastery was enough to curb even the most stubborn man in his pursuits.

Perhaps Blythe was just too tired to keep her walls reinforced this round. Instead of readying for a fight, she felt like she was meeting him halfway along the road to some harrowing destination.

"It was him," Blythe began. "Andrew Kenwood. Andy."

She tried to ignore how heavy her breathing became as the words trickled out of her.

Across from her, Lugh held still, as if he feared the slightest movement or lapse in attention would make her stop talking.

"I walked out of the bar late, after everyone else was gone. He was waiting for me."

He nodded along with her, hanging on her every word. "At Tanya's Place?"

"Yes. Andy Kenwood. A couple others, and Elitia."

She didn't know why she was whispering. She'd never been a quiet person, and with Sly's influence, she'd only gotten louder with age. But in the cozy atmosphere of the library, in a prestigious vampire home, with Ezra Lugh's focus trained on her and a wealth of hopes and fears buffeting her from all sides, Blythe couldn't help it. She whispered.

No. She seethed. In the quiet and anticipatory stillness, she let the ever-present temper fly with none of the self-directed shame and internalized fear that so often brought her to tears. She told him everything, from the foggy memory of being under the influence of unknown drugs, to the wretched details of how she relieved herself while trapped in the cage. Her voice cracked when she detailed the imaginary forest built inside a prison, but she didn't succumb to the misery; she never stopped talking. She spoke of Gregoire and his hateful rhetoric, his threats and convictions that twisted in on each other and warped his view of reality. She spoke fast and harsh and kept the bubbling rage to a simmering hush.

It was far from a smooth delivery. Her tongue twisted on every other sentence, her throat closing up intermittently with reluctance as she forced the story out into the open. It went in fits and starts, but at least it went.

She finished without shedding a single tear. Her whole body was feverish and shaking, and there was more than a touch of a savage growl in her voice by the end, but she did not cry.

"You survived," Lugh said with a fierce approval etched around his mouth and eyes.

It took a small eternity for her to collect herself, and he didn't rush her. When she managed to catch her breath and sit up straight, she was surprised to find him smiling at her.

"Ezra?"

His smile melted away as he relaxed back into his chair. "Yes, Blythe?"

"I know you have to return Polaris to her Harem"—Blythe swallowed the lump in her throat—"but is there any way I'll get to keep her by my side when this is over?"

When his smile reemerged, it had a sorry tilt to it. "I do not have that kind of pull with the Nocturni. Neither do you."

Blythe closed her eyes and tried to breathe.

"Look at the people who have flocked to your side, Blythe. Do you think because she isn't human, she does not need that support as well?"

Blythe gave a soft shake of her head and dropped her face into her hands. She didn't want to see his face while he crushed her hopes.

"I promise you, the Nocturni need that interconnection even

more than we do," Lugh continued. "Polaris needs more than you alone can give her."

With a soft mewl, Blythe pressed her palms to her eye sockets till the darkness hurt in its absolution. Blinded or not, she could still hear Lugh as he left his chair and made his way toward her. She felt his presence as he knelt close and placed a consoling hand on her shoulder.

"If the two of you can't handle some necessary distance in order to heal among your own families, what future do you really have together?"

Blythe shook her head harder. "But it's not necessary."

"Her Harem will disagree." He sighed, and his hand slipped away. "They already do."

POLARIS NEVER CAME TO BED THAT NIGHT. THE BUSTLE OF THE staff conducting their morning routine irritated Blythe out of bed without a wink of sleep, and still, there was no sign of the Nocturna.

Was Polaris still holed up with Balint?

Blythe dragged herself down the hall to the doctor's room without bothering to fix her hair or change from the silken pajamas the Harem insisted she claim ownership of. When there was no answer to her knock and no hint of continued weeping, she cracked open the door to find the blue guest room vacant.

The sight made the weary lump in her throat turn cold and heavy.

The sensation persisted as she widened the search for her lover. It twisted into something sharp and alarming when she finally discovered the vampire in the garden.

Polaris sat on the ground between the artful arrays of alien foliage with her hands folded in her lap. As she stared up at the sky, the swirling cosmos left haunting shadows on the pale gown fanned out around her. The starlight reflected off her silver hair and entranced eyes like an angelic vision.

Blythe sat beside her, brushing their shoulders together as she hugged her knees. She couldn't bring herself to ask why Polaris hadn't come to bed, hadn't sought her out. She wasn't sure she wanted to know what the vampire had spoken to the doctor about all night. She especially didn't ask what Polaris was thinking about.

She had a strong enough suspicion already.

"What do you want to do?" Blythe asked.

Polaris shrugged. She sat there staring at the stars, as if Blythe wasn't waiting on her. She said nothing.

"I talked to Lugh," Blythe said.

Polaris didn't react.

The words left Blythe's mouth slow and clipped, "He said . . . that is, he implied your Harem was on their way—"

Blythe shut up as the vampire's hand darted out to grab her ankle. Polaris's grip was almost bruising, but Blythe made no move to shake her off; she didn't like how those ever-blue eyes refused to look at her, still glued to the heavens despite the sudden arm movement.

Blythe studied Polaris's rigid form, with her disconcerting stillness and her refusal to acknowledge her true name and Harem connections. For once, Blythe felt like she understood it. It was an escape, a mental reprieve from the reality closing in around her.

Blythe reached toward her feet and held Polaris's wrist tight. She didn't pull or attempt to direct the Nocturna; she simply held her, returning the unrelenting pressure like a lifeline.

"We could pack up whatever we can carry and sneak away tonight while the household's asleep," Blythe whispered as she crouched and perched her chin on Polaris's shoulder. "We could steal another ship—"

Not the same one they nearly suffocated in, she told herself, that one was already covered by Lugh and his proverbial red tape.

"There's a colony on Mars. Want to go to Mars with me?"

She left it at that. In the safety of her own mind, Blythe longed to hear an answer that preserved her selfish fantasy of a life where they didn't have to worry about anyone but each other, but she wasn't bold enough to say it outright.

Polaris said nothing and kept staring at the stars, like her mind was out there with them. Only her persistent grip on Blythe's ankle suggested otherwise.

"It has to be your decision," Blythe insisted. "I don't care if it's Humans First, The Guard, or The Nine Bloodlines as a whole, we can't let anyone else decide our future for us, okay?"

Slow and so, so sad, Polaris closed her eyes. She did it without turning away from the endless galactic view.

With a sinking heart, Blythe let go of Polaris's wrists and sat down, hugging her knees tightly to her chest, Polaris's grip still on her ankle. "Whatever you decide, just promise me we'll do it together?"

Polaris didn't turn to face her. Blythe was too anxious to check if she even opened her eyes. Eventually, the Nocturna nodded.

Blythe deflated and succumbed to a full-bodied shiver. It wasn't the enthusiastic agreement she wanted, but it was enough. It had to be enough.

LUGH DIDN'T KNOW ANYTHING, BLYTHE TOLD HERSELF FOR THE umpteenth time while pretending to eat her breakfast three days later. Beside her, Polaris picked at her own pastry, not really eating so much as disassembling the food. Blythe didn't have the heart to pressure the Nocturna into feeding herself, so they sat there like a pot and kettle, silently steeping in turbulent thoughts and the ambient chatter filling the dining room.

Polaris tired of the pretense first. With a stifled sigh, she abandoned her fork and shuffled close to peck Blythe's cheek, whispering, "I'm going for a walk. Try to eat something."

Those were the first words Blythe heard from her in the past three days. The Nocturna said them, then she was gone without waiting for a response.

Since her little heart-to-heart with Ezra Lugh, Blythe found herself incapable of shedding the feeling that she had made a grave mistake. While Polaris's unyielding silence was a big factor, it wasn't the only reason for the anxiety. Blythe spent long hours, both in Polaris's company and not, berating herself for not knocking on Balint's door the moment she heard Polaris crying.

It didn't help that the Nocturna still hadn't voiced a decision about anything. Not to Blythe.

Blythe squirmed in her chair and glared down at her plate. No one else noticed her unease, not a single one of Walters's people, and their lack of reaction only irritated her further. Polaris was gone for mere moments before Blythe shoved away from the table; the chair legs shrieked over the floor, and the room hushed as everyone watched her storm off.

Did no one realize they were running on borrowed time? Was Blythe the only one who cared?

She just didn't want to keep sitting at that noisy table, feeling like an outsider among the close-knit throng. She was no more a member of Walters's staff than she had ever been a part of Tilla's crew.

And according to Lugh and an onslaught of unnamed vamps, she didn't belong with Polaris either.

Blythe rounded a corner and collided with another hustling form.

"Shit!" they squeaked in unison.

Reeling back to regain her balance, Blythe reached up on instinct. She stopped Sly from tumbling to the floor before her conscious mind recognized him.

"Where are you rushing off to?" she demanded, holding on till he regained his balance.

He shrugged her off in the demeanor of a child caught with their hand deep in a pile of off-limits sweets. "Oh, uh . . . I was looking for you, believe it or not."

Blythe stared him down as her hands went to her hips. "I'll go with not."

His eyes darted around the empty hall, and for a split second, Blythe wondered if he was going to try to make a run for it. It wouldn't be the first time she had to chase him down for a tough conversation.

Except Sly didn't run away from whatever he was dreading. He was the same boy who made her annoy hard truths out of him on a semi-regular basis, but with new life experiences she had no hand in. Despite his shifty gaze, he squared his shoulders and faced her.

"Maybe we could take this somewhere more private?"

Blythe's insides shriveled. Her hands dropped from her hips to hang at her sides like deadweights. "Why?"

"Just trust me."

As she led him to her guest room, Blythe wasn't so sure that she did.

With the door closed and sealing them away from the rest of the manor, Sly seemed more nervous than ever. He was always a bit twitchy, but the gnawing at his lip and wringing of his hands went into overdrive.

He wouldn't quite meet her eye as he said, "I spoke to Kahled."

"Nice. How's your vampire holding up without you?"

"He wants me to come home."

Blythe sat down on the corner of the bed with a huff of sardonic laughter. "Of course he does."

Sly winced, and his wrist cracked from how hard he shook his hands. "I should rephrase; Kahled says I have to head back by the end of the week."

"I didn't realize you guys had that kind of relationship."

Sly flushed as he rolled his eyes. "We don't. If it was up to him, I could stay indefinitely, but . . ." He deflated as he trailed off. "Blythe. Hun. I may only be his Companion, but he's descended from The Nine! I belong to the Harem just as much as he does."

He joined her on the bed. They were close, pressed together from shoulder to hip, but the distance felt vast.

"Lugh's been in contact with every last Harem with a presence on Luna in the past two centuries."

Blythe sighed as a swooping sensation yanked at her gut. "You told him Polaris's name, didn't you?"

He shook his head almost violently. "I didn't need to. She's not a random loner who got caught in the wrong place at the wrong time, Blythe—"

"I'm aware," Blythe snapped as she heaved herself to her feet.

"Are you?" he pleaded. "Because what happened to her is terrifying, Blythe. And I don't mean scary on a personal level. The Nocturni are shaken. Your disappearance was bad enough, with your connections to me and the Vauqeulins by extension, but *Tanya?*"

"That's not her anymore!" Blythe sighed and rubbed at her temples, hoping to ward off the ache throbbing to life in the area. "For all we know, she doesn't want anything to do with her Harem again."

Sly cringed as he scratched his neck and avoided looking at her. "Harem Heirs don't get to fuck off to wherever they want—"

Blythe cut him off with a deadened laugh. "Right. Because the only part of this situation she actually wants is me. She's not Tanya Troy. She's Polaris. She's *my* vampire."

Sly hung his head. "Maybe in a few years, the Troys will sponsor her in a Companionship—"

Blythe's next laugh startled them both with its harshness.

Sly raised his voice over her. "—when the people responsible are in custody, and she's healthy—"

"We're not *Companions*," she spat the word like a vile insult. "You think that's what this is? That this can be reduced to a black-and-white transaction where all I am to her is a blood bag?"

Sly paled as he shot to his feet. "That's not what I'm saying—"

"You know what? Fuck you, Sly! Fuck you, and fuck The Guard, and fuck Balint—"

"Calm down—"

He tried to take her wrist, and she smacked him away. Her palm stung as he stumbled backward.

"What about me, Sly? Maybe I need her just as much as she needs me. Maybe that's the way it should be! Look at everything we've done together!"

Hot furious tears obscured her vision, but she was moving, thinking, feeling too fast to care.

"We're alive because we were together! I'd be dead three times over if it weren't for her, and if I hadn't been there, Polaris would still be in that fucking zoo or starving while she waited for Humans First reinforcements to find her. Either way, she'd still be there!"

Sly sat down again, staring at her with his shoulders slumped and a fist over his mouth. Blythe noticed him like a beast of burden notices a gnat; real and annoying, but insignificant in the grand scheme of things.

"She trusts me!" Blythe insisted, practically hissing in his face. "Has she told anyone else her real name? No!"

She was vibrating out of her skin. There was more sweat streaming down her spine then there'd been the last time she stepped off a stage, and her empty stomach sizzled with enraged acids. Her heart was sprinting at a record pace, and she envisioned herself coughing it up with the deluge of upset preparing to make a forceful exit from her body.

"They can't take her away from me," Blythe cried as she crashed to the floor in a hyperventilating heap.

Sly waited till she was too burned out to push him away, then he hugged her close and rocked her like a squalling babe. He didn't reassure her. He offered no empty promises.

For the first time in their lives, Blythe thought she hated him.

CHAPTER 19

After kicking Sly out of her room, Blythe treated herself to a long, cathartic nap. She probably shouldn't have.

"For the love of the moon!" Reese Walters's voice shrieked in her ear. "What are you doing?"

Blythe flopped over in bed with a groan, shielding her ears as she glowered at him.

The librarian wasn't actually screaming into her ear; that was just her cat DNA being helpful for a single unfortunate moment. Reese stood in the open doorway, a hovering suitcase bumping into him as he barred it from entering the room with his hands on his hips. The shiny metal of the luggage wasn't enough to distract Blythe from the vivid pink scars decorating Reese's throat.

"There's no time to be lying about!" Reese scowled as he ushered the suitcase in and shut the door. "You need to pack."

"What's going on?" Blythe fumbled out of bed as she gaped at him.

Reese shook his head, looking harassed and distracted as he began reallocating her unsolicited wardrobe from the rack to the luggage. "Honestly, why no one woke you earlier is beyond me—"

Then Madam Walters's voice drowned out his grumblings as it boomed from down the hallway, "I don't care what Sylvester says! He no longer needs the master's room, and the Troy Harem Heir is on his way here as we speak! We'll be hard-pressed as it is to have enough rooms prepared for his entourage, and I will be damned before I let a Companion displace a Harem leader!"

Blythe came to full alertness as she rounded on Reese. "What the fuck? Leopold Troy is coming here? When?"

"He'll be here for supper, from the sounds of it," he answered without breaking stride on his way to her dresser.

Meanwhile, Walters's volume seemed to increase as she marched through the guest wing, yelling, "Stars and moons, no one's going to care about the cleanliness of our baseboards! Focus on the rooms! I would rather not risk our Harem's reputation if we can help it!"

Blythe was nearly trampled when she stuck her head out the door as a line of servants rushed by with mounds of linens overflowing from their arms. She dumped herself against the wall and tried to keep from shaking. The final man in the line stumbled to a halt in front of her with his jaw dropped.

"Ms. Ramos!" he squeaked, caught between an indignant demand and a concerned plea. "Why aren't you dressed?"

"Keep moving," Reese ordered the man as he took her by the shoulders and led her back into the room. "My sincerest apologies, Ms. Ramos, but it seems lines of communication have gotten a bit tangled in all the commotion—"

"Where's Polaris?"

Reese urged her onto the corner of the unmade bed with a hand on each shoulder. His harried expression went taught with sympathy as he opened his mouth to speak.

"Why am I packing?" Blythe cut in with a devastated warble to her voice. Stars above, but it sounded like she was speaking through a gag. Or maybe there was cotton crammed in her ears.

Reese bit his lip as he gave her arm an awkward rub. "Oh, well, the thing is . . . we're tight on space—"

"I doubt that," Blythe wheezed, fighting against the constriction in her throat and chest.

"I don't have the details, but once he confirmed Polaris's identity, he simply had to inform her Harem—"

Blythe launched off the bed. "Where is she?"

Reese tried to set her back on the bed, but she wheeled around him. He latched on to her wrist to keep her from bolting out the door.

"Stars above!" Blythe cried. "Lugh, that bastard! Did he even warn her before he went and told—"

"Lugh wasn't the one who made the call!"

Blythe froze. She stared at Reese, demanding answers without words.

He winced, but he answered without hesitation, "It was your friend. Sly."

"No, it wasn't."

"He's Master Kahled's Companion," Reese implored. "He was honor bound to notify our Harem the moment he became certain we harbored another Heir—"

"Bullshit."

"Ms. Ramos, wait!"

But Blythe couldn't—*wouldn't*—wait. She was out of his grasp and flying down the hall in a mess of rumbled clothing and wild limbs. She didn't know where she was going, but she gave into the insurmountable urge to run all the same.

Why oh why hadn't she pressed the Nocturna harder for an answer sooner? Now there was a host of vampires heading straight for them, and Blythe couldn't shake Lugh's warnings from her mind. Did Polaris know her kin had already been alerted? Barely anyone had bothered asking Blythe about what she wanted out of the mess, but had anyone ever considered asking Polaris?

Had Blythe? When it really came down to it, had she ever given Polaris the same freedom of choice she wished she could have?

The realization almost made Blythe trip mid-sprint.

She recovered her footing and paused to do the same with her breath. Feeling small and ill, Blythe wobbled her way through the manor to the garden, but Polaris wasn't there.

The Nocturna was nowhere, in fact. Blythe rechecked the guest wing, only to find nothing but staffers hurrying about. She checked the kitchens and the dining room, but Polaris wasn't there either. She wasn't in the library or any of the first three lounges Blythe thought to look in.

Blythe told herself there was no way Polaris would hide from her, that Polaris would never let Blythe leave without a proper goodbye. In the end though, she came to the frigid realization that she hadn't known Polaris for that long or, really, that well.

She had no idea how the Nocturna would respond to the imminent reunion with her Harem.

Too late, Blythe considered the likelihood that Polaris had sought out Doctor Balint again. Blythe carved a sluggish path back toward the guest rooms when her spliced ears decided to make themselves useful for once. She heard the commotion outside the scion's office from several rooms away.

Oh, Blythe thought, feeling like a first-rate idiot. The scion's office.

When she arrived on the scene, the office door stood solid in its frame, despite the two men attempting to break it down.

"What's going on?" Blythe demanded as she pushed Lugh back from the door. In the next breath, she was ready to pry Dr. Balint's fingers from the handle, but the smaller man had the mind to take a step back on his own.

"Polaris. She's upset, but she won't talk to me." The doctor was out of sorts, his hair mussed and shirt collar uncharacteristically crumpled. Blythe didn't like the deep frown lines carved into his forehead and under-eyes as he stared from her to the door. "She threw me out. She . . . she actually picked me up and threw me out . . ."

Before Blythe could process that information, Lugh grabbed her by the shoulders and spun her toward the office.

"Talk some sense into her," he hissed in her ear.

Blythe shook him off and planted herself with her back against the door. "Back off, all right! She hasn't said a word to me in days! What makes you think she'll talk to me now?"

Lugh glowered at her like he thought she was being intentionally difficult.

"You're the most trusted person she has," Balint interjected. "If she won't talk to you, she won't talk to anyone."

Blythe flushed and crossed her arms across her chest like a shield. "What does she have to talk about?"

She met their eyes one at a time. The Guard glared back at her before throwing up his hands and proceeding to stomp his way down the hall, but the doctor lingered with a distinct pinch around his kind eyes.

"I was only trying to prepare her," Balint murmured.

Blythe laughed in his face, and he flinched. "What did you tell her? That Sly sold her out before she could even try sorting things out for herself?"

His face turned scarlet. "It's not like that. If she's going to have any chance of reclaiming her life, she needs to go home and be with her family."

"Did you bother asking how she feels about reconnecting with her Harem? What if she doesn't want to reclaim anything?" Blythe snapped. "Maybe all that healing you keep pushing isn't possible, and there's no going back for either of us!"

Balint's face fell as he stroked his beard. The shadows under his eyes seemed to darken as he looked at her.

"Why can't you let her be?" Blythe croaked. "Why is that so

wrong? Of everyone in the known universe, doesn't she deserve to choose where she goes from here?"

"Blythe," Balint said, soft and heavy, "I know how deeply you sympathize with her, I do, but you have to remember, Polaris isn't human. She's Nocturni."

"As if that matters!" she hissed under her breath, seething as she collapsed against the door.

"It does."

"Bullshit. She's no more animal than I am—"

"That's not the point, Blythe." She fell silent when he took her face in his gentle hands. "The average Nocturni lifespan is 5.6 centuries. Do you know what that number falls to for loner vampires?"

Blythe shook her head. Her jaw hurt, it was clenched so tight.

"Three."

She flinched away from him.

"You must know how long ago she went missing," Balint said without following. "Without the support of her Harem, she could be on the last stretch of her life."

Blythe turned her back to him, her face in her hands as she fought back tears.

"Even if Polaris weren't so mired in trauma, as a loner, there's a good chance you would outlive her."

"Stop," Blythe whispered as she began to shake.

"But let's say that doesn't happen . . ." Balint continued, his words rushed and fervent. "Let's say you don't live a long and healthy life but succumb to any of the millions of accidents that befall humans in this galaxy every day. Do you really want your legacy to be her following you into an early grave?"

"No." Her clenched fists shook.

"Is that what either of you deserve?"

"We deserve each other!"

"Yes, Blythe."

He came up behind her then. She felt the warmth of his hand before he touched her, but it was an insufficient warning; when he gripped the nape of her neck with utmost care, the contact still made her jump.

"If I could snap my fingers and magically resolve this whole mess, I would." Balint's voice remained quiet, but the unprecedented edge of ferocity to it smoothed over something raw and ugly in Blythe's heart. "I can't work miracles, Blythe, but I will do everything in my power to encourage her Harem elders to sponsor a Companionship. It might not be this week, or this year, but I'll try—"

"Enough."

Blythe twisted out from under Balint's touch to stare at the open office door.

Polaris stood there, her soft curves drowning in pink fabrics that matched the sore skin around her eyes. She trembled as she blocked the doorway, and part of the near-indestructible frame creaked under her fingertips as she studied Blythe, her irises such a pale blue, they almost shone white.

Balint gasped aloud. "Polaris? Your eyes—"

"Enough," she repeated while her gaze remained locked on Blythe's face. "No more fairy tales and empty promises, Lyall. Tell us honestly, after leaving this place, what are our chances of ever seeing each other again?"

With utmost reluctance, Balint muttered a soft, "I don't know."

"Then you have nothing to offer us right now."

Without breaking their gazes, Polaris stepped aside and gestured for Blythe to enter the office with a regal tilt of her head.

Blythe didn't hesitate. She rushed past the Nocturna before she pulled the door shut on the rest of the universe. When Polaris flipped the lock without uttering a single word, it startled a relieved sob from Blythe's throat.

The mattress from Polaris's unfortunate period in lockdown

remained stationed along the wall, its far edge crushed against the lower shelves of a bookcase. It seemed the staff either hadn't noticed or disregarded Polaris's unceremonious return to Blythe's guest room, because the bed was neatly dressed in fresh sheets. A tea tray sat on the corner of the desk, the unused cup overturned on its saucer and the pot full of steaming liquid.

It was a pretty cup, painted with intricate flowers and vines. Blythe imagined Balint offering it to Polaris like a paltry offering as he told her the future had already been decided by so many faceless people. In a spike of irritation, Blythe flicked her nail on the cup's side, and the shriek of the rim against the saucer was booming in the stillness of the office. Blythe's ears were no more attuned than any other human's at that moment, but the noise was still startling.

Then Polaris was there, lifting the tea tray away in a graceful sweep like a trained housekeeper. She set it down on a distant shelf with a sharp clatter, as if it offended her on its own, without Blythe's help.

"Did they tell you?" Polaris said in a stony voice.

"I've been told nothing," Blythe admitted with a nasty snort.

"The Hare—" Polaris choked and restarted. "My Harem is refusing to cooperate with The Guard for now. Not until they ascertain my condition for themselves."

Blythe croaked a cold bitter laugh. "Is that how your Harem talks? Like you're an asset and not a person?"

Polaris issued a short, sad laugh of her own. "It doesn't matter."

"It does." Blythe crossed the room to cup that perfect face in her palms. "It matters to me."

The Nocturna's eyes welled with tears as she smiled. She nuzzled into Blythe's hand and said, "Lugh promised me he'd get you home safely."

"I don't want to leave you," Blythe whimpered back.

Polaris slid forward and into her arms in the next moment. The fine points of her claws pricked the sides of Blythe's neck as the Nocturna held her in place for a deep, soulful kiss.

"Then don't," Polaris whispered against her lips. "Don't leave. Stay with me. Come home with me. I can't face them without you."

Blythe hushed her with an open-mouthed kiss. It did nothing more than delay the oncoming dread, but it was a delay they were equally desperate for. The one kiss turned into two, then many, many more, and Blythe's concern for the outside world was banished to the shadows as she tore the fine dress from her vampire's back.

There were no more words worth speaking. There was nothing but skin and emotion and this burning, aching need begging to be met.

Blythe gasped as her blouse was removed in ribbons, only the faintest streak of pain crossing her back as Polaris shredded the garment. It wasn't unpleasant, but distracting as Blythe arched her back and craned to catch sight of any raising welts. She never got a good look at the superficial damage, though.

In a display of superhuman strength, Polaris gripped Blythe by the thighs and lifted her off the floor. Her ass hit the desk, and before Blythe could appreciate the texture of the smooth mahogany against her skin, Polaris was lavishing attention on her breasts. Blythe's nipples pebbled, and her breath hitched. She sank back onto the desk with her eyes closed and let her vampire have free rein.

Polaris was always eager for contact, bordering on touch starved even after weeks of constant exchanges—both innocent and lustful. She was never so aggressive though, never so forceful in the way she clung to Blythe's hips and buried her face in Blythe's chest. Each and every jaguar spot decorating Blythe's shoulders was licked and nipped, worshiped as the vampire's hand slipped between her legs and zeroed in on Blythe's clit. The first touch was a zap of electricity to her core, and Polaris wasted no time in urging that spark into a lasting burn.

Polaris wouldn't slip lower, never delve deep, until her hand and Blythe's thighs were drenched. When she finally did, Blythe tossed her head back to find her skull hanging over the far side of the desktop. There was no point in trying to lift it again; all her remaining strength was funneling into her lower body, to where her legs held fast around Polaris's waist and low in her abdomen where the external pleasure sank deeper and deeper.

Blythe went breathless and nonsensical, overwhelmed by the onslaught of Polaris's unbridled adoration. There were bruises blossoming on her ass from where Polaris held her too tightly, and more than once, Blythe expected to feel the sharp pinch of fangs sinking into her breast or throat. It hurt in the most delightful of ways, from the unforgiving wood beneath her, to the relentless movement of the powerful body above her.

When she came, it was explosive. It left Blythe weak and sweaty, splayed out across a piece of furniture worth more than the blood in her veins.

As she lay there useless, Polaris backed off with that effortless grace. Blythe shimmied back to the edge of the desk so it could support her head, and she saw the way the vampire was watching her. Standing tall and shamelessly nude, Polaris surveyed her spent body with a greedy gaze that was white-hot in the office lighting.

No. Wait. That wasn't quite right.

Polaris uttered a low, animalistic purr as she leaned down to grip Blythe under each knee. In one sharp tug, Blythe was brought to the edge of the desk. Polaris dropped to her knees, and there was more than raw intent gleaming in her eyes.

Blythe gaped at her vampire as she rose on one elbow. "Polaris? Your eyes . . . they're glowing— Ah!"

Her meager warning fell on deaf ears as Polaris lapped over her folds. Blythe was still thrumming from the first orgasm, and the renewed attention short-circuited her brain. Coherent thought became next to impossible.

Before Blythe could reach a second peak, Polaris stood up between her legs and planted one foot on the desk by Blythe's hip.

"Mine," Polaris growled as she pressed their groins together. "Always mine."

Blythe groaned and grabbed a handful of that silver hair to yank her lover down for a kiss. The rolling motion of Polaris's hips never faltered. Blythe licked into the vampire's mouth and felt an unexpected fang scrape her tongue.

"Mine," Blythe rumbled back as they ground together with increasing speed.

"Yes!"

When the bite finally came, the pain went unnoticed beneath a rising tide of pleasure and visceral joy. Blythe arched into it, offering herself as if there weren't already fangs clamping down on the curve just above her nipple.

"Yours!" Polaris whimpered as she found release. She collapsed on top of Blythe's trembling form a moment later, licking the blood from her lips as she whispered, "Always yours."

There was a suspended moment in time where they lay there, recovering. As the sweat and slick dried on their skin, Blythe closed her eyes and imagined they were somewhere else—anywhere else. There didn't have to be a bed or top-tier air filtration and atmosphere controls; they could be in another facsimile forest, for all she cared. The place of her fantasies didn't matter a bit, so long as it harbored her vampire.

But fantasy had no influence on reality.

They lay together on the desk till Blythe's feet started to go numb. Her grip tightened around Polaris's back, and she ignored the tingle of discomfort.

"Is this why you wouldn't give them your name?" Blythe asked, voice thick with tears. "You knew the moment your Harem discovered you were alive, it would mean the end of us."

Polaris hardened in her arms.

"You should have told me at the beginning."

"I know," Polaris whispered. "I'm sorry, Blythe."

It took all the strength Blythe had to raise her head, but she did it so she could kiss the top of Polaris's fair head. Then, she unwound her arms, and the vampire crawled off the desk, off of her, and Blythe found herself naked and alone on the hard wood surface. Blythe hugged her knees to her chest and watched Polaris collapse onto the nearby cot.

"What happens now?" Blythe asked.

Polaris's lower lip trembled. "I'll go home. Either to Lunar-1 or our estate on Kepler."

"Kepler." A hot flash of anger stole Blythe's strength, and she swayed. "With the colorful garden?"

Polaris turned away, a hand over her mouth. She didn't face Blythe again before resuming.

"I don't know when, but someday, they'll want me back at the head of our Harem." Her voice was somber, almost lifeless, and Blythe couldn't look at her while she spoke like that. "I was born for the sole purpose of leading my Harem in my father's footsteps. That won't change just because I made a single reckless decision in my youth that happened to detour my life for a couple centuries."

Blythe swallowed a lump of revolting anger and heartache. "I was wrong then. This was never your decision at all."

A stifled croak came from Polaris's direction, but Blythe didn't look over to see what it might mean.

"What about me?" Blythe asked. Without waiting for an answer, she continued, "If you asked me to, I would be your Companion."

"Companionship requires Harem affiliation and approval," Polaris said, prompt and deadpan. "That won't happen until I've been proven stable and reinstated as Heir."

Blythe huffed. "You've thought about it, then?"

"Frequently."

In the following silence, Blythe's shoulders drooped. Her breath came a little heavier.

"I stopped hoping long before you were ever born."

Blythe closed her eyes and shook her head. "Don't tell me that."

"You have no idea how badly I needed to believe you were my future," Polaris continued in that soft, terrible voice. "Finding you and coming here, it's been like a fever dream. Too good to be true."

Blythe squeezed her lids shut, but the tears escaped anyhow. "Why didn't you answer me about Mars? Why didn't we leave while we still could?"

"I don't know." Polaris sniffled. Her breath hitched. "I'm so sorry, Blythe. I was so scared, I still am—"

"Yeah?" Blythe laughed as she hopped off the desk and began gathering her ruined clothing. "And what? You think I'm *not* scared?"

Polaris paled and made an aborted motion to reach for her. "Of course, I know you are—"

"No, you don't!" Blythe cried, clutching her clothes to her chest as she rounded on Polaris. "I don't have a Harem jumping to have my back, Tanya!"

Polaris blanched.

"I don't have a family or some grand life waiting for me," Blythe continued as she yanked on her clothes. With every word, her voice got louder and her movements sharper. "But for one fucking minute, I deluded myself into thinking I at least had you!"

Blythe braced her hands on the bed, caging the vampire between them. Even then, Polaris didn't meet her eyes.

"And the whole time," Blythe accused, "you knew we were never going to last."

Polaris shook her head, and her tears speckled the jaguar spots on Blythe's arm like a bullseye.

"What am I supposed to do now, Polaris? Go back to work for Phink or Tilla until some magical day when you can convince your Harem to let you run your own life again?"

Blythe stood up straight and waited for Polaris to collect herself. She watched her lover's face smooth out till she once again personified an untouchable deity carved from precious marble. Her inaudible weeping was the only sign Polaris consisted of living flesh.

Blythe gulped back air and made her final statement on the matter, "You said it yourself; you have *centuries* to make up for. Who's to say I'll even be alive by then?"

"I'm sorry," Polaris whispered. "I love you, Blythe."

Blythe nodded as her face crumbled with misery. "I love you too."

BEFORE BLYTHE KNEW WHAT WAS HAPPENING, THE GUARD'S PORT-issued star cruiser was prepped and ready to launch. Phink met her in the reception hall not ten feet from the entrance to the hangar bay.

"Ready?" he asked with forced cheer as he hitched his travel bag higher on his shoulder.

Blythe didn't give him an answer. From the bags under her eyes to the slump of her posture, it was obvious she wasn't ready for anything.

"Where's your stuff?"

Blythe gave him a deadpan look. "I didn't bring anything with me. Remember?"

He winced and cast about for something else to say. His eyes stopped on something over her shoulder, and his expression shuddered into relative blankness.

He cleared his throat. "I'll just go get my stuff settled with Lugh's gear, then, huh?"

Blythe frowned after him, and the expression only deepened when she realized why he rushed off.

"You're really going to leave without a goodbye hug?" Sly teased.

Blythe tensed. She spun around, and he seemed to shrink a few inches under the force of her glare.

"You blabbed to Kahled and ended my relationship without warning," she scowled, "but you still expect a hug?"

Sly's eyes widened with confusion. "It's not like that, Blythe. I was trying to help—"

"Well, you didn't."

He reached for her, shaking his head. "You don't understand. I didn't tell the Harem, per se, but I had to tell Kahled—"

"No, you didn't!"

"Yes, I—"

"You did not!" Blythe screamed as her temperature spiked.

He gaped at her as her voice echoed through the empty reception hall. He let the noise fade, and the air in the room grew heavy with her anger. It was more than an uncomfortable silence; it was hateful.

Then it was shattered.

"She's Cursed, Blythe."

Blythe's lungs stopped working.

"I thought you knew," Sly continued in that sad, simpering voice. "I thought that was why you were so against talking to The Guard—"

"No," Blythe said. "Polaris isn't Cursed. She's nothing like Kahled."

"Her violent streak and glowing eyes say otherwise," Sly said.

"But . . . But . . ." Blythe floundered, staring about the room like it was hiding a glimmer of hope. "She has control over her splicing abilities—"

"Blythe?"

Blythe felt numb and off-kilter as she whirled around to find Dr. Balint standing mere feet behind her. The depleted set of his shoulders and drooping bags under his eyes made her whine.

"Tell me it's not true?"

"I'm not an expert when it comes to Nosferatu's Curse, Blythe," he said without his usual reassurance, "but I can corroborate Sly's suspicions to a point. She may not be manifesting many involuntary phenotypes yet, but her control is slipping. Did she tell you she's been trying to alter her hair for years, with no success?"

Blythe tried to take a full breath as she shook her head, but it was painful and shuddery.

"And your account of the escape is much more detailed than hers, despite the severity of her actions," Balint continued. "She blacked out."

Blythe's voice quivered. "And Reese?"

"Probably another episode," Sly interjected, wringing his hands. "Stars above, I wish I was wrong, but . . . I'm so sorry." He reached out for her like he wanted to give her a hug.

Balint held up a hand to stop Sly in his tracks. "Blythe? Look at me, please."

Blythe did. She had never distrusted his kind gaze more, not even the first time they met.

"She's early stages," he said. "With the right treatment, the side effects can be mitigated for a good long while. With her Harem's support, she could live decades longer without hurting anyone else."

Blythe couldn't keep listening to his mild tone and hollow words. All she could think of were Polaris's eyes—blinding, but not the faintest traces of blue left in their white-hot light. She tried to count the times she played it off as a trick of the light or a neat reflection of the stars. There was nothing normal about the ethereal cast of her lover's gaze as they made love for the last time, though.

Stars above, but how could she be so naïve?

"No," Blythe whimpered as she stared down at the black-and-gold markings on her arms. "If she's Cursed, then she . . ." She turned to Sly with wide beseeching eyes. "She'll need the purest blood she can find. Someone like you."

Blythe didn't have the pure human blood that might combat Nosferatu's Curse. Polaris didn't have the health benefits of a solid connection to her Harem. They had none of the advantages that Sly and Kahled had; quite the opposite, in fact.

In the end, Lugh was right. What future did they really have together?

CHAPTER 20

The flight back to Lunar-5 was uneventful and quicker than Blythe wanted to think about. It took a matter of days, not the weeks it would have taken on board The Zephyr. Blythe spent most of the journey peeking out of every window she could, hoping—and also dreading—that she would spot an abandoned compound built into the rocky landscape, but she never did.

Then they were on the ground. They were home.

"I have a friend in the Human Services Department," Lugh said as he joined them on the station floor a stone's throw from his aircraft. He gestured for Blythe's wrist, and the moment she raised it, he began tapping at her comms. "His name is Murray. Giving him my name won't do you much, but he's a good investigator, and he has experience with the strictly human side of the Humans First problem."

Blythe scoffed at his underwhelming phrasing as she tried to pull her wrist free. His grip tightened, and his fingers flew across the interface as he input a string of code into her contacts.

"This is my personal comms. Just in case," he said with a wink.

"I'll be preoccupied with the Troys for a while, but if you remember anything I should know about Tanya's confinement—"

"I thought the Harem wasn't letting you near her?" Blythe snarked.

He shrugged. "For the moment. I think I'll make myself available around Lunar-1, just in case."

And that was that. Lugh helped Phink unload his bag and the suitcase Reese filled with Blythe's new and unwanted wardrobe, then he strode off into the crowd with a careless wave above his head.

Phink brought her the rest of the way home, right up to her building, then to her floor. He left her there while he hustled back to the superintendent's office to recover a copy of her key card, then he practically carried her through the door.

The apartment was just as she left it, complete with cheap carpeting and a pile of laundry that made her gag if she got too close. The layer of dust on her counters was new, at least.

Phink dropped her in the tiny lounge room and took it upon himself to unpack the various items Walters and her people forced on Blythe. At some point, he set a plate of food in her lap and signed her name to the waiting list for the baths. When she trudged back through the door in damp skin and yesterday's clothes, with her hair covered in a hasty wrap, he bullied her into putting on some clean clothes.

He offered her a fitted top and sweatpants from her bedroom. Blythe's stomach rolled at the sight. Without explanation, she ghosted past him and changed into the first thing she saw that wouldn't remind her of the scent memory of ammonia. She ended up in one of Walters's pajama sets; it felt silky and wrong on her skin.

Phink tucked her into bed, and Blythe was too exhausted to comment on the uncharacteristic tenderness.

"I was thinking," he said as he perched himself on the bed by her shoulder, "I could stay the night. I'll hang out on your sofa and help myself to one of those fruity spirits you keep under your kitchen sink. Huh?"

"Sure."

He sighed and stayed put.

Blythe closed her eyes and rolled over to bury her face in a pillow. She expected dreamland to claim her in record timing, but it didn't happen.

Phink never moved from her side.

"I don't know if you remember," Phink muttered under his breath, "but we've done this before. You and I."

Blythe opened her eyes to study the patchwork of plastered wall inches from her face. She kept quiet, wondering what to make of this new subdued tone of his.

"I'm not talking about that time Sly's old man kicked you out on your ass either," he said with a touch of disgust speeding up the words.

Blythe held her breath. She almost wished he'd stop talking and go grab himself that drink.

He sniffled and cleared his throat. "You were thirteen the first time we met; you were this scrawny kid with more energy than sense, and HEPP all but dropped you at my feet when all I was trying to do was whip a failing House into shape. If I wanted kids, I would have made them the old-fashioned way, but HEPP didn't care. You didn't care."

He trailed off into a muted chuckle.

Blythe sighed and grumbled into her pillow, "I wasn't yours. HEPP left me at my parents' place and paid you to make sure I didn't starve. There's a difference."

The bed shook with Phink's galvanized chortles, hushed as they were, and Blythe felt the corner of her mouth lift without permission.

"Yeah," Phink let out a nostalgic breath and patted her hip. "The port had no room for you in the orphanage, and HEPP figured you were old and adept enough to be on your own, for the most part. I don't think you agreed with that, though."

Blythe gave him a dry snort of humor.

"I never wanted kids," Phink repeated, "but there you were. I had a show to run at the House, but the moment I opened that door and found you curled up in your folks' filthy bed, I said to hell with it."

Blythe rolled over again so she could loop her arms around his waist. Well, she tried to. He was too thick around the middle for her fingers to meet.

His hand settled on her shoulder. The fur coating his palm was thin enough to tickle rather than scratch.

"I did right by you," he said with an air of bravado. "I got you up and moving, taught you what you needed to know. I did right."

"Yeah," she whispered. "You did."

"I'll get you through this too."

Blythe nodded. She didn't speak. If she did, she was bound to ruin the moment and drag him down to her level, and Phink didn't deserve that. She wouldn't do that to the one soul in the universe who hadn't abandoned her.

PHINK LET HER WALLOW FOR AS LONG AS HE COULD. HE LEFT periodically to do what he could for Tanya's Place and to maintain his personal matters, but he always came back. Blythe wasn't sure why she kept expecting him to stop.

When he finally forced her out of bed and back to work, it was done with obnoxious amounts of whining from both sides.

"Go on," Phink huffed, nudging her forward with his shoulder.

Blythe nudged him back with her elbow. "Give me a minute."

"You've had ten already."

Blythe threw her head back with a groan and reached for the door to Human Services.

Phink followed her inside, and together, they headed for the reception desk tucked in the corner beneath a modest sign announcing HEPP's presence in the building. Someone had taken the time to handwrite "The Human Existence and Preservation Project is here to help!" on the sign, but the space behind the counter was void of any activity or life.

They were halfway to the desk when Blythe stopped in her tracks. Phink's belly bumped her forward a half step before he caught on.

"Oh, right," he said, correcting his course toward the rear of the building.

With a minor sneer on her face, Blythe fell into step beside him, and they went for the manned desk that spanned the greater length of the room. There was no handwritten signage, but the words "Human Law Enforcement" were carved into the front face of the counter in giant professionally blocked letters.

The woman stationed there was heavily spliced with a patchwork of fur on her hands and cheek. She turned an expectant face to them as they approached.

Blythe set her elbows on the counter and her chin on her fist as she forced a smile. "What does a girl have to do to press charges against a former boss?"

The agent reached for something beneath her desk, saying, "Workforce disputes are—"

Phink cut her off with a sharp clearing of his throat. He gave Blythe a bracing pat on the back.

"Oops," Blythe said, her grin starting to hurt. "I meant to say, how do I press *criminal* charges against my former boss?"

BLYTHE WAS NOT A FAN OF PAPERWORK. BY THE END OF THE WEEK, her wrists ached, and she was going cross-eyed from staring at too many screens. When Phink burst into her apartment one day with a pair of carry-out mugs steaming away in his paws, she shoved the very official and heavy digital pad aside with a relieved wail.

"I have good news and great news," Phink said as he joined her at the kitchenette counter.

Blythe's apartment only had space for a single stool, so Phink dropped a drink in front of her and dragged her oversized armchair around to sink into. She had to lean over the counter to see more than the tuft of wayward fur on the top of his head.

Blythe scooped up the mystery drink and sniffed. "Thanks for the . . . tea?"

It was hard to tell, considering she never drank the stuff before visiting the Vauqeulin Harem's Lunar base. Her nose itched with a bit of feline sensitivity, but all it told her was that the cup contained plenty of cream, sugar, and something dark and musky. It smelled ten times better than anything Walters ever served.

Phink gestured for her to drink. "That old hag said it's good for you."

Blythe snorted before taking a sip. It tasted as good as it smelled. "I don't think this is the same as the stuff Walters serves, but okay." She took another drink and waved him on. "Talk. What news?"

"Human Services agents finally made it around to Tanya's Place today."

"Nice," Blythe deadpanned. "Is the great news that they arrested Kenwood?"

The peach skin visible around Phink's eyes tightened. "Not quite. They talked to her for a good long while though, and she didn't look so good when they left. That Murray guy promised me he wasn't done with her."

He said nothing while Blythe stood up straight to drain her cup and proceeded to crush it into the counter beneath her fist.

"She hasn't asked about you," Phink said after a contemplative moment. "It's been two weeks since we got back, and she needed a badge shaking in her face to let the rest of us know she remembered your name."

"I don't care," Blythe said, swiping the ruined cup to the floor. "We can talk about Elitia-fucking-Kenwood again once she's locked up. What's the great news?"

Phink wiggled into a more upright position in the armchair and gulped from his cup before telling her.

"I heard from Sly."

"That's nice. I haven't."

He rolled his eyes but didn't bother repeating his dearly held belief that Sly was trying to give her some much-needed space.

"We got this harebrained idea in our heads," he said with feigned nonchalance. "He's worried about you."

"No shit."

"I'm worried about you."

She smirked at him as she resumed leaning on the counter. "Old news."

He heard her—she could see it in the way he refused to smile—but he pretended he hadn't. "Like Sly promised, Kahled Vauqeulin has been talking to Master Troy."

Blythe pushed off the counter with a scoff.

"Kahled is head of his Harem in all but name," Phink continued, "and whatever authority he lacks, he makes up for with his intimate knowledge of Nosferatu's Curse."

Blythe nodded, glaring downward as she finished flattening the carry-out mug under her heel. "That's super great news, Phink, but it has nothing to do with me."

"Why's it always all-or-nothing with you two?" Phink

demanded. "You and Sly, you operate like the world's imploding every time you're asked to practice a little patience."

Blythe barked a mean laugh. "Seriously? That's your take on this situation?"

Phink raised his drink like he was preparing a toast instead of spouting nonsense. "I'm just saying: everyone's got to compromise sometime. You, me, Sly . . . even vamps."

"Phink," she admonished.

He gave a contrite nod and corrected himself. "Vampires, then. My point is, the groundwork's been laid for you to sign up to work for Polaris's Harem. Just because it won't be in a Companion capacity doesn't mean you won't get to be near her."

Blythe stomped on the carry-out mug, but it was too squashed to provide any satisfaction.

"What are you going to do instead, Blythe? You can deplete the savings Sly left you on rent and food, but eventually, you're going to need another job. You won't work for me for obvious and valid reasons, either."

Blythe turned her back to him and occupied herself by kicking the destroyed take-away cup back and forth.

"Look," Phink said, "sooner or later, the Troys are going to overstay their welcome with Walters, and when that happens, the news that Tanya's alive is bound to get out. You and I both know they'll be keeping the Curse quiet for as long as they can, though."

Blythe hummed noncommittally when he paused for her to comment.

He sighed. "The Harem is going to need new staff to accommodate her. Staff they can thoroughly vet and guarantee are trustworthy."

"Good luck to them."

"All you need to do is reach out to Master Troy, and you could be on your way to Lunar-1 tomorrow. I'll still be here to keep an eye on Elitia, while you set up a homecoming party for your vampire. Think about it."

Blythe thought about it, all right. She thought about the bandage on Sly's throat after his Cursed lover nearly killed him in the bed they shared. She thought about the way Polaris clung to her the last time they made love, the unexpected ferocity of it all and the disquieting glow to those baby-blue eyes. She thought about Tanya's Place and the memorial that may or may not exist there, how she was afraid to ask Phink about it, how she was petrified to ask how the Harem intended to deal with the first ever occurrence of Nosferatu's Curse to emerge within their esteemed bloodline.

Questions she took such care to avoid creeped along the edges of her mind. Would the Troys follow the Vauqeulin's lead and risk keeping their Cursed Heir alive? Would they adopt the historical precedent for cutting their losses before too much harm could be done, or would they jump aboard the modern train of radical hope that the Curse's growing frequency was a blessing in disguise, the next step in Nocturni evolution? And then what? Was Sly really a good enough example to convince Leopold Troy that Companionship was the safest route to maintaining his cousin's sanity?

And ultimately, what good would any of that do Blythe, when her spliced blood couldn't provide a cure?

It was a vicious cyclone of concerns. Blythe didn't have the stomach to deal with it long.

She spent more and more time daydreaming. They were stupid, wishful dreams leading to nothing but dangerous hopes and dead ends. More than once, they got the best of her, and she'd wake up to find herself eyeballs-deep in piles of information she had no business digging into.

Lunar-1 was the first of the moon's sustainable colonies, and the human population there was limited entirely to Harem employees and transient associates. Fifteen well-to-do Harems called the port home and routinely funneled their resources back into its accommodations, and that included no less than three of the original Bloodlines. HEPP's presence in the port was virtually nonexistent, with zero interest or need for a House or recruitment stations. Employment opportunities in housekeeping and administration were easy enough to find, provided a person had their foot in the door with a residing Harem. She wasted hours looking for job opportunities in the realm of entertainment.

Somehow, she doubted cleaning toilets and scrubbing floors would put her in much direct contact with any elite vampires, Cursed or otherwise.

Her hopes were only further dampened when she looked into the Troy property on Kepler. The dwarf planet was one of several Nocturni-run experiments in recreating Earth-like atmospheres. There were no statistics about the planet's human population, and it took her too long to confirm the reason why.

There were no humans on Kepler. Tanya's parents lived there now that their nephew was leading the Harem from Luna, but no humans did.

Blythe stopped snooping on the Troy Harem after that.

～

"Murray and his partner came by again," Phink said one day after forcing her out of bed and practically spoon-feeding her a bowl of oatmeal.

"Hmm," Blythe mumbled around her mouthful.

"Elitia's still out and about," he continued, "but this time, she was throwing a fit as they left. She seemed mighty unhappy."

"Hmm."

"Half my staff was hanging around the bar, hoping to see her throw something at Murray's back. If she had, maybe she'd finally be in cuffs."

The sound of Blythe's teeth scraping on the spoon with her next bite was sharp and purposeful, but she gave no other acknowledgment.

Phink sighed. "We're filling seats easier, now that word's getting around about what happened to you. Vampires, humans, they all come in hoping to see you on that stage, and the cheap drinks keep them there for an hour or two after they realize why we're not charging extra for a minor celebrity showing."

"There's an idea," Blythe said as she stabbed at the oatmeal and mushed it against the sides of the bowl. "I'm surprised you're not capitalizing on the opportunity. It won't last long."

Phink flinched despite her lack of censure. Blythe had to replay her words a few times to figure out why.

"Shit." She sighed, throwing her cooling meal to the side. "I'm sorry, Phink. I didn't mean anything by it."

At least, she didn't think she did. It was Phink's idea to market her as pure-blooded when she first started working for him, and she was young enough not to question him about letting Humans First sympathizers become regular clients. She didn't have jaguar spots back then, and her spliced senses were easy enough to disguise; there was no harm in taking their money, or so they thought.

Blythe studied the wretched expression on Phink's face and felt something cold and pitiful wrap around her heart.

"This isn't your fault," she said.

He nodded, but he didn't look very convinced.

A MONTH AFTER CRAWLING INTO HER OWN BED AGAIN, BLYTHE woke up to a near constant buzz from the comms on her bedside table. She got one look at the holographic display through sleep-blurred eyes before she threw the device across the room and put herself back to bed.

Tanya Troy's discovery was officially public knowledge. Intergalactic news. A freaking media sensation.

Blythe wanted no part in it. Her stomach soured, and her gorge rose at the idea of the public's reactions.

Would there be celebrations for the former Heir's recovery? What an insult that would be to the horrors she survived. How would society at large react to whatever details were released? Blythe didn't know which would be worse for Polaris: the desperate victim blaming or the inconsiderate idol worship. What if Lugh was right, and Polaris was being inundated by galvanized vampires and threats from human bigots, all while Blythe curled up in her bed and slept through the chaos?

There was no good way to look at it, so Blythe didn't look.

Someone knocked on her door. They kept knocking, and she kept ignoring them.

On the far side of the bedroom, on the floor where it landed in a cracked hunk of metal, her comms wheezed to life. Blythe left it there and pulled a pillow over her head.

The knocking eventually ceased. The comms fell silent a while after that.

Blythe told her gurgling stomach to shut up and went back to sleep.

In the end, her bladder won the fight. Blythe clawed her way out of the blankets and stumbled to the toilet, and when she finished relieving herself, she felt almost human. Her mouth was coated in fuzz, and her right boob was scarred with creases from the sheets. Her sense of smell spiked with hyperawareness to alert her to her body odor, then went immediately and pointedly dormant, like her very DNA was trying to spell out some very poignant messages.

Blythe rolled her eyes at herself and trudged back toward bed. She tripped over something cold and hard, and she cursed.

It was her comms. It blinked up at her from the floor like a discarded friend, trying to make her feel guilty. She considered stepping over it and face-planting in the mattress, but the moment she thought about it, her nose twitched, and she noticed the stench on the sheets.

With a sigh, Blythe bent to retrieve the comms. It was cold as it settled on her wrist, but the sensation was only half as startling as the message glowing from her display.

It was from Phink. It read: Where the fuck are you? Charges against Elitia were dropped. Lack of evidence.

Blythe stared down at the communication without comprehending. She read it twice over, then again. And again. She was still trying to make sense of it when the comms chimed with another incoming transmission.

She didn't recognize the number, but she was too numb, too confused, and she answered the call on autopilot. She didn't have the capacity to react when the comms projected the least likely face before her.

Master Leopold Troy gave her a strained attempt at a polite smile. "At last, Ms. Ramos."

"H-hello?" Blythe shook herself and tacked on the honorific title, "Master Troy. What can I do for you?"

"I haven't yet thanked you for your part in recovering my cousin," he said, words crisp and polite. "As a show of personal gratitude, I wanted to make you an offer."

Above the busted comms unit, his likeness flickered. While the image reassembled, Blythe could see Phink's message through it.

She felt nothing. Not relief. Not anger. Not hope. Nothing. She said in a monotonous murmur, "You're offering me Companionship, then?"

His carefully bland expression slipped. For a split second, his eyes and mouth made a series of perfect o's before he managed to stow his surprise.

Master Troy scoffed. "Ms. Ramos, me and mine are eternally grateful for all you've done, but it would be in poor taste for me to accept you as my—"

"What? No!" The implication rocked Blythe back on her heels and into reality. "I don't want you. I want Polaris! If you're not looking to sponsor a Companionship between us, I can't imagine why you're contacting me."

"Ms. Ramos . . ." The skin around Master Troy's eyes and lips looked pinched as he said her name with utmost gravity. "I don't know how aware you are of Tanya's present condition, but even if she were well enough for such an agreement, our Harem does not make Companions from just any Earthling we happen to take a shine to. There's a very strict and lengthy vetting process—"

"Then what could you possibly have to offer me?" Blythe spat, cutting him off.

He made no attempt to disguise his affront as he sneered at her. "I beg your pardon?"

"You have nothing else I want," she said.

His chest puffed out as he gaped at her. "I am the head of my Harem, I assure you, I have—"

"Nothing. Else."

He nearly bared his fangs at her as his lips parted for a reply, but Blythe never heard whatever he had to say.

The projection twitched out of existence for a heartbeat, then he was back with utter confusion whipping the disdain from his face.

"Master Troy?"

"One moment, Ms. Ramos," he said, gaze darting to the side as he frowned. "There seems to be a disturbance—"

His words cut off. She could still see him, but his image warbled as if he were on the move.

"Master Troy?" she repeated as he disappeared from view.

For a long moment, the transmission picked up no visuals, only background noise. Blythe could hear footsteps and the shuffling of fabric as someone hustled across a floor, but that was all. She thought she heard a dull thud at one point, but it was too faint and easy to write off.

She still didn't have a visual when she heard Leopold Troy gasp.

"Master Troy?" Blythe gripped her arm as if she could reach through the comms to pull him back to the conversation.

"Stars above," he whispered, still beyond sight.

Then the transmission was ended.

Blythe was left standing in the middle of her unkempt bedroom, holding her arm and staring down at Phink's message. Her mind and heart raced, each organ fit to combust in its own right. She didn't know what to think about Elitia Kenwood or Leopold Troy. She didn't know what to think about anything.

It was less a thought than a feeling; it sat heavy and dark in her gut. Anxiety? No. Dread? Whatever interrupted Master Troy just seemed too coincidental, so soon after the universe learned Tanya was alive.

Blythe tried to ignore the sickening sensations telling her something was wrong. She bribed the bath attendant to let her skip the waitlist, then busied herself for a bit drying and styling her curls, but the scent of products mixed with her nerves made her feel nauseous. She set about cleaning her room in fits of motion, only to keep stopping to do some conscious breathing. She made food she couldn't eat; everything smelled and tasted noxious, and when she did swallow something down, it tended to lurch right back up in short order. She retreated back into the cool enclosure of her bedroom to change the linens, but she barely managed to strip the bed before the sorry attempt at distraction was brought to an abrupt end.

Her comms blew up with emergency alerts. Her hands shook hard enough to blur the bold red words projecting in front of her, but Blythe still found a way to read it.

ATTENTION: Troy Harem Heirs Abducted for the Second Time

CHAPTER 21

"Where is she?" Blythe demanded as she shoved the front door to Tanya's Place open.

The throng of employees crowding the bar leaped to attention as she stomped their way. It was hours too early for the lounge to be open to the public, but the evening's barkeepers and servers were already done with most preparations, and a good number of performers were out on the floor in various stages of dress.

For the love of the cosmos, but was everybody who worked for the House creeping around the bar for a pregame drink?

Blythe shelved such questions for another time and raised her voice, "Elitia-fucking-Kenwood. Where is she?"

Instead of answering, the staff swept themselves out of her way to give her a clear shot at Phink. He was seated at the bar with his back to the room, his form hunched over. He was the only one not staring at Blythe like she was a descending demon about to wreak havoc.

"Phink!" Blythe snapped, grabbing his shoulder.

His weight threatened to topple off the stool as she twirled him around to face her. As limp as the rest of him was, at least his arm was steady as it brandished a glowing comms between them.

Blythe recoiled.

Tanya Troy stared back at her from the hologram over Phink's wrist. It was the same snapshot from Leopold's locket depicting a round-faced brunette adorned by her Harem's gems. As Blythe stared, the image began to morph: the coiffed hair was released from its clips, and its color drained as it grew long and unkempt; the face grew leaner, making the pointed features that much sharper; the smiling mouth thinned into a blank expression, and the skin around the eyes tightened and creased with wariness.

It was a startling transformation, and it stole the air from Blythe's lungs.

She knew what the rolling ribbon of text beneath the image would say long before she forced herself to look at it. Polaris's face shrank into the corner as Leopold Troy's overtook the center frame, and Blythe's heart spasmed as she read the caption again.

Latest in Troy Tragedies: Lunar-1 Seeks Emergency Aid in Wake of Unprecedented Attack as Harem Sequesters on Kepler.

Blythe's sense of reality went a little funny at that point. It was like the world around her was muted, her ears ringing with some undefinable sound that left no room for anything else. Her eyes were open but tracking nothing. She was aware of being upright, on her feet, but she felt disconnected from it, as if her mind were drifting away from her physical being.

Then a door opened, and the whine of the hinges flung her back into her body with the effectiveness of a sonic cannon firing next to her ear.

Elitia Kenwood stood in the doorway leading to the back rooms.

Blythe went for her on autopilot. No one intervened. No one dared. Or maybe they did, and Blythe just didn't notice.

Either way, nothing got between Blythe's fist and Elitia-fucking-Kenwood's face.

The bigger woman went flailing back through the doorway, and Blythe's ears started working again. The crash of Elitia hitting the floor was almost drowned out by the commotion of bystanders screaming. There were gasps and cheers and alarmed cries, but Blythe ignored them in favor of the frantic wailing of the woman crawling away from her.

"I should beat all that makeup off your fucking face," Blythe snarled.

Was this what Polaris and Kahled felt under Nosferatu's sway? This unrelenting bloodlust? This indomitable rage?

Blythe didn't know—she didn't want to know—but she didn't let that stop her.

Her foot came down on Elitia's ankle with a satisfying crunch, and she heard the exact moment when Elitia's shout changed from pain to fury. She was ready when the sharp point of a high heel came flying at her head, and she was glad for the spliced reflexes that kept it from blinding her. Blythe ducked under the projectile, and she nearly reached Elitia's throat with her nails before the other woman shoved her back.

For the first time, Blythe thought the spots on her skin weren't enough; she longed for a jaguar's claws.

For all her animalistic rage, it got her nowhere. Blythe launched herself at Elitia without thought toward their substantial height difference, or the fact that Elitia was fully clothed in her precious silver suit while Blythe's flimsy sleepwear left her so exposed. Blythe never considered how Elitia's familiarity with the bar might tilt things one way or another.

In her need to do something—anything—to alleviate the apprehension rotting away inside her, Blythe was blindsided by a plastic mop. Elitia never made it off the floor, but she managed to kick the cleaning supply station with enough force to send the pole crashing onto Blythe's head. The mop broke, and as Blythe yowled with a hand to her skull, Elitia made a bid for escape.

The big woman was stopped at the open door. Blythe could make out Phink's fuzzy form filling the frame beyond Elitia's bulk.

The sharp end of the broken mop whistled through the air as Elitia brandished her makeshift weapon at him. "Move it!" she shouted.

"Calm down, Elitia," Phink said in a soft, trembling voice Blythe didn't recognize.

"Calm down?" Elitia mocked, volume soaring as she jabbed at him. "You let this little whore loose on me like the feral animal she is, but you want *me* to calm the fuck down?"

"Just set the stick down—"

Elitia gave a wordless snarl and pulled back her arm for a mighty thrust, and suddenly, Blythe's head didn't hurt. She was up and moving, faster than she'd ever moved across a stage. Her fingers clamped around something long and solid, then she rammed into Elitia's back.

Someone turned up the volume on the world. People were shrieking, and Phink was sobbing her name, and the universe was spinning into hyperdrive.

The two women tumbled into the main lounge and smashed a table to splinters beneath their combined weight.

"Stars above!" a performer squealed, racing for the exit.

"What did you do?!" cried another.

"She stabbed her!"

"Oh my stars, someone call The Guard!"

"Not The Guard, you idiot. Call Human Services—"

Blythe yanked herself free of the table's remains. The business half of the mop was in her hand, the dried-out bristles hanging loose below the point where she held it in a white-knuckled grip. The pole broke off inches above her fist, creating a clean, wicked point.

"Fuck me," Blythe whispered as her stomach dropped at the sight of blood. What had she done—?

"Blythe?" Phink hissed her name as he crept up behind her.

"How the fuck did you manage to miss? Not that I'm complaining, but really?"

Blythe tuned him out as her brain caught up with the adrenaline coursing through her. There was blood, yes, but not much. None of it was on the pointed tip of the broken handle. A sliver of material from the table was sticking out of Blythe's forearm. It was a superficial hurt, and Blythe found it easy to ignore in favor of the relatively clean mop.

Elitia clambered to her feet with more huffing and puffing than Tanya's Place had likely seen in years. Her blonde hair stuck up in all directions, and she clutched her side as if she were nursing a grievous wound. There was a scratch on her cheek surrounded by purples and blues in the shape of Blythe's knuckles, and some bruising on one ankle where the fancy suit didn't cover her properly. Otherwise, there was nothing obviously wrong with her.

Blythe's fury was drowned by a wave of bewildered disappointment.

Elitia glared at Blythe with the force of Earth's sun. "You nasty little—"

Blythe stabbed her with the mop again.

"Ow!" Elitia wailed, seething as she swatted the mop away.

Blythe felt nothing but confusion as she prodded at Elitia's thigh with the sharp plastic tip to no real effect. She did it again, then again, but much harder. With each jab, Elitia's shrieks got louder and more inflammatory, keeping up with Blythe's souring mood.

"Okay, that's enough," Phink said as he wrestled her for the mop.

Blythe only fought for a moment before she let him stumble back with the broken thing clutched to his chest. She ignored him as she shoved an accusing finger in Elitia's face.

"You're sick!" Blythe sneered. "You and your fucking family!"

Elitia puffed up her chest, face going red. "How dare you!"

"You know who else has clothes like this?" Blythe snared the lapel of Elitia's magnificent jacket and nearly uprooted the woman as she tugged her forward. "The wackjob who kept me in a cage for a month!"

Blythe shoved her, and Elitia caught herself on a nearby table as the bar erupted with shocked conclusions and heated whisperings.

"Okay," Phink said as he puttered around behind Blythe and addressed the onlooking staff, "I think we've all had enough drama for one day, huh? We should stay closed tonight anyway, out of respect for the Troy Harem—"

"Yeah!" Blythe snapped at Elitia. "Speak of the vampire, what do you think Master Troy will think about you wearing your grandpa's clothes in front of him, knowing they were made out of his missing cousin's hair?!"

There were no murmurs or gasps in reaction to this outburst. The room collectively held its breath as Elitia seemed to inflate, appearing taller than ever as her face turned an interesting shade of puce. Her jowls shook as she sputtered at Blythe.

"You got what you deserved," Elitia hissed. "You and that vamp. It's no wonder you get along with their kind so well; you're just as much a rabid animal as they are!"

This time, when Blythe swung at Elitia's face with deliberate force, Phink never intervened. No one screamed in dismay or called for any authorities. This time, when Blythe's heartbeat finally stopped pounding against her ear drums, and she allowed the rage to ebb, there was more than a little blood dotting the floor.

Blythe's fist was bruised and aching. Her toe hurt from one kick too many against Elitia's armored middle. The blonde was a mess as she lay in a pitiful moaning heap on the lounge floor, hands holding her broken face together. Blotches of crimson soaked into the front of the perfectly intact suit.

In the far reaches of her mind, Blythe noticed how quiet the room had gone. More distantly still, she could hear Phink ushering people out the front door with hushed assurances that Agent Murray was already on his way. She was aware of the growing void surrounding herself and Elitia as the witnesses cleared out, but she was in no state to appreciate it.

There was no one and nothing around to stop her as she wound her fingers in that blonde hair and gave it a yank.

"You're going to tell me how to find your Humans First friends," Blythe said, "and if I don't find my vampire alive and well, you can bet your ass I'll be back to finish you off."

Phink was waiting for her outside. He was perched on the front steps staring at the bottom of the giant illuminated letters proclaiming the House as Tanya's Place. He didn't react as she crouched down next to him.

As she sat beside him, Blythe felt a chill steal over her body. The feverish anger that had sustained her for the past hour or more was fading fast, and in the stillness of the aftermath, she wasn't sure what to think. She was far less sure about what Phink thought.

Throat tight, Blythe left him to his silence while she tried wiping Elitia's blood off her hand with her shirt. The sleep shirt was a pale lavender, almost white in the port's street lighting. She ended up dropping the cloth with a resigned sigh and hiding the offending hand between her knees.

"I'm sorry," she said lamely. "I shouldn't have done that."

Phink heaved a breath that was too powerful to qualify as a sigh. "No. You shouldn't have."

"I can't undo it."

"True."

"I doubt I would if I could anyway."

He said nothing.

"I don't know what happens now," Blythe admitted, and her voice began to thicken with emotion. "I have to do something. I can't sit here and wait for The Guard to figure it out. They've already had centuries to try, and I can't leave her to . . . I just can't, Phink."

Phink nodded without looking at her.

Blythe folded forward to press her forehead to her thighs, hiding her face. Her hair was still loose, and a few curls bounced into her view with a wet, red smack to her nose. It didn't feel like the shield it once was when she used to hide from Gregoire's stares.

The minutes dragged, and eventually, she felt a furred palm land on her back.

"I lied to my staff," he said. "I haven't called Murray yet."

Blythe bit her lip and went frigid under his tender touch.

"She told you where to go?" Phink asked.

Blythe nodded. "Gregoire has another property in Lunar-1. The bastards were there this whole time laughing it up right under the Harem's nose."

Phink shuddered. The hand on her back delivered a gentle thump before sliding down her spine and disappearing.

"How do you plan to get there?"

Blythe groaned and shoved the hair out of her face. "I guess I'll reach out to Tilla—"

"The Zephyr's long gone," Phink interjected without emotion. "Besides, I reckon they've done us enough favors for a while."

Blythe's stomach dropped. She cleared her throat and scratched at the drying blood on the back of her hand. "Don't suppose you know how much a charter costs?"

"At short notice?" He huffed a sorry little laugh. "More than you can afford."

"Ah."

Phink made a gruff noise as he shifted his weight. Blythe nudged him with her shoulder and tried to think of the least cringeworthy way to ask for his advice. Before she could get a word out, he was clambering to his feet and digging into his jacket's inner breast pocket.

"Before I give you this," he said, "you promise me you won't get yourself killed, yeah? That's the only thing that would make me regret this."

Blythe frowned at him. "What?"

Phink pulled a shiny black card from his pocket and turned it over in his fingers as he avoided her eye. "HEPP issued this to me the last time I was put in charge of a Lunar House. I doubt they realize I still have it."

He offered her the card, and Blythe took it after a moment's hesitation. There were no words, no images, but an intricate spiral of code was engraved on one side.

"It's a boarding pass," Phink said, pouting at the item in question. "One of the perks of being senior management. It won't get you off the moon, but it should get you to Lunar-1 all right."

Blythe jumped up and flung her arms around his shoulders.

"Don't you start." Phink bristled and patted her shoulders as he pried her off. "Even if HEPP doesn't look too closely at what happened tonight, giving that to you will probably get me fired, and I'll have to forfeit my retirement plan."

"Oh! Phink—"

He stopped her from giving back the pass with a vicious shake of his head. "You and I aren't the brightest stars in the sky, Blythe, but our hearts are usually in the right place. This is the best I can do, and after you rescue your vampire, you better make it up to me. Fair?"

Grinning through her tears, Blythe said, "Fair."

He accepted one last hug, and if he held her back just a little too tightly, neither of them commented on it. The embrace lasted far longer than it needed to, and when he finally let her go, Blythe wasn't sure what to make of the smile on his face.

Of all the goodbyes they'd shared, this was the only one that felt so bittersweet. It felt . . . final.

CHAPTER 22

*A*t first glance, Lunar-1 was much the same as Lunar-5. The commuter station was a bit cleaner, the metal walls of the building a little taller, and there was a noticeable shift in balance between species demographics, but for the most part, Blythe was underwhelmed. She half expected to see The Zephyr parked ahead of her every time she turned a corner.

Then she exited the station and got a good look at the moon's longest standing port city.

The place gleamed like a polished gem. It wasn't a matter of neatness either; yes, the roads were clear of debris and uncongested with too many bodies vying for personal space, but every walkway and structure was meticulously maintained, to the point that Blythe imagined the whole city was reconstructed from scratch every decade. Unlike Lunar-5, the domes that shielded the city from the moon's natural atmosphere were so far reaching and detailed that they blended into the sky and seemed to fade out of existence.

Blythe drew a deep breath of sterling oxygen, and her Earthling tongue translated the taste to something sweet and incomparable. It would take time to get used to it, though, and time was one of several fleeting resources. Blythe shook herself and ducked into the nearest shadowy corner between buildings. The vampires casually strutting by could still see her, and many shot her curious glances, but the illusion of privacy was enough for her to raise her comms to eye level.

Ezra Lugh didn't answer her signal. That was just as well, considering how astute Nocturni ears were, regardless of diet. She probably should have thought of that sooner.

"I am in way over my head," Blythe muttered to herself.

Clearing her throat and fighting down a useless blush, she typed out a message to The Guard instead. It was direct and brief, and frankly more than her nerves were ready to provide. She input her name and a single address courtesy of Elitia Kenwood and sent it off before she could doubt the wisdom of handing law enforcement written evidence of her involvement in whatever shit was about to go down.

She had neither the time nor the interest to dwell on it.

Hours after landing, Blythe had to begrudgingly admit Gregoire might have had a point about vampires owning the moon. Lunar-1 was undisputed vampire territory. She stuck out in too many ways; she was at minimum a head shorter than the smallest Nocturni, and the asymmetry to her jaguar spots was an oddity that earned her several stares. More than once, someone paused her on the street to ask what she was doing wandering around without an escort from her Harem, as if humanity carried an infantile connotation. No one attempted to harm her, though one Nocturna did ask if she could bite into Blythe's neck. Despite the general politeness, Blythe became embarrassingly aware of her vulnerability.

The tension turning her back and shoulders into carved stone didn't let up when she finally came across other humans. Their presence only made her stomach churn faster, though. It could only mean one thing: she was getting close to Humans First.

If the port itself belonged to the Nocturni, this street belonged to Gregoire.

By the time she caught sight of the bar from Elitia's descriptions, Blythe had assimilated into Lunar-1's meager human population without much effort on her part. She walked down the street under the disinterested gazes of overtly spliced individuals, and no one seemed to care that her face was unfamiliar, or her steps were a touch too quick compared to everyone else. The baggiest of the jumpsuits from her time on The Zephyr was of no particular interest to anyone, though she did get an appreciative side comment from a few passersby for the cornrows holding her hair out of the way. Her solitude wasn't uncommon either; the humans in this city seemed disinclined to travel in pairs or groups. She was simply one among the few isolated hundreds.

Blythe stepped in front of The Lighthouse and wondered if she was the only one who thought the bar looked an awful lot like Tanya's Place. It wasn't an exact likeness. Blythe couldn't quite say what element reminded her of the HEPP House, but it felt like a mockery.

Then again, maybe she was projecting.

At any rate, it was cleverly disguised. Despite its outdated fashion, the building was as crisp, clean, and well-kept as the rest of the port, and there were no blunt signs or vernacular that might suggest the vampire majority were unwelcomed. The windows were darkened over, with the exception of a detailed artwork spanning the largest center frame. It was an old-fashioned pinup girl straddling an Earthly rocket.

Blythe recognized the character. Teeth clenched in distaste, she reached for the front door.

It was dark and barren inside. Laminate tables and benches

filled the space, and the bar was equally bland and unassuming. There were two men seated in a corner booth nursing their drinks and playing with an abused deck of cards; Blythe didn't need the years of splicing to smell the alcohol and worse substances seeping from their pores from the doorway.

The only other occupant was the barkeeper. Blythe made a direct line for the diminutive and plump woman behind the counter. She had narrow, single-lidded eyes, and her ebony hair sported random streaks of discoloration that might have been intentional if the texture weren't so coarse. Blythe wondered if the woman despised her hair the way Andy despised his armadillo skin.

Blythe noticed the men in the corner shooting her hopeful glances and promptly threw herself onto the bar in front of the worker.

"Hi." She grinned, deliberately careless with her volume. "What's a pretty thing like you doing in a place like this?"

Behind her, she heard one of the men scoff as the other chuckled. They refocused on their game in due course.

The barkeeper turned a bored expression on Blythe as she retrieved a glass from beneath the counter. "I'm uninterested, and they're harmless. What would you like?"

Blythe shifted her ass along the edge of a barstool and hesitated. When the mild interest in the bartender's expression waned further, Blythe leaned forward and hazarded an opening, "A friend of mine said I might be able to find someone here. A special acquaintance, if you know what I mean."

The bartender responded with a lazy blink.

Blythe bit her lower lip to hold back her cringe as she said, "I'm looking for Gregoire?"

Another long, slow blink was all the reaction she got.

"Elitia Kenwood sent me," Blythe said as panic began tingling up her spine. "From Lunar-5. The HEPP House there. You know Elitia, right?"

"Nope."

"I know Elitia."

Blythe's desperate smile froze in place as one of the men slid onto the barstool beside her. He leaned an ostrich-skinned forearm on the counter with the familiarity of a frequent patron. Blythe glanced toward him, but she couldn't bother to take note of his features or clothing. She had the sudden and petrifying thought that she wouldn't be able to function if she recognized him from anywhere.

"Another beer for me, darling," the man said with a tap to the countertop. As the barkeeper bustled off, he called after her, "and one for my new friend here."

"I can buy my own drinks," Blythe said.

"'Course you can," he said as he lifted the tail end of a braid from her neck and rolled it between his fingers.

Blythe shoved away from the bar with a protective hand over the braid in question. She hoped he couldn't see her shaking as she glared at him.

The man leaned away with his hands raised in innocence. "Just welcoming you to the port. I know a newcomer when I see one, and you did say you were looking for someone—"

"Gregoire," Blythe spat, all patience burned out. "I'm looking for him, not you."

"Maybe I know him—"

"No, you don't."

"I do!"

"You do not," the bartender announced as she dropped a full glass on the bar between them. She slid it toward the man and gestured for Blythe to step away with her. "Come on. It's almost time for my break anyway."

Blythe didn't need further encouragement to get moving. With a final glare at the unhelpful man, Blythe stormed down the length of the bar. Despite the lumpiness of her chosen jumpsuit, she could still feel his gaze burning holes into her backside.

She put his gawking out of her mind and followed the bartender through an unmarked door into a back room. Falling into step behind her, Blythe passed through a maze of stacked barrels and cartons of inventory, passed an overflowing trash bin, a crowded bulletin board, and a hastily stowed folders of receipts. It was an irritatingly normal back room to an ordinary bar, and Blythe's anxiety started to quiet under an inkling of doubt.

She followed the shorter woman down a skinny hallway with cold cement for walls and floor, and her worries came back with a vengeance.

A door awaited them at the end of the hall. The busty caricature from the front window was painstakingly rendered across the full surface, winking at them with a saucy little smirk on her cartoon face. But this one was different from the one on the front window. She held a long stick with ruby-red droplets falling from its pointed end in the fist resting against her cocked hip. Dangling from the dark hair wrapped around the fingers of her other hand was an emaciated head with a gaping mouth full of fangs.

It was a small miracle Blythe didn't trip over her own feet when she realized what she was staring at. Said miracle didn't extend all the way to her mouth.

"They could have wrote 'Humans First' on the door in neon lights, and it might have been less obvious."

The bartender made a vague noise of amusement and stopped walking. Blythe walked straight into her and got a face full of rough hair that was decidedly not humanoid. Blythe spat the stuff out of her mouth as she backpedaled.

"I don't know what you're doing here," the barkeep said, without inflection or turning around, "I don't know how you know Gregoire, and I don't care to know, but I do know that everyone who waltzes through that door runs the risk of never coming back out."

Blythe shifted her weight from foot to foot as she waited for the other woman to turn around or speak further. She did neither.

Blythe swallowed the saliva flooding her mouth and gave the woman's arm a gentle poke. "Any suggestions on how I can improve my chances?"

The barkeep quirked her head to the side in silent thought. Maybe it was the way the woman moved, or the dim lighting or the coldness emanating from the cement, or the illustrated murderess winking at them from the door; regardless of the reason, Blythe was overwhelmed by sudden appreciation. There didn't seem to be many females hanging around Gregoire's properties—human or otherwise.

The hairs on Blythe's arm stood on end. She reached for the woman's shoulder. "Hey. Are you okay?"

The smaller woman slipped away to crack the door open. "I'm fine," she said as she began walking back the way they came. She never once looked at Blythe as she retreated.

Blythe listened to her footsteps fade as she stared at the slim space between the painted door and the cement wall. It wasn't wide enough to tell her anything about the space beyond, just that it was dimly lit and decorated in darker colors than the hall.

With her eyes locked on target, Blythe called over her shoulder, "What about those suggestions?"

No one answered her.

Blythe blew out a breath and squared her shoulders. She gripped the door's edge.

"Stop broadcasting your fear."

Blythe turned. The bartender was nearly at the opposite end of the hall, staring at Blythe from just outside the back room of the bar. Her face and eyes were void of all emotion.

It made Blythe's heart hurt to witness. At least with Polaris, she could assign some context to the expressionless shield.

"Also"—the bartender sighed—"whatever it is you're after, don't expect to get it for free."

Blythe nodded, and then she was left alone in the chilly hall, just her and that damn pinup.

With the unsettling sensations of a sinking gut warring with the heart lurching into her throat, Blythe opened the painted door.

The place beyond was nothing like the compound where she and Polaris were held captive. Despite the utilitarian creepiness of the hallway, the room beyond was cozy and warm. It was a bit crowded with furniture and fixtures, but not untenable, and the couch set was well worn and lumpy in a way that was almost inviting. The far left-hand wall appeared to be made of stone, with a digital fireplace crackling away in its center. The fire wasn't real, but as Blythe drew closer, she learned it gave off more than surreal ambiance; it gave off heat.

"Huh," Blythe murmured to herself as she studied the rest of the room. "It's no phony forest, but I have to admire the dedication to theme."

It was like stepping back in time, into a mythical log cabin designed with contemplative retreat and ultimate human comfort in mind. Farthest from the hearth was a stone-like counter with a deep sink and a plethora of weathered cupboards. Stretching between the counter and the couches were floor-to-ceiling shelves, discolored and occasionally warped with age, but they hosted the sort of leatherbound tomes she expected to see in a Harem library.

That was where the homey illusion began to crumble.

There were other items on display beside books. Blythe was forced to acknowledge her misgivings when she noticed the antique scythe erected on its own shelf beneath a delicate spotlight; the blade was stained with more than rust. Several feet away from there, she discovered a prized scrapbook left open on a stand to reveal pages packed with disturbing images.

Blythe gagged and clapped a hand over her mouth as she backed away from it.

"Disconcerting, isn't it?"

She whipped around, and there he was. Gregoire.

"They look almost human on the inside, don't they?"

His fancy cane was planted on the floor in front of the fluffy slippers covering his feet, and the magnificent silver robe she last saw him in had been replaced. He wore simple trousers and a simpler top, with a thick receiving robe over his shoulders that sported the imperfect patterns of a handmade garment. There was no silver in his attire; Blythe checked.

The bald goon who stationed himself by the door was no more familiar than Gregoire's outfit. A motley assortment of quills and fur patches dotted one side of his skull, right above the one eye that was halfway through manifesting a new phenotype. He gave no sign of noticing Blythe as he braced his muscular back against the wall and began swiping his thumb over the barrel of the pistol at his hip.

"Who's your new minion?" Blythe asked as her feeble hopes plummeted another foot or two.

Gregoire did not respond, nor did he return her steely regard. His ancient face remained benign and composed as he stared past her at the wretched scrapbook. He folded both arthritic hands over the carved head of his cane and nodded at it with his chin lifted.

"This document is older than the longest surviving vampire," he said. "While the rest of our ancestors allowed our race to be bastardized for the sake of progress, a brave few had the sense to protect themselves and their legacies. I like to think of them as the first true vampire hunters."

Blythe glanced from the imposing stranger to the gruesome photographs, and she promptly decided his ugly mug was the easier sight to stomach. "So that's . . . what, a book of institutionalized serial killer souvenirs?"

Gregoire chuckled. "Not at all. They're simply the first recorded vampire autopsies. Nothing more, nothing less."

The clap of his cane on the floor made her flinch as he started toward her. The way the armed man remained unfazed and disinterested by the door did nothing to help her control the reaction.

"They were mere younglings, of course," Gregoire continued in the cadence of a wiseman lecturing a disciple, "an understandable oversight on behalf of my forebearers. Back then, they had no way of knowing that vampires could live so far beyond a single century."

Blythe shut her eyes out of unwillingness to take in any more of her surroundings. "You're proud of having pictures of dissected children up on your wall, are you?"

"I wouldn't say that. I'm sure our ancestors presumed these specimens were fully matured at thirty-or-so years old. Besides, while their youth was unfortunate, we can hardly call them children. They weren't human."

He came to a stop alongside her and stretched out one of those wizened fingers to turn a page. Blythe's eyes flew open to dart after the movement without her permission and despite her nausea. The next pair of pages were somehow worse than the first ones. Blythe swallowed a mouthful of bile, her fists aching at her sides as she skimmed over the full-color images of a spread open chest cavity.

"Are you familiar with the phrase 'knowledge is power,' Ms. Ramos?"

Blythe bit her tongue. She was hyperaware of the shadowy hulk of flesh by the door and the way he eyed the repeated clenching of her fists. She tried to shake out her hands again, but it was fast becoming a futile practice.

Her uneasy silence meant nothing. Gregoire never needed a participatory audience to carry his own conversation.

"Humans First wasn't always the foundation for social justice that it is today."

Blythe almost laughed at the sincerity in his tone, but she found it impossible to make a sound as she watched him lift the cane from the floor so he could hold it lengthwise across his middle. He raised it in both hands like an offering to the sordid shelves.

"In the beginning," he said, words dripping with grandeur, "we were a sanctioned group of skeptics. We preceded the Human Existence and Preservation Project, and we were the first to recognize and uphold the legitimate concerns of the public. We encouraged our fellow men to defend themselves against the rise of Homo nocturni."

Those age-spotted hands twisted the stylized wood in opposing directions. Blythe shuddered as a sharp creak rent the air.

"Humans First," he aggrandized. "The first true vampire hunters."

The cane came apart in his hands with a gentle tug, and Blythe gasped. The pieces slid apart, and the bottom half revealed a shaft of polished wood that tapered down into a wicked point that was as sharp as any fang.

The room spun as Blythe's head swam with foggy memories of Andy's body and a broken cane. But no, that was wrong; it wasn't broken. It wasn't a cane.

"It's a stake?"

Her disbelieving whisper brought a smile to his face. "I nearly lost this when The Guard raided our compound. Fortunately, a friend of mine managed to reacquire it before relinquishing the accompanying bodies to the authorities."

Gregoire slid the weapon back into its sheath with a short click that threatened to pierce Blythe's eardrums. She jerked back, but the flash of sensitivity was over before she finished raising her hands to either side of her head.

"Poor boys. Especially Andrew." Gregoire sighed. "He let his temper get away with him and fancied himself a vampire slayer. He never had the presence of mind to ask me how to wield it."

He twirled the cane around his withered wrist, and the length of wood spun in a graceful sweep before he brought its sheathed end back to the floor. There was no click or clank of contact being made, not a whisper of sound.

"It's an archaic and ineffective weapon, of course." Gregoire snickered to himself. "But I'll admit, I find a certain nostalgia in carrying it."

Blythe's blood boiled. "This is how you people kept a Nocturna cowed over the centuries, then? Every time you showed her your face, you came strutting in with the most racist weapon you could imagine and dressed to the nines in clothes woven from her hair."

"It was strategic," he said with a fond pat to the weapon's handle. "The hair, however, was a commendation. I thought she deserved to see the product of her resources, especially after all the time and trouble my parents invested in fine-tuning her diet and physiology for the right effect."

He turned to her with an excited gleam in his eye, and Blythe wished cats had the ability to turn off their hearing entirely. Her plain old human ears wanted nothing of the words he continued spewing.

"Did you know," he said as their eyes finally met, "spider DNA is highly incompatible with human biology, so it's a bit ironic that the Darwin Bark Spider produces such indestructible silk. Fortunately, there hasn't been a species yet that the Nocturni haven't managed to absorb. I know generations of women like yourself who wouldn't mind risking their purity for hair like hers."

"You're sick."

"No." He shook his head with a sorrowful and unsurprised

expression enhancing the lines on his brow. He gestured toward the revolting scrapbook and the bloodied scythe as he justified, "I take no joy in the necessity of these works, Ms. Ramos. Like all other men in this cold universe, I must make the most of what few resources I have."

"People," Blythe sniped. "They're not resources."

"Are we not a resource for them? Do they not pay for and steal from us the very blood in our veins?"

"Sounds like you're willfully misrepresenting Companionship, to me."

"As you misrepresent me, I'm sure." A touch of profound impatience infused his sigh. "If the Nocturni race were wise enough to take themselves to a far-off world, I would be the first to applaud them. We only wish they would return Earth and her moon back into the hands of honest humanity, along with the other rightful fruits of our technological labors."

Blythe stared at him in disgust.

"Their parasitic nature is not their fault," he continued. "Much like the dogs that were once bred to attack on command, they have become what they are due to the folly of men. We created our worst enemy—and our strongest competition—in those bygone labs."

Blythe snorted. She thought she heard a click of a cocking gun, but when she cast a hasty glare at the door, the henchman was unmoved.

Gregoire refolded his palms over the handle of his disguised stake. "Clearly, you have no greater respect for my perspective now than you did on the dark side of the moon. Why are you here, Ms. Ramos?"

Blythe redirected her glower to the elder. "Figured you already knew."

He huffed a nasty little laugh. "So, dear Andrew was right after all. Our Doll's affection is reciprocated!"

"Her name is Polaris."

"You can rename a pet as easily as anyone. It's what my grandfather did," Gregoire said as he made his way toward the fireplace. "In the end, the animal is still an animal."

He settled in the lone armchair within the fire's light, and Blythe practically teleported across the room to loom over him.

"If she's nothing but a pet to you, why would you risk keeping her around?"

"My dear, what makes you think she's here?"

Blythe jerked a thumb over her shoulder toward the disgusting shelves. "You like keeping trophies."

A quiet cough sounded from the doorway. Blythe's spine straightened with the reminder that they weren't alone, but she didn't back away from Gregoire.

He grinned up at her. "I like this version of you, Ms. Ramos. I felt pity for you before, when you wept, but now . . ." He wagged a gnarled finger at her, like a proud grandfather granting an upstart youth a point. "Oh, now, you've discovered your spine."

"I don't care," Blythe said through clenched teeth. "All I want is Polaris."

"And how do you expect to obtain this vampire, hmm?"

Blythe brandished her wrist in his face till the metallic gleam of her comms reflected in his milky eyes. "Elitia Kenwood. You haven't seen the state I left her in, but I won't touch another hair on her head if you hand Polaris over. You give me Polaris, and I tell my people to let Kenwood go. Hell, I'll even do you one better and close out her family's indenture."

As far as bluffs went, it was a weak one. Phink was hardly taking orders from Blythe, and whatever pull she once had with HEPP was withering away with every second since she took a swing at Elitia and trashed their House. But Gregoire didn't know that. Probably.

He smiled a small secretive smile that made him appear sicklier than ever. "Andrew was a friend. Not a particularly good one, mind you, but a friend, and a useful constituent. Miss Kenwood was his cousin and a sympathizer, but that's all."

"Yeah?" Blythe braced her elbows on the arm of the chair and hissed in his face. "Do you dress all your sympathizers in vampire-hide materials, then? Do they all know your home address?"

The crinkled skin around his smug eyes tightened with displeasure, but his smile never faltered. "What a pity things didn't work out last time, Ms. Ramos. You would have been a pleasure to work with."

"Elitia for Polaris," Blythe said, hoping he couldn't pick up on the angry flush swarming her cheeks. "She's a loose end for you, at best, and damning proof of centuries of hate crimes at worst. Let me take her off the moon, and you'll never hear of us again."

Finally, he dropped his smile. "I may have misjudged you, Ms. Ramos."

"Yay for me."

"Have you given any thought to the other one? The male?"

Blythe shoved away from the armchair, away from him. "Excuse me?"

"Leopold Troy," he said, giving her a mild frown as he steepled his fingers together beneath his chin. "He's the current Heir to his Harem. By now, I imagine he's far more valuable to the Nocturni than his cousin, but you would happily have him take her place, wouldn't you?"

"No." Blythe shook her head. "No, that's not—"

"You needn't lie to me, dear girl," he said with a scowl of parental disappointment.

Blythe gaped at him. She started to speak, then croaked as she realized she didn't know what to say.

"I am an intensely curious man, Ms. Ramos."

With a strained puff of breath, Gregoire gripped his cane and rose to his feet.

Blythe backed away from him as he did so, until she felt the rearmost of her braids brush against the behemoth of a man behind her. She bit off a yelp and twitched forward again on reflex, but then the goon's unoccupied hand pinched shut around her bicep. Before she could give a token of resistance, Gregoire was breathing in her face and demanding her attention.

"Curious, indeed. What did that mouse of a parasite do to earn such loyalty in so little time?"

Blythe spat on him. A nice big glob landed on his wrinkled cheek, and the Humans First leader froze as he blinked away his shock.

The lackey at her back made a rude noise and shook her.

Gregoire put an end to it with a casual lift of his hand. Once she was still, that same hand reached forward to grip her chin.

The touch made her skin crawl, and Blythe figured she might as well take her shot; she bit him. Rather, she tried to.

The geezer tightened his hold with alarming strength and mused aloud, "What is it about you? Of all the gifts I've given Dolly over the years, you were the only one she showed any interest in. So much wasted blood in her enclosure, but it was only after you that she dared to fight me. What did you do?"

Blythe's words were warped from the pressure of his fingers against her jaw, but her disdain was evident as she spat, "Fuck you."

"They told me you arrived alone, with no Guard in sight, and I truly hoped you were here to make amends," he said, speaking with the voice of a bereaved lover having his heart broken for the final time. "I thought perhaps you understood, now that not one, but *two* illustrious Harems—the Vauqeulins and the Troys—have washed their hands of you. After all you've done for them, after the personal sacrifices you made as a misguided child to acclimate to the failing society they built, where has it gotten you?"

He tossed her face aside, and the force behind it made Blythe laugh.

"You fucking hypocrite," she cackled as the goon tried to tug her off-balance. "You really had me convinced."

"I think we're done here."

As Gregoire crept toward the same shadowy door he entered through, Blythe sneered at his back. "You can hide behind the decrepit old man image all you want, but I know spliced strength when I feel it, asshole!"

He made a flippant gesture over his shoulder, and the goon shoved her to the floor.

"Suffice it to say, Ms. Ramos, but this will be the last time you compromise my operations," Gregoire announced as he opened the door. To the goon, he said, "I'm afraid I won't be able to stay long enough to supervise, but I want Dolly and the male sedated and prepped for off-world transport within the hour. Finish up here and help Lin lock up the bar, then the two of you can join the others downstairs."

The minion grunted his acknowledgment, and that was all the warning Blythe got before his foot came flying at her face.

CHAPTER 23

The beating turned out to be rather anticlimactic.

The first blow left the side of her face throbbing and brought a burst of blood pouring from her nose, but it was a half-hearted assault at best. After spitting a mouthful of crimson onto the floor, Blythe ran her tongue over her teeth and huffed an inaudible laugh of relief when everything seemed intact. The next kick caught her in the gut, and she dropped onto her side, but Blythe almost didn't notice the bruises. She had a half second of reprieve where her arms instinctively shot up to protect her head, then that blasted boot stomped on her shoulder to put her on her back.

As his toe pinned her down, Blythe's stunned brain whirled around the possibility of dislocating her shoulder for the second time in a matter of months. It was a good thing the present abuse was landing on her uninjured side, she decided.

Then she heard the click of the gun preparing to fire.

"Shit!"

Blythe tucked her chin and shielded her face and exposed throat with her arms clamped together, and not a moment too soon. The first bullet blasted above her and rammed into her forearm. The brutal force shoved her arm aside and stunned her into a silent scream.

There was no chance to recover. She was still caught in the disbelief of the first shot when the second collided with her sternum. It shoved the air from her lungs with relentless pressure, and for a moment, she thought it was over—she was dead—the bullet had cut through her and punctured a lung, surely, because she couldn't suck in another breath. The mind-numbing awareness of her approaching death made her immune to the final shove of the goon's boot.

Her body rolled away from him, and she clutched at the chest wound as the blood kept gushing from her nose, shrouding her face.

That was all. It was over.

WHEN BLYTHE GOT AROUND TO ACCEPTING THAT SHE WAS STILL alive, she unfurled from an ineffective fetal position and fell limp onto her back. She was alone. The fire was still crackling away at the heart of the domestic setup, and Blythe lay there, limp and panting in its warm glow.

She was alone, bleeding, and alive.

"Wow," Blythe gasped, trying to inflate her chest to max capacity just to reassure herself that she could.

She turned her head to the side to rid her mouth of a saliva-and-blood mixture and noticed she was close enough to the hearth that her spit landed on a rug she hadn't noticed earlier. With a groan, Blythe heaved herself up onto her elbows and gave the geometric weave work an exhausted sneer.

"Evil fucker," she muttered, still catching her breath. "He would have great style."

Blythe gave herself another moment to breathe before pushing herself into a fully upright position. She groaned as the motion summoned a fresh throb of pain to her face and a concerning tightness to her chest, but she didn't let it stop her. Her hands shook as she unzipped the throat of her jumpsuit and tugged the loosened collar up to wipe the blood out of her eyes. The first dab had her nose shrieking with agony, but she didn't stop.

She already wasted all the time Polaris could afford.

It took an unimaginable effort, but she got to her feet. Her legs wobbled like wet noodles as she blundered over to the nearest shelf to brace herself. Her ribs felt eerily concave, still holding on, but like they might splinter apart with each consecutive breath. Still, she didn't stop. She'd come too far and lucked out too long to stop now.

That is, until she did stop.

The door sporting the travesty of a pinup swung open, and Blythe's feet froze as her hand latched on to the first object it found.

"What the fuck?" The ugly bald henchman gaped at her from the doorway.

The bartender stood by his elbow, staring at Blythe with a subtle frown that seemed almost bored.

"How the fuck ain't you dead?" the man blustered, stomping toward her with a finger raised in accusation. "I shot you! Twice!"

Blythe summoned whatever strength she had left to answer him. She didn't bother with words. She shrugged, and the simple motion morphed into a lunge that conveniently brought her occupied hand swinging across his front.

"Holy shit," the barkeeper whispered.

"Holy shit," Blythe agreed as she let Gregoire's prized scythe clatter to a halt at her side.

The blade was sharper than it looked. Despite its age and concerning discoloration, despite Blythe's compromised position, it cut a clean dark line across the man's body. The wound streaked clear across his front, from the height of one shoulder, over the base of his throat and curving around the opposite pectoral. He fell backward, still gawking at Blythe like he couldn't believe his eyes.

Once his substantial weight hit the floor, the wound opened up, and the line of blood became a brief and silent geyser.

Blythe and the barkeeper stared at the body for a moment before lifting their gazes to each other.

With fresh blood smeared all over her front and dotting the edge of the scythe, Blythe set her back against the spot-lit shelf for support and hefted the weapon as high as she could muster.

"Just curious. How well does Gregoire pay you?"

The barkeep didn't so much as blink. "You're here for the vamps?"

"Do you care?"

Blythe followed the woman's stoic gaze to the rear door where Gregoire made his dramatic exit.

"You'll need an access code to the holding cells."

Blythe sighed and pushed off the shelf. She lugged the scythe up onto her shoulder; as graceless as it was, it was at least better than dragging it on the floor behind her. "I'd really rather not use this again."

The other woman snorted, unconcerned and bored as ever. She pointed at the body laying between them.

"I'd take his gun, if I were you."

"Good idea."

"Obvious advice is one thing. I don't hand out information for free."

Blythe let go of the weapon's handle, and it rolled off her shoulder to embed the blade inches into the floor. "Naturally. What do you want?"

"That," the woman nodded to the scythe, then trained her eyes on Blythe's chest, "and that."

Blythe gripped the scythe's handle with the intent to pass it over, but the floor held the blade with a stubbornness the minion's flesh didn't have. She gave up and settled for making a rude gesture at the immovable object.

"Go for it."

"And the suit. The silver one."

Blythe ground her teeth together in reluctance. She shucked the spacefarer's jumpsuit off her shoulders, but hesitated when her fingers found the topmost button of Elitia's business jacket.

"There's a maze of tunnels between here and the hangar." The woman spoke in the tone of someone commenting on the continued existence of atmospheric domes covering the Lunar cities. "You'll need directions."

"And you expect me to believe I *won't* need some body armor?"

"Maybe."

Blythe studied the other woman's face, but it told her nothing. "I'll give you the pants," Blythe decided as she shoved the rest of the jumpsuit down her legs.

Just like that, the bargain was struck.

BLYTHE HATED TO ADMIT IT, EVEN IN THE SAFETY OF HER OWN head, but the jumpsuit was significantly more comfortable without extra layers of fabric clumping up beneath it. It was once again loose on her legs and backside, and after tying the sleeves around her waist, she had enough padding to don the fallen lackey's belt and holster without it falling off her hips every few steps. She looked ridiculous with the man's belt separating the spacefaring gear from the magnificent suit jacket, but she figured no one would care when she was sticking a gun in their face.

She kept the gun in her hand as she descended the stairs leading to the labyrinth beneath the bar and hoped she looked like she knew what to do with it. The metal handle was cold and bulky in her palm, and her finger flittered in the vicinity of the trigger with a nervous tremor she couldn't get under control.

The first person she met in the tunnels didn't notice her

discomfort with the weapon. He got one look at her, and the spliced bug-eyes on his face grew to cartoonish proportions. With a frantic shake of his head and hands raised in placation, he scurried by as if she were nothing but a recurring phantom of his imagination.

Blythe let him pass unmolested. They never traded a word.

What was the protocol for a one-woman siege on a terrorist's headquarters when the underlings were being so cooperative? The question would have to wait for another time.

Blythe rolled her shoulders back and pushed onward, counting her steps till she reached the turn she needed. Before long, she broke into a cold sweat that never seemed to seep through Elitia's fortified jacket.

If the poor barkeeper were still around, Blythe could have kissed her for the succinct directions. The tunnels were a mess, nothing but intentional chaos, but Blythe knew where she was going. She turned a corner and clapped eyes on a pair of steel doors, reinforced by a heavy bar and locked with a digital display on its front.

A spike of adrenaline seemed to shake her ears and nose awake the moment she spotted the doors. She became suddenly and intensely aware of the coppery stench of spilled blood mixing with the vileness of unfamiliar chemicals. Until that moment, the rhythmic beeping of the locking mechanism went undetected, but suddenly it was tapping her ears with the consistency of a ticking bomb.

With the gun raised in one hand, Blythe approached the doors. Her finger trembled beside the trigger as she fumbled with the display to input the barkeeper's code.

There was no way of knowing what was waiting for her on the other side. Once the barrier broke, she was inundated with noises and scents that were too convoluted and bizarre to tell her anything useful. Blythe swallowed her nerves and squished her body against the door as it swung inward. She led with the barrel of the gun.

There was no apparent reaction to her intrusion. A minimum of two masculine voices carried on a conversation unperturbed among a background of metallic clatter and meaningless beeps.

"—I don't make the rules," one voice was saying.

"Whatever," said another. "If the bloodsuckers were so important, the boss should have taken them with him. Now we're left with two of the fuckers to deal with."

Blythe jumped at the sharp thud of knuckles cracking on plexiglass.

"Hear that, Doll Face? Not so special after all."

Blythe rushed in without thinking. The door crashed into a wall, and she had a split-second impression of large, white blocks lined up along one side and the gray openness of everything else. Then someone was shouting at her, and Blythe's finger cinched on the trigger before she knew what was happening.

It was a lucky shot. The bang was instantly followed by a series of screams, and the bland surroundings were suddenly awash with spraying color. Blythe stood in the doorway like an idiot and watched the guy nearest her clutch at his arm where the bullet grazed him, but she was too distracted to put anything about him into her memory.

The second man was known to her.

Blythe gaped at the familiar tiger stripes of one of her abductors, and her shock was mirrored on his face as he keeled over. She watched the blood bubble out of the neat hole in his throat without understanding what it meant.

The rest of the world didn't wait for her to catch up with it.

"Blythe!"

Polaris's voice snapped her out of suspension with barely enough time for her to twirl out of the way of a third goon. Blythe didn't recognize him as he swung, though her nostrils twitched from a hint of something memorable yet elusive. She got a better look at the fourth guy over his shoulder and uttered a sharp squeak of alarm at the convolution of fur and scales growing from the side of his jaw and neck. She wasn't proud of it, but Blythe raised the gun toward him on instinct and managed to shoot off a few rounds before his buddy swatted the weapon out of her hand.

"Bitch!" the grotesque man wailed as he crumpled to the floor.

Before Blythe could determine how injured he was, the nearest henchman lunged at her again. He was fast enough to make contact, but she was faster; the blow hit Blythe on the shoulder and threw her off-balance instead of hitting her face and knocking her out cold. It was a small favor she was unashamed to take advantage of.

She was on her ass, weaponless, with a man twice her size looming over her, but she had no fear. There was no room for it. All she felt was resolve haloed by the white-hot chill of exhaustive resentment.

"How the fuck did you— Ugh!"

Her foot shot up in what might have been the most beatific and powerful arch of her career, and she kicked him straight in the nuts. He went down with a strangled cry as Blythe swiveled to her feet with an ill-contained cheer.

A gun went off.

Pain. Sharp, ringing pain zapped her ear and reverberated through her skull. It was so bad, Blythe first assumed she'd been shot. But that didn't make sense. Nothing made sense. The agony lancing around her head took a small eternity to relent into a discombobulated throbbing.

Then she realized the shouting and gunfire had degraded, as if hidden behind layers of cotton. Blythe blinked her eyes rapidly and gave a cautious shake of her head, but the noise remained muted.

What just happened?

She could hear a commotion, but it was distant and vague. All she could see was gray cement and cold walls. She could feel movement around her, sense a frenzy of activity, but her brain wasn't working the way it should. She squeezed her eyes shut against the lingering pain and tried to recalibrate.

What went wrong?

She discovered she was kneeling on the ground, crouched low with her hands clamped over her head. She felt no wetness when she patted at the braids, but she couldn't piece together why that seemed important. Then it wasn't important, because lowering her shaking hands from her ears to the cool floor did nothing to clear up the surrounding nonsense.

There was a whistle. It was small and dismissible at first, but it didn't stay that way. It seemed to be coming from inside her, and once she acknowledged it, the sound swelled in volume and intensity. Blythe gasped as the whistling spiked into a javelin set on piercing through her eardrums.

It lasted seconds, or maybe eons, but when it ended, Blythe was gasping with her forehead flush to the tile floor and puddles of tears spreading beneath her face. She stayed put as her auditory sense began to recover in increments, paralyzed by confusion as much as wariness.

She wasn't shot. Over a series of deep, cleansing breaths and a frazzled mental pep talk, Blythe realized it must have been a very close call indeed. At least there wasn't a bullet in her head. Yes. The shot missed. She was still alive.

But . . . how?

It wasn't as difficult to raise her head as it had been to peel herself off the floor after being shot in the chest, but it was still an experience she never wanted to repeat. A touch of dizziness chased her as she crawled to her feet and took stock of the situation.

The first dead body lay several feet away. Farther still, she spotted the guy with the nasty splicing side effects, who had dragged himself out of the center of the room to prop himself against a far wall. He was still awake, but his breathing was labored and his glare lackluster as he held his hands over a bloody spot on his side. She couldn't see Henchman Number Three, but she could hear his limping stride and ceaseless whimpering as it faded into the tunnels.

The fourth lackey, the one she grazed on the arm, was nowhere in sight. Neither was Polaris.

Blythe's ears were still flipping in and out of usefulness as she made her way over to the wall of white blocks. Her balance was pathetic, and it took far too long for her to reach the plexiglass wall so she could lean against it and keep upright.

Now that she could focus on them, the bright cells with their transparent fronts were horrific. They were cold, built with relentless lighting and inhumane exposure as the top priority. There were a lot of them, all lined up along the one wall. Blythe didn't bother counting. Blythe knew of penitentiaries with more comfort in their designs.

She could already tell which cell was recently occupied.

Blythe leaned against the only slate of plexiglass that wasn't perfectly smooth. Fighting the urge to cry, Blythe traced her fingertips over the web of cracks spreading throughout the barrier. She found the tail end of a line inches beneath the glass where she pressed her cheek, then she traced it. Her finger pricked the jagged edge of a bloodied hole.

It didn't make any sense.

Where was Polaris? Clearly, someone had broken free of this cube of a prison, but when? How? Why didn't they come to Blythe after getting free?

Blythe didn't have the energy or the smarts to figure it all out. She barely had a grasp on which questions were worth asking. She'd come all this way, soiled her hands and conscience, and she never even set eyes on the Nocturna.

"You were right here," Blythe murmured as she dabbed the fresh blood from the shattered glass. "I heard you."

She was no more a genius than she was a fighter, but Blythe

wasn't dumb. The outward protrusions of broken glass and blood placement was telling. It was Polaris's, and it might very well be the last piece of her Blythe would ever find.

"So close," Blythe whispered, only to have her voice crack into depleted sobs on the last syllable.

Her knees gave out, and she crumbled, the skin on her tear-soaked face pulled taut against the glass as gravity dragged her down.

This was how it ended for them.

"Ms. Ramos?" someone whispered. "Is that you?"

Blythe stiffened. Warily, she pressed her back to Polaris's cell and eyed the vacuous room. There was nothing, no one around. Even the minion with the gut-wound had gone still and silent. By all appearances, she was alone.

Maybe that shot by her ear had done more damage than she thought.

The space was so devoid of life, Blythe was sure she imagined someone speaking to her. She was about to write it off as wishful thinking when it happened again, quieter still.

"Ms. Ramos? Are you . . ." the voice faltered, "alive?"

Blythe's brain clearly wasn't working at top speed, because it took her an embarrassingly long moment to place the voice. With a gasp, she scrambled to her feet, shouting, "Master Troy?!"

She recognized his voice much easier at full volume as he moaned, "Thank the stars!"

Blythe's legs wobbled with the first few steps, and a fresh wave of dizziness turned her stomach. With an impatient groan, she planted her palm against the plexiglass and used it as a guide to hurry down the line of cells without waiting for her equilibrium to sort itself out.

Leopold Troy met her in the foremost corner of his very own cage, three empty blocks away from where Polaris broke out of hers. Blythe caught sight of him and immediately let loose a string of curses as she turned away.

The Nocturnus was naked. He had the decency to hold a hand over his crotch, since he didn't have enough hair to help preserve his modesty like his cousin once did.

After a pause, the vampire cleared his throat. "I don't suppose you have any spare clothing on you?"

Still facing away and braced against the glass, Blythe shook her head.

"Ah. Well . . ."

Blythe pulled herself together and took a breath. Without looking back at him, she asked, "What happened to Polaris?"

He didn't answer.

Blythe jerked her chin over her shoulder in his general direction and snapped, "She was here. I know she was. I was out of it for a minute though, and now she's gone. What happened?"

He answered this time, but it was more of a non-answer, rife with reluctance and pity. "You shouldn't worry yourself over her any longer, Ms. Ramos."

Blythe squeezed her eyes shut. The hand on the glass wall curled into a clenched fist. "What. Happened?"

"Tanya—she—" He sighed, and something in his tone made her stomach curdle into a series of knots. "She's Cursed, Ms. Ramos."

"I already knew that—"

"I witnessed it," he cut her off with the deadly quiet of his words. He sounded unbearably young and fragile as he said, "They ransacked our home and took us hostage, and I was useless. She tried to fight them off, and I just stood there—"

"I don't care." Blythe whirled around, and the wrathful blush warming her body left no room for awkwardness over his nudity. "This isn't about you. What happened just now? Where is she?"

Leopold Troy's brow furrowed, his lip giving a minute tremble as he stared at her. He set his palm on the barrier between them as if reaching for her shoulder.

Blythe stepped back. She abandoned the plexiglass support, and to her surprise, her legs held strong and sure.

The vampire said, "She lost whatever reasoning she had left when she woke up back in a cage."

Blythe shrugged and hugged herself. "So? Kahled had repeat episodes before, and since Sly—"

He shook his head. "This wasn't an episode, Ms. Ramos."

"You don't know that. The stress—"

"How long has it been since we went missing? Weeks?"

Blythe's heart sank with empathy even as she physically reined in her impatience. She ended up telling him in an emotionless drawl, "Less than four days."

His mouth pulled into a harsh line, and he persisted with a warbling tone that suggested he was close to losing all composure.

"Fine," he said softly. "I've spent the past four days then, doing nothing but listening to her rage. She never spoke, though she was as vocal as any beast in existence. She rarely slept and never ate because they were too afraid to risk opening the cell after she made the first cracks in the glass. I tried to speak to her, and she never once acknowledged my existence."

"Okay," Blythe whispered, willing him to stop talking.

"Then you appeared, shedding blood right in front of her. She was already lost to the Curse, but that sent her into a frenzy—"

"I get it," Blythe snapped, biting her lip and raising a hand to warn him off.

"Cursed episodes burn hot and fast. Kahled Vauqeulin told me so himself. But this . . . There was no end to this."

"I said I get it!"

"I am sorry, Ms. Ramos," he said, and his shadowed eyes and trembling lip proved the sentiment was genuine. "You were too late."

CHAPTER 24

The barkeeper's code was worth the cost of Elitia's pants. In next to no time at all, Leopold Troy was free and reluctantly donning the bloodied clothes Blythe stripped off the tiger-striped body. The shirt and pants were far too small, exposing most of his lower legs and a strip of abdomen, and his feet remained bare, but at least he was covered.

The same could not be said for Polaris, assuming they ever found her.

They found Gregoire's fourth minion, at least—or what was left of him. Blythe only recognized him by the superficial bullet wound she caught him with earlier; the arm was otherwise intact, albeit a full six feet down the tunnel from the rest of the body.

"We should summon The Guard," Leopold said, breathing down her neck as he tiptoed around the severed limb.

Blythe didn't tell him about the message she sent Lugh so many hours ago. Instead, she forced the Nocturnus out of her personal space with a jab of her elbow and grumbled, "What do you expect them to do? Gregoire's long gone, and we haven't seen another living human in over an hour. The only thing left for The Guard to do is put a silver bullet in Polaris's head."

Blythe's steps didn't falter, but she felt the Nocturnus's presence retreat a little as he mumbled a half-hearted correction. "It wouldn't have to be silver. That's a myth—"

"Stars above," Blythe groaned, "I know!"

The Harem leader didn't check her on the blatant disrespect. He resumed his self-imposed role as her silent shadow, following her through the dimly lit halls with a scant foot or two between them. She noticed his steps quickening into brief skips whenever she turned a corner, but it wasn't till her finicky ears clued into the haphazard pacing of his heartbeat that she realized he was afraid to lose sight of her.

The longer they roamed the abandoned labyrinth, the shorter the path between Blythe's brain and her tongue seemed to get.

"You know," she snarked without glancing back at him, "if you're so concerned about my well-being, you're welcome to take the lead. No one's stopping you."

Leopold tripped over thin air. Blythe heard the stumble with a full appreciation for how disturbingly neat Gregoire kept his properties.

"Oh . . . No thank you?"

"Maybe you could get off my ass, then?"

She turned to shoot him a pointed look and stopped cold mid-stride.

Leopold Troy looked nothing like the put-upon aristocrat who once tossed a priceless heirloom in Phink's face like it was a cheap trinket. His hair was greasy and unwashed, standing on end despite obvious signs of repetitive finger combing. The skin beneath his eyes was bluish and creased with raw weariness. He didn't appear injured, but the way he held one arm close to his body, hugging the joint with the other hand as he shied away, was concerning.

Four days since their comms conversation was interrupted, and that entire time, Blythe never once considered what was happening to the current Heir of Polaris's Harem.

Blythe's shoulders slumped. "Are you okay?"

He blinked at her in apparent surprise. "Why would you ask me that?"

"Forget it." She sighed and resumed walking. "Just stay close. She knows me better than you, anyway."

After that, neither of them spoke for a long while. Blythe didn't tell him about the time she witnessed a Cursed vampire destroy several trained Nocturni bodyguards on a whim. In turn, Leopold voiced no reminders that her feeble mortal self didn't have a hope of stopping a vampire who so recently tore through a prison wall meant to confine monsters.

No, it was better that they didn't speak at all.

THEY FOUND THE SORRY BASTARD BLYTHE TRIED TO NEUTER earlier. It was a simple matter of following her ears to the only discernible sounds she couldn't readily explain. He was hiding in a storage closet.

"Nope," he said when she opened the door and immediately grappled for the reclaimed gun on her hip. He raised his hands high. "I'm just here to follow orders and get paid. This isn't it."

Blythe palmed the gun anyway and pointed it in his general direction. "Then make yourself useful—"

"Tell us the way out of here," Leopold demanded as he loomed over her shoulder, bumping into her.

"No!" Blythe threw her shoulder back to bounce him off her and snapped at the goon, "Polaris, the Nocturna. Where is she?"

"How should I know?"

Blythe didn't know what possessed her, but in the span of a heartbeat, her arm moved. She lowered the gun to the side, squeezed the trigger, and amid a chorus of ricochet and shattering tile, she resumed her previous aim.

Both males jumped a foot or more into the air. Blythe watched the henchman plaster himself to the rear of the closet with his hands hiding his face, while Leopold's alarmed squeak sounded in her ear.

"Tanya Troy," Blythe sniped, shaking the gun at him like a rattle. "How do I find her? Don't you guys have a surveillance system or something?"

Yeah, she thought, a surveillance system was a good idea. Wasn't that what Sly did when he tried playing the knight in shining armor for his vampire?

"Only upstairs," the lackey rushed to explain. "For bar security. The port wouldn't issue a liquor license without it—"

"My stars, I don't care!" Blythe yelled. She was tempted to fire off another warning shot, but considering she didn't have a clue how much ammunition was left nor how to refill the weapon, she decided against it. "I only care about Polaris. You can either find a way to help me, or I can put a hole in your leg!"

She stepped into the closet and pressed the barrel of the gun to the thick flesh right above his knee. She had poor aim and a shaky hand, but they were in close range, and the guy was too cowed to try wrangling the weapon away from her. Blythe was determined enough to take the risk, and she was sure it showed on her face.

The goon wasn't as stupid as he looked; he got them moving again without further comment.

"Gregoire really needs to invest in more loyal underlings," Blythe murmured to Leopold half an hour later. "Seriously. How in the cosmos has he survived this long as a criminal mastermind when half his people are just waiting for a chance to clear out and hand over info on him?"

"Perhaps we shouldn't give Humans First any professional development advice?"

Blythe rolled her eyes and handed him the gun. "Your turn. My arm's getting tired."

She left him standing in the middle of the hall to get comfortable with the thing and crossed over to where the goon was weighing his options before a fork in the path.

"If you're about to get us lost," Blythe said, "I'd rather turn around and go back to the bar."

It wasn't ideal, but she didn't want to trap herself down there, and they might be in for a long wait for Lugh to show up with reinforcements. At least The Lighthouse was abandoned and locked up, as safe as they could likely get. Blythe figured she could hold the henchman at gunpoint while sitting down just as easily as she could in the underground maze.

She would just have to hope Polaris didn't find herself another exit. She didn't want to know how Lunar-1 would react to a crazed Nocturna wreaking havoc on the streets.

"Not that simple," the goon said. "I know what's where, but not who."

Blythe pointed down the left tunnel. "What's down there?"

"Bunker rooms, a couple firearms cabinets, and a few years' worth of provisions," he said with a shrug, "in case of a siege."

"Naturally," she scoffed. "And the other way?"

"Archives and the main armory. Oh, and Gregoire's personal collection."

An inexplicable chill trickled down Blythe's spine. She took a step toward the right-hand passage without thinking. "What kind of collection?"

"Don't know. Never been inside."

Wordlessly, Blythe started down the tunnel. She didn't want to know what a man like Gregoire would value to such a degree, but there was an itching need in her gut that couldn't be ignored, and Blythe wasn't interested in trying.

Her days of turning a blind eye to Humans First dealings were long gone.

Blythe opened every door along the way, and just like the lackey said, she found several rooms stacked with shelves of computer hard drives and documentation, and no less than two massive gates barring access to more armaments than she cared to know existed. Too much of it looked militaristic, and she wouldn't be surprised to learn some of it was capable of large-scale destruction. It was the second time in her life she'd spied a Ratheon cannon in person, and the circumstances surrounding the sighting were no better than last time.

She felt cold looking at it, but this was something for Lugh and his people to deal with. Blythe abandoned the latest armory gate and led the way farther down the tunnel without a backward glance.

The door at the end of the hall was normal and unassuming. There was a digital lock, and Blythe didn't expect the prison cell code to work on it.

It did.

"You've got to be kidding," Blythe muttered under her breath.

With a disbelieving chuckle, she braced herself for fresh horrors and shoved the door open.

It was both more and less than she expected.

The room was spacious and uncluttered, dimly lit by an extravagant chandelier that might have cost more than the whole of Lunar-5's inhabitable real estate. Items of various materials and importance were staged along the walls, each haloed in its own overarching light, like a private museum. There was a floor-to-ceiling shadowbox of dried plants and seedlings frozen at various stages of sprouting. Farther down was a detailed diorama of a seaside mansion, complete with a backsplash detailing ancient blue-prints of the original Earthly abode and archival photographs of sun-kissed mortals frolicking on beaches. A series of life-sized anatomical models were posed in their own dedicated alcove, showcasing the unaltered musculature and skeletal systems of mankind from childhood to adulthood. An eye-catching glass pyramid sat on its own pedestal, filled with layers upon layers of differing sands from areas of the mother planet that hadn't been accessible in a millennium. The matching pedestal across the way sported an amazingly intricate cross, golden and bejeweled in the manner of long-gone Earthling religions.

The majestic homage to ancient humanity ended there.

A few more steps forward, Gregoire's collection morphed into an extension of the macabre vampire hunting theme from the first room, minus the homey veneer. A full four feet of wall was dedicated to rows and rows of extracted fangs, and the next anatomical model consisted of actual flesh and bone amateurly skinned and partially stripped of substance before the body had been encased in some form of resin.

Blythe's heart and stomach turned leaden at that point. She stopped looking too closely at the revolting paraphernalia mounted on the walls.

"Monsters," Leopold whispered from somewhere behind her.

Blythe couldn't force her agreement past her lips. If she dared try, she was certain she'd be tossing more than words.

The display room was long and substantial, and Blythe discovered a desk and shelving built into the rear wall that wasn't visible from the entrance. All the furnishings were relentlessly white, almost blending into the walls, and that included the throne-like chair settled behind the desk. Blythe refused to sit in it as she tapped the tabletop and summoned the holographic desktop to life.

Blythe had never handled such a large device, but it used the same basic interfacing as any modern comms. She swiped through images and text with the same intuitive ease she would check messages from the unit on her wrist. No firewalls or password requests stopped her.

A hot flash of incredulous disdain heated Blythe's face. She realized Gregoire, in all his experience and so-called wisdom, felt no need to safeguard his hideous passions here. He had no shame, not here in what probably passed for his home, right underneath the masses of blissfully ignorant vampires inhabiting the city above him.

Blythe flipped through folders and files without comprehending much. What she did learn put a sour taste in her mouth and inspired a bloodlust Blythe didn't know humans were capable of.

She found design plans for a rapid-fire crossbow and a lengthy list of potential ammunition: laser darts that could rival the sun's heat and miniaturized stakes crafted from artificial wood, silver, and all the nostalgia of a sick-minded folklore fanatic.

There was a substantial listing of equations and notes that culminated in a formula labeled "Holy Water." It had liquid and gaseous options.

She found notes upon notes on Nocturni splicing abilities, shortly followed by files containing sketches and plans of various clothing items and blades. A dagger caught her eye, and Blythe swallowed a rush of bile as she read about the harpy eagle claw it was made from after being "harvested" from a conscious and unmedicated Nocturna. There was a disgustingly attractive leather jacket made from the kangaroo hide of a skinned Nocturnus.

When she found the sketches and annotations concerning Polaris's hair, Blythe froze. The whole of what she was, body and soul, crystalized into ice and summarily shattered.

"They didn't cut it," Blythe whispered in horror.

"What?"

"Her hair." Blythe couldn't bring herself to explain further. She read on with festering nausea turning her gut.

Humans First never cut Polaris's hair. They couldn't. Once

Polaris's cooperation was secured, the hair strands of an evolved species were reinforced by the might of a Darwin Bark Spider's silk, and the resulting phenotype was impenetrable. They had no choice but to remove the scalp and free the follicles by soaking the skin in acid.

For the love of the cosmos, what had they done to her to make her compliant in her own torture?

Blythe smacked her palm through the suspended imaging to move on to the next file, then the next, and the next after that. She didn't read any more, couldn't see through the furious tears blurring her vision, even before she lost the fight with her gullet and doubled over to hurl onto the floor.

She was still gagging and bringing up noxious-smelling chunks when Leopold cried out.

"Impossible!"

Blythe trembled as she whipped the foulness from her mouth. She was vaguely aware of Leopold jabbing his hand into the projected screen from the opposite side of the desk as she stared at yellow-tinged puke smearing the silver cuff of Elitia's despicable jacket.

"Oooh!" she wailed, swaying into a shelf as she began clawing at the buttons running down her front. If her choices were between an indestructible shield or never touching such awful material again, she would gladly eat the next bullet to fly her way. It left her wretchedly exposed, with only a sweaty athletic bra and lumps of bruising to cover her chest, but she didn't care. She wouldn't touch the damn jacket again.

Her devastation was lost on Leopold.

"What have they done?" he gasped.

Blythe kicked the jacket as far as she could and faced the desk with her fists clenched at her sides. If she was looking for a distraction from the horror, she was well and truly out of luck.

She could see Leopold through the display. He navigated back and forth between two or three pages with a slack jaw and terrified eyes. Neither of them spoke until he paused on a document of colorful symbols, unintelligible paragraphs, and lines of complex code.

Blythe frowned at him through the transparent jumble. "What is it?"

Instead of answering, the vampire tapped his fingers together in quick pinching motions and zeroed in on a section of the screen. Tanya Troy's name filled the air above the desk, swiftly followed by a string of annotation that made no sense save for one bolded word.

"Nosferatu," Blythe read aloud, her voice thick with incomprehension.

"Nosferatu's Curse," Leopold corrected, sounding distracted as he swept a hand through the words and let his eyes dart all over the document in its entirety.

"Wait." Blythe set her palms on the desk, arms fully extended as she leaned on it. "They knew she was Cursed?"

"Yes," he breathed. Then, as the color drained from his face, he said, "No."

Blythe threw up her hands. "Well, which is it?"

Leopold didn't answer as he hurried around to her side. He started opening drawers, and on the third try, he located the hard drive wired into the desk. One good yank was all it took, and the holographic images snapped out of visible existence. Blythe stared as the vampire plucked the small dark block out of the drawer with shaking fingers and cradled it against his chest.

"Humans First didn't merely know about her Curse." He met her gaze, his own wide and wet. "I think they gave it to her."

Blythe stared at him. "Excuse me?"

His mouth worked frantically to explain with a fitful start. It got them nowhere, only stretching out the ugly moment till his suspicion overwhelmed his ability to communicate completely. Leopold swayed on his feet, and before he could collapse into the available chair, Blythe grabbed for his arm to redirect him onto the desk.

He landed hard, and though the weight dump didn't move the desk, it shuddered. Something solid and metal clattered to the ground.

Leopold jumped back to his feet with a pitchy gasp. At the same time, Blythe turned toward the sound with her hand going to the holster on her waist. Her gut sank as she remembered it was empty.

"Where's the gun?" she demanded as she whirled toward Leopold.

He was clustered along the rear wall with both hands clutching a treasure trove of digital information over his heart.

She followed his panicked stare back to the desk. She could hear him hyperventilate as she stretched clear across the tabletop. Sure enough, she found the gun, dark and damning on the floor.

Without climbing off the desk, Blythe glared back at the vampire and demanded, "Where's the guy?"

"Who?"

"Gregoire's man," she hissed, gesturing around the unmanned and ever-creepy room. "The asshole who led us here! The one who's supposed to be on the other end of that fucking gun!"

His eyes turned bulbous. "Oh no."

"You know"—she wagged a finger at him as she rushed toward the distant doorway—"for a Harem leader, you're really not good at operating under pressure."

Blythe sprinted back through the grisly gallery with the Nocturnus two steps behind her. His legs were longer, and he was sure to have at least as much spliced speed power in his limbs as she did, but he never overtook her. Blythe was too busy figuring out how they lost their tour guide to bother calling him out on it.

Leopold still caught up to her too fast when they hit the start of the tunnel. Blythe flew through the doorway into relative darkness and promptly tripped over something. As she fell, she heard

Leopold skid to a halt and catch himself on the doorframe. His brief, wordless cry punctuated the wet smack of her hands catching her weight on the floor.

Two rapid-fire blinks later, Blythe's eyes adjusted to the dimness of the passageway.

"Stars above," Leopold gasped.

Blythe couldn't summon the air necessary to repeat the sentiment. She was lying in a pool of blood, one ankle still hooked over the motionless form of their would-be tour guide. His body remained in one piece, technically, but the fangs that tore out his jugular had ripped loose a substantial strip of chest muscle too.

Cold washed over Blythe. She never heard him whimper, never caught a hint of him leaving the room and meeting his end.

She never heard Polaris approach.

"We should leave," Leopold's voice trembled as he inched around the mess on the floor.

Blythe climbed to her feet in a blustering series of squelches.

"Polaris?" she begged of the lifeless passageway.

"Hush!"

Blythe pushed Leopold's arm out of her way before he could cover her mouth. "Polaris? Where are you?"

"Ms. Ramos!" he pleaded in a panicked whisper. "Please!"

There was no sign of the Nocturna. No flicker of motion or the shadowy cast of a figure.

"I don't understand," Blythe muttered, heedless of her volume. "Why didn't she come after us too?"

"Who cares! Let's go before she changes her mind!"

"Wait! If she can discern between us and them—"

"That might be worth your life, but not mine!"

Blythe whirled to stare at him. For the first time, she saw his fangs bared in her direction, and all it inspired in her was a wealth of disgusted pity.

"She's your cousin! Your family," Blythe reminded him, and

something in her tone made him flinch. "You," she spat, "are her Harem's Heir. You're supposed to be responsible for her. Care for her!"

To his credit, Leopold seemed to shrink in on himself under a tidal wave of regret. He wouldn't meet her eye as he took care pocketing the stolen hard drive in his pants pocket.

"I cannot value her life above all the rest of my people's. My Harem needs a viable scion"—his voice broke on those words, but he finished with—"and my species may very well depend on the information I now hold."

He proved her suspicions about his physical capabilities then. Without a second glance in her direction, Leopold flew by her with ghostly stealth. She blinked, and he was gone.

She was alone. Again.

Blythe sat on the cold tunnel floor in the narrow streak of light coming from Gregoire's gallery. She sat, alone and quiet, and tried to figure out her next move. It felt like she spent hours racking her brain, too numb and too tired to panic or renew her search.

The final henchman's body was still warm when her feline nose twitched with the faintest recognition of decay. The blood was still drying on her jumpsuit and flecking off her palms. It didn't have time to begin itching. Sighing, Blythe knocked her head back against the passage wall and began scrubbing her hands clean on her thighs without the vigor necessary to achieve the task.

"I can't do this without you."

Blythe's voice carried down the hall with the dull echo of an aimless comment, no inflection, no emotion, just fact.

"I don't know if you can hear me, Polaris. If you're close enough, or cognizant enough, or if any of that even matters."

She trailed off into a sad chuckle and closed her eyes before another useless tear could fall. She imagined Polaris lurking around the next turn, eyes aglow and alien as they considered the best angle to get at Blythe's veins.

"I owe you an apology," Blythe said.

No one answered.

She raised her voice a bit. "I put too much pressure on you. I wanted to cut and run while we had the chance, but instead of owning up to it, I put that decision on you. I should have been stronger for us. I should have insisted. Maybe it would have ended badly, but at least we wouldn't be here. We'd be free."

Still, no one answered.

"I was stupid. Weak," Blythe admitted.

Her back straightened as a slight sting zipped from one ear and through the other. It was a sound, a movement, but it didn't have the same clarity she expected of a cat's hearing; her ears were still smarting from the too-close gunshot for her to discern anything meaningful.

Still. It was a sound. A sign of life. Blythe set a hand over her heart as if the gesture would soothe the needy spark flickering there.

"I'm used to people leaving me," she croaked. "I guess a part of me assumed you would too, and I did nothing to fight it."

Blythe caught her breath, and the dull ache in her ear canal ebbed away. There was no mistaking the sounds of stealthy movement in the near distance then.

Blythe's throat constricted, and her pulse lurched, but she held herself lax and reposed on the floor, refusing to open her eyes and give in to the urge to seek out whatever was coming toward her.

"I love you," Blythe whispered.

The silence was deafening. It held her fast, trapping her to the soiled floor with a finality that made her question if she hadn't fallen deaf for real this time. She could hear nothing and sense no one, as if all her senses had been muted and buried under her grief.

"I love you, Polaris."

Blythe waited. She didn't know what she waited for, but she waited nonetheless. A part of her expected to be wrapped in a tremulous embrace, reminiscent of the victimized Nocturna who once sought Blythe out with innocent tears in her ever-blue eyes, despite the raw brutality staining her porcelain skin. Another part of Blythe's mind expected nothing but pain as claws or fangs ripped into her.

With a mild grin, Blythe realized she didn't care how the next moment went. She found Polaris. Polaris found her. Either way, they were together again.

The worst was over.

The indistinct sputter of disturbed fluids nearly startled her into opening her eyes. It was close. Blythe's foot twitched as she instinctively retreated from the nearby corpse, but she didn't move far.

There was no sound as a clammy touch graced her ankle.

Blythe froze and opened her eyes.

The vampire was a fearsome vision. The light from the gallery doorway wrapped around her naked form, shrouding her in a cloak of shadows and blood. Her eyes were painfully bright, sparkling with an otherworldly gray glow that put the starlight of her hair to shame. The fangs protruding from her mouth were twice the length they should have been. The fine lines of her face seemed carved from marble, and she almost appeared expressionless except for the animalistic twitch of her upper lip.

Slow and easy, Blythe extended her foot again, and Polaris yanked her fingertips from Blythe's ankle like a startled beast. Blythe's toes tapped the edge of the pool of congealing blood, inches from where Polaris knelt.

"I'm sure you've had your fill by now," Blythe said, "but if my blood could do anything to restore you, anything at all, you can have it. All of it."

The weariness in Blythe's limbs didn't stop her from prying the strap of her compression top to the side. It was easy to tug the fabric in the opposite direction she craned her neck, to expose a larger stretch of brown skin and golden spots. It was so very, very simple.

"You chose me," Blythe said, watching those inhuman eyes trace over her throat. "And I'll always choose you. If it's the last thing I do."

It might have been a trick of imagination, but Blythe thought she saw the luminous orbs of Polaris's eyes flicker from her throat to meet Blythe's gaze. The irises were too vivid to tell, the pupils all but eclipsed, and there was no change to the hungry expression on the vampire's face. Still, Blythe hoped.

That hope clogged her airways and made the corners of her eyes go tight and raw as Polaris crawled toward her through the gore.

"I love you, Polaris."

The vampire straddled her thighs, and a filthy hand cupped Blythe's cheek. For all the tenderness of the touch, the prick of unsheathed claws was distinct as it threatened to gouge a black-and-gold mark from Blythe's face.

"I love you. My Polaris."

The vampire made her move. The eerie mask of calm covering her face was at odds with the fathomless hunger burning in her stare, but her movements were deliberate and unrushed as she turned Blythe's face farther to the side. There was nothing savage in the way Polaris leaned into her, like a lover delivering a farewell kiss.

The fangs sank deep, and only then did Blythe let the last of her tears fall.

CHAPTER 25

*B*lythe's death was a good death, she decided. It had meaning. Even if she didn't return Polaris to sanity, at least she tried. She showed up. She didn't abandon her, not then, when Polaris needed her most, and not ever again. Maybe it was too little, too late, but at least she tried to do right by her vampire.

She tried.

"Hush, my love."

She tried, and maybe that was enough to earn her a little peace.

"I'm here. I'm right here with you."

The fingers combing through her hair were gentle and sweet, dragging their now blunt nails over her scalp in a way that made her purr. The lips peppering kisses along her jaw and shoulder were dry and petal soft. Every sweet word murmured against her skin was melodic and heartfelt, quiet yet powerful.

A short lick swiped over her lower lip, and Blythe moaned as she opened her eyes.

Her vision was filled with wonder. A golden nebula of active stars danced overhead, haloing the smiling face of an angel. Their surroundings faded into darkness, save for the cosmic spotlight raining down on the lovely, loving vision that was Tanya Troy. Polaris.

Blythe smiled and reached up to hold that precious face in her hands. The satin feel of a pale cheek was all the confirmation she needed to believe in Heaven.

Polaris turned into her touch and kissed her palm. Her eyes were bluer than blue and wet.

"There you are," Blythe murmured.

She was floating on a cloud, bathed in starlight and a bone-deep comfort she never experienced in life. The physical sensations were secondary to the soaring relief in her chest as she stroked over the clean flesh of Polaris's throat, tracing over the line of a sharp collarbone and graceful curve of a breast.

There was no pain or fear, no horror or worries. Not here, in this place of beauty and peace, where nothing bad could reach them.

"Rest, Blythe."

The Nocturna gave her a kiss that lingered for an eternity, branding her lips with the gentlest warmth. Blythe hummed into the feel of it and tried to chase after the contact when it lifted away.

"Hush. Rest."

Before Blythe could argue, those tender lips swept over her brow, then over each eyelid to encourage them to remain closed. It was so soft and nice, Blythe couldn't imagine doing anything else.

"I'll still be here when you wake," Polaris breathed against her temple.

Blythe was carried away on a haze of relief and unreality, and the reprieve was nothing short of glorious. Once she was ready to face the fact of her continued existence among the living, she could almost imagine her time spent in Lunar-1 as nothing more than a bad dream.

The luxury accommodations of Leopold Troy's interplanetary aircraft were helpful to that end. Blythe didn't know enough about the caliber of the ship or its heading to know where they were, but she was swarmed in such princely wrappings that she couldn't be bothered to dwell on it. The circular mattress beneath her maintained a perfect degree of warmth, and the bronze sheets with their golden filigree complimented the jaguar spots on her skin with a peculiar humor. The wall opposite the bed curved up and overhead in a spectacular view of the Milky Way, and the browning sphere known as Earth was too small in the distance to intrude on the majesty of all that starlight. The cozy lump of Polaris's body heat resting against her side was the finest detail of all.

Blythe couldn't imagine a scene more heavenly. It just didn't feel real.

At least, it didn't feel real until Ezra Lugh materialized at her bedside, hands on his hips and an unenthused scowl on his face.

Blythe frowned at him. "Where'd you come from?"

He snorted.

Polaris shifted in her sleep and uttered a low grumble of complaint against Blythe's shoulder. Blythe stroked the silvery hair from the Nocturna's face till the animalistic curl of her lip smoothed back into a mild and sweet visage.

The Guard stayed silent, shaking his head as he stepped backward. Maybe he wasn't there at all. Maybe she was dreaming.

Blythe was content to let him disappear into the background, to fade away from her awareness, so she could lose herself in Polaris and the stars. She found she couldn't hold on to the fantasy though, not when she tucked a strand of hair over her vampire's shoulder and discovered an inch's worth of skin roughened with the first signs of emerging scales.

"Is this real?" Blythe asked, her eyes locked on Polaris's mutating skin.

Lugh nodded in her periphery. "She's in the early stages of

Nosferatu's Curse, but they tell me she's stable. They also told me not to get too close; apparently, a perceived threat to you is the surest way to push her into another episode."

"Who's 'they'?"

He shrugged. "The Troy Harem and their doctors, a few folks on loan from the Vauqeulins. The higher echelons of The Guard, too."

With a sigh, he settled into a chair stationed a few feet away from the bed. The furnishing was as dark as the room, nearly as dark as his skin, and for a moment, Blythe imagined he might still vanish from her awareness entirely.

"They're putting together a task force," Lugh said in a dry, unassuming voice. "Not The Guard, but the Harems. The Nine, specifically."

Blythe jerked her head up to look at him. "The original Bloodlines? Why?"

He shot her a deadpan look. "Seriously?"

Blythe relaxed back into the bedding and huffed. "Let's pretend I'm still reeling from shock or that I'm only half as quick on the uptake as you seem to think I am. Yeah?"

He hummed under his breath, and Blythe thought she detected a hint of wry amusement.

"Reeling or otherwise, it seems you had a better handle on the situation than I did. Did you know Gregoire was effectively waging war against the Nocturni?"

"Nope," she admitted. "Guess that means you were as unprepared as I was to see what was under that bar."

"That's an understatement," he said, before his voice adopted a mild admonishment. "You knew about Nosferatu's Curse, though. You knew the Vauqeulin had it, and Polaris too, but you never so much as mentioned it to me."

Blythe shrugged. "I figured you knew."

"No one knew," he countered. "Not until I called on the Troy elders for backup. None of their vampires were left on Lunar-1, but they put me in touch with a few remaining locals in the know."

Blythe followed his considerate gaze down to the vampire snuggled into her side. "The Guard really didn't know about the Curse?"

"Not officially."

Blythe didn't have the strength to delve into the wry disbelief flavoring his voice. She cleared her throat and changed the subject instead. "Did you find Gregoire?"

"No."

"Figures."

"We found enough to put his name on every Guard's radar from Earth to Ethos, though."

"Great."

He inched forward, elbows on his knees as he peered at her. "He's still out there, but you should know you're coming out of this on top. You won, Blythe."

Blythe bit her lip, frowning down at the faint scales emerging from Polaris's skin. "Did I?"

"Thanks to you, the Humans First presence on Luna has been completely unveiled with two of their main hubs seized. And now the whole galaxy knows better than to underestimate them; Polaris might be the first Nocturna to be intentionally poisoned with the Curse, but I doubt she'll be the last."

Blythe raised a hand to stop him. "Why are you telling me this?"

"Isn't it obvious?" Lugh gestured to the pretty picture Polaris made, tucked into bed beside her. "You're part of this. Part of her."

Blythe swallowed the hopes clogging her throat. "She's still Cursed, and last I checked, I'm still an unattached Earthling with delusions of grandeur."

Lugh stifled a scoff and leaned back into his chair. "Don't cut yourself short. The Nocturni want to see Tanya Troy returned to her

Harem, for everyone's sake, but the second-most popular opinion seems to be that you're the key to making it happen. They're calling you a hero."

That startled a gust of laughter from her. Blythe smacked a hand over her mouth when the noise summoned the briefest of snarls from Polaris. With a subvocal grumble, the Nocturna wound her arms around Blythe's waist and tugged her close. Blythe grunted and rubbed at Polaris's topmost arm, willing its iron grip to ease.

"All right, there?"

"We're fine," Blythe replied, ignoring the discomfort of Polaris's grip compressing her bruised ribs.

Lugh made a soft, considerate noise in the back of his throat. Blythe was happy to let him keep his musings to himself.

"You need to speak with Master Troy," Lugh said as he rose from his seat. "He didn't bring you aboard this ship by chance, Blythe."

With an impatient sigh, Blythe restated, "Still in shock and not as quick as you're expecting."

He chortled as he strode toward the exit. "Remember that boy you like so much? Sylvester Spurgeon?"

"I love that boy," she corrected him.

Her heart gave a resounding pang beneath her sternum, a complicated mix of regret and relief, and Blythe realized the words were true. He wasn't with her anymore, and their last interaction left a sour taste in her mouth, but it didn't sit so heavy and untenable as it had a few weeks ago.

Lugh spoke with a note of smugness, "People say he gave his all to restore his vampire's humanity, right? Blood, mind, and body. Who can say you're not doing the same?"

Blythe was too exhausted to refute the jolt of possibility his careless supposition inspired in her. She almost smiled.

Lugh paused with his hand on the door. "When you speak to Troy, you might remind him that he owes you his life. I think you'll find him much happier to sponsor a Companionship between yourself and his cousin than he was previously."

He left her with those parting words, and Blythe dared to believe her afterlife fantasy might intersect with reality after all.

~

BLYTHE WAS BACK ON HER FEET BEFORE ANYONE ELSE HAD A chance to intrude on the little pocket of paradise she seemed to exist in.

"There's nothing to fear now," Polaris muttered in her ear as she brought their bare bodies flush together.

Blythe wished she could believe her, and her longing for such affirmation was almost strong enough to quiet the doubts itching at the edges of her consciousness. Almost.

The point of Polaris's chin dug into Blythe's shoulder as the Nocturna joined her before the floating mirror in the far corner of the scion's cabin. Her pale form blanketed Blythe's shape like a phantom, bright and superhuman as it framed Blythe's body with its swollen bruises and sundry jaguar markings. The yellows and oranges of the spots seemed imbibed with a life of their own against Polaris's ethereal presence. The longer Blythe studied their entwined reflections, the more she realized how striking they looked together, bruises and all.

Much like the chair Lugh sat in earlier, the mirror went unnoticed for far too long. The same could be said for the mechanized bar that slid in and out of the wall, and the several feet beside that where the darkness occasionally succeeded to an outrageous display of garments and accessories, most of which was designed for a male vampire.

Blythe blamed the surreal spacescape and her slew of near-death experiences for the lapse in her situational observation. It made a convenient, if all too realistic excuse.

Polaris's body was a solid warmth against her back, and that, if nothing else, was worth putting her trust in. With a sigh, Blythe gave the Nocturna the greater part of her weight. Polaris accepted it without complaint as she smiled against Blythe's nape. The transparent bandage on Blythe's throat crinkled as Polaris pressed against it.

The bite wound was pink and puffy, but far along the path to healing beneath the artificial skin. She could feel the warmth of Polaris's mouth, though not the moistness as a careful kiss was placed over the injury.

"I promised you a new comms once," Polaris said, soft and sweet as her hands traveled from Blythe's waist to her wrist. "Do you remember?"

Blythe answered with a noncommittal hum as she leaned her face against the other female's. She closed her eyes and reveled in the sensation of Polaris's fingers drawing errant patterns over the fragile skin of her inner arm, from wrist to elbow.

"I swore no one would be able to take it off you," Polaris continued in that heavy, serene tone that made Blythe think of untouchable fates and all-powerful deities.

"I don't need a comms," Blythe whispered back. "Just you."

Polaris stilled, but she didn't retreat. After a moment, her casual caresses resumed, and she said, "I'm told possessiveness might be a symptom of the disease. If I asked you to, would you still wear it?"

As if her meaning were in any way unclear, Polaris's hand encircled Blythe's wrist and clenched tightly. It didn't hurt, but the pressure teetered on the edge of discomfort.

Blythe didn't need to think it over. With her arm still locked in Polaris's grip, she twisted around to face her.

"Curse or no Curse"—Blythe nudged their noses together as she whispered—"I'm here for you. I'll wear whatever you want, so long as you're mine too."

"Always," Polaris vowed, smiling as she sniffled.

Blythe kissed away the tear rolling down her cheek. "Vampires don't have a monopoly on possessiveness, you know."

Polaris's laugh was quiet and strained, but it sparked a light in Blythe's chest.

〜

THERE WERE THIRTEEN SCALES GROWING AT RANDOM ALONG Polaris's shoulder and clavicle. Blythe counted them all, more than once, and as the days dragged on without further mutation or incident, she could almost convince herself the new phenotype was insignificant.

Conversely, Leopold couldn't seem to notice anything else in the rare moments he deigned to exist in the same room as his cousin.

"No one knows what to expect," he said with his eyes narrowed on the faint blemishes on Polaris's collarbone. "Nosferatu's Curse has never been weaponized like this before."

The two vampires gave each other a wide berth. Blythe and the enormous bed filled the void between them. Leopold remained near the doorway, watching warily as Polaris paced along the farthest wall, as if she neither noticed nor cared about his discomfort.

Blythe sat on the corner of the bed, stiff as a trained sentry, and stared at him with no such pretense.

"Our Harem has no real experience with any form of the disease either." His eye gave an involuntary twitch at the admission, but he carried on, "So, for now, we will be relying on the Vauqeulins and their . . . *expertise.*"

Blythe scoffed, "Well, the Vauqeulins have a history of using Companionship to treat the Curse, so . . . ?" She threw up her hands, letting the point hang open-ended between them.

"HEPP is drawing up a contract as we speak. It should be ready for you to sign by the time we reach Kepler." At last, his gaze left

Polaris to study Blythe with a pinched expression. "You're aware of the risks?"

"I don't care." Blythe rolled her shoulders back and met his stare. "I love her."

Behind her, Blythe felt Polaris go still.

Leopold sighed and dropped his gaze with a baffled shake of his head. "I cannot guarantee your safety as a traditional Companionship would dictate."

"I'm not asking you to."

He stared past her to Polaris. Blythe had no way of knowing what passed between the two vampires then, but she had a front row seat to the effect it had on the Harem leader. His jaw tensed for a moment, then relaxed, taking with it the creases in the skin around his eyes as he seemed to settle on a conclusion.

"I don't understand you Earthlings," he said, glaring at the floor with a frustrated sigh. "You and Spurgeon. The most recent incidents of the Curse are unprecedented, yet here you are, committing all that you have to a vampire you barely know."

In the stilted silence that followed, Blythe slid to her feet and took an imploring step toward him. "Kahled Vauqeulin is still alive and mostly humanoid because of Sly. Don't you think Polaris deserves an opportunity like that?"

He frowned. "You can't cure her."

"We don't need a cure," Polaris interjected. She sidled up to Blythe's back and enveloped the woman in her arms in the next heartbeat. "I just need her."

Blythe patted the arm crossing over her middle and smiled at her vampire.

Leopold studied them with wet eyes. After a long moment, he nodded.

"This is what you want, Tanya?" he asked.

Polaris said, "Yes."

Blythe shivered when the breath of that single word caused the hair on her neck to flutter. Then Polaris placed the meekest of kisses on the spot, and her hand found Blythe's like they were corresponding puzzle pieces.

"I lost myself long before I was Cursed," Polaris said, "but Blythe found me anyway. After repeat abductions and so much bloodshed, in the end, she found me. Don't you see, cousin? You're not protecting me from hurting her, merely making it harder to enjoy the peace I have left."

The fingers wrapped around Blythe's tightened. Without thinking, Blythe squeezed back with enough pressure to match the rush of emotion tightening her throat.

"I owe her all that I am, and all that I will be," Polaris said with finality. "She'll never be just my Companion. She's my hero."

ABOUT THE AUTHOR

K.R. Bady is a queer sci-fi/fantasy fanatic with a love for art and story telling that has resulted in a flourishing career in visual art and novel writing. Her first original written work was published in Fall 2022 with the release of *Companion,* which quickly hit Amazon's Best Seller List in LGBTQ+ Science Fiction.

As a queer woman who was raised in a religious American household, she aspires to write the sort of novels she wishes were more readily available to anyone who felt similarly disenfranchised. Since making a difference in the real world seems impossible at times, she happily indulges in her obsession of exercising change in fiction by envisioning worlds where people are free to be who they want to be.

www.ingramcontent.com/pod-product-compliance
Lightning Source LLC
Chambersburg PA
CBHW051122300726
48981CB00021B/509/J